TWICE
A BROKEN
BREATH

LISETTE BRODEY

Published by:

SABERLEE BOOKS
Los Angeles, CA
United States of America

Editor: D.L. Savvides
Preliminary copy-editing: Kenneth Brodey
Cover design: The Cover Collection

ISBN-13: 978-1-7340894-7-9 (paperback)
ISBN-13: 978-1-7340894-8-6 (e-book)

To Cynthia G. Pecoraro, my dear friend of many decades.

Thank you for always being such a caring, supportive, and loving presence in my life .

"Never confuse a single defeat with a final defeat."
— *F. Scott Fitzgerald*

"The only person you are destined to become is the person you decide to be."
— *Ralph Waldo Emerson*

ACKNOWLEDGMENTS

To D.L. Savvides for being such a phenomenal editor;

To Kenneth Brodey for his superb preliminary edits and brotherly support;

To Deborah Nam-Krane for being an outstanding, invaluable beta reader and friend;

To Lisa Wentworth for being such an amazing friend and doing so much to support the writing and production of this novel. You always believe another book will follow. I hope you're right again;

To Charles Roth for his endless love and support;

To all of the following people who lent a hand with my research: Cynthia and Mike Pecoraro, Janet S. Selden, and Eric Yahyayan;

To Kathleen Harryman, for creating such a wonderful animated cover and video for me;

To Stephanie Bauerlein, Shykia Bell, Dody Cox, PattiAnn Cutter, Dionne Lister, Tonya Staufer, Virginia Talamantes, Sheri A. Wilkinson, and Leigh Ann Wilson for their ongoing support and kindness;

There are so many people who have supported me in so many ways. I wish it were possible to thank each and every one of you. I hope you all know who you are. And last, but not least, thank you to my fellow authors for your support, advice, inspiration, and friendship. You all mean so much to me.

TWICE
A BROKEN
BREATH

CHAPTER ONE

I'm having trouble breathing. Panic constricts my throat. I can't speak. I've never been so scared—or have I?

The bank teller repeats her words, "I'm sorry, sir. Both accounts were closed this morning." She watches me struggle to breathe again. "Can I call someone for you, Mr. Tallamore? You look quite unwell."

Yeah? You think? My eyes speak for me because the words won't come. I brush my inner shirt sleeves against the sweat on my cheeks and it leaves wet spots on the light denim. There's no way I can go back to work. I move away from the teller's window. Some customers are staring at me. They probably think I'm a psycho. I'm pissed, and I feel the urge to say something—to every person looking at me—but I won't. I'll let my angry words retreat. Strangers eyeballing me is the least of my worries.

I pull my phone out of my back pocket. My hands are so slippery with perspiration that it falls to the floor and slides over to hit the side of the lavender comfort shoe worn by an elderly woman who hasn't taken her eyes off me. Damn.

Unlike the others, she looks sympathetic, bends down to retrieve it from the floor, and hands the phone back to me. I manage half a smile, and she nods. I text my boss to say I have a personal emergency and won't be back from lunch. Thirty seconds later he wants to know what's wrong. If I wanted the sonofabitch to know, not to mention everyone in the damn auto-parts store, I'd have told him.

Now to call Carly. My escalating pulse tells me that my greatest fear is seconds away. A digital voice confirms it. "The number you have reached is no longer in service. If you feel you have reached this recording in error…."

I knew it. Stick me with a fork. I've got to get home and cancel my credit cards before she can do any more damage, but far more importantly, I need to check on my daughter, Rayelle. She's usually at her friend Kayla's house on Friday afternoons. I'm praying she's safe and having fun. I hope Carly let Kayla's mother know that she needs to stay there until I can pick her up. But I know I'm deluding myself. If Carly is gone, Rayelle is too. All of the wishful thinking in the world won't change that.

I get into my car and drive the five minutes to our house. I'm trembling but driving with extreme caution. The last thing I need is to complicate this situation with a ticket, or worse, an accident.

I'm stunned to see Carly's car in the driveway. Really? She's wiped out our checking and savings accounts and she's still here? I pull in next to her and get out of the car. Wait. Oh, God. What if I'm all wrong about what it appears she's done? What if someone forced her to close our accounts—then hand over our money and shut off her phone? What if our precious Rayelle was kidnapped, and she had no choice? If someone has laid a hand on my daughter or my wife, I'll fucking kill them. My son, Oliver, is away at college. He's twenty now and is Carly's biological child. I adopted him when he was eight. I think he's on summer break, but I haven't been able to reach him for nearly two months. Nobody has. I miss him and so does my Ray-Ray. Carly said he's just asserting his independence by going off the grid for a while. Who knows? How will I reach him if my worst fears are confirmed?

"Carrrrly!" I scream as I look around for a trail of blood or something out of place as though I've stepped into the opening scene of a *Criminal Minds* or *NCIS* episode. Nothing. I run upstairs and into our bedroom. Everything is immaculate. The bed is made. I run to the sliding closet doors. I push them aside so hard that I hear something crack as I expect a bloodied skull to roll out. Ah, just a plastic hanger on the floor. Shattered. I don't have a spirit animal. Just a spirit inanimate object: a plastic fucking hanger in little pieces. Jesus.

Her side of the closet is completely empty save for a few old shoes and that blue-and-green Hawaiian dress from her mother that she despises. She wanted to cut it up and use it for dust rags, but her mother keeps asking her to take photos in it. Says it makes Carly's dad happy when she acknowledges her Hawaiian heritage. Why do I care about the damn dress? I have to keep breathing.

The disappearance of my wife and child isn't feeling so involuntary anymore. More like Operation Precision. I look over at her bureau. Most everything is gone. With both hands, I lift the gold-framed painting of Maui from the wall and lay it on the bureau. Almost forgetting the combination, I tremble as I open it. It's empty. Damn her. We're the only two people who knew about this. Fifty grand: gone.

I run into Rayelle's room—my precious eight-year-old pumpkin who is the light of my life. Her handmade rag doll that sits against her pillows is gone. Of course it is. Her favorite toy, Paddington Bear, is nowhere to be seen. I jerk open the closet door that always sticks. Nothing there except hangers and a few old shirts.

My rage intensifying, I yank open each bureau drawer. Empty. Empty. Fucking Empty! I don't see any of her other toys or favorite trinkets. The only thing left, sitting atop the bureau, which I wish *was* gone, is the recent photo of the two of us on her eighth birthday at Mill Hill Park. It's the same one I carry in my wallet. It's our special photo. Why didn't she take it? "Didn't you want it, Ray-Ray? Or did Mommy make you leave it?" Where the hell are they?

"Carly! Rayelle!" I scream over and over. I know they're gone, and I know they won't answer, but where are they? Everything is so neat. Nothing looks hurried, only planned. It had to be.

Rushing back into our room, I sit on the bed, pull out my two credit cards, and look for the phone numbers on the back. I call the first one, plug in the last four digits, then my date of birth. "Please wait while I pull up your information." This needs to be done, but what an insane waste of time. Now I'm getting a bunch of information I don't need, and the voice won't shut up. "Agent!" I scream. "Representative!" Nothing. Just more standard nonsense about my available credit, last payment, and other things that mean nothing now. I can feel my blood pressure rising.

Wait! I remember reading that if you hit the zero twice, it will bypass this mess and get you to an agent. It works. A human voice answers, and then, because it's such a happy day, the call gets disconnected, and I have to start all over again. The new agent sounds a bit mistrusting of me, but I explain my distressed circumstances as best and as quickly as I can. She believes me. Assured no one can use the card, I call the second company. Pretty much a repeat of the first scenario. Argument with a voice, only with zeroes to the rescue, I don't waste as much time—and luckily, no disconnection. Done! I'm already exhausted.

I stumble going back down the steps and whack my ankle against the base of a balustrade. Damn that hurts. Red-hot, burning pain. Just as I stop to let it subside, in that second, I see an envelope with my name on it, sitting on the drink table by my chair across the living room. My gut is flipping like pancakes and again, I can't breathe. Twice a broken breath in a half an hour. That has only happened to me once before—I just can't remember when—but I'm sure the incident, and my subsequent inability to recall it, has somehow defined my life.

I fall into my chair and prepare to read something I know is going to kill me. Carly should have left a drink on the table with it. She had to know I'd need one, except if she had, by this point, I wouldn't trust that the drink hadn't been poisoned. I stand and walk to the small dry bar against the wall. I grab a bottle of Johnny Walker and pour a shot. Now I'm sitting again. I stare at the envelope; then I tear it open.

Liam,

I know you're feeling confused and devastated. I know you're bouncing off walls now. I know you are missing Rayelle, but sorry because right now, I can't say when you can see her again. I knew when you went to cash your paycheck, you'd learn I'd closed the accounts. I hope you didn't go apeshit crazy in the bank and get yourself arrested or thrown out. You're really good at making a scene in public places. I know what you're thinking as you curse me out. I didn't just close the accounts, I cleaned them out. And yeah, I took the emergency money in the safe. But I signed my car over to you so there's that. Because I'm a good person.

Also, you have investments and parents who will help you. You have a job. You'll be okay. I had to take the money. I don't owe you any explanations. I know you'll miss Rayelle way more than the money. I know you're pissed off and really hurt. You're probably too angry to even cry. I didn't do this to hurt you. I did it to reclaim the joy that's been missing from my life. I have a right to be happy.

I married you because at heart, I know you're a good guy and I needed a stable home for Oliver. Yes, you can be funny and loving. You've been a good father to our daughter and my son.

"I adopted him twelve years ago. But he's not my son too? That's bullshit, Carly!"

There's always been something missing for me in this marriage. Can't believe you haven't noticed. And hello, your paranoia makes me crazy. You're always looking for something ominous around every corner.

"Maybe because it's actually there, Carly! You just kidnapped our daughter, and you call me paranoid?" My hands tremble as I read on.

You've never been comfortable in your own skin. You say you can't remember most of your childhood. But your parents told you all about it. You had a head injury playing ball and lost your memory. Sad, rare, but it happens. But no, you're obsessed with finding something deeper and darker than what you've been told. You know what else you've been obsessed with? Lying. Pretending to be confused so you can get away with whatever crazy behavior suits you. That's bullshit. So ask me if I feel I'm doing a terrible thing here. No. I'm tired of your sickness. Bubbling under every surface and oozing from every pore of your body. Did you ever think how it's been for me? Of course you haven't. You're totally thinking of yourself right now. And who knows what self that is – you're so many people rolled into one. And I don't like most of them. So yeah, I'm thinking about myself. But at least I can admit it. That makes us even.

I'm not going to tell you anything else except that I'm back with the true love of my life. Don't look for us. Let us be. One day, if I feel it's okay, you can probably see Rayelle again. If you fucking call any form of law enforcement, I'll make sure you never see either of the kids again in your lifetime. And I'm not messing around. I finally have what I've wanted since I was fifteen, and damned if you'll ruin it for me. I'll have divorce papers sent to you soon. Sign them, and there's a much better chance you'll see Rayelle. Not messing with you. Just do what I say. I'm proud of myself for writing this letter and explaining as much as I have. I've done the right thing so I can sleep at night. Aloha, Liam.

"NOOOOOOOOOO!" I scream so loud, I feel my soul bending in half. No, I can *hear* it snap into two pieces.

She took my daughter. The most precious thing in my entire life. And she tells me that *if* she feels it's "okay"—some fucking day—that I'll be able to see my child again? "NOOOOOOO!" That's kidnapping! She won't get away with it. I won't let her. She left that picture here to help Ray-Ray forget me. What a calculating bitch. "It takes more than leaving a photo behind, Carly!"

That car was no gift. She's afraid that taking it could lead the police right to her. I'll find her all right—and whatever sonofabitch she's holed up with. My poor Ray-Ray. What is she thinking? Is she frightened? Does she believe I've stopped loving her? Did Carly tell her I didn't want to see her anymore? An eight-year-old child is smart enough to know better. Isn't she? "I'll find you, baby. Daddy will find you. And I'll find your cruel, self-centered, holier-than-thou, kidnapping bitch of a mommy too."

I pull my phone out and call Kayla's house. Maybe Carly slipped and told Kayla's mother, Lisa, where she was going. Or confided to her. Doubtful, but I need to call.

Nope. Lisa tells me that Carly called days ago to say Rayelle wouldn't even be in school today: family trip. Hearing my distress, Lisa asks what's wrong, but I don't have time to tell her. She sounds really worried, and I know she's in the dark too.

I run to the dining room, grab a chair, and drag it over to the bookshelves. Standing on it, I grab a copy of *The People of Czechoslovakia* and jump down with the book in one hand. Swallowing hard, I open it. Thank God! My emergency six grand and burner phone, still in its original packaging, are intact in the hollowed-out book. I always thought I might need them some day. When you have no memory of the first fourteen years of your life, it does something to your head. You prepare for things even though you don't know why. It's just that way. At least for me. I don't know anyone else who's lost most of their childhood. Most people who have an accident like mine eventually get their memory back.

My mind races. Thank God I was able to cancel the credit cards before she could max them out. I would never have used them. I don't want her to know where I am or what I'm doing.

I look at the fake book. Found it at a yard sale years ago. It served me well. I put it back where I found it. The chair too.

Now back upstairs to change my clothes. I'm drenched in sweat. I need to take a quick shower so I don't draw attention to myself, and I'll stuff a light change of clothing and a few other things into my large olive-green backpack. I take a handful of quarters out of my side pocket, along with my folding knife, and drop them on top of my bureau, making a mental note to transfer everything to the side pocket of my post-shower pants. I can't go to New York City wearing these sweaty, look-where-I-work-and-see-how-nice-my-name-looks-in-embroidery DiNello's Auto Parts' clothes. I'd stand out in the worst way.

New York. That's where I'm going. That's where she is—with my little girl. I know it. They're somewhere in that concrete jungle of millions, back where she came from. It's the only place that makes sense. The true love of her fucking life couldn't be anywhere else.

I pick up her letter and read it one more time, just to make sure that I haven't missed anything in my state of shock. What's this? She's written something at the very bottom of the page.

P.S. We're leaving the country in 24 hours. And again, call law enforcement, and you'll be sorry in more ways than one. Leave things be. Do. Not. Look. For. Us. It'll be better for everyone.

"What the fuck!" Not for me, Carly. And not for Rayelle. I'll see you soon. And no, I'm not calling law enforcement, but only because there's a loud voice in my head that tells me to handle this myself. And it's not because you threatened me. Nobody cares as much as I do, and I have the best chance of finding you. I know some people would think I'm reckless and stupid, going it alone, but I'm compelled to do it my way. I don't know how I'll find you, but I will. Count on it!

CHAPTER TWO

I pull into a space in one of the private lots by the Trenton Transit Center. Grabbing the parking ticket, I slip it into my wallet. I unhook my seat belt. I reach for the door handle but freeze before I grab it. *Not so fast, Liam.* I scan the lot to make sure no one is standing too close or watching me. I reach deep into my side pocket, grab a wad of cash, and sandwich half a grand between each foot and the insoles of my Nike Air Maxes. Five hundred is already in my wallet. Gotta spread the cash out on my person and in my backpack. Just to be safe. I'm angry with myself. Why didn't I think to do this at home? Maybe because my life had just been shattered by my wife.

Sticking half a grand in each side of my boxer briefs, I watch as people walk by me with briefcases, luggage, and weary faces. My mind is racing, and I'm thinking one dumbass thing after another. None of it matters. I've never had a reason to go anywhere with so much cash, but it's common sense not to keep it all in one place. That's basic survival. Am I going to survive this nightmare? I don't even have a plan beyond arriving at Penn Station. I've got to think. Purge the clutter from my brain. Except for the voice that tells me not to call the police, to *never* call the police. Where does that come from? It's real, powerful, and unidentifiable. And it's right. I have to find them myself.

I check one more time to make sure my phone is powered off. It is. I check to make sure the burner phone is in the backpack. I've only done this at least six times.

I run into the station, buy my ticket, and make it onto the top level of a silver double-decker train—just in time for the 3:11 to New York. So glad I found the last window seat. I pray no one sits next to me, but that's the least of my worries. And people are still boarding, so my luck is going to run out.

"Ahoy, mate!" says a voice next to me. "I'm Captain Bob." He nods to indicate the window. "How about you let me have that winder seat so I can watch for pirates? Them seas can be rough."

My eyes narrow and evince disgust. I turn to see a sixty-something-year-old man with a full head of gray hair under a red flat cap wearing a blue rain jacket and holding a folded red umbrella on his lap. I wonder if he's wearing red Wellington boots, hoping to emulate Paddington. Rayelle loves that bear more than anything. I'm happy he didn't stay behind with our photo. I know he comforts her. I choke up as I picture her and "the Padster" in an embrace. I bought him for her fifth birthday. Never saw a child love a gift so much. I remember to breathe, then emerge from my happy-memory coma with a full-on desire to release my smoldering rage. "Maybe you'd like the experience of having that umbrella …." I stop myself from finishing the sentence. Punishment a bit too harsh for the crime. And this man isn't the one who's done me wrong. I'm embarrassed, but understanding my unfinished sentence, I watch him scan the car for an empty seat, but there isn't one.

"I reckon I'll be fine sitting right here." He looks down. "Just thought a little humor might snag me a winder seat. Didn't mean nothin' by it. What are you? Thirty-something, young feller?"

"I don't know what your game is, but this old-man-country-bumpkin bullshit isn't going to get you anywhere with me."

He's unaffected by my words. "Back when I used to ride these trains into work," he drawls, "they had gray-speckled floors that looked just like the floor of my old dentist's office. Darn floors outlived him. They sure did."

My hand morphs into a tight fist, but I unfurl it. I have a bad habit of getting angry too quickly. A co-worker once told me I had a pugilistic personality. I didn't know what that meant, but I wanted to punch him for saying it. Anyway, Captain Bob is not my enemy nor is this a battle I need to fight or even think about. I've got until 4:44, when this train pulls into Penn Station, to figure out my next move. But that doesn't mean I'll allow my thoughts to be derailed by some Paddington Bear wannabe or his red umbrella. "Do I strike you as someone who wants to chat?"

He puts his palms up and laughs nervously. "Don't be strikin' me." He looks like he's got more to say.

I turn sharply and stare out the window as the train begins to move. He mutters something, but I tune him out. The scenery messes with my head. I see out-of-commission commuter cars sitting on old wooden tracks. Grass and weeds growing over what was once functional. So much litter, broken glass, and God knows what else. I feel confusion growing over my once-semi-functional brain.

The train picks up speed and hurries past an old warehouse. Seems abandoned. Probably just down on its luck—like me. Who knows what the hell is inside? Where will I go first when I get to New York? Why is the old man carrying an umbrella? Is it raining there? It's starting to rain here. I've got my answer. Damn.

Everything outside is screaming at me as the first few drops slide down the window. The train speeds past low buildings of industry with green-glass windows, storage units, and a long aluminum building with hundreds of tiny-paned windows. It's a place where dreams never come true. How could they?

What is my little girl thinking? What did they tell her? Does she miss me? Is she crying for me? Will she believe their lies?

The train races past a large parking structure. Now, suddenly, fields of crops. Thousands of trees behind them. So many leaves to drop in the fall, but evergreens to keep nature's colors alive. What's going to keep me alive? I can't lose my breath again.

We pass a housing community. Thousands of homes. Replicated dreams, cloned families—a different shade of paint the only marker of individualism. Another housing development, and then another. How much land was raped? I stop to remember something. Carly said she was raped at a sweet-sixteen party, bringing Oliver into the world. I run the entire scenario over in my mind. Wait! The rapist conveniently fled never to be found again. I asked her a few times whose name she put down as the father on Oliver's birth certificate. Each time, she'd get visibly nervous, defensive, and change the subject. Then there was the time I asked her if she ever had a serious boyfriend before me. She got really pissed, and asked me if I wanted to run a background check on her. I felt terrible and apologized for the question. But I'm remembering little things she'd say to her mother on the phone. They made no sense, but now they do. Like the time she said "He still doesn't know about Oliver." She fucking blanched when I walked into the room, then later said she and her mom had been discussing some black-sheep uncle. I should have known then, but I was in love with her—and in denial. My breath becomes slightly labored as realization dawns. Why didn't I see it before? She wasn't raped. I feel disgust hugging me, squeezing all compassion out of my system. I take a useless deep breath. She got pregnant by whoever she's with now and wants to protect him, even though he left her twenty-something years ago. That makes so much sense. Her parents never would have stopped looking for a rapist. Ever. How could I have believed the woman who had the audacity to call *me* a liar?

Thirteen minutes have passed, and the train stops at Princeton Junction. A sea of cars outside my window—signs of affluence and education everywhere. Advertisements for banks, colleges, energy drinks, real estate, donut shops, and psychiatric clinics. At least the blue-collar neighborhoods have character—rusting cars disintegrating in at least one yard on every block or so. Tacky lawn ornaments, silly decorative flags. Not to mention when they put up those blow-up Christmas scenes in December— the ones that light up at night and in the daylight look like they're victims of a drive-by shooting. Nothing screams festivity like plastic puddles on the lawn.

I'm hoping that Captain Bob will get off here, but no luck. He mumbles something about having a cousin who graduated from Princeton and went on to embezzle from a law firm years later. I pretend I don't hear him as his rambling fades into nothingness and the train moves on. Another land-raped, landscaped development. But this time, all of the houses are gray as if built for an alien compound. I've always thought aliens, if they existed, would be colorblind. Where do I even begin to look for my family? For my daughter? I can't waste any time.

Seeing miles of telephone lines, I try to imagine how the years of conversations have actually traveled through them. My father's cousin was a scientist. Once I asked him how it all worked, but when he began to explain oscillating pressure waves, one look at my face told him I wasn't receiving what he was transmitting. So we just talked about the Mets and the Yankees—and none of this is important now. I know what those phone lines must feel like with all of the never-ending voices moving through them. I'm surprised they don't all scream. Or self-immolate.

In that letter she left, Carly said I pretend to be confused about the first fourteen years of my life, and that I'm obsessed with finding something darker than what I've been told, all so I can get away with crazy behavior. That's *her* lie to get away with *her* crazy behavior. She's using this garbage as a bullshit rationale to kidnap our daughter, when her reason for everything is to reunite with her old lover. All I've ever wanted is the truth. I thought she accepted me as I am.

I actually believed she loved me, even though she hasn't wanted me to touch her for over two years. Said she was having female issues, and I believed her, even though everything else changed too. And now, I don't know how worried I should be about her threats. A tiny part of me considers calling the police, but the rest of me hears that voice admonishing me to *never* call them. I agree with it. What Carly did is illegal, but I don't want to call law enforcement anyway, especially the Feds. They'll only get in the way. They'll tell me to stay out of it and let them do the work. No time to complicate things, nor contemplate what Carly might do if she learns I've sent anyone after them. I have to take her threats seriously. I'll handle this myself. I can't trust the most important job of my life to strangers. I would never be able to sit still and wait. And maybe I'll have to make a crazy scene or two. But oh well. I'll do whatever it takes to get my daughter back.

The rain is coming down harder now as we pass another godforsaken development with ugly dark wooden porches. A truck yard with empty cabins and a trailer park next door. Beyond that, another bland cookie-cutter community, a water tower, idle machinery sitting on the tracks, mountains of gravel, smokestacks, wires, towers, and parking lots. America the Beautiful running parallel to train tracks.

"Hey, young feller. Might you be in a better mood now? Wanna hear some jokes I made up?" I jump at his voice. I'd nearly forgotten he was sitting next to me. "Did ya hear about the workshop tools that got together for a party? The hammer says to the nail, 'Hey, you know the drill?' Then the nail gets hammered, and the hammer gets nailed for pounding a screw. Get it?" He laughs. "Made that up when I was working in my dad's garage, many moons ago. Got an even better one about a rake dating a hoe. Bit risqué though. Bet you can figure out the nuts and bolts of it."

Expressionless, I look at him again but say nothing.

His voice *grows* a bit more serious as the train pulls into another station. "Ah, New Brunswick. Home to Rutgers University. Remember that embezzling cousin of mine, the one who went to Princeton? Well, his partner in crime went to Rutgers. Damn shame that fellers like them, lucky enough to get such a good education, threw it down the hopper like they did. Both got a whole bunch of years. Wives divorced them. Kids hate them. Yep. They both got sentences. Period. Full stop." He laughs again, awkwardly, but stops when I show no reaction.

I turn toward the window. It's still raining. In my peripheral vision, people hurry onto the train, shaking their now-closed umbrellas in the aisles, creating a mock shower, and pissing off the people who believe that rain belongs outside. A kid behind me is kicking my seat while yammering to a kid next to him. *Gotta keep cool, Liam*.

The scenery is nicer here. An old stone church with stained glass windows. Modern office buildings, a river running through the town, and the train is moving again.

Captain Bob just did me a favor. Apparently, his seat was being kicked too. Just told the kids' father to "settle yer young folk." The man asks where he's from, and Captain Bob says he's originally from the Trenton area. The man calls bullshit and says something ugly. Bob is hurt. And look at me, bloody fool, I'm actually feeling sorry for him and happy I said nothing at all.

Finally, the train is pulling into Penn Station. Before it comes to a stop, Bob taps me on the shoulder. His entire countenance is different. Unnerving actually. He looks into my eyes. They're not the same eyes that looked at me before. "You know that cousin I told you about, the one who graduated from Princeton and went on to become a thief?" His voice is completely different. Educated. Refined. "That wasn't my cousin; that was my son. Robert Fitzgerald Dansworth Junior. The other man—my nephew. Both have shamed our family. I dreaded talking to people, even strangers, who inevitably would ask my name and possibly make the connection. Then the intrusive questions, unwelcome commentaries, and judgments would come. Horrible." He sighs, and I can see he's in pain. "It was a high-profile case. Made the national TV shows. My beautiful wife, Janine, died of a broken heart."

I'm stunned by the transformation in his persona. I can only listen. I remember the story in the news about those men. They embezzled millions and destroyed a lot of lives in the process.

"Six months after Janine died, overcome with grief and feeling angry with and ashamed of my son and nephew, misery clung to every ounce of my being. One night, I decided to watch a silly old movie to help me forget for a couple of hours. It was nothing I ever would have looked at before. And to my own great surprise, I found myself talking like the main character. Everyone liked him. His life was simple but happy. And I thought, Bob, why not be like Captain Elmer! He has so few worries. Wakes up happy every morning." Looking forlorn, he slowly shakes his head. "And that's how Captain Bob was born."

I falter trying to speak, but he doesn't wait for the words he knows I don't have.

"But when people meet me in this part of the country, somewhere between Philadelphia and New York or any other cosmopolitan metropolis, hearing me speak in that silly voice and saying absurd things—it amuses a good number of them but baffles many too. Just as it did you and that cruel man behind us. For a while, it seemed worthwhile. Nobody ever asked my name, wanted to know me, or made the connection to the shame my son and nephew brought onto my family. It's hard, my reluctant friend, when what you love most destroys you. Bobby was our only child. The pride of our life. And he's still rotting in prison where he belongs. In fact, we just passed his current city of habitation a few stops back: Rahway. That's right; my son and his cousin live in Rahway State Prison. And me, I'm in my own prison. For various reasons you don't want to hear, I'm all alone in the world. It's tough. Don't even want another woman. Just a good friend or two. A roommate would be nice."

"Well, I...."

"I can see you've got something heavy on your mind. And no, I'm not suggesting you talk like a silly old country man to escape it. But I caution you: don't let the opinion of others change who you are. In the end, pretense is not your friend. You'll only come back to yourself anyway. Stay strong, and fight your demons." He pauses. "They're fighting to overpower you right now. I can see how frightened you are. I'm sorry I didn't notice when I first boarded the train. I was insensitive."

I don't know what to say to him. I don't respond because I have no appropriate words, but Bob instinctively understands this.

"Thank you for listening. I'm going to take my own advice and retire Captain Bob. It was fun at first. Till it wasn't. When all is said and done, it does nothing to soothe the pain I carry, though there were moments when I believed it did. Sure doesn't ease the loneliness. I need to deal with my pain as me. This train ride put the final nail in Captain Bob's coffin. You were the catalyst that set me thinking straight." He looks down. "And this silly red umbrella." He hands it to me. "It's raining hard out there, and you don't look like you have any time to shop for umbrellas. You take it. I've got all the time in the world to replace it with something that suits me."

Before I can thank him, the train has stopped and he's up and hurrying toward the steps to the lower level.

I look at the red umbrella and think of Ray-Ray and Paddington Bear again. I glance at his empty seat as I replay his words and find a business card lying there. Robert F. Dansworth, Attorney at Law. I stuff the card in my pants pocket.

I'm in a huge hurry. If only I knew where I was going.

CHAPTER THREE

I run out of the Seventh Avenue exit to a sea of blurry yellow cabs in the rain. Taking cover under my umbrella, I quickly snare one. The driver tells me, "I stop for you because I like red umbrella. Happy color."

Not knowing what to say, I offer a nervous smile.

"Where to, mister?"

As if I'd known my destination all along, I tell him I need to get to a pub on Broome Street in lower Manhattan. I don't know the address, and I can't remember the name, plus it may have changed ownership since I first walked in the door over a decade ago. I just know it's in the middle of the block, not too far from a sign for the Holland Tunnel, adding that I remember there's a lot of red-brick, four-story buildings on the block, all with storefronts on the ground level. "And a lot of trees."

He laughs. "Could be many street. But I get you there. Good you get cab on Seventh Avenue. Already going that direction."

Now that he mentions it, I left by the Seventh Avenue exit because it only goes one way: downtown. I didn't think I knew that. A vision of a boutique across the street from the pub comes to mind. I give the driver a description.

"You lucky, mister. I think I know where you mean." He turns his head and flashes a smile. "I know New York well. I drive here for twenty-two year."

I'm grateful he understands when I can't give him an exact address or anything he can plug into the GPS.

As soon as he pulls away from Penn Station, the rain intensifies. It's blinding now, and I worry that we'll get into an accident before we can find the place, or that we'll just sit in traffic forever. I look out the window. Construction and scaffolding everywhere. People with umbrellas trying to avoid one another as they hurry along the crowded streets.

There's a loud skid of tires as the cab in front of us stops suddenly, veering to the right as it narrowly misses a jaywalker and another cab. Some crazy person is crossing through traffic, likely figuring it's slow enough that he can avoid walking to the corner. Isn't that illegal? As if New Yorkers care. Isn't kidnapping my daughter illegal? I've got to find Carly and Rayelle. Damn this traffic and this rain.

The cab driver tells me that the pedestrian and the cab driver who slid to a halt are having a middle-finger, shouting war. "Stupid people. I see people get hurt bad when cross street like that. Maybe dead. Never know what happen when you have to keep driving. Harder to see in rain. Not driver fault. Stupid people."

"You're right. People are idiots." I try to be kind. I'm lucky I got this driver, and I wonder how much more time I have to find my wife and daughter. Where in the world are she and her lover planning to take my child? The same thoughts come back to me. Kidnapping is a federal crime, isn't it? Yes! But I'm not calling the FBI. Even if I were so inclined, I'd have to make sure I know what I'm talking about. I have Carly's letter in my backpack, but that's not enough. They might not even believe she wrote it and maybe think I'm trying to use federal resources to resolve a domestic dispute. No, I can't trust anyone but myself. There's no time to waste. And, yes, I still believe I can do what they can't. I just know she's in this city. It's her hometown, and seeing how she had Oliver at sixteen, it has to be his too. If her lover's come back from wherever he's been, he's here.

Turning to my right, I see we're now in front of the Fashion Institute of Technology. What a massive building, extending two city blocks on the west side of the street. Halfway down, there's an opening at 27th Street that goes under the building and an entrance to the subway on the right. Just as I'm looking at the back of a woman holding a child's hand, wondering without logic or reason if it's Carly and Rayelle, I see an old woman slip, landing on her back as she turns off Seventh Avenue to find shelter under the building. Two men rush to her side. One of them implores a nearby pedestrian to call an ambulance while the mystery woman and child disappear down the stairs. What if it's them? It can't be them! *You're losing your mind, Liam. Stay focused.* There are well over a million and a half people commuting to work in this city per day. Not to mention the residents, tourists, and students. I have no clue how I know these statistics. Guess I heard it on the news once. I remember random things. I can't help what my brain decides to store, but today of all days, it needs to focus.

Get a grip. That poor woman fell hard. I hope she's okay. My Ray-Ray better be okay. Traffic is moving … slowly, but it's moving. I'm glad to see the driver focusing on the road while my brain is taking every conceivable detour.

We stop at the light at a large intersection: 24th Street and Seventh Avenue. A man comes running out of the supermarket on the northwest corner. Holding two bags with his left hand, he's knocking on the passenger side of the cab with his right, making a frenetic gesture with his hand for the driver to lower the window as the rain drenches him.

The driver does so, but just enough to hear what he's saying.

"Please, sir," the man begs through the small opening. "Get rid of the passenger in the back. I'll pay you triple. I need to get home. I have a sick child. Please!"

"I have a *kidnapped* child," I tell the driver in my most urgent voice. "I need to stay in this cab. I'll pay you whatever he was going to pay."

The light turns green, and the driver raises the window and keeps moving. "Many more cab can take him. And he rude to say get rid of you. I see you in trouble, mister. You very nervous. Hope you no rob bank."

My instinct is to feel insulted and speak harshly to him. I stop myself. That would be the stupidest thing I could do. "No. I'm serious. My wife left me and took our child."

"Oh. Sorry. You never know in this city."

We get to 23rd and Seventh. The ugly brick building on the southwest corner is the Chelsea Savoy. There's a bank that runs along the street level. A man in a suit buys drugs from a dealer in a dark hoodie. Only yards away, a hooker in a curve-hugging red minidress and black stilettos shivers under a large black umbrella. Finished with his deal, the man who bought the drugs approaches the hooker, says something, and they walk north together as the cab keeps going.

At the corner of 22nd Street, I see a woman's briefcase spill open. Papers and documents scatter all over the sidewalk, turning to wet mush as she looks at them and cries. Probably a lawyer. An older woman in a Burberry raincoat yells at her—likely for blocking the middle of the busy sidewalk. Yeah, like she did it on purpose. Thought it would be hilarious to watch the contents of her briefcase become one with a sidewalk puddle while a random person screamed at her. What's wrong with people? The "lawyer" lady goes ballistic on her. I get a visceral pleasure watching this as the harassing woman hurries away. I didn't hear a word, but it's clear what was going on.

I'm sure that in my brain, there must exist a universe parallel to the madness I see. So many thoughts and scenarios are swirling, dancing, flying, falling, screaming, and jumping inside my head. I have to focus. I have to breathe.

"Is this it, mister? This the place you want?"

I'm stunned as I come out of my semi-stupor to find this brilliant man has delivered me to the right pub. I don't know what it used to be called. It was some Polish name I could never remember. It's now Sweep's Pub. Probably because it's on Broome Street. Now, if I can just get as lucky inside as I did with this driver.

I reach into my pocket and hand him a hundred-dollar bill. "Keep it."

He looks at it, then at me. "Hmm. Big bill."

Oh, shit, he might really think I robbed a bank. "My emergency money," I tell him. "Kept it in a safe. It was too late for me to change it into smaller bills before I jumped on a train to New York. I had to close my credit cards too. My wife took my child, and I can't trust her. Not to mention, I don't want her tracking me. I just need to find my daughter!"

His concerned expression is gone. "My wife leave me eight

year ago for working too many hour to support her with good home. How you like that?" He looks angry as he remembers, then smiles. "But I have girlfriend now. Much nicer. You give me another hundred, I break it for you. Most days I don't carry money. You lucky."

I hand him another hundred. True to his word, he gives me a handful of smaller bills. "Thank you. Really. Thank you." I feel guilty that despite liking this man, a part of me wondered if he would keep the second bill.

"Thank you for very big tip. Hope you find your daughter and wife. I say prayer for you."

I thank him, make sure I have my backpack and umbrella, and jump out of the cab. Now for the hard part.

Friday, 5:34 p.m.

The place is more crowded than I imagined. Stuffing my wet umbrella into the zippered pocket of my backpack, I look around, wondering why I imagined it would be far less crowded. It's Friday evening, it's pouring outside, and people are getting off work. Don't they want to get home? I remember that I don't give a damn, but the larger crowd is making things a bit difficult for me to see if Carly might be here. For that reason alone, I'm agitated, but I can't imagine she's anywhere I'd know to look.

Halfway through the room, the bar begins and goes all the way to the back wall. Trying to be as casual as I can, I scan the table crowd for Carly and Rayelle. Before I get to the bar, I stop at the vintage jukebox, admiring the colored lights on the outside, looking at every nuance of the retro design, and hoping I don't look too obvious. I want to see as many faces as I can before I blend in with the bar crowd.

Why did I have the cab driver bring me here? Because this is where I met Carly. Twelve-something years ago. I was working for a restaurant supply chain and had a substantial order to deliver to this place. My first time alone in the city. New York had always overwhelmed me for some reason, but when my boss sent me here, I pushed through my uneasiness and drove into the city. It was crazy, but the traffic almost made it easier for me. I was able to go slowly and get my bearings. It would have been easier to park in one of those big lots on the New York side of the Lincoln Tunnel and take a cab the rest of the way, but with a big delivery, that was near impossible. Not to mention chickenshit and pathetic for a grown-assed man. I cursed my way here, but I made it. Losing my New York-traffic virginity improved my life.

There's some tall scruff of a guy at the far end of the bar who appears to be fixing his gaze on me a little bit longer than he should. I don't like it, but I pretend not to notice while my gut churns and I look to see what songs this machine can play. "Remember (Walking in the Sand)" by the Shangri-Las sounds like a good bet. I stick some coins in and enjoy as it begins to play. I have a bad habit of letting my face reveal too much. Can't do that now. Oh no. Oh no no no no no. Not this time. Too much at stake.

I catch my breath before it can leave my body. Just being here is tough. Memories of my first visit to this place overwhelm me. That was the day I met Carly Victoria Kawai. She was working as a server, but she was a friend of the owners and was trained to do much more. When I came in, pushing a dolly stacked with boxes, she hurried over to greet me. I'd never seen a more beautiful and exotic-looking woman. Her dad is Hawaiian and her mom Italian and Greek.

It was so ironic. Carly was an only child, and her parents wanted the best for her. So they sent her uptown to a private school. She did well there, but because of that, she never knew many people in her own neighborhood. The first time we met, she told me she'd always felt like a fish out of water, and, on bad days, an outlier. That's when we really bonded because I'd always felt that way too.

We started dating, and while I visited the city many times, I only came into this establishment one or two times more. We'd meet somewhere else, or she'd come to Jersey. When I learned she was a single mom with a seven-year-old son, I was good with that and thought it wise to not ask any questions about his father, knowing that she would tell me when it was comfortable for her. Several months later, she confessed that she was raped by a stranger at a friend's birthday party. I felt intense anger. I wanted to track him down and beat the crap out of him—and worse. I kept my fury under wraps because I didn't want her to think I was a loose cannon.

That's when Carly disclosed that a lot of people in her neighborhood had always thought she was a snob because she'd been sent to private school. But when she got pregnant, they made fun of her and said she was a little slut, no better than anyone else. She told me she never tried to be superior to anyone. She just wanted to be herself. And she really hated being around people who'd gossiped about her for years.

That's when I really fell for her big time. I introduced her to my parents, and they did too. A few months after that, they told me they'd buy us a house if we got married. That was all I needed. I proposed. Carly had always dreamed of having her own home in a good suburb, especially one that was close enough by train or car to her parents in New York … yet far enough away from the judging eyes and loose lips that regularly taunted her. She wanted a place where Oliver could grow up as safe as any kid can in these fucked-up times. When he turned eight, I adopted him. Four years later, she became pregnant with Rayelle, and I learned all over again that I had a capacity to love in ways I'd never imagined.

I have to find my daughter. And I don't know where my son is now, but I'm praying he's okay. I miss him something fierce.

How is this song over already? Wow, it's a short one. I see "Bohemian Rhapsody." Almost six minutes long. That's a better choice. I feel like I'm standing naked in this crowded place and every eyeball is on me. Queen to the rescue.

Carly and I had so much fun together. We laughed a lot—but there were many times when nothing was funny. I'd be lying if I said we didn't have our problems, but seriously, what couple doesn't? There was one time, early on, when she seemed to tune out of our marriage for several months. She said it was a family thing she couldn't discuss. Even after I found out what it was, I still thought her evasive behavior said a lot about how she felt about me—or didn't feel. It hurt. And it's hurt for the past two years when she stopped letting me touch her, but I believed she had health issues, and I didn't want to make it all about me. I thought that's what good husbands do. I never imagined it was because she was back in touch—and in love—with Oliver's biological father.

There's fear in the pit of my stomach that's unlike anything I've ever known. I want to hold my daughter and never let her go.

That dude at the end of the bar gives me the once-over again.

I rock to the music and pretend I'm oblivious.

I wonder how I can be full of rage, sick with worry about Rayelle, and still be intoxicated with the woman who kidnapped her. That's the really messed-up thing about love. It doesn't take a hike when you need it to. It loiters, taunts, and confuses. There's this recurring hope, running wild through the incongruity of my thoughts, that she was forced to write the letter that way. Maybe things aren't as they appear. What if she's in trouble? Should I be so quick to condemn her?

Someone taps me on the shoulder. I jump. *Fuck it, Liam. Chill.*

A hipster chick in her late twenties with massive fake eyelashes is looking at me. "Hey, sorry to startle you, but since you're not having a conversation with anyone, I thought you might take a minute to help me. I'm down from Washington Heights to meet this guy from Tinder. We both swiped right and all that. Yesterday, he texted me to come here, but I just saw he texted me again to say he was at Marge's Place and to meet him there instead. Didn't even give me an address. Is that a bad sign?" She waits for my answer, but I've got nothing. She pouts. "Well, I guess I can Google it and all, but still. I wonder if that was rude of him and like yeah ... what kind of place does he want me to meet him in now?"

I can't help this woman with her online dating dilemmas, nor do I know much about anything in this neighborhood. Before I can bullshit my way out of answering, another woman turns and joins our conversation. While she gives directions and a personal review of Marge's Place, I listen for ten seconds, then turn away and tune out.

Okay. No more wasting time. I've got to go to the bar and find a way to casually ask about Carly. I'd better order a drink first, then ask as an afterthought. Yeah. That will sound better. But if I were the bartender, I wouldn't tell me squat.

As I gently push my way through the two-deep bar, I inadvertently end up standing behind the scruffy guy who'd been staring at me. He looks stressed. Probably why he hasn't shaved. He speaks to the female bartender. "You see any thirty-something-year-old dudes in here ... ones you've never seen before, if they ask about anyone, you don't tell him fuck all, keep him here, and then you get my attention. In fact, if anyone at *all* asks, you do the same thing. Got it, Lexi?"

She looks slightly concerned, nods, then goes back to pouring a beer from the tap.

I've got to come up with a Plan B. This won't work. I turn to go and feel a tight grip on my shoulder. My normal get-your-fucking-hands-off-me response isn't going to cut it. But I pull away and reveal my dissent with a look. Can't help myself. Scruffy man is way scarier close up because he's angry. Maybe that wasn't the best choice. I relax my face. Playing dumb is better than aggressive. Definitely.

"I've never seen you here before," he states, as if seeing a stranger in New York City is a fucking crime or anomaly.

I have my trigger finger on my sarcasm gun, but I reconsider. He doesn't wait for my answer. He's not done talking. "Why don't you tell me why you picked this place?"

Of all the gin joints, in all the towns, in all of the world, he walks into mine. I want to say it, to mock him, but I don't think quoting *Casablanca* or any other movie is going to help me out of this one.

He puts his hand back on my shoulder and squeezes. "I'm

waiting for an answer, motherfucker."

Wow, that escalated quickly. I panic as he shakes me.

"Well?"

I change my entire countenance and embrace timidity as I break into a goofy grin. "Well there, feller, only reason I find myself in here is because there's a mighty rain outside. Them seas are treacherous. Just came here to see if a winder seat up front might be openin' up. Sure would like to have my chow at one of them there tables. I'm a sea captain, you know. Gotta keep my eyes on the water and all them sailors walkin' by." My insides freeze in fear.

The guy looks stunned and says nothing until his friends start to laugh. He's still not convinced. Damn. Wasn't that enough?

"I'm Bob. What's yer handle?" I continue to grin while I fantasize about punching him and wonder where my wife and daughter are. I feel as if I'm made of glass, falling in slow motion to the tile floor, anticipating my demise, knowing I'll shatter into a million pieces.

Wait! I've convinced him. His expression changes, and he waves me away. "Go on. Get the hell outta my face, nutjob."

Not needing to hear him ask twice, I hurry toward the door. Who the hell is he? He had to be talking about me to the bartender. Carly must've known I'd come here looking for her. It's the most obvious place to start my search, even though I didn't think of it at first. She's figuring out my moves as I try to figure out hers. I've got to be more careful.

I've just dodged a speeding bullet, and I know it. And I'm no closer to finding them. Time is running out.

CHAPTER FOUR

I hurry out of Sweep's like I'm running from the law. I don't know if that guy really bought my Captain-Bob routine or if he just pretended to because his friends were laughing. I wasn't going to wait around to find out.

I'm not the fucking criminal here. Carly is. I think. I need to find them. The rain has temporarily subsided. At least I can keep the red umbrella out of sight for now. I was planning to take Ray-Ray to the Farmer's Market tomorrow and then surprise her with a movie. Now she'll be surprised if she ever sees me again. What the hell has she been told? How could they do this?

I'm walking fast and have no clue where I'm going. But I'm petrified of being followed. Within minutes, I'm hurrying down the much-narrower Crosby Street. I keep going until it dead-ends at Howard. Which means nothing to me. What do I do now? *Think, Liam, think!* Wait, that woman who asked me about Marge's Place. I thought I'd tuned out the gabby woman who came to her rescue, but now I remember hearing the words, "Marge is an icon in this neighborhood. Knows pretty much everyone. Just don't get on her bad side."

That's where I'll go. Where the hell is it? I start to pull out my phone and then remember I don't want to turn it on for fear of being tracked. I have a burner phone, but it's still in the original packaging. Not going to mess with that standing on a street corner. I run into a

grocery store and pick up a pack of mints. Casually, I ask the cashier
if he knows where Marge's Place is.

"Heard of it for sure. But I don't know the address." He yells
to someone in the back. "Yo, Jay, know where Marge's Place is?"

I'm paranoid. I don't know who's watching, and the last thing
I want to do is broadcast what I'm asking or where I'm going. I know;
I'm in New York City. There are millions of people here, and I'm a
nobody. But I just learned in Sweep's that it's a good bet people are
looking for me. Probably not-so-nice people too. So no, I'm not
paranoid. I'm careful.

I get an address on Houston Street, but luckily, now speaking
with his indoor voice, Jay comes up front and tells me how to walk to
Marge's Place. Somehow, I remember Houston Street runs east and
west across Lower Manhattan. Luckily, where I need to go isn't far. I
thank them both and hurry out. If I'm grateful for anything, it's that
the rain has stopped long enough for me to get there. Just as I arrive,
it starts again.

The green awning has the name prominently displayed.
Walking in, I get why that woman's Tinder date wanted to meet her
here. The place is softly lit and has a completely different vibe. While
Sweep's was more of a place *to* meet someone, Marge's Place appears
to be more the spot to go once you already have. Across from the long
walnut bar, there are a line of romantic nooks along the opposite wall,
booths on either side of a table and tied-back red curtains framing
each entrance, just waiting to be freed.

Lots of people at regular tables too. A fair number of them
appear to be work colleagues letting loose after a long week. About
nine or ten loners sit at the bar, but they're most likely regulars. I'm a

walking sore thumb in this place. Maybe this was a bad idea. Problem is, I don't have a better one.

At the empty end of the bar, the red-headed woman in her mid-fifties standing behind it is looking at me, motioning for me to come over. Oh, shit. That must be Marge, and she's already suspicious of me.

I force a smile as I approach. I've never been too good at nonchalance when I'm feeling anything but. Would have been a crap actor.

"Sit your ass down," she says with a wink, waving off the bartender who's walking our way.

I can't read her, but that's one hell of a greeting. Something about her feels familiar, but I'm paranoid by nature and often suspicious of a lot of people … but still. I force a pathetic "Hello."

She must know I'm wary. "Don't worry. I don't bite." She thinks. "Not unless someone gives me a reason to."

"Don't want to do that," I struggle to say.

She's studying my face now. "I'm Marge. Owner of this place. But you've probably figured that out."

"Yeah."

"This is the part where you tell me your name."

Shit. Like I said. I'm a crap actor. Even worse at improv. "Sorry, I'm Liam."

She doesn't say squat. Just stares at me like I'm an oddity in some museum as she comes around to my side and sits on the stool next to me. Her entire countenance changes. "Where's home, Liam?"

"Trenton."

Nobody has ever looked at me with such intensity, except

maybe that guy back at Sweep's.

"Straight-up truth time, Liam. What brings you here?"

Oh fuck! She must know that guy from Sweep's. What? Is there a red alert out on me for coming to find my kidnapped daughter and my maybe-but-probably-not-kidnapped wife? "Just looking for someone."

Her look softens. "I called you over here because you look out of sorts. You still do. Only want to help. Why don't you talk to me?"

I exhale, trying not to be obvious. Maybe she's okay, but that's one hell of an intense stare. It's almost like she can see my insides. It's creepy in a way.

"What can I get you?"

"Got some good beer on tap?"

"I'm Irish. This is an Irish pub." She smiles. "Of course. How about a Guinness?"

"Sure." If she'd offered me a Shirley damn Temple, I would have agreed.

She gets up and draws my beer, slaps a coaster on the bar, and puts the beer on top of it. Grabbing whatever unfinished drink she has behind the bar, she comes around and sits next to me again. "Wanna tell me what's going on?"

I don't know how to respond.

"Really. I just want to help you."

"Why? I'm a stranger."

She nods in the direction of the tables and booths. "Look over there."

I take advantage of her offer as an excuse to scan every face I can.

"This is lovebird city. For the most part, anyway. Ya hear me, Liam? Not a lot of men who look like you haul ass into my place. Not alone anyway. You stand out. But you already know that. Something heavy is weighing on you. I've been around the block a few times and then some. Maybe I can lend a hand. You're not here looking to get laid. That's obvious."

"No. Not at all." She's sharp, but I feel a bit insulted as if she's saying I couldn't if I wanted to. That's the last thing on my mind, but I'm glad I don't come off like some horny pub crawler. I take a few sips of Guinness, knowing that I need a lot more than liquid courage to help me through this nightmare. I don't know if I should confide in her, but I've got absolutely nothing else. I have to place a huge bet here, trusting that Marge is for real. Just gonna pray I come out on the winning side. Plus, I feel oddly drawn to her.

"Come on, Liam. You can do it." She looks into my eyes. "You *can* trust me. I know, famous last words of every liar on the planet, but you can."

I take a huge breath, which oddly seems to please her. This feels insane and bizarre, but I have to go with it.

She's looking at me with kindness. The kind I don't think you can fake. I've got everything to win and everything to lose. What a fucked-up predicament. But with zero options, I trust my gut and accept her at her word.

"Okay," I tell her. "Here's what happened." I'm hyperventilating, but by some miracle, I'm able to stop. "So, it's like this." I pause to see that she's with me. She is. "Earlier today, I went to the bank after lunch to cash my check." I'm thinking this afternoon already feels like a million years ago. I cut the narrative in my head and resume speaking to Marge. "That's when the teller informed me that both of my accounts are closed. My head was spinning so hard I thought it might fly off and hit the walls of the bank, maybe taking out a few customers with it." Damn, I'm being dramatic as fuck. *Watch your words, Liam.*

I look at Marge. She's waiting for me to continue.

"That's when I hurried home to find my worst fears realized. My wife was gone, and she'd taken the love of my life, our precious eight-year-old daughter, Rayelle, with her." I pause for a moment to slow my breathing. "Everything gone—in the blink of an eye."

"Oh, hell no." Marge clenches her fists, but I doubt she's aware I've noticed.

"The house was neat, like always, and it was obvious she'd planned everything. Damned if I know for how long. When I went downstairs, I found a letter she'd left me, and it confirmed what I'd already figured out. And then some." I stop and struggle to catch my breath.

"You're doing fine, Liam. Keep talking." She splays her hands on the bar as if she's done it before—like it's some method for keeping her anger in check.

"Well, it appears that the money in our checking and savings accounts wasn't enough for her, so she took our entire emergency savings from the safe. Didn't leave me a wooden nickel as my father likes to say." I stop to fume. "I canceled our credit cards, found the small stash of my own that I'd hidden, and made my way to New York."

She's not saying anything. I've never had such a rapt audience. I keep talking. "In the letter, she told me that she's gone back to the love of her life and that I'll only see my daughter again if *she* fucking decides I will. Oh, yeah, and that she's leaving the country in twenty-four hours."

Marge is genuinely alarmed. "What time did she leave you the note?"

My face drops. "I don't know. I saw it sometime after one. I was counting twenty-four hours from then. Didn't even think about that. I might have way less time than I first thought."

Someone taps me on the back, and I nearly self-eject from the stool. I turn to see the woman from Sweep's.

She gives me a big smile. "Well, as you can see, I found my way here." She lowers her voice. "So far, my Tinder match is a real doll baby. Glad I came. Who says online dating doesn't work?" She twists her mouth. "Hey, you, I thought you didn't know this place. Were you messing with me?" She talks playfully now, and it sure as hell looks like flirting. I want to throw up. "Maybe hoping I'd stay at Sweep's with you instead?" Damn. She's batting her fake, heavily mascaraed eyelashes at me.

"Did you come over here to talk to this gentleman?" Marge asks her. "Because if you did, I don't think 'doll baby' will be happy about it. Do you?" She challenges the woman with a hard stare.

"Oh, no. I'm just on my way to the ladies' room, and I—"

"Keep walking, and you'll find it on your right," Marge tells her. "Atta girl."

"Thank you," I say to Marge as the woman hurries away.

"Tell me more, Liam."

"Strangely enough, if it weren't for that woman,"—I nod in her direction—"I wouldn't be sitting here. I met her in Sweep's, and she asked me if I knew where this place was. I didn't have a clue; some woman told her. Said a few things about you that made me think to come here."

Marge bites the inside of her lip. "Like what?"

I quickly summarize all that happened and explain why Sweep's was the first stop on my not-so-magical mystery tour. She exhales—as if a weight as been lifted from her shoulders.

"Well, then, I'm glad she was good for something. Divine intervention comes in strange packages. Glad you followed your instincts. More than you know. Go on."

Marge doesn't interrupt me as she soaks in every word. I get the feeling she actually cares. I look for malice in her eyes, but I don't see any, despite knowing she doesn't suffer fools gladly, and I'm sure as hell feeling like one. When I finish talking, Marge takes the last swig of her drink and slides it to her right. "Want something to eat, Liam? My treat."

My stomach is growling, but I decline her offer.

"Listen, kiddo. If you're going to be out all night looking for your wife and kid, you damn well need some sustenance. Now, what will you have? I'll grab a menu for you."

"Not necessary. If you've got a cheeseburger and fries, that would be great. Thanks."

She calls the bartender down, gives him my order, and asks for a bowl of soup and a sandwich for herself. As he walks away, she turns back to me. "Listen, the short version of your story isn't going to help me help you. Hear me? I need to ask you some detailed questions if we're gonna get anywhere."

I have to trust her. "What do you want to know?"

"You said you met your wife at Sweep's when she was working there over a dozen years ago. What's her name?"

"Carly. It was Carly Kawai." The look in her eyes gives me hope. "It's Carly Tallamore now."

Marge turns pale. "I knew it. I knew it." She's muttering to herself as if I'm not even here.

Not knowing why is freaking me out. Why would my wife's name have such an impact on her? Panic in the pit of my stomach is working its way to the outside. I can't show her my fear. I clutch my hands together so I won't flail my arms like a lunatic. Something is off-kilter. But what? I still trust Marge as well as I can, but there's more to this. I think she's right about divine intervention bringing me here. I lean forward, feeling sweat forming on my brow. "You knew what? My wife? What does 'it' refer to?"

Whatever caused such an emotional reaction in Marge has reset itself. She's back in full control now. "I didn't know the lady personally, but I knew the Kawai family. I knew the situation. Let's put it that way." She pauses. "Sweep's was Kowalski's when you met Carly, right?"

"Yes!" I say emphatically. "That's it. I couldn't remember the name." I see the wheels turning in her head.

"I'm going to tell you what I can, Liam. But I want you to understand that while I grew up in this neighborhood and have known a lot of people—and still do—can't say I have a full timeline of events in my head. Though I know that Carly went to school uptown, so I wouldn't have seen her hanging much with the local kids anyway."

"Right, she went to school uptown." Marge is correct, not sure where she's going with this. I just want to know what she has to say about Carly. But she's getting off the subject with her personal history.

"I wasn't always a model citizen. The hubs either. We've both done a few stints in the hoosegow, pokey—if you get my drift."

Not expecting this, I try to be cool. What about *Carly*?

"No need for pretense here. I can see you're shocked. Never murdered anyone. But I've led a pretty messed-up life. Several years after my second release, my uncle, Lorcan O'Toole, God rest his soul, gave me a job. Yes, he waited quite a while to make sure I didn't repeat my past mistakes, but even then, I don't know how that man ever found it in his heart to believe in me as he did. But working here turned my life around. I never knew he was auditioning me to see whether I'd be fit to entrust this place to one day. But I was a different woman. After many more years, he passed, and I became the owner. Still got the mischief in me—that'll never leave—but I'm an honest woman now. As honest as anyone can really be."

I'm fascinated, but I'm also impatient, worried, and hoping she'll get back to what matters. I just know I can't push her.

The bartender comes over and puts paper placemats, napkins, and silverware in front of us. Reaching under the bar, he pulls out a bottle of ketchup along with a wooden salt and pepper holder. After he promises to be right back, I force myself to ask Marge an uncomfortable question. "Is there a reason you want me to know this?"

"Yes." She touches my hand, then pulls away. "Putting myself in your shoes, well, you've got enough on your plate without wondering who's legit trying to help. I thought if I shared some cold, hard facts about myself, it would help. And also, you'll better understand why I know some things and not others. And why I recognize a person in trouble. Seen far too many of them."

She's right. Telling me this makes things feel less one-sided. I look up to see the bartender putting our food in front of us. I thank him, sprinkle salt on my fries, followed by a heavy squeeze of ketchup, then shove a few of them into my mouth. Marge is smiling at me, but oddly, she looks like she wants to cry.

"You *are* hungry. My still-legal-but-not-for-long husband likes to eat fries that way. Only he'll shove two or three times as many into that big mouth of his. Gluttonous bastard. I used to stop him when we were together, afraid he'd choke and stop breathing. Now I don't care what he does or where he goes. Just know he's out chasing tail...." I can see she's momentarily gone to another place. "Never mind."

She's fully focused on me again. Sounds like she's got a lot of crap to contend with on the outside, but still far better than being locked up. I take a few sips of Guinness, then smother ketchup on the burger before I shove it in my mouth. I have a bad habit of eating like this when I'm hungry. I turn to face her. "My mother always tells me I look gauche when I eat this way. She says I should eat more artistically. She paints watercolors ... trees, streams, and mountains ... so I guess she wants me to eat like a mountain stream."

Marge laughs and takes a few sips of her roasted-garlic and tomato soup, but I know her peripheral vision is focused on me.

I can't hold back anymore. "I'm sorry, Marge. I don't want to be rude, but I really need to know about my wife. You said you knew her."

Laying her spoon down, she looks at me. "This is some heavy stuff I've got to tell you, Liam. I'll try to be ... well ... *artistic* about it."

I smile. Her humor calms me a bit, but my heart rate goes up. "Whatever it is, please tell me. I don't have a lot of time."

"I'll get to the point."

Shoving another fry into my mouth, I nod.

Marge motions for the bartender to bring her another drink. I'm surprised to see him fill a glass with only tonic and put a piece of lime on the top.

"Liam, the Kowalski family, who owned the joint now known as Sweep's Pub, were the best of friends with the Kawai family. Lived in the same ten-story apartment building, not too far from here. Anyway, the event I'm about to tell you about had to have happened several years after you and Carly got hitched."

"Okay. Go on."

Marge takes a cocktail napkin and wipes her brow with it. "Every few months, as you no doubt know, your wife would bring your son to New York to see his grandparents, and when your daughter was born, she'd bring her too."

"Yeah. Carly would visit as often as she could. I was always working, especially when I could get overtime. Always wanted to give my family everything."

She offers a sad smile. "You're a good man." Crumpling up the napkin, she momentarily stands, pitches it with ease over the bar into a trashcan, then continues her story without missing a beat. "From what I heard, Carly, the kids, and your in-laws were in Kowalski's having lunch when a former neighbor, who had moved out of the immediate area years before, Sandy Magel, approached the table. Expecting to engage in small talk, Carly was surprised when Sandy boldly asked about the boy …."

"Oliver. I adopted him when he was eight."

"Right. Okay." She nods. "Well, Sandy wanted to know who Oliver's father was and if was she keeping his kid from him." Marge readjusts her position on the stool. Her expression quickly changes. "Can you believe the gall of that tripe? None of the damn bitch's business, I tell ya, but Elaina Kawai panicked. Instead of telling the woman to mind her own business or kick her ass like I would've done, she gets up from the table and pulls the nosy bitch aside. Elaina was afraid Sandy would keep pushing if she didn't offer some kind of answer, so she tells her Carly doesn't know the father's name. Goes on to repeat the same story the family had told a select few about the boy's paternity. That Carly was raped at her friend Jani's Sweet Sixteen party at the Kowalski's home. Their two-bedroom apartment, mind you. And that supposed friend of Jani's had brought an uninvited guest with her, a guy nobody knew, and that he raped Carly in Jani's bedroom, fled, and nobody ever saw him again. And that Jani's friend claimed she didn't know him, but came in with him thinking he was invited. And nobody would say who *she* supposedly was." Marge's face reddens. "Because *she* was a phantom friend." She fumes. "Pisses me off something fierce that Elaina shared this bullshit lie. Sandy would have been flat out on the sidewalk for sticking her nose in someone else's beeswax if I'd been at that table. Wiping the blood off her face and pulling a hot poker outta her sorry ass if it didn't decide to take up permanent residence there."

My head feels like it's spinning. "The rape story is the same one Carly told me. And I believed her until I read her letter. When she said she'd gone to be with her first love, I knew it had to be Oliver's father, and that she'd obviously been lying to me since day one. I always thought her parents would have searched the ends of the earth to punish a rapist. And stupidly, I believed I was her first true love."

"Maybe the first love she could be *honest* about," Marge says. "The most shocking part of this story, to me, is that the few friends the Kawai family confided in actually kept their traps shut about her supposed rape. Carly was apparently so damn tight-lipped about her baby daddy, that to this day, I don't think even her besties have a clue. The only person who would know—"

"Who! Who would know? Please, Marge. Give me a name!" I wipe ketchup off my face, then start furiously balling the napkin with my left hand until I catch myself and stop. This woman needs to know I'm sane—or close to it.

"You see, Liam, while Carly's bogus rape story stayed secret all of those years, like all secrets, they eventually get exposed. See, that day in the pub, Carly didn't appreciate her mother giving Sandy the time of day, much less giving her any information at all. She told her dad to watch her kids, then got up from the table and told Sandy to get the fuck out. But she didn't want to leave, and it turned into quite the public spectacle. And that's how Sherita Kowalski, who was only a few yards away, came to hear the story for the first time. She's a damn fine woman, Sher, and believe me, nothing went on in their home that she didn't know about. There's no way on God's green earth that something like that could have happened at her daughter's birthday party. A stranger wouldn't have made it through the front door, much less stayed for more than thirty seconds. Not only that, Sherita'd taken a ton of photos. Carly was in nearly every one, and there was no one in any picture who didn't belong. That damn rape nonsense is an implausible scenario. Total bullcrap. A donut with nothing but the damn hole."

"Oh, shit." Yeah. That's all I can say. My heart is racing, and time is passing.

Marge understands this. "I'm gonna cut to the chase so you can scram."

"Where am I 'scramming' to? I don't have a clue."

"You will." She takes a bite of her sandwich. "Okay, see, so that was the end of an era right there. Sherita and her hubs had been Carly's parents' best friends. Imagine how they felt, knowing they told that lie involving her and her daughter's party. Boy, you never saw a friendship break up so fast." She coughs, and I'm guessing she used to be a smoker. "After that public argument, the story made its way around the hood something fierce. Gossip-hungry idiots believed that Sherita had let a rapist come to the party. I've never seen her so angry—not to mention hurt. And her hubs ... don't even get me started on what he would have done if Sherita didn't hold him back."

"This is unreal," I say, stating the obvious.

"Yep. Anyway, in no time at all, Kowalski's Pub went up for sale, and they moved somewhere in Midtown and got jobs at a hotel off Times Square."

I feel like it's raining puzzle pieces, only not nearly as many as I need.

There's another tap on my shoulder just as a crack of thunder booms through the room. "What the fuck?" I say loudly as I simultaneously jump and turn around. Oh, no. I can't believe the Tinder chick is here again. She's crying, but I have no time for her.

"Look, I'm sorry to bother you. My name is Fancy, and my date just took my wallet. That's why he wanted to come to this place.

You know, the soft lighting and all." She pouts. "It was all too good to be real. I thought I'd found true love, but instead, I just had my wallet lifted. And now, I can't pay the tab or get home."

I feel a twinge of empathy, but I'm angry that she's dragging me into this at the worst possible time. Marge is seething and responds to her before I can say squat. "This isn't a good time. Why don't you call the people who named you Fancy, tell them they owe you big for that silly appellation, and get a credit card number to pay the check with. Not letting you skip out, Fancy Pants. Now get out of my face so I can finish business here. You hear me?"

Fancy doesn't move. She looks at me as if she expects me to save her.

Marge is furious. She catches the bartender's attention, gives him some kind of hand signal, and he calls the woman down to the middle of the bar.

Damn, I need to get going.

Marge sees that I'm in a state of panic. She touches my hand like she did before but says nothing for a moment.

I catch my breath as she watches me. I look at her. "I know exactly when everything you just told me had to have happened. Carly came home from New York one night, really messed up, but she kept trying to hide it. When I pushed her to talk, she said she had a fight with her parents. That was weird because they got along so well, but maybe not as well as I'd thought. She was in a bad way for months but never said why. Even my parents noticed. Then, one day, her mom and dad announced they were moving to Hawaii because her dad missed his home, and Carly told me that the move is what caused all of the upset. It made sense, except I never understood why she didn't just tell me that from the start. But I let it go."

Marge nods. "Yeah. They moved to Hawaii. And yeah, your bullshit radar was fully functioning."

I look at the clock. "I've got to go! It's nearly seven."

"Seven o'clock." She looks at me. "Time is Irish once an hour. Did you know that? It's why they call it O'clock."

Somewhere, I've heard that before, but it's hardly worth thinking about. All I want is to find my daughter.

Marge takes a swig of her drink as if she's re-setting again. "Okay, I'm going to tell you what you need to know and send you on your way."

I'm feeling so many emotions at once that I can barely identify them. Fear and hope have one hell of a way of blending themselves into one miserable sensation. "You gonna tell me where to 'scram' to?"

"Sure am." She glances down the bar to make sure that Fancy is in her seat.

"See here, Liam. Sherita and I are good pals. We go way back. Anyway, getting back to that day when Sher first heard Carly's lie. My friend isn't the kind of person to let some shit like that slide—especially when it ruins her reputation and harms her family. So, while they were working to sell the place, she started digging. With a big ole-assed shovel too. Found out that Carly had a boyfriend, a few years older, who got her pregnant at fifteen, then went to prison three months later for second-degree murder after he killed a grocery store owner in a robbery. Got twenty-five years. That was when ...."

"When what?"

Marge looks out of sorts. "Well, that's when she learned they all lied because she didn't want the felon to find out he had a son.

Elaina and Don Kawai didn't want the other grandparents claiming the boy. That's why they went along with the sham of a story, and that's why they never looked for a rapist who didn't exist." She takes a swill of her drink. "Guess it was statutory rape, considering Carly's age, but she never saw it that way."

"I can't fucking believe this. I really don't know the woman I'm married to. Who the hell is this guy?"

"Marge!" the bartender calls.

"Hold on, Liam. Rico needs something."

What's happening? I need something too. Why does Rico look so worried? He and Marge exchange a few words, and she hurries back to me.

"Liam, Rico just told me that my miserable old man is on his way over. I can't tell you anything else now. The bastard is drunk, and I don't want you involved with his shit. You go see Sher. She works nights. Front desk at the Curtain Call Hotel on Eighth Avenue. I'll call and tell her to expect you. She's short, about five one. Reddish-brown hair and glasses. A little spitfire with a Chicago accent. Grew up there. She can pick up where I left off. She knows more than I do anyway."

I stand and hug Marge, surprising myself. "Thank you. Thank you so much."

"You're welcome. Now listen, I want you to let me know how this works out. Promise you'll come see me again when you find your daughter. Anything you need, call me." She reaches over the bar and grabs a card and a pen, then scribbles on the back of it. "Now you got the bar, my cell, and the address of the hotel. Get going."

I reach into my pocket and pull out some cash.

"You're not thinking of paying for that burger and fries you wolfed down, are you?"

"Yeah, actually. I—"

"Save your money, boy. One more thing before you leave. Be careful. That lady sitting nervously at the bar. She's a damn con artist. And her name ain't Fancy, but she's a fancy liar. I should know. If she doesn't pay up, she's gonna meet New York City's finest. She was hoping you'd take pity on her so she could lure you out of here to some place where she could rob you blind. Be careful who you show sympathy for. Even a little."

Marge is scary perceptive. "How did you know how I was feeling?"

"I saw it in your eyes. Practice your poker face, boy. It could save your life. And one more thing."

"Sure, what is it?"

"See that big guy by the door? That's my friend. Ken. Does all sorts of things for me. Tonight, he's working the door because we had a few undesirables in here earlier … folks a bit scarier than our fancy con artist sitting over there. Ken's known by many as 'Karma Ken,' and nobody wants to mess with him. Nicest man in the world, though. Tell him I said to reach into the closet up front and give you my old man's blue jacket. You'll need it in this weather. You hear me?"

"I hear you. Thanks, Marge."

"Go on now. Scramola."

CHAPTER FIVE

It's pouring again as I step out onto Houston Street. The jacket Marge insisted I take is really helping to repel the rain. But it's still wet as a mother out here. Normally, I'd walk to Times Square and not bother with a cab. But it's two-and-a-half miles uptown, and this weather is insane. Marge's friend at the door told me I'd have better luck getting a cab if I walk a couple of blocks to Sixth Avenue.

I take his advice. By the time I get there, the rain is coming down with a vengeance. The fury of the raindrops hitting my umbrella and me feels almost personal. But I won't let this deluge stop me from getting a cab and getting where I need to be. I'm hoping my red umbrella will stand out like it did earlier. "Earlier" feels like it was days ago.

I see some cabs coming my way, and think I might get lucky. Just as I raise my arm to wave one down, my backpack is snatched from behind.

I spin around to see a thirty-something-year-old guy in an oversized designer hoodie clutching my backpack, smiling like a homicidal clown. What the actual fuck? Most thieves grab and run, but this dripping-wet sonofabitch stands there laughing while I dork out with my red umbrella.

"There's nothing in there but a change of clothing and some personal items. Nothing of any use to you." I panic, knowing there's a few grand hidden in the clothing, but hope a quick inspection wouldn't reveal that. "Give me my fucking backpack. I didn't do anything to you."

The dude still wears that sick smile. Almost as if it isn't raining where he's standing, and he's got all the time in the world. "There's where you're wrong. You could have helped my friend pay her tab back at Marge's, maybe offered her cab fare home. But no, you couldn't be bothered to help a lady."

"Says the guy who stole her wallet?" I regret the words the minute I speak them. This is "Doll Baby." He didn't steal anything from her. It's like Marge said—she's a scammer. One who doesn't work alone, obviously. She probably would have lured me out here. I crush my own thoughts. I don't want to see where they go, and I don't care what game these people are playing. I need to get to Midtown. I'm not letting this bogus yuppie punk take what's mine because it's what he does.

He looks at me, his eyes threatening. "Empty your pockets. Give me your wallet and every cent you have, and I'll give you back your big-ass purse." I press my lips together and seethe while I desperately try to figure out what to do. He bursts out laughing. I can't stand being laughed at; I won't let him get away with it. I close my umbrella and drop it. Infuriated, I lunge at him. Before I can get my hands around his neck, his expression, eyes now bulging, changes to that of a raging maniac, and I feel the sharp edge of a knife at my neck as my hands drop to my sides. My instinct is to reach for my pocketknife in my pants, but I know he can slit my throat before I ever touch it.

I freeze. If there was ever a time not to act without thinking, this is it.

"Hey, purse boy, did you think I was fucking playing around? This ought to convince you I'm not!" He cuts me lightly on the back of my neck, but it's enough that I feel blood seeping out. "That's a warning. I can go for the carotid next. Believe me; I won't fucking hesitate."

I gulp. I believe this bastard. I'm not going to die over my wallet. Besides, he doesn't know I've got a ton of money in my backpack, not to mention I still have a bunch of it stuffed on my person. I have to give him my wallet, but I can't quite bring myself to do it. *You have no other choice, Liam! Give it to him or die!*

Just as I'm about to give in, a big hand grabs Doll Baby's wrist, squeezing it so hard that he drops the knife. It's the guy from Marge's. Karma Ken. He told me he helps people get what they've got coming to them.

Ken pulls down Doll Baby's hood and grabs him by a fistful of his thick mop of brown hair. "Give the man back his backpack, or you'll be singing soprano in the rain. And there's nothing I have in mind that'll resemble an old Hollywood movie. No tap dancing or happy splashing. You hear me?"

The guy drops my backpack into a puddle. I pick it up and sling it over my shoulder. Reaching down again, I grab my umbrella and open it.

In a move so quick, I didn't even see what he did, Ken is now standing in front of the guy, pointing a gun at him.

"How the fuck?" the punk says as he recognizes his face.

Ken snorts. "How'd I find your thieving-apparently-also-violent ass? Maybe because your partner in crime followed this man out of Marge's with her eyes, then sent a text the second he was gone.

Talk about a surefire bet some crap is going down. Amateur shit."

"Okay, okay. You got me, you big fucking oaf. Just put the gun away."

I want him to take this loser con artist away, but I wish he could do it without a gun. They terrify me.

"What did you just call me, asshole?"

"Nothing." Doll Baby is cowering now.

"You call me that again, you'll be tasting an oaf-knuckle sandwich. That's all I got on the menu except this piece. Hear me?"

Ken pauses to watch the sniveling coward shaking before him, his once-gelled hair looking like overcooked angel hair pasta. From meeting him earlier and observing him now, I know he's only doing what's necessary. He just wants this loser to think he's enjoying himself. "I have no intention of shooting you. Unless you make me. Just a friendly escort back to Marge's where the finest in law enforcement will take you and your con-artist girlfriend away."

"Come on, man!" Doll Baby's countenance does a one-eighty, and he's now in aggrieved-yuppy mode. His entire body does some kind of apologetic slump, and his pathetic eyes look at Ken with desperation. "Just say you couldn't find me. I'll give you a hundred bucks … two hundred … three!"

"From the man's wallet that you lifted in the men's room? No thanks. And it's not yours to give. That and I don't take bribes. Especially in the rain."

"W-what?" Confused and stammering, Doll Baby is fresh out of bullshit, and I think Ken's a pretty cool guy. I just hate that he carries, but I know it's necessary.

I come out of my temporary fog, shake off the uneasy feeling the gun gives me, and remember I've got to find my way uptown. "Thanks, man," I say to Ken. "And please thank Marge for me too."

"Hold up, Liam." Still pointing the gun at the punk, he drags him off the curb as he steps into a stream of rushing water in the street. With his free hand, he puts his index finger and thumb in his mouth and hails a cab for me with a whistle that nearly splits my head in two. "Get going, man … and hey, take care of yourself."

"I owe you," I say as I hop into the back of the cab that's stopped for me. As we pull away, I look over to see Doll Baby squirming as Ken directs him down the street with a gun at his back.

Speaking of guns, I just dodged another speeding bullet. This is the worse day of my life, and somehow, I'm catching breaks. Can't last long. Nothing ever does.

Friday, 7:48 p.m.

The Curtain Call Hotel lobby is more mellow than I expected. Wait. I didn't give it a second's thought, so how can it be different from what I never thought about. Now I'm thinking about my twisted logic and getting nowhere. It's just that the amber lighting and the lobby seating, especially this one empty couch, call to me. If I sat down, I could fall asleep. It's not quite eight, and it's already an endless day.

I turn to my right and see an animated crowd in the bar. The music and chatter momentarily drown out my thoughts. I'm here to see Sherita. Where do I find her? There's a huge Reception sign on the wall to my left. A woman fitting her description is talking to a guest. I never thought I might have to wait to speak to her. Shit. I hope she's not super busy. Do people check in this late? I wonder if Ray-Ray had dinner. If she even feels like eating.

Sherita looks like she's Marge's friend. Just has that air of no-nonsense confidence about her. The guest at the counter is gabbing in unrestrained detail about the Broadway musical she'd seen the night before. As soon as she sees me, Sherita's countenance changes. With a quick smile, she tells the woman her description was fascinating, but she's got to help another guest.

The guest turns, looks annoyed that I'm behind her, and walks away. Sherita gestures for me to come to the counter. "Liam?"

"Right. That's me."

She nods toward the guest who just left. "I have a big pin badge that says 'Go Fascinate Someone Else' and I'd love to wear it, but if I put that sucker on, I'd be wearing it to the unemployment office." She looks over at a man whose window is closed as he does some paperwork. "Lewis! Take over for me. Got a quick emergency."

Sherita leads me to a quiet corner of the lobby, and we sit. I tell myself she's looking at me in the same odd way Marge did, but I dismiss the thought. I'm paranoid by nature, and I'm not exactly in ordinary circumstances here. Why wouldn't she check me out before she helps me? Damned if I wouldn't do the same thing.

"I'm Sherita. You can call me Sher if you want. Or Sherita. Just don't call me Rita, and we're good. I begin to say something, but she's already on a roll. "I know you're in a hell of a hurry. You're lucky I talk fast. That sucks rancid swamp water about your wife and kid. I'm going to tell you everything I can to help you find them. Just wish I knew where they were. So Marge filled me in on everything she told you. You already know why we moved out of the neighborhood. Your wife's parents, well—"

"I'm really sorry they brought your name into their lie."

She glances over at the reception desk to make sure Lewis is covering her spot. "They could have still used their bogus rape story and said it happened somewhere else, you know? But nah, Elaina thought dragging her best friend into the story gave it more realism. Fuck that. I have no time for fake friends. Them doing that was the most hurtful thing that ever happened to me. I can be a pissed-off little spitfire, but I was a fuming-mad-better-get-out-of-Dodge-before-I-kill-someone spitfire." She takes a breath. "People who know me call me that." She pauses, looking angry with herself. "Sorry, that's not why you're here."

I offer a nervous smile. "I'm desperate to find my wife and daughter before they're no longer findable." I wince at the thought. "Marge said you did some digging to find the guy who got Carly pregnant."

"Damn straight. I wanted to find 'the impregnator' and have him and Carly tell people the truth so the people of the hood could take our names outta their mouths after they went and fucked themselves for believing it in the first place."

If I weren't so despondent, I'd laugh. This woman is funny. "Marge said you found out who he was and that he went to prison for twenty-five years."

"I did. Most of us in the neighborhood knew all about him, especially after he committed such a horrible crime. We also remember when he went to prison; we just didn't know that he and Carly had any connection at all. And just now, on the phone, I told Marge something she didn't know because … um …"

"It's okay," I reassure her. "Marge told me she did a couple stints in prison. Well, she didn't use that word."

Sherita looks around to make sure no one is listening. "Hoosegow is her preferred vocabulary. So here's the thing. Marge told you that a former neighbor, Sandy, one who'd moved away years ago, was in my pub. Right?"

I nod.

"And when she saw the Kawai family at the table, she went over and stuck her nose into Carly's business as if she had some right to it. And that's the day I found out about the 'Kawai lie.' Our lives changed forever."

"That's just what Marge told me."

"Like I said to her: who runs into a former neighbor and presses them for that kind of information?" Twisting her lips, Sherita leans toward me. "Nothing random about that. Sandy didn't just 'run into' the Kawai family; she came looking for them. See, the father of Carly's son who impregnated her at fifteen, also had a few other gal pals he could legally fuck. Excuse my Polish. Sandy was one of them. She was still in love with the guy, even with his ass in prison for a quarter of a century, and she wanted to know if Carly's son was his. How she knew they were even a thing isn't important now. But that's why everything exploded as it did."

"That sucks, but it makes a lot more sense now." I nonchalantly glance at the wall clock as I feel time running away.

"I know you're in a hurry." Her sympathetic eyes look kindly at me.

So much for feigning nonchalance. "Sorry. Do you know his name? Where he is now?"

"His name is Raymond Oliver Royce, Junior," she tells me.

I feel a punch to my gut that couldn't hurt more if Karma Ken had punched me with his massive hands. My God. Carly named our daughter after Oliver's father, her real true love. And Oliver has his father's middle name. I'm sure Sherita can see my pained face, but I'm not going to explain.

"Good thing Marge called me before you got here, Liam. Gave me time to make a quick phone call." She blows out a puff of air in exasperation. "I thought the guy was still behind bars, but it seems he was paroled five years early." She makes a face. "For freakin' good behavior. Got out about two months ago."

I close my eyes and drift back for a moment. Two months ago is approximately when Carly started sneaking out of the house with one excuse after another. But the excuses made sense—sort of. No time to deliberate on that now. I raise my head and look at Sherita's sympathetic face. "I don't suppose you have an address. You know, where any of his family might live."

She gives me a sad shake of her head. "Nope. I know the Royces were mortified when he killed that lovely man during the robbery. I think he panicked when he pulled the trigger, but the man was dead all the same. Got me right here." Sherita pounds her chest with her right fist. "So, like we did, they moved out of the neighborhood where everyone knew them. From what I've heard through the grapevine, that marriage went down the crapper quickly, and they split up. Their son going to the hoosegow changed everything. Manhattan has millions of people, but a residential neighborhood might as well be a small town. Hear me?"

Captain Bob pops into my head and the shame he felt when his son and nephew embezzled millions. Poor guy having that story on the national news. I don't have time to think about him now. I just know a lot of people do messed-up things, and I need to focus. "I hear you, Sherita. Listen, I'm scared to death that I'll never see my daughter again. I'm worried about my son, too, but I believe he's safe. If you don't have an address for the guy's parents, any thoughts about where I might begin to look?"

"I do. And it's not far from here. See, the father, Raymond Senior, was part owner of one of those big souvenir stores right off Times Square. Has the name Tiger in it. But that could have been changed. And I don't know if he still owns it or works there, but I remember someone telling me that he first worked for his brother. Then I heard he bought into the place. Like I said, can't be sure. Speculation ain't fact. You know?"

A thought occurs to me. "Wait. Carly's letter said they were leaving the country. But if the guy's on parole, isn't that illegal?"

"Sure is. But getting a passport isn't. Unless you have a warrant out for your arrest, you're free to apply. I learned all about that when Marge and her husband … well …."

"So this Royce bastard can't legally leave the country?"

Cocking her head to one side, Sherita looks at me. "You can't legally rob a store and kill the owner, Liam. But that didn't stop him. You think breaking parole in an overburdened system would stop a guy who wants to get out of the country?"

"I need to get to that souvenir store." I stand but remembering something, I sit again. "Wait, when I was in Sweep's, there was some guy checking me out. I'm almost sure he was expecting that I'd come looking for Carly and Rayelle." I'm angry that my own daughter's name momentarily puts a bitter taste in my mouth. "If Senior is still working at the souvenir store, it's not impossible they might be waiting for me too."

Sherita stands. "Walk with me, Liam."

I follow her to a rack of brochures where she shows me one for Circle Line Tours. As a bellhop walks by, she begins talking. "This boat goes all around Manhattan. Takes two and a half hours. Maybe try it on a day it's not raining. It leaves from Pier 83. Midtown. West Side." She rolls her eyes at having to pretend I'm a tourist, and I shove a brochure into the pocket of Marge's husband's jacket to complete the act.

"Sorry about that. Had to move you over here. If I sit too long with a stranger, people get suspicious, and they talk. Sort of like in my old neighborhood." She steals another look at the reception desk. "I don't think you're wrong that someone might be looking for you. A person can't be too careful. Maybe you should disguise yourself."

A ridiculous sigh escapes my lips, and I apologize profusely. "Shit. Who knew I should have stashed a fake beard, mustache, or wig along with my emergency cash? An emergency stache."

She laughs. Just as she's about to say something, a guy in a full suit of armor walks up to us. "Hey, got a room for a knight?"

"Go clank on back to your round table," Sherita tells the man. She rolls her eyes as he walks away. "That's Sir Effin' Lancelot. Met him last night. Here with some Round Table group. Can't be nutty enough in their home cities, so they rendezvous in New York once a year. Because you can never get enough crazy here, right? Sir Lancelot's wife is staying at the Big Apple Royale because she's attending a Furries convention there."

"Never heard of them," I say.

"They're a group of people who geek out over dressing like animals. Okay, all good. To each their own. Except two years ago they had their annual meeting here, and on the last day, at night, a bunch of them were roasting in their costumes and de-furred in the conference room. They headed to the bar, got plastered, and never came back for their furry alter egos because they were all rushing to catch planes the next day. Still got those giant creepy costumes sitting with some other unclaimed property we just can't bring ourselves to chuck."

I wonder if Carly and Ray are rushing to catch a plane. Every muscle in my body tightens as I visualize this happening, my Ray-Ray in tow, scared out of her mind.

Sherita is still talking. "Got an unclaimed woman down there in a storage locker too. She's still waiting for the husband who left her here and ran off with her best friend. Just kidding. She's not here. We threw her out after forty-five days. Anyway, you didn't come here to hear me yammer. As for these clanky knights, I'm hoping they'll all go out into the rain, and by tomorrow, their blabbers will be rusted shut. Like the Tin Man." She sighs. "Where were we?"

I want to laugh, but I can't. "I was saying that I really need a disguise." I look in the direction the knight has gone. I force a smile. "One a little less obvious."

Sherita laughs. "I know a guy. Rents a ratty-ass studio apartment not far from here. Out of work. Used to do wardrobe for one of the big theaters. Survives on odd jobs now. If you've got a few bucks to throw his way, I'm betting he can help. I know he's got a stash of stuff. I can find his number. Come on, kiddo. I'll call him for you and get you on your way."

CHAPTER SIX

Was it really only this morning, in DiNello's Auto Parts store, when I spent fifteen minutes with this preppy dude who wanted to know all about rust removers and rust inhibitors? If anyone had told me then that in twelve hours I'd be in some ramshackle Midtown studio apartment, listening to an unshaven, wild-eyed, long-haired, greasy guy called Spike, telling me how to use spirit gum for prosthetic facial hair, I'd have had them committed. This is the most surreal day of my life—at least that I can remember. I don't think I'd be this way if something more surreal hadn't happened. I just can't think about that now.

Spike is giving me his best sales pitch. "They got these beards with the adhesive strips, you know, stuff you just press on, but if you're looking to fool people close up, maybe this ain't your best option." He sniffles and wipes his nose on his sleeve. Aware I'm watching, he makes a face and explains what I don't need to know. "Nothing came out. Sleeve's clean. Sucked it all back up into the schnoz."

I won't have this insane conversation. I can't bring myself to call him Spike. "Look, man," I say, ignoring his last sentence. "I'm not planning to rob anyone. I just don't want to be recognized. So it's important that I don't look like I'm in disguise. Is there something easier I can do?"

"Yeah. Got a couple of cheap wigs. You've got brown hair, so I'd go with red and maybe black. These are meant for actors to wear on stage, but if you put a hat on, even a beanie, no one will see the seam. And I got some cheap-but-effective press-on staches you can get away with. Oh, and glasses always help with a look, you know?" He pulls a pair of heavy black glasses out of a box. They're hideous. "Like these babies."

"How much do you want for two wigs, two hats, two pairs of glasses, and a press-on stache?"

This bozo strokes his chin as if I've just asked him to explain the Theory of Relativity. Sonofabitch is trying to figure out how desperate I am. He's pissing me off. "If you don't want to sell, I know someone else."

"Fifty for everything," he blurts out. "It's not the best quality, but it'll do for what you need."

"I'll give you a clean hundred. As a thank you for seeing me so fast."

He tries not to smile. I'm angry at myself that I even played this game when my daughter's life is at stake. Why did I even take two seconds to haggle over price? Probably because I was afraid he'd want a grand or more, sensing my desperation, so giving him double what he asked for seemed like a good bet. I hate being taken for a fool. Right now, it shouldn't have mattered, but I've got this rage inside that doesn't want to sit any shit out. I need to let my common sense, if I have any, take the lead and put everything else on the back burner.

Spike is staring at me. Oh, yeah. Money first. I reach into my pocket and hand him a hundred-dollar bill. "Sorry, man. Don't have time to fish around for smaller bills."

"Not a problem." He rubs it between his fingers, tilts it back and forth, looks at the serial numbers front and back, then holds it up to the light. "Nope. Not counterfeit." The human bill detector then roots through his stash of godforsaken junk for the items I just bought. He shoves them into a grocery store bag and hands it to me. "Better put these in your bag there. Keep 'em dry. You're welcome to put your first disguise on before you split. Would be the smart thing to do. I'm happy to help."

"Appreciate it. I'll start with the black wig, beanie, and those black frames."

He offers a cocky smile. "Won't even recognize your damn self. By the way, gonna write down my cell for ya in case ya run out of disguises. I do take-out and delivery." He grins. "Let's step into the living area for a quick transformation."

This guy's apartment is a trash heap. The last thing I'd ever want to do is live here.

Friday, 8:52 p.m.

I'm standing at the north corner of Times Square. The heavy rain is only a drizzle now, and I've never seen so many people in one eyeball intake. These seizure-inducing electronic billboards are pissing me off. I feel completely disoriented as if I'm watching twenty-five movies at once. There must be a million tourists scanning the area with their phones. Every square inch of real estate has an ad plastered on it—still or animated. Every Broadway show, TV series, makeup brand, cell-phone carrier, athletic shoe store, chain clothing store, fast-food restaurant and on and on is represented in one way or the other. Even those animated M & Ms. Especially the green one.

A guy with a heavy New York accent is explaining to some

people that the spot we're all standing in is called Father Duffy Square. Apparently, Father Duffy is the guy immortalized with the statue that stands on a pedestal. He was a military chaplain for the "Fighting 69th." This isn't story hour, and I need to stop listening.

Behind Father Duffy are red bleacher-style seats that also appear to double as the roof of the discount ticket office. I wonder if the statue comes alive and performs. Maybe the petrified priest tap dances his way through the crowd. Nothing would surprise me anymore. This feels like freak city. No, it doesn't feel like it. It is.

The man starts giving his friends the history of another statue, and I tune out completely. Everything is dizzying, confusing, stupefying, and I don't know where to begin finding a souvenir store with the name Tiger in it. I figure most of the stores are clumped together, but not where I'm standing.

My breathing is erratic, and I fear a panic attack coming on. Why didn't I ask Sherita to look up the address for me? I answer my own question. The woman was on the clock at her job. She wasn't sure of the exact name or even if it still existed. Nice enough that she took the time she did for me. I was so happy to get a clue that I didn't ask any more questions. I should have. No, I shouldn't have. She was in the middle of work. I take a few deep breaths. *Do not let yourself lose it. Not now.*

A cop is standing to my right. I ask him where to find a souvenir store with Tiger in the name. "I could tell you, but I'd be lion," he says. "Sorry, bud, I don't know."

I didn't know cops made jokes. Wish I could have laughed. Nice guy. He has no idea where it is but points me to the closest big store. Bet the police get asked dumb shit all the time.

A pretty young Asian woman hurries over to me. She's smiling and pointing to her phone as she's gesturing toward her boyfriend. I know she wants me to take photos of them together. She can't take a selfie because she wants the whole Times Square throng in the background. She giggles as she tries to explain that her arms aren't long enough to get the shots she wants. I don't have the time, but I smile and take four shots before handing her phone back to her. I can't expect others to stop and help me if I don't pay it forward.

I know I need to walk faster now on the off chance another tourist sees reason to stop me. I can't even remember what the cop told me, but when I get to Broadway and 42nd Street, I see a giant store with the I Heart New York name. It's right under this massive billboard of a cheeseburger. It's a good thing I had one at Marge's. My stomach is too upset to put anything in it now.

My God. I forgot about my parents. I'm hoping they haven't tried to call me. They'll be a wreck by now if Carly or I haven't answered our cell phones or landline. Even more so if they hear the recording that Carly's number is no more. I've got to turn on this burner phone the first chance I get. I'll call them and make up some story. I remind myself that far less time has elapsed in reality. My parents won't be worried yet. No point in dragging them into my nightmare unless there's no other choice. Besides, they're such calm and sweet people. Me, I'm the apple who fell far from the tree, rolled into a swamp, and who ironically is having a breakdown in the biggest Apple of them all.

The minute I walk into the souvenir shop, I know it's a mistake. It's crawling with tourists, and the register line is long. I see a lot of people holding "I Heart NY" rain jackets, hats, and umbrellas.

There's not one employee here who has a spare moment, much less to direct me to a competitor. I'm not going to waste my time. I'll just have to keep walking and looking. On my way out the door, I pass a couple with their five-year-old daughter. She's wearing a Paddington Bear rain jacket. My eyes well up as I wonder where Rayelle is. I hope Carly hasn't tossed my pumpkin's Paddington Bear because it was a gift from me. I didn't think my heart could break any more. I was wrong. This is the worst pain I can ever remember feeling.

I continue walking. All of a sudden, bursts of color go up in the crowd as the rain starts again and people open their umbrellas. I take mine out of my backpack, almost by rote, and open it. I can't think of any place I've ever been with so many stimuli. This is insane. Other umbrellas bump into mine, and I want to release my rage at people who don't deserve it. It's even more difficult to see the names of stores with umbrellas blocking my view.

Twenty-five minutes have passed. My face is wet as if I'd been crying. Maybe God knows I'm too angry to do it myself. There's enough water out here to rival the Atlantic Ocean. My squishing Nikes tell me I'm stepping into small lakes. Clouds are dumping buckets of rain on me. I'm soaked. Everyone is soaked and blurry, especially behind these grotesque black glasses. I feel like I'm in a car with broken windshield wipers and about to crash.

I put the umbrella away—it's easier to snake through the crowd without it, and this jacket Marge gave me has a hood, for whatever that's worth. I've passed by at least seven souvenir stores. Maybe one of them is the one I'm looking for only with a name change? If that's the case, I'll have to search the entire area before I start going into each store for a history lesson nobody will be inclined to give me. And that will be way too time-consuming.

Twenty more minutes pass. I won't lie. There are millions of people here, and I've never felt more alone in my life. I'm invisible. I could let out every bit of rage I have, and I doubt anyone would notice. I've been here for an entire hour without any—wait—I see it! The Souvenir Tiger. Here it is. I have no time to complain about lost minutes. I've just got to get inside.

It's a corner store. Massive and crowded like the other place. So much junk to behold. Statue of Liberty figurines for every taste and every budget. Damn, there's one almost as big as the lady herself. How would someone even get that out of here? Why would anyone want that?

In less abundance are Empire State figurines. With or without King Kong on top: your choice. I've got to get to the counter and see who works here. I didn't go through all of this to leave with nothing. Yellow metal taxi cabs with moving wheels, bobbleheads of famous people, snow globes with skyscrapers inside, mugs, teddy bears with tacky I Heart New York patches on their chests, frames, baseballs, shot glasses, rock glasses, sunglasses, ceramic bells, piggy banks, T-shirts, hoodies, and on and on. It's like a dry version of what's outdoors. Chaotic, colorful, crowded, and fantastic in its existence. I move past racks of postcards and the tourists who mindlessly examine every card before plunking down money for them.

Finally, I see some employees, but they're way too young to be that bastard's father. Wait. A tall, well-built man in his early sixties stands by the glass display case where the more expensive items are kept. He looks frazzled as if he wants the crowd to thin out as much as I do. A line forms to his left. Perfect. I'm standing to his right and pretending to contemplate the pricier earbuds and headphones. The man explains items to customers, loath to make eye contact with most of them. Why is he so nervous? His cell rings, and he signals someone to take over as he moves to the end of the counter.

I move with him but keep my distance as I look at the framed prints and posters high on the wall. This is my chance. Fate had me walk around for an hour in this wet hell so I'd be here when this call came in. I know it.

The man looks annoyed. "Thanks for taking care of everything. Guess I'll keep you on my payroll. But I told you not to call me now. Yeah. I feel confident about this. They're well hidden."

He's talking about Carly, Ray-Ray, and his son. It couldn't be any more obvious. I don't need a ton of bricks to hit me over the head. But where the hell are they "well hidden?" I hear someone call his name. "Raymond." How anti-climactic. I already know it's him, and I know what he's doing. I just need a location and God knows what else. Now. He's growing impatient. He's eager to say something else to the caller.

I remember to breathe as I continue to faux admire the art. I can't crane my neck much longer.

He listens. "Believe me, nobody comes in here asking about vintage postcards. I'm telling you. They're safe. The antique market isn't exactly booming these days. You know? I'll be in touch." Annoyed, he ends the call, and I'm about to end all hope.

I heard what I wanted—what I *needed* to hear. Nothing more. This man is in the souvenir business. He has some expensive vintage postcards he's worried about someone stealing. Maybe an employee who knows their value will take too long in the stockroom. Yeah, he probably wanted to hide the valuables. The actual scenario neither matters nor concerns me. Why won't my mind shut up? What does matter is that I just walked through a concrete rainforest for absolutely nothing.

I feel embarrassed in front of nobody but myself. Distraught, I walk through the hordes of wet souvenir seekers toward the door. I stop. Through the window, in what is now a light drizzle, I see the scruffy guy from Sweep's. He's standing outside smoking a cigarette. He looks angry and uncomfortable. He finishes his smoke and drops it to the ground, barely bothering to crush it.

I can't risk bumping into him. I hide behind a rotating display of personalized-miniature license plates as he walks inside and hurries to the back. Coast clear, I leave the store, and find a spot outside to wait for him. Once he comes out, I'll follow him.

CHAPTER SEVEN

I didn't expect this guy, who I now refer to as Scruff, to come out of the store so quickly or to be looking so angry. From the street, I was able to see him hurry to the back, say something to Raymond, then leave. He's walking away from this circus environment with some kind of axe to grind and heading west. I'm keeping a healthy pace behind him, grateful that the rain has temporarily stopped—again.

I don't ever remember being this tired. I was wrecked the night Rayelle was born, but that was a good kind of wrecked. Now, my mind, body, and spirit are debilitated beyond comprehension. It's not even ten o'clock yet. Wait. Ten o'clock. Marge made some joke about time being Irish once an hour. O'clock. Where have I heard that before? It doesn't matter. There's only one thing that does—finding Carly and Rayelle.

We're now on Ninth Avenue, and Scruff quickens his pace before opening the door to another pub. Good. I know where he is, so there's no need to go in right after him. That would be way too obvious. I'll walk slowly, window shopping. A couple goes into the pub. A good sign. The more traffic in and out, the less obvious I'll be. Says the same idiot who just decided to browse in dark windows.

How the hell am I going to walk slowly enough to let ten minutes pass before I follow him in there? I know! I pull my cell out of the side pocket of my backpack. My phone is off, but there's no one around to notice. I'll stand against this bakery window and pretend

I'm on a call. This is my own personal theater of the absurd, but I can't be too careful.

After rambling on for seven minutes to an invisible audience, it's time to head into the pub. Just as I stick my phone back in the pocket, I realize someone inside the bakery has been watching me, in a fucking dark store, the entire time. What kind of maniac does that?

I always thought it was overdramatic as hell when people said they felt as if their heart was leaping out of their chest, but holy shit, mine is. Who is this sonofabitch? I'm not going to let him intimidate me. I pull my pocketknife out of my right pants pocket and open it. I'll let this bastard know he needs to keep his distance.

Oh, shit! He's got a knife too. I raise mine to show him I mean business, and he does the same thing. Son of a fucking … *reflection*! Jesus! I'm about to murder my damn self through a plate glass window. I'd forgotten all about my long black hair and beanie. And this jacket isn't mine, so how would I recognize myself? Still, I feel stupid. Imbecilic. But I look nothing like I did when I met Scruff at Sweep's. I wave at myself just to make triple sure it's me. Good, I waved back. I'm so polite.

I'm feeling pretty good, but what a fucked-up way to regain my confidence.

Friday, 10:05 p.m.

This place is narrow with a much larger restaurant area in the back. One look tells me it's jam-packed, but only three men sit at the bar. Scruff is sitting closest to the front door, which is my cue to sit six barstools away, leaving two guys between us.

He's just ordered a beer and something to eat. Good. He's staying put for a bit. Not that I know how that helps, but it gives me time to think. I order a beer and tell the bartender to hold it until I get back from the head. Damned if I'll drink out of any glass that's been sitting out.

I walk into the men's room. Once again, I'm startled by my own reflection. At least I know it's me. The last time I saw my face in a men's room mirror was at the Curtain Call Hotel. That was right before meeting Spike at his costume house of horrors.

I'm relieved there's a stall in here. After taking care of business, I finally remove the burner phone from its packaging. I'd better not make a call from inside the stall in case someone comes in. It'll only draw attention to me, and I won't be able to see who that someone is.

I exit the stall and toss the molded packaging in the trash. I bought this years ago, but I paid cash. That was smart. I wash my hands, then make a quick call to my parents. My mother answers. She didn't recognize the number and thought someone was calling to tell her I was in the hospital or worse. I apologize profusely and explain that Carly and I are taking a long weekend trip to Mount Tammany, and cell service is rare in our East Stroudsburg rental cabin. Not to mention Carly had to change her number, but I'll explain later. And that I've just walked a half mile to get a bar on a borrowed phone with better network coverage. Sorry I forgot to tell them we were going. It was so last minute. She's talking fast, asking, "Why did Oliver change his number?" and making me promise to tell Rayelle, "Grandma loves you," but I panic and pretend our connection is fading. I feel awful lying to her, but at least she and my dad won't worry. I hope.

If only I could call myself to offer the same reassurance. Why not? I mean, I almost fucking stabbed myself through a store window. Offering some self-affirmation should be a breeze.

I see my stache is a bit loose. I press it with three fingers and hold. That ought to do it. Oh, shit, I remember my mother asking if it was raining where we are. I have to let that go. She's got to be thinking we're nuts, going away in the rain, but she'll just assume I wouldn't have known if it's raining near Mount Tammany. Yeah, all that stuff is online somewhere, but my mother wouldn't think to look it up, nor would she think I would have done so. Rain is the last thing I thought about when I headed for the train to New York. Didn't occur to me until it started falling from the sky. My mind is rambling again. None of that is important.

I made the call. That's what matters. Glad I thought to tell them we were taking a long weekend. That'll buy me a day if I need it. I won't. I'm going to find Carly and Rayelle tonight. I'll tell my parents the truth after this nightmare is over. I have to believe it *will* be.

Two men walk in as I'm on the way out. I was lucky to get this room alone when I needed it. Another stroke of luck on the worst day of my life.

Friday, 10:12 p.m.

As soon as the bartender sees me, my beer is on the bar before I can sit again. Scruff has a large red plastic basket of onion rings in front of him on which he's liberally squirting ketchup. Reminds me of myself back at Marge's. What a nice lady. So kind, especially as I felt oddly comfortable with her. She must be wondering what happened to me. I can't worry about that now.

Scruff still looks like he's in a bad mood, but I can't look his way anymore. I sit in the black-leather barstool and take a sip of my beer, pretending I've been thinking about how good it will taste all day long. Yum, isn't this refreshing after a long day of work. I wonder if my faux pleasure shows on my face. This is a lot of work for a crap actor with no audience.

Oh, no. What if Scruff is pissed because he hasn't found me yet? No, that doesn't make sense. If he was still looking, why would he have come here? I realize I forgot to check the name of this place. Doesn't matter. Before I can continue this nowhere train of thought, the door opens and a bleached blonde in a purple vinyl raincoat walks in, shaking the rain off the umbrella she'd just closed. She looks to be about the same age as Scruff, and it's obvious she's here for him. Wow.

"Whoa, you look like shit," Scruff says after a mere over-the-shoulder glance. I'm glad he's speaking loudly enough for me to hear. It helps that the bar isn't that crowded.

"What the hell did you just say?" Her face tightens.

His voice is louder. "I said you look like shit." He swivels around to make eye contact. "Have you seen your face? Looks like your eyeliner and your mascara are having a race to see who can be first down your cleavage. Or maybe your makeup colluded with the rain to make a fast getaway. Holy clown face!" He turns back to his onion rings.

Now she's more embarrassed than insulted. Probably a mixture of both. She takes off her coat, hangs it on a wall hook along with the umbrella, then races down the bar past me to the ladies' room.

One thing's for sure. Scruff's not happy she's here. As soon as he and the bartender stop laughing, he leans forward, says something under his breath, and they both turn serious. The bartender nods as Scruff speaks. Sure wish I could hear what he's saying.

I face forward and read labels from whiskey bottles to focus my attention elsewhere. I can't help but think that much of the whiskey is about the same age as Rayelle. *Oh, pumpkin, I never thought I could love anyone so much. Daddy loves you, baby. I'll find you.*

The blonde has cleaned her face, reapplied a fuck-ton of makeup, teased her overbleached hair, sprayed herself with cheap cologne, and possibly looks (and smells) worse than she did coming in. No way I'd hit that. Not in a million celibate years.

She hurries to Scruff. She sits next to him and reaches for an onion ring. Her hand doesn't even make it to the basket before he slaps it away. "Don't touch my food. I'll get you your own, but hands off my dinner."

"That's your *dinner?*" She stares disapprovingly at his basket of onion rings.

He coughs, probably gagging at her cologne, looks at her face, then mumbles something I can't hear.

"Oh, and you're so hot to look at, you unshaven mess."

He mumbles again. I can't hear him, but I think he's saying, "Fuck you."

A couple who'd been in the restaurant catch the dialogue and laugh on their way out the door. Angrily, she mumbles something to them which only makes them laugh more. She turns back to Scruff. "People suck. And that includes you."

He shrugs in response—just barely, which I think angers her more.

The bartender is waiting to take her order, so I take advantage of looking in their direction as if I'm going to order another beer.

"I thought you'd be happy to see me," she tells him. "I walked forever in the rain to get here."

"I didn't ask you to meet me here, Sandy."

Oh, shit. Sandy? I wonder if this is the same woman who caused the scene in Kowalski's the day Sherita and her husband parted company forever with Carly's family. Has to be. She's the right age. Can't be a coincidence. I need to pay more attention. Now she's playing the coquette. "I know, Chazzy, but I like to surprise my man."

"Your face surprised me all right!" He laughs; then his face is serious. "And don't fucking call me Chazzy."

"Excuse me, *Chaz!*" She addresses the bartender. "Dewar's and soda, a grilled cheese sandwich, and a big-assed basket of fries."

Chaz finishes the last onion ring, savoring it, then turns to her. "I told you I was stopping by here to see Rick. If I'd wanted company, don't you think I would have asked?"

She snarls and takes a swig of the drink bartender Rick has just placed in front of her. "I thought coming here was what you wanted. Knowing that my presence means a hella good time later." Her tongue comes out of her mouth lizard-style and caresses her top lip.

He cringes.

The restaurant is thinning out. More people are heading toward the entrance and not one can look away from the trainwreck as they pass.

Chaz reaches behind him and starts putting on the rain jacket that he'd hung from the back of his barstool. He can barely stand to look at her. "Please don't ever refer to me as 'your man' anymore. I'm not. Never will be. I let you use me because I had a couple horny nights. Beyond that, we've got nothing. Never did. You know that. And we both know why you're so hot for me—or why you're pretending to be."

"That's such bullshit!" she says as Rick places a sandwich and basket of fries in front of her. "It's not what you think." She watches as he puts on his jacket. "Where the hell do you think you're going?"

"I'm going where I always go to calm down. Baradino's Tavern. To shoot some pool. But you already know that, Sandy. And I'm telling you right now so you don't show up and pretend you didn't know I'd be there. Do not fucking follow me. If you think I embarrassed you here, you ain't seen nothin' yet. You hear me?"

"I can't believe I've let you use me like this." Beginning with her shoulders, her body slumps dramatically in the barstool as if her world has been decimated and is unrecoverable.

Calmly, Chaz pulls money out of his front right pocket and puts it on the bar, a palm up to let Rick know to keep the change. "This isn't off-off-Broadway, and nobody is buying your act. And yeah. You *have* been using me, and we both know it. You're not the only one. But you're the last one. I'm not my poor misunderstood felon brother. Much to everyone's fucking dismay." He waves to Rick. "Later, my man." And he's gone.

I pick my jaw off the bar before anyone notices. I didn't know Ray Royce had a brother, but it never occurred to me that's who Scruff aka Chaz could be. Things are making some kind of sense. Yeah, he looked angry before he went into the souvenir store and even angrier when he came out. Maybe he's done with all of them. I'll bet Sandy waited all of these years for Ray to get out of prison, only to have him make tracks to Carly. He doesn't give a damn about her, but I guess she thinks fucking his brother is her so-called revenge.

For a hot second I consider how she might be of use to me, but I shoo the thought away. Nope. Not going near her. Leaving this chick alone. She doesn't think twice before messing up lives, past and present. Bad news.

Chaz just told her where he's going, and I believe him. There's no way I can show up right after him, just in case he's seen me. But then what? How will being in the same place get me closer to finding Carly and Rayelle? Am I really stupid enough to just walk in and introduce myself as the guy he's been looking for and wants to strangle—or worse?

I'm not sure what I'm expecting to happen at that pool tavern, but it's the only option I have, and I've got to keep going. The alternative is unthinkable.

I'll have another drink here, mull it all over, go somewhere to swap out disguises, and I'll be on my way.

CHAPTER EIGHT

Friday, 11:03 p.m.

I'm back in the men's room. Paid my bar tab and decided to swap personas in here.

I'm feeling a bit hot. Probably because I never took my jacket off. I remove it, just to let my clothing breathe, and I realize it's reversible. The other side is khaki green. Perfect. Back on it goes. An unexpected but welcome change to my appearance.

I don the red wig and the black newsboy cap. The fake stache comes off with half a yank. I don't think it felt at home on my face. I stick it inside a wet paper towel and throw it in the trash, return the black frames to my backpack, then take another gander at myself. Holy crap. The glasses and stache are gone, yet somehow I look more ridiculous.

This theater wig isn't meant for closeup viewing. And this cap looks like I should be standing in an old movie shouting, "Extra! Extra! Read All About It! Wife Steals Child and Takes Off with Old Lover!"

No time for any more sarcastic nonsense that doesn't matter, but I worry about my disguise. Then I remember I'm not in Trenton. I'm in New York City where individualism is the norm. But inside a neighborhood pool tavern, as my inner newsboy might say, well, that's another story.

One more thing. I pull out the burner phone and look up Baradino's Tavern. It's in the West 50s, off Eighth Avenue. Not too bad of a walk. I'll just leave with the last of the dinner crowd.

Convenient that so many New Yorkers eat late.

I'm stalling. If I don't hurry, Chaz may be gone, and where the hell will I be then? Literally clueless. And I can't let that happen. I've got to ... I'm *going to* find Rayelle.

I exit onto the street. Thankfully the rain has stopped, but there was quite the downpour while I was inside. Oh, and Sandy, she picked up some random guy and left with him twenty minutes ago. Glad I followed my gut and stayed away from her.

I decide to walk crosstown to Eighth Avenue, then head uptown. I'm halfway down the street when I hear loud voices in the open doorway of an old brownstone.

Some woman is chastising her teenage son who's halfway out the door. "Eddie! If you don't get back in here, your ass is grass! Mama don't mess around."

"I'm not your prisoner," he shouts back as he takes off.

"Eddie! I swear, boy, I'll have your ass locked up soon as I find you."

She stands in some old, pink-quilted bathrobe, in a puddle, on the sidewalk, yelling expletives he can't possibly hear. I can. I feel my entire body trembling in fear. The pounding in my chest is increasing, and it's as if I'm shrinking into myself.

"Eddddiiiieeee!"

Shut up, lady! I don't know what her issues are , but she's unnerved me to the core. I tuck into the recessed wall of a wall of a storefront and stand in front of the grate. It's happening again. My breathing. I'm gasping for air. Once a broken breath I can barely survive. But once again, and I won't be alive. Why does that rhyme? And what's the other version of it? Twice a broken breath means—

"Eddddiiiieeee!"

I fight to regain my breathing and stand across the street where she can see me. "Shut up! Just shut the damn hell up!"

The woman turns sharply to see where the voice is coming from. "Who the blazes are you? Mind your own effing business."

I want to tell her that she's making her domestic issues the business of everyone within earshot, but when I go to scream at her again, the words lodge in my throat and stick there. I feel dizzy. Everything is blurry. I can't lose consciousness. She's still yelling at me between the alternate calling out of threats to her son, but I've lost the ability to process her words. I feel as if the caution in her voice is stronger than her anger, but I don't know. *Stay conscious, Liam. Breathe.*

The rain has started again, but it's more of a heavy drizzle. Damn. She yells out one last thing before splashing her way inside as the puddle of dirty water makes contact with the hem of her robe. Ordinarily, I might indulge in the small pleasure of seeing such an occurrence, but I'm fighting to understand the bewilderment that's tugging at me, pulling me away from my mission. I don't know what it is. I've just got to get out of this alley. I'm lost. I'm in trouble.

No, my daughter is in trouble. I'm not in an alley. I'm on a street, standing up against a neighborhood nail salon. I've got to get to her. Where is she? Where was I going? Why was that woman yelling at me? She wasn't. She was angry with her son. It had nothing to do with me. So why did I yell at her? I didn't. That was someone else. No, it was me. I'm sure. Maybe not so sure.

A well-dressed couple in their fifties approach me. The man is holding the umbrella over his wife. He's looking at me with kind eyes. "Are you okay, fella? Can we call someone for you?"

I must look really bad. Maybe it's the flame-red polyester hair making me look crazy. What sane person would wear such a getup and cower in a doorway? I hope it's only my hair that concerns him. Besides, I'm not cowering. Am I? It's the hair. No it isn't. Don't be a fucking idiot, Liam. You look deranged.

I can't even get the words "No thank you" out of my mouth. I can only look at him.

"I think maybe we should call the police," the wife says.

Somehow, her words shake me from my semi-delusional state. "No, I'm fine. Sorry. I just got some bad news. I'm very upset. Just needed to stop and rest. I'm good now. I have to be on my way."

The man nods. "Okay, then. If you're sure. Sorry to hear that." He links arms with his wife, and they walk down the street. I can hear them discussing me. Did they make a mistake in not calling someone? A few steps farther and I can't hear a word, but they're still talking. Bet anything it's about my wig.

I need to move. If they look back and see me standing here, my semi-luck will run out on me, like Carly did. I've lost precious time. I only hope Chaz is still at the tavern.

Friday, 11:39 p.m.

I'm almost there. A few storefronts away. A couple of guys come out, and an old man walks in. This is definitely not the kind of place a random stranger visits. Maybe I should take off this wig. Then I remember. Chaz met me without it at Scruff's. I can't. He'll recognize me.

"Can you help me? Please."

Where is that voice coming from? I see nothing but a large black trash bag on the curb. I haven't exactly had the sanest half hour. But now I'm hearing voices.

"I'm so cold in this rain. I'm hungry."

The voice is not in my head. I'm not that crazy. Not yet. I walk over to the bag and see that it's not filled with trash. It's flat and empty with a homeless man sitting on a wooden box under it, spreading it over him for shelter. He appears to be in his fifties, but it wouldn't surprise me if he was younger. I've seen what living on the streets can do to people.

He looks up at me, his dark brown eyes begging for help. "I'm so hungry. I've been out here all night. Most people ignore me. They don't believe I'm hungry. They think I just want to buy booze or drugs. Can't a man just be hungry?"

"Yes, of course." Nervously, I look at the tavern door to make sure Chaz doesn't come out.

"There's a big pharmacy around the corner to the right. They stay open until one. Can you get me something to eat there? Please? And some smokes if that's not asking too much." He shows me his empty pack of cigarettes.

I want to help, but I don't have time. But the agony and fear in his eyes could be mine. "Okay, but I'll have to hurry."

"God bless you."

I can't wait to ask what he wants. I run past the tavern and turn the corner. Sure enough, the store is there, and it's open. I rush in, grab a basket, and find the refrigerated food section in the back. I grab

three sandwiches, a bottle of water and an orange juice, then throw a
bunch of snack bags in with everything else. On the way to the register,
I see a few souvenir hoodies with I Heart New York on them. I grab a
black one and throw it in my cart.

There's a woman in line in front of me bitching about the rain.
It ruined her romantic night. She should know what it's like to have
her child snatched or to be homeless, sitting hungry on a curb and
craving a cigarette because it's all you have. She keeps talking. The
cashier nods as she blabs, but I can tell he's annoyed. This woman
couldn't care less if anyone's behind her. Just like the woman gabbing
to Sherita who gave me a dirty look for existing. The cashier is
annoyed and finally says, "Can I help you, sir," tuning the woman out
as I'm trying to do.

She snarls and walks away.

I hate smoking, but I buy two packs and ask for a lighter, just
in case my new friend doesn't have one. I ask if I can pay with a large
bill as I don't have enough small bills to cover it. I do, but I can't give
up the small bills that cab driver gave me.

Luckily, the cashier says yes. He looks at the bill, sort of the
way Spike did, then puts it in the drawer and hands me change. I put
it in my pocket and keep a twenty in my hand. I'll give that to the
homeless man too.

Rushing back around the corner, I'm glad to see he's still there.
"Hey, buddy."

He looks up. "You came back!" he says in disbelief. Then he
looks upward to thank God for my return.

"Sure did." I hand him the bag. Got you a bunch of stuff. A
couple packs of smokes and a lighter. Oh, and I thought maybe you'd

like something to keep you warm. Got you a large so it would fit over whatever you're wearing."

He's looking in the bag, astonished by what he's been given. His eyes glisten with tears. "You're one of the few kind souls who hasn't treated me like I'm invisible. Homeless people are always invisible, to most folks anyway. God bless."

I hand him the twenty. "Here, hope this will help too."

"Thank you, my friend!" He looks to the sky once more, then blesses me again. I know he wants to talk, but there's no time.

My heart is warmed to see him reaching first for the hoodie and putting it on. It's nice and roomy on him. He smiles as the warmth envelopes him. "Someone is waiting for me inside." I nod toward the tavern. "God bless you too."

CHAPTER NINE

I stand in front of the big wooden door. The sign says they serve snacks until one. Good. I'm hungry again, and eating gives me something to do. I don't want to drink too much; I need to stay in control.

My stomach drops the moment I walk in. I hate being in strange places on a *good* day, and today is not that. I quickly assess the lay of the land. The place is dark. There are some booths and tables across from the bar, and from what I can see, three billiards tables in the back. About seven men and one woman are gathered around two of them. I can't make out any faces.

The bar is lit by cone-shaped hanging lamps. The floor, black-and-white linoleum squares, has seen its share of action, but the place still has charm, much of which I'm sure disappears in the light of day. Nothing is remotely new except the TVs. There are three of them mounted above the whiskey bottles and at least three more in the back. All of them on. Tuned to different stations. Kind of like I am right now.

Okay. Where is Chaz? Where should I sit? What should I do? How do I go look in the billiards area without unwanted attention. I gulp. I don't need to. Chaz is at the bar, deep into conversation with some guy.

I opt for a table, far enough away for him not to see me, but close enough that I can watch him. He doesn't look like he's ready to leave any time soon. So when a woman comes to take my order, I ask for fried mozzarella sticks and a Guinness. She's suspicious of me. I can see her looking at my so-called hair. Even in the low light, it must look ridiculous. She stares at me, then cracks a smile as she walks away. Just fucking great. My stomach flips. I don't even know if I'll be able to eat.

Almost immediately, she returns with the Guinness. Tells me the sticks will be another six or seven minutes. I nod my thanks. Don't want to get into any kind of conversation.

She's back with a tray exactly when she said she would be. "Here you go, Red." She has the nerve to smile as she looks at my hair, then puts a large basket of sticks in front of me, followed by a round dish of ketchup with chopped parsley sprinkled on top. "And here's some napkins for ya. These can get messy."

I can tell she wants to laugh. Like really laugh.

"You need any utensils?"

"No, thanks."

"Bon appétit." She chuckles as she turns to walk away. I intercept her departure and tell her I want to settle the check now. I'm still nursing the beer and tell her I'll pay again if I want another one. Need to be able to bolt at a moment's notice, so I can't be running a tab. I want to stiff her for laughing at me, but instead I give her a generous tip, hoping she'll drop whatever stereotypes are going around in her head. She smiles and says, "Thanks, Red." It takes everything in me to be cool. Rayelle is what matters. Not this cocky bitch.

I look over at the bar. The bartender's been watching the entire time. He's laughing along with a female customer who's sitting in front of him. Damn. And I thought I could be weird in New York and it wouldn't matter. Not true. I knew this place would be different, but I was out of options. What the hell was I supposed to do?

I look at the clock and am somehow shocked that it's after midnight already. Almost twelve hours since I learned Carly's taken Rayelle. Are they still in the country? They *have* to be.

I feel stupid sitting here alone with half a beer. I look at the empty table next to me. Someone's left a copy of The New York *Daily News* there. Great. I can pretend to be reading. Absorb my interest somewhere. Can't even pull out a phone and pretend to be on that. Don't want to turn either of them on.

I find myself reading a short piece about the Mets home series with the Astros this weekend at Citi Field. Friday's game's a washout, and Saturday isn't looking too good. Yeah. Didn't need a newspaper to tell me that.

"What a surprise to see you here," a man says.

I look up to see Chaz sitting across from me. I can tell he's had a fair amount to drink. "I didn't expect you to be in a place without a 'winder seat' where you can't look out at 'them seas.' You're a captain, isn't that right, Captain Obvious? Then again, that's not why you're here, is it?" His eyes dare me to respond. Only he's not laughing like that server was.

One response after another pops into my head, but every one of them is useless. He knows who I am. How? I looked completely different at Sweep's and again at the previous bar with my black wig and beanie.

"Tallamore, you have the worst fucking disguises I've ever seen. In case nobody ever told you, the point is to blend in, not stand out like a circus clown at a convent. You look ridiculous. I don't know if you have any more dollar store wigs left, but the charade and the stalking ends now. You hear me, bro? I don't wanna have to repeat myself."

I still don't say a word. Is he going to take me out back and kill me? What should I say? He knows my name. I'm fucked. I've got to be real with him. It's the only option I have. Maybe he's capable of empathy. I'm about to find out.

I push the newspaper to the side, and it falls off the table and scatters its many pages into a holy mess.

He stares at me, eyeballs the floor, then me again. Oh, shit, he's telling me to pick it up. Okay. I can do that.

I quickly reassemble the paper and put it on the next table, out of my nervous reach.

He stares, challenging me to speak.

I straighten my posture and lean toward him with authority. "Look, you know why I'm here. If your brother wants to run off with my wife and she's good with that, nothing I can do. I hate it, but I can't fight it. I only want my child." I make eye contact, but he's unreadable. "And yeah, they took all of my money, and that doesn't mean I don't want my share back, but I'm not here for that. Just my daughter. Maybe your brother and my wife don't know that kidnapping is a federal offense." I'm feeling brave enough for a bluff. "It might be time to call the FBI."

His entire body language changes as I say, "FBI." He sits up straight, loses the hint of cockiness, and his eyes bore into mine.

Oh, shit. I don't know when to stop. Why did I go from being a surprised clown to a threatening sonofabitch in thirty seconds? I've always been prone to extremes. Why don't I have better control? Why didn't I pause to at least gauge where he's coming from? I'm about to find out.

I don't know this guy, but he's got a crap ton of responses swirling in his brain, and he's trying hard to choose the right one. His eyes are slightly bloodshot and I know he's weary like I am, but not for the same reason. He hasn't taken his eyes off me for a fraction of a second. Wish I could read him better.

"Lissssen." That's the first word he's slurred. "You try to do everything you can for your old man, for twenty fucking years, but the prodigal son returns from the prodigal prison, and it's like the fucking messiah returning. And then you're s-supposed to bow and do his dirty work."

I see anger rising within him. I recognize it easily and realize how I must look to people when I'm angry. It's scary, but unimportant to me at the moment. I still have no idea how to respond. So I just wait for him to say more.

"You didn't even know I existed, did ya?" He wags his finger at me as he squints. "I could blow your mind wide open right now, but I won't. You think I'm some motherfucker threatening you, but I've been your very best friend for a really long time. Decades. You just never knew it."

This guy must be more smashed than I first thought. He's completely lost me. I can't figure out what he is talking about, and I'm not so sure he knows. But he thinks he does. He's my only hope of finding Rayelle and Carly. I have to be cool.

"Yeah, I'm all thugged out 'n shit because I've been *instructed* to keep your ass away. I mean, anything for the jailbird, Ray Fucking Junior. Fuck me and everything I've done for twenty years. Doesn't mean fuck all to my old man. Not. Jack. Shit."

I'm understanding him a bit more. He's got a whole lot of family issues, but I really wish he'd get to the point so I know who or what I'm dealing with. My heart is racing. I hope he can't see it. My breathing is weakening, and he hasn't laid a hand on me—yet.

"So let that questionable brain of yours absorb what I'm gonna tell you now. You dig?" He stops to stare at me.

I don't know how he gets his eyes to darken on command, but damn.

"Personally, I don't give a rat's ass about any of this. I have two kids, a boy and a girl, and I'd be out in the streets chasing anyone who needed chasing if someone kidnapped them. I get it."

I'm relieved he understands.

"Don't be looking at me like we're buddies now, because I can still be your worst nightmare. And I won't hesitate if you give me a reason. While I have less than zero interest in being my brother's keeper or protector, I've got every interest in the world in inheriting half of the very lucrative businesses and properties the old man owns. And I'm not letting you or anyone fuck that up for me. So, while I'm gonna let you go now, just like I let your ass leave at Sweep's—I sure hope I'm not making a huge mistake. If I see your mug again, I'll make sure you don't have a snowball's chance in hell of finding your fam damily. You do what you gotta do, but you need to find a way that doesn't involve me. Got that? Ain't playing with you, Captain Bullshit. Don't even think about calling the FBI because they'll want to know your every move today, and I'm toast if you drag me into this."

He's looking nervous. Like he wants to retract what he just said. "Your tongue frozen, Tallamore? Cat got a hold of it?"

I'm going to have to lie to him. I hate doing it, but he's my only hope. "Okay, I'll leave. I'll find another way. One that has nothing to do with you. And we've never seen one another. I get it. I appreciate the slack you've cut me."

"You're damn lucky the crowd at Sweep's thought you were a full-on whack job. Couldn't have let you walk out if they hadn't fallen for your act. Now get the hell out of here, and don't forget what I said. Look for them all you want, find them, but without any help from me. You hear me? If I catch your ass within a mile of my person, it's game over."

I nod, put on the jacket, grab the backpack, and head for the door. What the hell will I do now?

CHAPTER TEN

The rain is brutal and unrelenting. It makes everything more difficult. No. Maybe it doesn't. It's actually been a helpful distraction. Why am I thinking about any of this? I don't care and neither does the rain. I only know one thing: it's not happy. Nothing and no one can cry so much without feeling grievous pain. The rain's crying for me because I don't have that luxury now.

I'm standing outside of Baradino's knowing the clock is ticking and Chaz will be outside soon. What will I do? I look at the spot where the homeless man was. He's gone. I'm surprised by how gutted I feel. Hopelessness overwhelms me.

"Friend! My friend! Over here!" the voice says through the torrential downpour.

I don't see him at first. Then I do. He's not gone. He's moved to take cover in the recessed doorway of a small store, wrapped snugly in the hoodie and blanket I gave him. I hurry over.

"My friend." He looks up with a bright smile. "My name is Isaiah."

"I'm Liam." I try to take shelter as I stand under the small awning in front of him, but it provides little. I'm glad to see him. I was worried, and I let him know. But I still don't have time for small talk.

Luckily, he doesn't want to make any. Just wants to know how he can help me, and I quickly summarize my ordeal. "The bottom line," I finish, "is that I have to keep tracking Chaz without letting him know I'm doing it. And that's pretty impossible seeing that he'll be looking for me. Not to mention he's threatened me."

Isaiah nods as if he's formulating a plan. He reaches into one of his bags. "Take this old shirt. And this hat. Put them on and go sit on the sidewalk." He hands me a black garbage bag. "And cover yourself up with this, my friend. Darned if I'm not a fixture in that spot. Chaz be seeing me every day." He pauses. "I don't do shelters. Even in the rain. Everyone knows that. Only reason I'm sitting in here's 'cause you gave me some real nice presents, and I don't want them getting wet. But nobody looks in dark doorways with a mind to hand out money. Scares people, and rightly so. See, I usually get some help from a few people when they stumble on out at closing. I need help bad, 'cause like I said, I'm invisible to most people. After the tavern locks up, I go to my place back in the alley. Storage shed behind this very store. Locks from the inside. Got permission and all. Matter of fact, the owner bought it secondhand—just for me. Sometimes pays me to do odd jobs. I'm a lucky man. Now, you go sit in my place, Liam. Ain't nothing gonna look out of the ordinary. Sad to say." He thinks. "But I'm still a lucky man. I've got it better than many."

I'm overwhelmed by his attitude, kindness, and quick thinking. I grab the black cap from my head and hand it to him. "Here, we can trade." I yank the red wig off. "Anything you can do with this nightmare?"

He laughs. "You got a nice head of hair under that thing. Sure, I'll take the goofball wig. Never know when I can use it. Least now I know why you were wearing it. Thought you might be a performer or something." He smiles, then gestures toward the sidewalk. "Go on, now. 'Fore you lose the chance to be me. And don't forget, Chaz leaves the same way he comes in. Just lives a few blocks away. Got no clue where, though. Or if he even goes straight home."

I reach into my pocket and hand him another twenty, promising to also let him have anything I'm given. While he offers effusive thanks, I put the trash bag over my head, run to his spot, and sit on the box.

Isaiah called that red mop a goofball wig. He's right. What the hell made me think I wouldn't stick out? Would I have been better off if I'd just combed my hair differently? No. I remember that Chaz recognized me in Sweep's. Nothing would have made a difference. But I pray this does.

As soon as I'm seated, I reaffirm my resolution to find Rayelle. Nothing will stop me. I don't care about what Carly wrote in her note. I'll deal with the loss of my marriage another time. But I won't lose my Ray-Ray. She's a very intuitive child. She has to know something is wrong. I wonder if she's able to sleep. But where is she sleeping—or lying awake?

Isaiah's eyes shone with gratitude when he told me where he sleeps. Well, as I'm literally in his place, I can understand why the shed would be a big step up from sleeping on the sidewalk. But it's horrible, and I hate that anyone has to live this way.

Isaiah told me which direction Chaz walks home. I poke a small hole in the left side of the bag so I can keep watch. *And then what, stupid?* Even if I successfully follow the man home, how will that help me find my family? I don't know why, but I'm sure they're not at his place. I can only hope that maybe they'll come to him. But why would they? Especially well after midnight. I remember seeing that the Souvenir Tiger stays open late, but it wouldn't be open now. There's no point going back there unless Raymond's still in the building, and I could follow him when he leaves. But he's probably left. If he hasn't, odds are, he's gonna hop in a cab or more likely, he has someone to pick him up. It wouldn't surprise me, but who knows? Too many possibilities, and too many unknowns. Plus, I'd be lucky to even hail a cab, and chase scenes don't work in real life the way they do in movies, especially in the rain. The more I think about it, the more I realize how grim my prospects seem. Going back there is a ridiculous plan. My head hurts. But I won't give up.

I curse as a cab drives too close to the curb and splashes me, but I take it as affirmation that I need a better plan.

"You'd think this loser would get a job already," a young woman says to someone as they pass behind me. Without missing a beat, she changes the subject. "Two weeks until I turn twenty-one, and you know what that means. Full access to my trust fund! Yay! Whoopee! Cancun, here I come, baby!"

I peek through the hole. She's carrying a gaudy Louis Vuitton umbrella, and I see the back of the young guy with her, walking under his non-designer umbrella. I hope he parties big time on her money. I don't know how many millions await her, but it wouldn't surprise me if the spoiled brat blows through it all. My anger is interrupted by kind words.

"Here you go, young man."

I glance up to see an older woman looking at me with sympathetic eyes. She hands me three dollars as she grips her multicolored umbrella with the other.

"Thank you very much."

"I can see the pain in your eyes. You've had a hard life. Just like that God-fearing Black gentleman who usually sits here. Such a lovely person. Where is he anyway?"

I don't want to draw her attention to Isaiah sitting in a doorway.

"Sleeping," I think. "He told me I could borrow his box tonight."

"Isn't that just like him?" She offers a sad smile. "Sure wish I could truly help. You look about the same age my son would be if he were still alive. I'll pray for you."

"You're very kind. I'm sorry about your son. Please, get out of this awful rain."

She lowers her eyes a bit. "I want to say the same thing to you, but that would be terribly insensitive, not knowing your circumstances. Goodnight now."

"God bless you." I say that because Isaiah does, but I also mean it.

Only sixty seconds have lapsed, yet, in that short window of time, on a rainy street in New York after midnight, I've seen an extraordinary contrast of humanity. It hurts my heart, but I must stay focused.

More people walk by. Another cab splashes me. Instinctively, I curse and brush the dirty curb water away. *Damn it, Liam. No physical reactions. You need to sit here as inconspicuously as Isaiah does.* In the distance, a police siren wails followed by a clap of thunder. Jesus. Will I get hit by lightning?

I turn to look out the hole, and I see what I believe to be the back of Chaz and another man. Good! He's moving down the street with his friend. The guy is tall like he is, only he looks like a vintage refrigerator from behind. Chaz thinks I'm gone. I'll wait a minute before I follow. I crack my knuckles to push through my fear.

There's a loud crash of metal on metal. Damn, there's been an accident. My eyes search the street until I see a dark sedan that has plowed into a yellow cab. Even from here, I can see how pissed the cabbie is, and he's yelling, his voice echoing through the rain and honking of horns. He looks like he wants to take the sedan driver and throw him—after he beats him up.

My attention is instantly diverted. "What the hell?" I scream as I feel two sets of arms pulling me up. They turn me around. It's Chaz and the other man. My heart is racing as the two of them glare at me.

"You've got massive cojones, Tallamore!" Chaz is pissed. His face now matches his bloodshot eyes. "Is this your interpretation of staying a mile from my person? I cut you a break, motherfucker, and now you'll be lucky if I don't continue what God started and cut the rest of your ass in two until half of it falls to the ground and gets swept into the sewer." He glowers at me, wobbling ever so slightly from the alcohol. "You think I'm kidding."

"Um, no. Actually, I don't."

"You were gonna follow me. Weren't you?"

"Well...."

"Yesss or no? I'm not gonna ask again."

"Yes. But only because I have no other way to find my family! For God's sake, man, this is my daughter we're talking about. Carly and your brother may be on their way to the airport for all I know. If they're even still in the country. They've got my daughter! Why can't you understand that?" I feel my heart getting ready to explode out of my chest.

The goon standing next to Chaz snarls at me. I think he wants me to cower in fear, but I'm not going to give him that pleasure. From the front, he looks like the vintage Kelvinator my grandmother had. Only it just kept food cool. It didn't have threatening eyes or flaring nostrils.

Chaz keeps talking. "And finding your fam damily could fuck me and mine up forever. That money is my kids' future. It's our security. If my old man and his prodigal felon spawn find out ... aww, shit. I'm dead in the sewer water. Just like you might be. Speaking of half-asses, that's what I've been. No more mister nice guy from me."

The goon's tongue gives his lips an anticipatory lick as if Chaz is speaking his language.

"I'll find another way, Chaz. I'm really sorry."

"You lying bastard. Like I said inside, I've been your best friend for two decades. You just don't know it."

I've changed my mind. Now I think he does know what he's saying. That wasn't drunken rambling earlier. Not to mention he appears to be sobering up. But this isn't the time to figure out what he's talking about.

"You know what, Captain Liar, you almost got away with this ruse. I thought you were Isaiah under there. Then my buddy here, Mack, tells me he just saw Isaiah sleeping in a doorway and wondered why he's not behind the store in his shed. And I'm thinking, well Isaiah must be quite the magician to be in two places at once." He turns to look in Isaiah's direction. "Still sleeping. See him?"

"Yeah," Mack grumbles. "See 'im?"

I take a good look at Mack. What a hoodlum. He must spend

half his day in a gym. Looks like a guy who would work for the mob. The scowl on his face is frightening, and to complete the stomach-churning vision, there's a smirk bubbling underneath. He's totally getting his rocks off thinking about the possibilities for fucking me up.

Chaz turns to Mack. "What should we do with this guy?"

Mack chuckles. "Being in da waste management business, I know just what to do."

Oh, no. I know that "waste management" is a euphemism for the mafia. Why am I not surprised. They're going to kill me. There's no way out of this.

"Please, guys. I'll disappear. Just let me go."

Chaz shakes his head. "That ship has sailed, Captain Bullshit. I cut you a break, and you betrayed me within minutes. Fuck you. I've had a lifetime of doing the right thing and being fucked over, so no way I'll let you join the fuck-over-Chaz club when I can stop your ass here and now."

Their arms still clutching me on either side, they start dragging me away. I'm barely holding onto my backpack, but I'm determined not to let it drop.

"Hold onto dat garbage bag." Mack chortles. "It's da standard dress code where you're going."

"Sure is," Chaz says.

As they drag me through the rain, around the corner, the few people who pass us don't so much as bat an eye. Probably a common thing in New York. Sadly, I wouldn't look either. Who wants to be a witness to this shit?

They drag me up the street a bit, past the large pharmacy, then turn into an alley. Despite my resistance, they pull me along as if I weigh all of ten pounds. We finally stop at a trash dumpster.

"You'll be spending some quality time here," Chaz informs me. "In Solitary. Gen Pop is at capacity. And just to be sure you don't play any games, let me have your phone."

I don't dare tell him I haven't been using it. "But it's all that I have. I've kept it turned off all day to save the battery. Please, it's my only contact with the outside world."

"Duh," Mack says. "Exactly why da man is asking for it."

I reach in and pull it out of the bag, letting my face reveal as much angst as I can. "Here." I hand it to Chaz and drop my head in defeat.

Mack lets go of me, takes the trash bag, opens it at the top, and lowers it to the ground. All aboard da garbage express. Hop in."

"Oh, come on, guys. Is this really necessary?"

"Get the fuck in the bag!" Chaz violently kicks the ground and takes a step toward me. He's almost in my face. "You heard the man!"

I step into the bag. I can't believe where my life has gone in roughly twelve hours. How the hell will I find my daughter now? Mack quickly ties the yellow loops at the top. Before I can beg for mercy again, they lift me and drop me into the bin. Bastards! If it wasn't for the one bag already in here, I would've hurt myself even more as I land with a thud on the bottom. There is a silver lining; my pants aren't touching the grime.

"Just tucking you into bed, Tallamore. Don't let the cockroaches bite."

They laugh, but Mack's clearly enjoying this the most. I'm seething inside this bag. Sure, I can claw my way out of plastic, but I'll still be in the damn bin. This bag was just to degrade me. I'm humiliated, but I can't stop to wallow in my feelings. Finding my daughter is the only thing that matters. I sigh. One place I won't find her is in here. That's for sure.

"Putting the top down," Chaz says, as the heavy lid thuds like I did. "And while we don't have a padlock handy, this gravity lock bar will make it impossible for you to get your ass out. When the men come for the trash on Monday, or maybe Tuesday, once they turn this baby upside down, you'll go up in the air, then fall out automatically. Into the truck. Until then, well, there's no place like home."

I want to jump out of my skin—and out of this hallucination. This can't be real. But it is. It fucking is.

CHAPTER ELEVEN

I have no time to lament the absurdity or gravity of my situation. Ripping my way out of the bag, I immediately try to stand. I gauge the dumpster to be about four feet high. I have to squat to push the palms of both hands against the inside of the lid. I try the other side. It doesn't budge either. Not that it matters. Chaz told me he was putting the lock bar down, but I'm human. I had to try. I can't dismiss anything as impossible. Sonofabitch!

There isn't a soul in the alley, and with the heavy rain, nobody will hear me scream. But that doesn't stop me from doing so. Yelling "Help!" sounds like dialogue from a bad movie. So does "Let me out of here!" but I repeat them both several times to no avail. If a better choice of words would free me, I'd find them. They won't. This is fucking surreal.

I still have my burner phone. I could call the police. But they may haul me into the station, and while I'm answering all kinds of questions, Carly and Ray will be taking my daughter out of the country. I can't risk it. That's a last resort. *Think, Liam, think!*

I sit on the bag of garbage that arrived here before I did. While it cushioned my landing a bit, the damn thing also split open when I fell on top of it. It's dark, and I can't see anything. But the smell. Damn. Covering my mouth, I stop short of gagging. The fetid remains of all that's been tossed is making my stomach flip and churn. I pull out my burner phone, turn it on, and use the light to see if there's anything useful in this heap. I really don't want to touch anything I don't have to. Coughing, I look at empty paper coffee cups, soda cups, smashed soda cans, crumpled McDonald's bags, old newspapers, discarded flyers, miniature liquor bottles, dirty napkins, plastic bags of dog shit, cigarette butts, a parking ticket, a sweaty shirt, and a damn used condom. There's a banana peel next to what looks to be a baby's diaper. My nose tells me I'm correct. Three horrifying objects catch my eye: two dead rats and a used needle. Holy fuck!

I'm going to die in this noxious contraption. Sitting here in garbage, absorbing this stench is already driving me insane. I turn off the burner and stash it in the zipper pocket of my backpack. I squat again and try to push the lid open on both ends. "Let me out of here!"

Why do they always lock me in the dark and tell me to be quiet while they take care of business in the kitchen? Who are these people that come to my house? They won't let me just go into my room when they do because the place is small, and I might overhear whatever illegal shit they're talking about. So what? There are rats down here. I've seen them. I remember the first time one brushed by me. I stopped myself from screaming just in time. I knew I'd be beaten later if I made any noise.

They keep me down here so long some days. I never get free until the lady screams at the man to unlock the door. Where is she? Who is she? Why isn't she screaming now when I need her the most? I'll never escape without her. I'll be here forever. It's just a matter of time before the rodents come for the garbage. Why does she let him put me down here in the first place? I remember. He's not very nice to her either.

I hate this basement. And there's not enough oxygen in here. I can't breathe very well.

Wait. Get a grip, Liam. This isn't a basement. It's a garbage dumpster in an alley. Where did I just think I was? It felt so real for a moment, but it wasn't. No, it was. It was very real. It's just not real right now.

My knife. Yes, I have a knife. I almost stabbed my reflection with it. Leaning back, I finagle it out of my side pocket. *Brilliant, Liam. You're going to cut your way out. Won't Chaz be surprised!*

I open the knife and go in for the kill. The moment it stabs the thick, hard-plastic lid, I realize I'm an idiot. This knife can sear flesh, but it won't hasten my departure. *Yeah, right, Liam. You're Superman in a back-alley dumpster, all tucked in for the night, but you still think you're going to rescue your daughter. You're delusional.*

No, I'm not. I'll get out of here. I just can't let myself pass out from the stench. Not to mention the claustrophobia. That can't happen. I know I've been through worse. I can feel it. Wait, I'm feeling raindrops on my face. How is that possible?

"I've got you, Liam."

I look up. Isaiah is peering over the bin and looking down at me. "Can you climb out of there?"

"Sure can." I stand on the trash and do exactly that. Compared to the unbearable stench inside the dumpster, I might as well be in a field of lavender now. But I can't take joy in anything until I find Rayelle.

"Sorry I couldn't come quicker."

I'm now standing face-to-face with the real Superman. Isaiah's new hoodie is soaked, but he's put the new blanket into a garbage bag to keep it dry. Meanwhile I hold my hands out, palms up, to let the rain wash away the grime from the edge of the dumpster I clutched in the act of freeing myself.

"I'm so grateful to you, Isaiah." I rub my hands together. "How in the world did you know I was here?"

He pulls me over to stand underneath a metal awning behind a store. "Saw them put you in here." He shakes his head in disgust. "When I heard them talk about how I was sleeping, I thought to myself, Isaiah, you can follow these men 'cause they won't be expecting it. So I did. Stopped when they got to this alley, then waited a few seconds before I took a peek and I saw what they were doing. Man, was I steamed. Would have rescued you right away, but there was no time to lose. I thought you'd prefer me to follow Chaz before coming back for you."

"Oh, hell yes! Thank you! You're brilliant. What did you find out?"

"Well, the second they locked you in there," he says, visibly angry, "they split up. Mack pulled out his phone, said it was later than he thought, and he had to take care of some shady business." Isaiah grunts. "I threw that word 'shady' in there because I know darn well that's what it is. Anyway, Chaz walks to the end of an alley, then, like it was a second thought, he walked backward into a doorway and pulled out his phone. He tells someone, 'Tell the old man I'll check on them later. I need to get laid now. It's been a hell of a day.' He listens to the person for a real quick few seconds, then cuts them off. You could tell. Then he says, 'Just because you don't use your plumbing much, my faucet needs to be turned on regularly. It's my only release. Knocking a few back isn't enough for me.' Then he mumbles something I couldn't make out and ends the call. Seems like the other party was still talking, but he didn't care. Then he lit a cigarette and walked away, real quick like."

I put my arms out and clutch his shoulders. "You're truly a godsend, Isaiah. I *knew* I was right to keep tailing him. Sounds like he's been told to protect his brother along with my wife and daughter. And that's exactly what he's going to do after he has a go at it." A wave of relief sweeps over me. "This means they're still in the country. They're still here!" Desperate for more good news, I look at the brave man before me. "You don't happen to know where Chaz is now, do you?"

Isaiah reaches into his pocket and pulls out a crumpled-up flyer. "He's in an apartment building over a wash house on Ninth Avenue." He opens the paper and reads it. "Guess most folks call them laundromats. My grandma always said 'wash house.' Anyway, the entrance to the place is a glass door to the right of the establishment. There were a few flyers on the front window, 'bout laundry specials or something, so I just pulled one down so you'd have the right address. Memory ain't what it used to be, living on the streets. I'd never have forgiven myself if I'd forgotten it."

I almost want to kiss him. I've got to get going, but I need to return the items he gave me. "Man, I'm really sorry that I got your shirt and hat all stinking of garbage. But I guess it's this borrowed jacket that took the biggest hit. Hope the rain will wash it off." Feeling shame, I take off the jacket, then his shirt, handing it back to him before reaching into my backpack for a clean one. "I'm really sorry."

"Don't be. I take my clothes to the wash house. Just like folks with homes do. I'll be okay." After putting on my clean shirt and Marge's husband's jacket, I reach in my pants pocket and hand him twenty-three dollars. The three dollars are from that lady. She knows you and thinks you're a good man. The twenty is from me, to do your laundry. But when this is over, I'm going to come back and help you more. I just can't part with any more money now, not knowing what's ahead."

Isaiah's eyes fill with gratitude again.

This man amazes me.

"My friend, Liam. You've done more for me than any soul ever has. And just being able to help you, well, it makes me feel more like the man I used to be. Medical debt from years of my wife's cancer treatments threw me into this mess. Did everything I could to save her, but nothing worked. Sure do miss her. Miss my Nellie, our life, my wonderful job, and our modest home. Lost it all. Not here because of alcohol. Don't do drugs either. I'd gladly give up the smokes if I had a real life. Don't really like them. Just started smoking because they give me something to do while I try to catch a break." He nods down the alley. "See that wooden shed up against the building? That's where I sleep, but you can pretty much find me where you met me."

"I will definitely come back and—"

"You have a daughter to find. Don't be worrying about Isaiah Calbert Jones. Despite everything, I'm still a lucky man. Go on, now, friend. God speed and God bless."

Saturday, 1:11 a.m.

The rain has thankfully stopped. I hurry to the address on Ninth Avenue. I get there in six quick minutes. I see the laundromat and the glass door Isaiah was talking about. So now what? There's no clear place to hide. It's after 1:00 a.m. There's a wooden tree guard only yards from the building. But it's made of slats, not solid wood. I can't be like the cat or dog who hides behind the drapes with no clue their tail is sticking out or that the fabric is transparent.

Across Ninth Avenue, there's another tree guard. It's painted bright red, and the tree it surrounds is much leafier. I can easily stand behind that one with my red umbrella. I'll blend right in, and I honestly don't think Chaz will look in that direction or see me if he does. Especially since he thinks I'm still in dumpster captivity. Bastard.

I'm feeling good about my decision. I cross the street, and it occurs to me. How stupid am I going to look with an open umbrella when there's no damn rain? Exasperated, I look upward. "Hey, Sky, now would be a really good time. Help a guy out?"

"Sure, what can I do you for?"

"I need you to rain again."

"What the fuck?" I turn around and some thirty-something-year-old woman has dumped half a bottle of water on my head.

She and her boyfriend laugh like it's the most hilarious thing they've ever seen.

"Not funny," I tell them.

"Dude," the man says, still laughing, "I've seen a lot of drunks in my life, but never anyone who asks the sky to bring more rain in the middle of a monsoon."

"I'm not drunk!"

"Yeah, you're real sober. That's why you want more rain and believed I was the sky talking back to you."

"It wasn't like that," I protest.

"So, what did I get wrong?"

Just as I'm about to tell him off, I remember I can't take my eyes off the door across the street. *Priorities, Liam. Rayelle is all that matters.*

"Yeah." He smirks. Mocking sonofabitch. "Like I thought. You don't have an answer."

Just as the woman is about to add her two cents, the rain comes back. She isn't happy. "What the ever-loving—"

"See, the sky heard me," I tell them, hoping it will shut them up.

"Where's your umbrella?" the woman asks her boyfriend.

He looks down as if he expects an umbrella to appear in his hand. "Oh, hell, Gina, I left it at the bar."

"Well that's just great! Real swell." She tries to swat the rain away like it's a swarm of flies. "Do you know how much it cost me to do my hair today?"

I want to laugh, but I understand futile actions. Hope that teaches them a lesson. With great pleasure, I open my red umbrella as they hurry off, bickering their way down the street, becoming more soaked with every step.

There aren't a lot of people around at this hour, so I can get away with standing here. In the daytime, I would be far more noticeable. But maybe not by too much. After all, it's not unusual to stand and wait for someone—and I am. He just doesn't know it. How much longer can he be? Definitely sounded like a wham-bam-thank-you-ma'am kind of thing from what Isaiah overheard. He should be out soon. Or does he rest up a bit and go again? I have zero interest in his sex life. I just need him to lead me to Rayelle.

Five more minutes pass, and my anxiety is ramping up. I shift from foot to foot as if that will produce Chaz. Could he have possibly left before I even got here? Nah. I've got to give it more time.

What the hell. A male voice is singing the stupidest lyrics I've ever heard. I turn around to see a stark-naked old man with a bar of soap, lathering up his body as the rain falls, standing not too far from me. "Scrubby scrubby scrubby, I don't need no silly tubby!"

My mind has played all kinds of tricks on me today, but this?

He's now washing his privates with soap, still singing. "Got a happier demeanor 'cause I got a cleaner wiener."

Oh, hell no. Nothing screams "Look at me!" like this guy does. If he's still here when Chaz comes out, it's going to make my red camouflage a whole lot less effective.

Wait, someone is coming to my rescue. A middle-aged woman is running out of a building with a large blue towel in her hand. "Dad! For the love of God, get back inside! I can't leave you alone for two minutes to make a phone call." She hurries over to him, wraps a towel around him, looks apologetically in my direction, and escorts him back to their building while he entertains her with a rousing chorus of "Splish, Splash, I'm just taking a bath."

Why does this shit happen to me? I'm not on a crowded street, yet in ten minutes … I stop the internal dialogue. Getting wound up over people who don't matter will get me nowhere I need to be.

Another five minutes pass, and I'm questioning my decision but remind myself I have no options. Wait, I see someone. It's Chaz. He opens the glass door and leans up against the wall under the laundromat's blue awning. Pulls a pack of cigarettes out of his jacket pocket and lights up.

As soon or before he finishes, he's going to start walking. I'll stay on the opposite side of the street. I pray he doesn't turn onto a narrower crosstown street. Hiding won't be impossible, but it will be more difficult.

I prepare myself to leave. This has got to be the break I've been waiting for.

CHAPTER TWELVE

Damn. He's crossing the street at the corner and heading west down 52nd Street. I follow him at a distance. So far, so good. At the end of the block, he turns south onto Tenth Avenue. That's a much wider street, but I can't press my luck and continue walking behind him. Luckily, the light turns when I need it to, and I cross to the west side of Tenth Avenue as he stays on the east side. I hurry a bit to catch up with him, but we're now walking parallel to one another. *Good, Liam. Luck is still on your side.*

After walking several blocks, he appears to be absorbed in thought. He isn't checking his environment. Maybe getting tossed in the dumpster was a blessing in disguise—or in garbage. The rain has already washed most of the stench from the jacket and my backpack. I'm breathing better. He moves fast and we're already in the forties.

Oh, no. He stops at the end of the block. Holding his umbrella in one hand, he reaches into his side pocket with the other. I think he's getting a call. He's fumbling and looks annoyed. He finds the phone, but a wad of bills falls onto the wet sidewalk, and he squats down to pick them up. Can't hear a word, but I know he's cursing as the money goes in all directions.

I hope he's not on the call long. I'll look suspicious if I stand here at the same time he's stopped. *No, Liam, he thinks you're still in the dumpster. Chill.* Ah, great. His call wasn't more than two minutes. He keeps walking and within no time at all, we've gone several city blocks. He's just crossed 44th Street. Great. He's going to keep going. Not so great. He turns to walk down the street, walking east while I'm heading south on Tenth Avenue. Walking perpendicular to one another isn't gonna work.

Luck isn't on my side this time, and my escalating heart rate frightens me. I look at the pedestrian crossing signal. The red hand is lit, and I can't wait for the walking man to come on. Checking traffic way too quickly, I wait for an approaching cab to pass and rush across the street. A second cab comes out of nowhere, narrowly missing me. He lays on his horn. Shit! I nearly jump out of my skin. That was close. A honking horn is not an anomaly in this city, but far more noticeable at this late hour when there isn't much traffic. I just hope it didn't register on Chaz's radar.

I've got no choice now but to follow him down 44th Street, which is much narrower, but I'll walk a safe distance behind him. I'm a bit shaken from almost getting hit. I look to make sure that cab is gone. As soon as I turn to walk, the rain lets up a bit and I can clearly see there isn't a soul on the street.

That's impossible! I was distracted for a second. There's no way he could have made his way into any building, and even running, he couldn't be at Ninth Avenue yet. But why would he have walked down Tenth only to go back where he was. I'm lost. Chaz and this city are both confusing me. I might as well be in the middle of the Sahara Desert, because I have as much chance of finding my daughter here as I would there.

Think, Liam, think! There's a modern condo building on the corner. He could have gone through the revolving glass doors at the entrance, but my gut tells me no. Besides, if he did, he's already out of the lobby, and I'd be conspicuous as hell walking in there, and I'd have nowhere to go.

The rain has now stopped completely, and so have I. Reaching up, I close my umbrella and stick it in my backpack. I didn't want to close it as it's helpful to hide behind, but I'd look ridiculous holding it now, especially as its bright red. Too many streetlamps on this block. I'll just keep walking. Maybe there'll be a clue. Maybe he rushed into a building and will be rushing out. *Please, God. Let him think I'm still in the dumpster!*

I pass the second building on the street. Between that and the third building is a large black metal gate with No Parking and Tow Away Zone painted across both sides. It's partially open. Before I can contemplate if this means anything, Chaz emerges from the open space and grabs me with brute force, a fistful of my loaner jacket in one hand, his other tight around my arm. Feels like those blood-pressure cuffs when they tighten. Damn. He's gonna cut off my circulation.

"Well, if it isn't Houdini Fucking Tallamore! You're wondering how I saw you, aren't you?"

"Yeah, it crossed my mind," I manage to choke out.

"I'm sure you saw me drop some money back on Tenth. Well, looking around to make sure I had it all, what did my peripheral vision see? A genius with a red umbrella, across the street, stopping the exact moment I did. I knew right then and there it was you. But that's a wide street, so I just waited until I got here, knowing you'd be fucking following me. When I heard someone laying on a horn, I was sure that was because you crossed the damn street in a hurry to come after me."

His grip is really strong. "Geez, will you let me go? I'm not going to run anywhere. You're my only clue to finding my daughter."

I'm stunned as he shoves me up against the concrete wall to my left, pinning me against it with both hands. The uneven texture of the concrete cuts painfully into the back of my hands. "I should've had Mack hold you in the alley while I ran into the store and bought a padlock. If I had, you'd still be in the dumpster. How the hell did you get out?"

I can't tell him the truth. No way I can betray Isaiah. He risked a lot to help me. "I'm so stressed; I can't remember."

"Fucking bullshit! You tell me, or I'll turn you around and squash your face against this wall until your nose falls off. Not playing, Tallamore. You've got three seconds."

He starts to turn me around. I'm hyperventilating. "All right! I'll tell you." I pause to breathe. "Okay, um, so there was a guy huddled in the alley. Nobody I've ever seen before. Young kid really. He saw what you and Mack did and let me out about fifteen minutes after you left. You know, just to make sure you were gone."

Chaz narrows his eyes. "Is that fucking so?" He nods in slow motion. "And you just happened to find me all over again in New York fucking big-ass City. Is that your story?"

"Oh, I guess I forgot part of it."

"What in the big ole book of lies might that be?" He presses his knee against my thigh for a tighter hold.

That hurts, not to mention the back of my hands pressing even harder into the concrete. "The kid said that if he knew where you'd gone, he might get a reward if the cops were looking for you. So he followed you to that apartment building next to the laundromat before letting me out."

"Bullshit!" He takes his right hand and makes a fist with it, raising it to my face. He holds it there while he stares at me, then puts his hand back on my shoulder. "You can tell 'that kid,' Isaiah, that he'll never get another handout from me or any of my buddies again. We don't take kindly to fucking betrayal."

I'm devastated for Isaiah. Ashamed that I couldn't think of another way to explain my escape. I have to make it up to him somehow, but right now, I have to find Carly and Rayelle.

"I don't see you denying anything, Houdini. But damn, there's nothing you won't lie about, is there?"

Sweat forms on my brow. "Chaz, please. You said you have a son and a daughter. Are you telling me you wouldn't lie to find them if they were kidnapped?" I'm being ridiculously brave—or stupid. "Come on, man, you tell *me* the truth."

Chaz isn't swayed by my words. He just stares harder into my eyes. "Maybe you don't remember the part where I told you that if my felon brother or old man, or anyone else, finds out that I didn't stop your ass the one, two, now three times I could have, my kids' futures, not to mention my own, will be flushed down the toilet. I'm talking millions here, Tallamore. I feel your pain, but I'm not going to sacrifice my children for your child. Would you sacrifice your daughter's future so I could find *my* kids?"

How the hell do I answer that? "I only know I sure as hell wouldn't leave you floundering when I could help. I'd definitely give you another source of clues."

He's still pinning me against the wall. "But the 'source of clues' you want would still come from *me*. What part of this don't you get? I'd still be helping your ass. I can't risk it! Not to mention you've already shown me more than once that you can't be trusted. Do I have to pummel the crap out of you to make that point? I might not be able to push you through this wall, but it would be fun to try."

"No. I hear you. I do."

He stares intensely at me for another thirty seconds. Finally, he takes his hands away.

"Thank you. I really appreciate it."

Chaz snorts in disgust. "Oh, you're laboring under the misconception that I'm letting you go. Oh hell no, motherfucker. I've got some errands to run and then I'm locking your ass up where nobody can *ever* find you. You'll only get out when I let you out."

"Please don't do that. Look, why don't you take me to the corner of Tenth Avenue? You can watch me walk as far north or south as you want. And then, when you feel confident that I can't possibly find you again, well, then go about your business."

"Fool me once, shame on you. Fool me twice … not gonna happen. The only way to know where you are is to drag your ass with me. Gotta make some extra stops. Need to circumvent dealing with anyone who knows me or my family. And I also need to know one hundred percent that you're not out there round the next corner. Sorry, Tallamore, but by the time I let you out of the prison I'm going to put you in, your wife and child, along with my miserable brother, will be far away. And that's exactly where I want him to stay."

"I can't lose my daughter!"

"I feel your pain, but my hands are tied just like yours are gonna be. Maybe one day, your wife will see Felonious Hunk's true colors and come home to you. Daughter and all. Maybe you can find a way to track them down before that day—if it ever happens. Hire a PI. A psychic. Or call law enforcement. Whatever. But if you ever invoke my name in any way, you'll sorely regret it. That's a promise. You and me got something in common, Tallamore—we protect our own. And that's why I'm not letting you out of my sight until I take care of business. And that means until the three of them are safely out of the country."

Saturday, 1:48 a.m.

Chaz didn't turn down this block for no reason. Holding my jacket like he did when he first grabbed me, he pulls me across 44th Street to an apartment building that's not far from the corner. We stand under the green awning where he stops and stares at me. "You're just an associate of mine, and you don't tell anyone what that association is. Got it? Someone asks your name, it's Jack. Like as in you don't know jack shit. You hear me?"

"I hear you."

"I don't expect to be long. Just picking something up." He stares at me again. "Why do I feel like you're going to try something?"

I stammer before I can speak clearly. "Because I was a stupid ass before. And again after that. But you've shown me that you don't play. I get it. Really."

He looks at me suspiciously, but changes his countenance as we walk into the building. We take the elevator to the fourth floor and turn left when we get out. I don't know what I was expecting, maybe fire-breathing dragons, but the man who opens the door is middle-aged, wearing a monogrammed blue shirt with thin white stripes and a pair of creased designer jeans. I can't help but notice the gorgeous art on the walls.

"This is a friend who can wait for me in the living room," Chaz tells him as the man turns several locks on the door. "Maybe there's someone who could keep him *company.*"

Understanding exactly what he means, the man calls out the name Dorothy, but nobody appears.

"Oh, hell. Excuse me." The man walks down a short hallway and opens the second door. A minute later, he walks back, a disheveled Dorothy, tying the belt around her blue robe and wiping the sleep from her eyes, behind him. The man shoots her a look.

"Oh," she says to me as the men turn down the hall to the first room. "Where are my"—she looks at a crystal clock on an end table—"two o'clock-in-the-morning manners? Have a seat on the couch. I'll sit next to you."

Two o'clock. Time is Irish once an hour. Why does that thought keep taunting me. I look at her but say nothing.

"What's your name, stranger in my home?"

"Jack. Jack Sh.... Just call me Jack."

She suppresses a laugh. "Sounded like you were going to say 'Jack Shit' for a moment. Probably because I'm half asleep. What is your last name?"

"Sh-Sheffield."

"Ah, that explains it. Guess my ears hadn't opened all the way." She nods toward the door where Chaz and her husband are. "How much money is your friend borrowing?"

So that's why Chaz is here. I wonder what the money is for, but it's got to have something to do with Ray and Carly and where we're going next.

"I don't ask him personal questions. That's the truth."

She lowers her voice. "I'm gonna say this quickly. I don't like my husband playing middle-of-the-night gangster banker. At least that's what I call it. There are some people, bad people, who know what he does, and they watch the front entrance. Saw someone today when I got back from the grocery. His eyes were fixed on our building, and it unnerved me. These people aren't necessarily enemies of my husband, but they likely have axes to grind with some of his customers, and they may not even know them by sight. I've never said a word to anyone before, and I hope I'm not making a mistake now. There's just something about you. I had to speak up. You and your friend need to be careful when you leave. And you didn't hear one word about anything from me. We talked about art."

"I hear you. Thanks for telling me. I won't say a word." What in the world is Chaz doing? What is the money for? Is this going to get me killed before I can find Rayelle? He said he was meeting with people who didn't know him or his family. Someone had to have sent him here. Maybe it was that call he got when he fumbled to get his phone out. This nice lady is trying to warn me. I'll bet she's scared on a regular basis. Can't blame her. She said she's never warned anyone else. Maybe the other people who come here don't look as out of place as I do. Fear crawls up my arms like an invisible army of bugs. I can't get them off me. I don't want to stay here, but I'm afraid to leave.

She looks up at the wall. "So, you like those two paintings of the beach?" She's speaking more loudly now. "Got them in Truro, Mass. On the Cape. Edward Hopper used to paint there. Lovely little museum with his work and his wife Jo's. These come from a gallery in town." She looks at me the way Chaz does. "Yes. That's what we talked about. Art. And now you can say so truthfully."

I hear Chaz and the man coming out of the bedroom. I turn to Dorothy. "When I was fifteen, my parents and I visited Cape Cod. I don't think we got to Truro, but yes, I do remember seeing a lot of art like this in galleries around town. Anyway, you have great taste. Everything is really beautiful." My stomach is somersaulting as I act like someone who's been invited to their aunt and uncle's home for dinner and pleasant conversation.

She smiles, pleased with my words. "Well, nice meeting you, Jack. If nobody minds, I'm going to bed—again." She shoots a dirty look at her husband and is gone.

The man walks to the door, unlocks, then opens it. He and Chaz don't even say good-bye. And as we walk to the elevator, Chaz says nothing at all.

A moment later, we're back out on the street. Dorothy's warning is repeating in my head. If I had physical alarm bells, they'd be ringing loudly and waking up everyone on this block. Only it's eerily quiet. I can barely hear the cars on Tenth Avenue. There's a police car parked at the end of the street. Probably chatting with his partner and having a cup of coffee and donut. If anyone's even inside the car, but I think there is as I see a flicker of movement. I feel bad for stereotyping cops. I'm sure not all cops like donuts. One may be a woman for all I know. What an asinine thing to waste thoughts on at a time like this. Something is wrong. I wish that car gave me more confidence, only it doesn't.

Chaz looks into my eyes. "Glad you didn't try anything stupid."

"I told you—I learned my lesson, and I meant it."

"Remains to be seen, Tallamore. But not on my watch."

The hairs on the back of my neck are standing up. Something's very wrong. I try not to be too obvious as I scan our surroundings. Across the street, in the flash of a second, I see a large male figure in a black hoodie coming out of the gate between the two buildings. Fuck! He's got a gun. He raises his right arm and points at us as he starts to cross the street. He wants to kill us before he robs us. I'm not waiting around to find out. I turn to Chaz and scream, "Get down!" I push him to the sidewalk, falling on top of him as he curses me out—right before two shots are fired.

The police car, lights flashing and siren on, speeds down the street after him. Guess he should have checked his surroundings too. Panicked, the shooter takes off down the street toward Ninth Avenue.

I get up, wondering if I got hit and couldn't feel it. I don't see any blood and I don't feel anything. I don't think he got anywhere near either one of us. "Chaz, you okay, man?"

Dazed, he sits up. Then, as if everything makes sense, he stands, grabs hold of me, and we run in the opposite direction. I guess he doesn't want to wait around to give a statement to any more cops coming to check on us. Standing on Tenth Avenue, where the traffic is going uptown, Chaz tries to hail a cab, but the first one he sees is off duty. "Fuck!" A second one passes. Chaz is freaking out. He pulls me out into the street and waves at a third one. This cab stops. Chaz opens the back door, practically pushing me in just as another police car turns up 44th Street.

I can barely breathe. Chaz tells the driver to take us to a street corner in the mid-sixties off Columbus Avenue. The driver nods and pulls the plexiglass partition closed.

Chaz looks at me and nods at the partition. "A lot of cabs got rid of these things so customers can chat with drivers. We're lucky we got one. We're not the chatty types, are we?" He takes a good look at me and lowers his voice. "How the hell did you even see that guy?"

I'm not gonna narc on Dorothy. If she hadn't said what she did, we might both be dead. I've got to think fast. If I don't answer, Chaz won't believe whatever eventually comes out of my mouth. "Well, you said you're gonna lock me up again, so I thought Mack might be around, waiting for us to come out. I had a bad feeling, so I looked across the street to that gate you dragged me through earlier, and that's when I saw him come from behind it. He pulled out his gun and pointed it right at us." I stop to breathe. "Maybe he was planning to sneak attack and rob us. But I guess he shot at us because he knew I saw him."

"Maybe. And some motherfuckers just want you dead so you don't put up a fight or can't testify against them. You know how many people get shot because the fucker thought they were someone else? No one with a gun asks for ID before they pull a trigger. If they get the wrong person, fuck it. Human life doesn't mean jack to them. I don't know why he shot at us, but we needed to get out of there, and that's enough questions." His tone softens ever so slightly. "Tallamore, gotta say it, you probably just saved my life. And I'm very grateful. My kids would be too. But sorry, I still plan to proceed with business as usual. After our next stop, I've got to lock your ass up."

I thought that if anything would get him to change his mind, saving his life might be the ticket to freedom.

"I haven't proved myself to you?"

"Man, hear me out. I know you're a good guy. You love your kid more than life itself. You'd do anything to get her back, and I can't blame you for that. But that's exactly why I can't trust you, even after you shielded my body with your own." He exhales. I can tell he doesn't like the words he's speaking. "Sorry, nothing's changed, except maybe one day, when this shit is behind us, I'll find a way to thank you. Until then. Sorry. Still gotta lock your ass up."

CHAPTER THIRTEEN

Saturday, 2:14 a.m.

We ride uptown in silence. Chaz sends out three different texts. I wish I knew what they said or who they're to, but I can't help but think at least one, if not all, directly concerns my fate. I don't dare ask, but I'm fidgety as fuck and desperate to know. Chaz is shaken, I can tell, but he's trying to play it cool. The driver lets us out at 66th and Columbus, and we walk several blocks after he drives away. We're somewhere in the 70s now. I guess Chaz doesn't want any cabbie to have a record of where he took us.

I'm grateful that it isn't raining at the moment. Chaz is once again grabbing a fistful of my jacket. He made me zip it up so I couldn't squirm out of it and run. We keep walking. I know he hates doing this, but he's not convinced I won't bolt, even though I've told him a hundred times he's my only path to finding my little girl.

I've never missed anyone more in my life. I'm trying not to think about her too much despite my love for her being the driving force behind everything I'm doing. When I find her, then I can free all of the angst that's bottled up inside me.

We stop in front of a building that has nine steps to the front door. Chaz turns to me. "Everything I said before applies now. Anyone asks your name, it's Jack, and you say nothing about our association. Got that?"

"I got it."

"You try to put out an SOS of any kind, even in the smallest way, it won't end well."

As I nod, I see his eyes darken like they did back at Baradino's. Only I sense more fear than anger.

I prepare to climb the steps, but instead, we go through a small wrought-iron fence to the right and down a couple steps to a basement apartment. There are two windows with black wrought-iron bars and a matching door which we stand in front of. Chaz doesn't knock or ring a bell. He doesn't need to because someone sees us through the window.

The woman who answers it is nothing like I expected. She's in her mid-thirties with well-done goth makeup, purple strands of hair mixed into the dark blonde, and is wearing a Bohemian-style dress with a paisley-and-floral design. She's wearing a ton of jewelry, her arms are covered in tattoos, and her purple Converse high tops complete the look. She smiles, and I don't know if I'm going to a party or to my execution.

The room looks like she designed it. It's low lit and has a comfortable vibe, but I'm feeling anything but. Still smiling, she goes to the door and locks us inside with a key that she wears around her wrist on a beaded, stretchy bracelet. Oh, just swell.

"I'm Jet," she says to me as if everything is normal. "Why don't you wait here on the sofa?" She looks at Chaz, and her tone is more serious. "I'll take you to him."

I collapse onto the overstuffed purple velvet sofa with about ten different-colored throw pillows on it as she disappears behind a door with Chaz. I wonder if she was told to lock me in or if Chaz and I are both being locked in. That turn of the key was likely just for me. He didn't look the least bit nervous when she did that. He looked relieved.

The coffee table in front of me has drawers underneath, and one of them is partially open. Sitting atop a stack of papers, I see a man's photo. It looks like it's two inches square. He looks kind of scary.

I avert my gaze before she returns. When she does, I look at her with a stupid hostage-like smile on my face. I can't think of a single thing to say.

She sits next to me. Noticing the open drawer, she shuts it nonchalantly with her right foot. "I didn't catch your name."

"Jack."

"Jack," she repeats. "Strong and powerful. A no-nonsense name."

"It's what they gave me." Wow, that was an idiotic response. I look at all of the interesting things around the room. I'll do what I did at the last place. Talk about art. "You've got some great pieces in here. I love that tapestry. And those baskets on the wall. Amazing." Turning toward some colorful, bold paintings, I pretend to be increasingly awestruck. "Wow, these are great. Are you an artist?"

"I am. I did those two paintings. I take pictures too." She points to a large, framed photo I hadn't yet noticed. "That sepia shot, the girl with the guitar, that's mine as well."

"You're a great photographer."

"Used to be." She looks a bit dejected. "Not as much time to chase the arts as I used to have." She stares ahead, and the conversation grinds to a halt.

My mind is just getting started. That small square photo in the drawer I saw. That's not photography. That's a damn passport photo.

Her boyfriend, or whoever the hell she lives here with, is a fucking forger. She's pissed because she has to take stupid photos all day and can't do what she enjoys. I know exactly what Chaz is doing. He's picking up passports and God only knows what else so that Carly and Ray can leave the country with my daughter. And that man on 44th Street lent him money to pay for this. That's the connection. Damn. Everything is making too much sense.

There's a knock at the door. Jet stands, peeks out the window, then opens the door. Holy crap! It's Mack, and he's looking right at me with a creepy smile on his face, the same way he eyeballed me before I was tossed in the dumpster. I can see that he's dying to say something, but wouldn't dare with Jet here.

His face loses all emotion. "I'll just stand here," he tells her, posing by the door like some damn Westminster Abbey guard. A red military jacket and a bearskin hat and he'd be good to go, excluding the fact that he'd still look like a goon. Sonofabitch. He's even standing straight like he's actually official. Official mob, yeah.

There's no doubt in my mind about the forged documents, but I decide to keep my suspicions from Chaz. The more he thinks I know, the more wary of me he'll be. I just need to be dumbass Liam from Trenton, New Jersey who wants to find his daughter. Really, that's all that matters.

I'm sure Chaz was texting Mack. If he's planning to lock me up somewhere, he knows he can't do it alone and tasked this bastard to help him. I wish I could get up, walk over there, and punch that mug, but he'd squash me like a gnat, and my pleasure, if I even managed to have any, would be extremely short-lived. Literally.

After another two minutes, Chaz comes out of the other room.

I never see who he was with. He nods at Mack, confirming my worst fears, and offers a quick half smile to Jet.

She gets up, says nothing, and unlocks the door.

Once again, the three of us stand together on the street.

"Well, if it ain't da little escape artist." Mack grins as he pulls a padlock out of his pocket. "I know da best dumpsters in the area, but nah, that's not a good idea. None of dem is isolated enough, and you'd cry like a little bitch for someone to save you." He looks at Chaz. "Of course, a big ole gag could easily solve da problem."

"No," Chaz says firmly.

Mack looks surprised. "What, you going soft on dis bitch?"

"No," he repeats. "I'm only trying to keep him away while I do what I need to do. He's just a man trying to find his child. That's not a reason to torture him."

"Really?" Mack grunts. "You didn't have no problem with da dumpster."

Chaz reddens as he presses his lips together, but he's holding his anger in. "Let's just take care of business, shall we?"

How the hell am I going to get away from them now? They're going to lock me up until Carly has taken Ray-Ray God knows where. "I need to use the men's room," I blurt out.

"Ya lookin' for one with a window to climb outta?" Mack says.

"I really do need to go. I'm not that stupid."

Chaz nods his approval to Mack.

"Okay, den, but consider me your bathroom buddy."

"Whatever." My bladder really is bursting, and I'm not stupid enough to think a trip to the men's room is going to save me.

"I know a pub down Columbus," Mack says. "C'mon. I'll take

youse. And den it's prison time."

Saturday, 2:43 a.m.

We come out of the pub, and Chaz is holding a brown bag, but I'm not asking any questions. He hails a cab that takes us what seems like five blocks south, then turns down a side street where it dead ends at Central Park West. Just like before, Chaz doesn't direct the cab to our actual destination.

My anxiety is mounting, and I consider creating a distraction that would enable me to run across the street and disappear into the park. *And then what, Liam? How the hell does that get you to Rayelle, if by some miracle you even managed to pull that off and get lost in the middle of Central Park at night?* They walk on either side of me, and I don't dare try to run. Besides, I know Mack is carrying, so there's that.

We start walking north on Central Park West in the direction we just came from. These guys are sure going to a lot of trouble to fool cab drivers who don't give a damn where we get out. Or maybe they're trying to confuse *me*.

"Down dis street."

Chaz isn't saying anything as we walk mid-block to a brownstone, not dissimilar to the building we were just in. Only I can see it's got all kinds of construction signs on it and is obviously being rehabbed or something. It's unoccupied, and this is where they're going to lock me up. The door to the basement has all kinds of locks on it and looking through the bars on the windows, I can see they're boarded up on the other side. They clearly don't want prisoners escaping.

We climb the stairs to the front door. Mack takes a key out of his pocket and opens it. Sure enough, the place is empty, and all kinds of materials lie everywhere. The floors are completely covered in paint-splattered canvases. There are several ladders, paint cans, and a bunch of other stuff that couldn't matter less to me right now. I've really painted myself into a corner.

You think that's funny, Liam? Making jokes to yourself when you're about to be imprisoned. Humor can save your sanity, someone once told me. Wonder who that was.

Oh, shit. They're taking me into the kitchen. Mack opens a door in the corner, which must lead to the basement. No fucking way. He points to some stuff on the counter and picks up this red metal bar. "Know what dis is? A security lock bar. Gonna install it as soon as you get settled in your new home. Ain't no one coming in or out."

I've seen those bars before. I know they're used a lot on worksite trailers to keep people out after the crew goes home for the day. A buddy of mine in construction uses them all the time.

Mack opens the door to nothing but darkness. I feel myself being pulled back in time with the force of a tornado. My earlier bouts of confusion seem trivial in comparison. This is like a lucid dream, only I have no control. Fear consumes me as my breath leaves my body.

"I'm gonna turn on da light for you to get downstairs. But den, I'm takin' out dat lightbulb so you don't be lookin' around." He turns to Chaz who appears uncharacteristically uncomfortable. "You still got his phone, yeah?"

"I got it. Left it somewhere safe."

With everything I have, I try not to let my consuming fear show. My breath is coming back, but I'm still trembling.

"Let's get dis show on da road." Mack nods to Chaz to lead me downstairs. The basement is completely unfinished. I see some patchwork on the concrete walls. Everything down here is probably going to be renovated along with the house, unless they're turning it into a torture chamber or prison. Maybe they'll end up burying people under the house. Just what I do *not* need to be thinking about.

I take a breath. I can't stress over thinking about what the future holds for this space. My own future along with Rayelle's is in jeopardy. I'm lightheaded. I slump to my side as if I'm going to pass out. *No, Liam! You can't faint!* I straighten as best as I can. *Are they seriously gonna lock me in here?*

"I did you a favor." Mack points to what looks like a bucket with a toilet seat on it. "Got you a camping loo." He snickers. "Actually, I didn't do nuttin' for you. My friends own dis building, and I don't want you soilin' it. Still, you got a place to go."

Am I supposed to thank this sonofabitch? I just look at him, then at Chaz, whose face is unreadable.

Mack's not done talking. "Got you a blanket and a pillow. No bed. This ain't the Ritz. You're lucky you're getting this. Took 'em from a homeless man's camp in an alley."

I know I should keep quiet, but I'm bursting inside. How reprehensible to steal from a homeless man. I dare to ask him a question. "What did I do to deserve this? Seriously. What?"

Mack scowls. "Oh, maybe not minding your own business. You're lucky you're only being locked in dis basement."

"I didn't know that looking for *my* kidnapped daughter was

minding someone *else's* business!"

"Da way you went about it sure is. Now you shut your mouth, or I'm gonna shut it for you."

Chaz gives me a warning look. I know Mack is a sadistic bastard who wouldn't hesitate to keep his word. I say nothing while anger burns in my body.

Mack grabs a wooden box and places it under the hanging light. He turns to Chaz. "You don't weigh as much as me. Stand on dis and take out da damn lightbulb."

"Got it." Chaz sounds tough, but I know he doesn't want to do it.

"Gimme dat." Mack puts the bulb on the ground and steps on it. "Be glad dis ain't your skull." I can see he gets a sick pleasure out of imagining that it is. He picks up the box. Obviously, he thinks it might somehow be of use to me here in the pitch dark.

Mack heads toward the steps and calls for Chaz to follow. "Don't be trippin' going up da stairs in da dark. Use your phone for light."

Quickly, Chaz hands me the bag he got in the pub on Columbus Avenue. "You just need to stay here, Tallamore. It is what it is, man."

In a minute, they're gone. Within another minute, I hear hammering. Mack is installing the security lock bar, and I'm doomed. Nobody will ever know I'm here. I won't get out of this nightmare until Chaz comes back for me or the work crew finds me next week. But if they work for the same people Mack does, they might be warned to stay away from the basement. It's very possible that I might die down here. Or that I'll get out way too late to ever find Rayelle.

I open the bag. I can't see what's inside, but I can feel. Chaz got me a sandwich, two bags of chips, and a bottle of water. These won't last long, but I'll have to ration. No, I won't ration anything because I'm not going to stay here. No fucking way.

"More pounding comes from upstairs. No doubt Mack is enjoying every smack of the hammer. There's no way out. There are no unblocked windows. Nobody lives in this building. No one will ever hear me. Someone has *got* to hear me. What was I thinking? I'm not even going to entertain the thought of never finding Rayelle. That's not an option. I don't know how, but some way or the other, I'm getting out of here.

CHAPTER FOURTEEN
Saturday, 3:08 a.m.

I sit in dankness and darkness. I don't yell out any clichéd cries for help. What's the point? In the dumpster, there was always the hope that someone would be walking in the alley and hear me. The chances were slim, I'll admit. I sure never expected Isaiah would come to my rescue, but I didn't feel as completely helpless as I do now—though close to it.

I eat a quarter of the hoagie that Chaz bought me. Only they're not called hoagies in New York like they are in South Jersey and Philadelphia. They're hero sandwiches here. I've been praying for a hero. Maybe I should have been more specific. I take a few sips of water. Yeah, I'm grateful to Chaz for the sustenance, but I feel my rage and fear escalating quickly.

It's the middle of summer, but it's a rainy night, and it's cold down here. I close the bag and find my way to the blanket. I sit on the floor and wrap it around me. But the smell is foul, way too reminiscent of the dumpster. I toss it to the side. I'd rather be cold. *Think, Liam, think!*

Wait! I still have my backpack and the burner phone. Why didn't I think of that sooner? I have no choice but to use it now. I open the zippered top and feel around for it. Fantastic. At least I have a bit of light too. Now, who should I call? I have Bob's card. I can call him. Anyone but the police. Never the police. I don't know why that's burned into my brain like a cattle brand, but I have to heed the warning. There's no way in hell I'm stepping aside and trusting anyone but myself. I stop to look at the phone. My breath feels like it's leaving my body again. This can't be happening. Nooooo! Fuck! There's no signal down here. Concrete can easily block them. There's no open window to stand by. I know all of this, but really? Now? Of all times? Seriously? Why now? I look toward the walls I can barely see … as if they can understand me. Kind of like the way I asked the sky to rain some more. I start to ask the walls to cut me a break, but I know that's insane.

Hmm. Walls. Cutting a break. Yes! Maybe I can do something with my knife. It didn't work in the dumpster, but I can start carving my way through the wall. *C'mon, Liam. This isn't* The Shawshank Redemption *or* Escape from Alcatraz. *You don't have that kind of time to dig your way out. Even if you could actually do it.*

I've got nearly six grand on me, but it's not like there's anyone here to pay off, is there? There are just times when money can't buy you anything. And there are things so much more valuable than money, like my Rayelle.

Thinking back, I remember the time when Ray-Ray was six and told me that Oliver was Mommy's favorite and then asked me why Mommy didn't love her as much. I told her that was silly, that Mommy loved both of her children the same, but I felt even then, she'd always showed favoritism to Oliver. Now I know it's because he's the son of her true love. Ray-Ray was right. Example after example is coming into my head. The biggest one of all is that a woman who truly loves her child wouldn't traumatize her by taking her away from a father who adores her and vice versa. I shake my head to get rid of nonemergent thoughts. I've got to get the hell out of here.

Fifteen minutes have gone by. Maybe more. I don't know. I turned the phone off. I'm starting to hear things that I know aren't real. A moment ago, I saw a kitchen. It was red and white. Retro-looking. Nothing like the one upstairs that's covered in canvas, the cabinetry and appliances gone, with only a paper-filled table and four chairs. In the retro kitchen, a bunch of people are sitting around the table drinking beer and smoking. I don't like them. They look mean, like the face of the man I saw in that passport photo. Like criminals. And now, a different man is putting me in the basement. He's done it so many times. It's not Mack or Chaz; I know that.

I'll be here until the woman yells for him to get me out. Why don't I hear her voice now? Who is she? Where is she? Why won't she save me like she did when … when what? I feel so confused. Maybe it's all just part of some recurring dream I used to have. Maybe it's all symbolism. Isn't that what dreams are all about? Only I'm not dreaming. I'm remembering. But maybe I'm remembering a dream. How can I really know?

Damn. I just dozed off. I think it was only for about fifteen minutes, but I can't be sure. I pull my phone out and check the time. It's nearly 4:00 a.m. I've been here just under an hour, but it feels like an eternity. I can't give into my body no matter how loudly it cries out for sleep. How do I know that Rip Van Winkle didn't start with a power nap? The guy went to sleep after drinking and didn't wake up for twenty freaking years. No. Not me. Not going to happen. I'll produce all the adrenaline I need to keep me going. Only death can stop me. But I won't let it.

I'm hearing voices again. That man and woman are arguing. They do that pretty often. They curse a lot. So do their associates. The man would lock me in the basement so I couldn't hear their *friends*. No, they were doing all kinds of illegal shit. Who were they? I know they weren't my parents. They're loving and only have the nicest of friends.

My stomach is in knots, but I need my strength to find Rayelle. I eat the rest of the hero sandwich, wash it down with water, then throw the two bags of chips into my backpack.

I turn on my phone again. I've been here over an hour. The sun will be coming up some time right before 5:30 a.m. Only I won't be the recipient of its light, because there is no way for sunlight to get in. It doesn't have a key to the basement, and it doesn't shine through concrete or wood. And the sun doesn't shine out of my ass, so that's not an option. Besides, even if this basement lit up like a night game at Citi Field, so what? How would that help? Trapped is trapped. *Shit, Liam! Maybe it* is *time to call the police. Sometimes 911 calls will go through without a signal. You don't have any better ideas.*

I keep drifting back to this time I can't remember as I fight to make a decision. Two minutes pass, and I keep falling in and out of hallucinatory hell. I hear voices.

"He has to be down there! Get him out now!"

That woman has come to rescue me. Just like all the times before. *No, you're hearing things, Liam. You're not.* Someone is fiddling with that door. Sounds like they're dismantling the lock. *You wish, Liam.* I am so worn. My body feels limp and wobbly, almost like jelly. I'm trembling from the cold and fear, but I didn't come this far to fall apart now. I'm going to call out. Yes. I am. "Help! Someone help me!"

"I knew he was down there."

She's real. I know her voice. But how is that possible? I hear the door open. Two flashes of light come down the steps. The woman is using the light on her phone, and there's a large man behind her doing the same.

"Liam!" she calls to me.

She runs over and grabs me as I grab my backpack. "We need to get you the hell out of here." She pulls me up the stairs. The large man is behind us now. I know he wants to make sure I don't fall backward into the dark pit of hell.

The kitchen light is on. I'm face-to-face with her. Holy shit. It's Marge. And Karma Ken. He picked the lock.

She touches my hair in such a familiar way. "You okay, Liam?"

Ken pulls out a chair. "Sit down. Catch your breath, man."

"Yes, always catch your breath, Liam."

I have so many questions. I don't know which one to ask first, but "How did you find me?" comes out of my mouth.

Marge touches the hem of my jacket and lifts it, inviting me to touch it. "Feel a little plastic thingy in there? It's a GPS tracker. Put it in there a good while back so I'd know who the hubs was banging and where he was going. He used to wear this jacket all the time. Such a Luddite; he never had a clue."

"Oh."

"When you left my place, I told Ken I'd be tracking you, and that if I saw you stay at any one place for too long, we were coming after you. Clubs and bars are one thing, but seeing you were on this residential street for over an hour, it didn't make sense. I had a hunch it wasn't of your own doing."

"That's great, but I'm confused. I couldn't get a signal on my burner phone. So how were you able to get one with this tracker? Isn't it all the same technology?"

"Like I said, I've had my eyes on you all night. There was nothing to block the signal when you arrived. But minutes after this address showed up, zippo. No signal. Trail went cold. When no new location came up, I told Ken someone was likely holding you against your will. And here we are." She lets out a long breath. "Thank God you're alive. I've never been more grateful."

I look into her eyes. They're watery, and she's doing everything she can to stay cool.

Pictures race through my brain like a slideshow going too fast to be properly seen. A weird sensation comes over me before I can respond to Marge. I wait a second for it to pass. Only it doesn't. I'm still looking into her eyes. "I know this sounds bizarre, but this isn't the first time you've rescued me from a basement, is it?"

She lowers her eyes, then quickly looks at me again. "Not a conversation to be had now. We've only got one mission: to find your daughter."

I take a deep breath. I have so many questions for her, but they don't matter at the moment. "You're right."

Marge pulls a chair out from the table with all of the renovation paperwork scattered on top. "Sit, Liam. We need to brainstorm—quickly."

I take a seat as she and Ken do the same. "I don't know where to go next," I tell them. "Chaz was my only hope. Time is running out. I know they're leaving the country."

Picking up a stapler, Marge puts two fingers on the end and her thumb underneath. "I used to make these things quack like a duck when I was a kid." She sees the confused look on my face. "Trust me, Liam. I'm busting my brain to figure something out. Just working off some nerves."

I'd do the same, but turning a stapler into a duck won't do it for me. Just the opposite, actually.

"After you left my place, I was thinking about that letter Carly left you. Said they'd be gone in twenty-four hours. I asked you about that, and you didn't know if it was twenty-four hours from when you read the note or from when she wrote it."

"Right." I'm pleased she's remembered the details. But that stapler "quacking" is messing with my last nerve.

She must recognize my escalating anxiety and puts it down. "Sorry, Liam." She pushes the stapler away. "Old habits and all that. So, listen, I've been thinking about what Carly wrote. You know, that they'd be leaving the country in 'twenty-four hours.' It just sounds a bit too precise. Too even. You know? Like she might've diminished the window of time to stop you from trying to find them. After all, she lied about being raped. I don't know the lady, but isn't it quite possible she'd lie or stretch the truth about this?"

"Under the circumstances, very possible and yeah— probable." I pause, then look down in pain as the realization of losing my wife hits me. "Clearly, I don't know the woman I married. I was stupid enough to think she loved me. So what do I know? I've put off thinking about her until I find my little girl. And I'd sure as hell like to know my son's whereabouts too for that matter. I hope he's okay."

"Sorry, buddy." Ken says, interrupting my downward spiral. "I know all of this really hurts. But, listen, from my perspective, for whatever that's worth, you may have a little more time than you thought. Key words though: a little." He contorts his face. I can tell he's determined to find them. He's angry. "I'll be here with Margie to help you to the end."

I'm overwhelmed with gratitude. "Thanks, Ken. I don't know why you're both doing this for me. I was a stranger to the two of you earlier this evening and now …" I'm getting emotional. No time for that. "I owe you big for saving me from that guy earlier." I sigh. "Feels like days ago."

"No problem. It was my pleasure. I've got little tolerance for punks like that. You've got way more important things to worry about now, but just know, the boys in blue took them away. Had warrants on both of their crim asses. No surprise. They're remarkably less clever than they think." He bites his lip. "So, let's figure out how to find Royce Junior and your family."

Marge, elbows on the table, is squeezing her head. "Come on, brain. Deliver the goods. Help me out here."

Her phone rings. "Better not be the old man begging me not to divorce his ass. Not that he gives a damn, but he'd love to catch me doing what he does all the time—just to have something to use against me at the 11th hour before our court date." She twists her mouth. "I've long stopped caring where the bastard sticks it, and he shouldn't care who …." She pulls her phone out of her pocket. "It's Sherita."

A twinge of hope warms my chest. Sherita wouldn't call Marge after 4:00 a.m. if she didn't have some kind of information.

"Sher," Marge says. "You got anything for me?" She listens. I can't hear what Sherita is saying, but I can hear her chattering quickly. Marge is staring at the table, nodding, and soaking in every word. "Somewhere on the Upper West Side? Good. We're already in the neighborhood. But she has no memory of what type of business it is? Not even a guess?" She pauses. "I see. Sounds like it would be less likely to be on a cross street, yes? More like Columbus, Amsterdam, or Broadway." She nods as Sherita pours more words into her ears. "Okay, north of Strawberry Fields. Got that."

I think Sherita's probably told Marge all she knows, and understanding the little I do about her, probably more. But I don't have a clue what they were talking about.

"Thanks for making that call, my friend. I owe you. You've given us a lot more than we had. Got to start somewhere. Okay, I'll tell him. Thanks."

"Any luck?" I ask.

Marge's tense face relaxes a bit. "First, Sher says she's praying for you. Now, about what she told me. While we still don't have anything remotely resembling an address, we're getting closer. About an hour ago, Sher remembered something else about Royce Senior. Did everything she could to follow up on it. Called her friend Eleanor in the middle of the night because she remembered Ellie was the one who told her years ago that she'd seen Raymond at another business he owned or managed on the Upper West Side. It was when Ellie's cousin was visiting from the West Coast and wanted to see the Imagine mosaic at Strawberry Fields. You know, the tribute to John Lennon in Central Park."

"Right near the Dakota," Ken says.

I nod. "I've been there." Why did I say that? I have no memory of when I would've gone.

"Okay." Marge crosses her arms on the table. "So Eleanor doesn't remember much, but she said when they came out of the park at 72nd Street, they walked west a block or two, then ambled their way uptown with no set agenda. Said they walked a gazillion miles that day and probably went into a gazillion stores. At some point, they walked into an establishment, and Eleanor was way surprised to see Raymond behind the counter."

"How did she know him?" I ask.

"Oh, he lived in our neighborhood before Ray went to the hoosegow. I knew her vaguely back when too, but she and Sher have remained good friends. Anyway, Eleanor can't remember where the store is, but she said it's got to be in the mid-seventies to mid-eighties and could be anywhere between Columbus and Broadway. They didn't go any farther north than 86th Street. Oh, and this is important: Eleanor remembers Raymond saying good-bye and disappearing through a door that went upstairs. She said it had to be to an apartment. She's really sorry she doesn't remember more. Seems they were weaving in and out of streets because Eleanor's cousin is a photographer who was stimulated by everything she saw." Marge chuckles. "Sher made a pretty funny crack, but I'll keep that to myself."

I feel hopeful and hopeless at the same time. I'm getting turned around with all of the street names, yet I can picture them and I don't know why. "So Eleanor doesn't remember what Raymond sold in his store?"

Marge shakes her head. "Not a clue. She said they visited more stores that day than she's visited in her lifetime and she was 'shopped out' for years after. All she knows for sure is that it wasn't a souvenir shop like he's got in Times Square. Don't think they even have many in that area anyway. Oh, and the store didn't have his name in it."

I look at Marge, then at Ken. "So what do we do with this

information?"

Ken stands. "My car is outside. I say we just drive around hoping to find lights on over a store. Sounds likely they've been hiding there. If they're going to leave the country, betcha they'd be hightailing it outta there before sunrise. It's not much, but we gotta go with what we're given." He sighs. "I know, it's like finding the damn needle in a haystack. We gotta try, though. And it won't be dark for much more than an hour and change."

CHAPTER FIFTEEN

We get into Ken's blue Ford Escape, and I give irony props as it's the car being used in hopes of thwarting Carly's escape. It's still unbelievable that Ken and Marge are going without any sleep to help me. I know they're used to very late hours, but still, I'm blown away by their kindness, not to mention Sherita making that call for me. I just don't know if all of the kindness in the world is going to help me find my little girl.

Marge jumps into the back seat and slides to the left as I sit up front in the passenger seat. Normally, I'd insist a woman sit up front, but she wants me to be able to have "prime viewing real estate" and to be able to easily get out if need be. I'm just happy to have eyes on both sides of the car while Ken keeps his on the road.

"Listen up, fellas," Marge says. "We've got to use every bit of logic we can. We know that Eleanor and her cousin left Strawberry Fields and started walking. They covered three avenues in their travels: Columbus, Amsterdam, and Broadway. Since Columbus is the first north-south thoroughfare they'd hit, loaded with all kinds of stores and restaurants, it stands to reason that would be their starting point. I'd say they started walking uptown around 72nd Street. Now, considering Eleanor said they'd been in a gazillion stores that day, that tells me it's highly unlikely that Royce's store would be near the spot they began their trek. I mean, if you've just left Central Park and there's a guy you know who owns one of the first stores you visit, that would be more memorable."

"Truth, babe," Ken says. "Makes sense. Sounds like by the time she saw Royce, the day was becoming a blur to her."

"Exactly," Marge says.

"But what if they doubled back to where they began?" I ask. "Does that mean we don't look at the buildings near 72nd Street?"

"No, it doesn't. We look everywhere. But logic dictates the store is more likely a bit farther uptown on Columbus, or somewhere on Amsterdam or Broadway." She's trying so hard to be positive. "Yeah, I know. Doesn't narrow it down much, does it?"

I swallow my fear. "This feels so impossible."

"Liam, you came into this city without much of a clue. Didn't take you long to find your way to my place—to someone who knew the Kawai family. That's the universe telling you it's on your side. I don't know how you managed to keep a tail on Chaz Royce all night, but you can tell me that later, after we find your little girl. All this didn't happen for you to fail. You've got to tell yourself that."

Ken starts the car. "Columbus only goes downtown, so we can't follow the route as they walked it. I'll drive uptown so we can check it out in reverse. You want to do that first?"

"Makes sense," Marge says. As we drive west, she starts to explain how Verdi Square and two subway stations, followed by traffic islands, pretty much split Broadway and Amsterdam where they come together. I can't follow. Too much information, but I know she's just trying to help.

Still, a part of my brain comprehends most of the nearly convoluted information. It's strange. I'm not from this city. Maybe I just need everything to make sense right now so I think I understand.

I've long given up hope of grasping my distorted thinking process and why I often can't decipher imagination from memory or real life. I'm a mess.

We're driving north on Broadway, and I see everything she just described. Despite Marge's confident speech, I'm feeling anything but. This doesn't seem right.

"Wait!" Marge says. "Something just occurred to me. Sher said that Ray walked upstairs to an apartment. No doubt, he had his store converted to access the unit. That's highly unlikely with so many immense apartment buildings here. We're looking for something that has maybe three or four floors. Maybe five. Just a guess, but I think it's a good one. My gut is telling me it's not on Broadway. Far more likely to be Amsterdam or Columbus. Got a strong suspicion."

Wow. We both had simultaneous feelings that we were in the wrong place. Then I realize that's no big deal. The odds that we're in the right place are slim to none.

"Okay," Ken says. "I'll go up to 88th and hang a right, then we'll come down Columbus."

I don't want to tell them that their play-by-play of the avenues and cross streets is dizzying.

As we drive down a few blocks, there's a light on in a first-floor window. "Right there," I say, "above the kitchen store. Someone's awake in that unit."

"They sure as hell are," Marge says.

"I'll find somewhere to pull over." Ken sighs. "So much construction and street repair everywhere. Damn near impossible."

The light in the unit goes out. "Oh, no. Either they're going to bed or they're leaving."

"Either way, we'll find out." Marge reaches forward and puts a reassuring hand on my shoulder.

"Go for it." Ken stops at the corner.

I hop out of the car. There's a woman with long, dark hair flowing down her back, holding two suitcases, walking quickly uptown. I run after her. "Carly!" I say breathlessly, still hurrying to catch up with her. "Stop! Where the hell do you think you're going, and where's my daughter?"

A Puerto Rican woman, in her late forties, turns to look at me. "Going to meet my Uber to JFK, and the name's Nadia. Before you threaten or scare the crap outta someone, you might want to make sure you've got the right person." She cocks her head to one side. "Ya feel me? Just some friendly advice. This is New York. Stuff happens when you surprise strangers—especially in the dark. If I didn't have a suitcase in each hand, there's an extreme possibility I might have tried to rearrange your face before I asked any questions. You're lucky."

I hope she's right. I need all the luck I can get, even though she didn't mean it that way. "Really sorry," I say, but now she's running to make up for the time she lost telling me off. My apology falls onto the sidewalk. I squash it and hurry back to the corner.

Oh, no! Ken's car is gone. Why would they leave me here? They wouldn't. Was this a ruse all along? I don't get it. I was so sure they were sincere. They rescued me. No, they're my friends now. I know they are. I feel it in my gut. Why does my brain always mess me up like this? Nothing makes any sense. They *are* my friends. I have to believe that. But then again, I thought Carly was a loving wife. No, this is different. There were signs with her; I just was too blind to see them. Am I being blind now? Maybe that woman … Nadia … was a plant to get me out of the car. Her hair was exactly like Carly's. Why would Marge and Ken be so cruel after being so nice? They wouldn't. They're good people. They care. They want to help me. I know they do. I don't understand why they left me though. Why am I so naïve? And what the hell do I do now?

Just as I'm about to melt down on the street, someone honks. It's around the corner. I turn right at the end of the street to see Ken's car. I can't get inside quick enough.

"Sorry, Liam. I had to move the car. No luck?"

"False alarm. Almost got my face punched in."

"Sorry, hon," Marge says. "Glad you didn't. We're going to have to go around in a loop. No way to get back onto Columbus."

I don't dare insult their kindness by telling them I thought they'd abandoned me and then some. Five minutes later, we're back in the same spot. I look at the various shops and businesses, but there are no lights on in any apartments above. Oh no. Fear courses through my veins. A major panic attack is going to annihilate any self-control I have. This one is a tsunami: way stronger than what grabbed hold of me in the dumpster or basement. Why is this happening now when I'm not locked up against my will? I'm visibly shaking. My breathing is labored. I know why. Because my chances of finding Rayelle are slipping away with every second, and that knowledge is physically manifesting itself. *Focus on the now, Liam.* "I-I don't see how looking for lights will h-help." I twist the fingers of one hand with the other until I feel pain. "They could be long gone. And if they're still there and getting ready to leave, maybe they don't want to attract attention to the apartment. Maybe they're s-sleeping and are planning to leave in daylight. I just don't see how we can possibly find them. I-I'm n-never going to see, to see my d-daughter again."

"Oh, honey, please. Catch your breath. You need to catch your breath."

Marge's words are hauntingly familiar.

"Please, Liam. Losing control is not going to help! Do you hear me?" She softens. "I understand every bit of your fears. But based on the limited information Sher got from Eleanor, we're lucky to know as much as we do."

"I-I know, but even if she had an ex-exact address, that doesn't mean they're hiding there. They could be in any b-borough, much less anywhere in M-Manhattan."

"No! They're not in any borough but this one!" Marge says sharply.

I turn around to look at her. Somehow, she verbally slapped the panic attack out of me. I'm breathing normally again.

"Sorry about that. I didn't mean to sound angry with you. I'm angry *for* you." She pauses for a quick moment. "They're in the city. I know it. Sher's told me the family has connections in Manhattan. All over. This isn't butt-fuck Egypt. There are a million places to hide three people."

"Yeah. Unfortunately." I turn and stare at my lap. Despair settles in to replace my fear.

"Don't you think about giving up, boy!"

I look at her again. Wow, she's not playing. She's really agitated. *For* me. Of course. "I won't."

The traffic is awful, but even so, Ken is driving slower than traffic permits. Horns of impatient drivers honk in a cacophony behind us. It's nerve-wracking.

"Listen." I spin around to face Marge. "I don't want any of these people messing with Ken or his car."

"Yeah," she blurts out. "Because they're going to get where they're going so much faster if he speeds up that one mile an hour. Not!"

"Right on, babe."

"Exactly." I glance out the window to reaffirm my game plan. "I think the only way to know we're not missing anything is to walk from 72nd to 86th Street and forget trying to see it all from inside this car."

"Good thinking," Marge says. "That makes sense. Especially if something stands out. Can't exactly stop the car. These are city blocks, Liam. If you don't know, twenty blocks equal approximately a mile, and we'll be doing thirteen. I'll walk on the east side, and you can walk on the west. Shouldn't take all that long."

"True dat." Ken nods as his eyes scan the street. "I'll find somewhere to park and come get you when you call."

Saturday, 5:24 a.m.

Marge and I walked the thirteen blocks. If there was something to see, we didn't find it. There's every possibility that we walked right past the store, but how would we ever know? I'm physically drained but my determination is not. The sun is about to come up. I've been awake nearly twenty-four hours, except for that short nap in the basement.

"It's time to check Amsterdam," Marge says. "I think it's best to drive uptown first for a quick sweep, then we'll walk like we just did if we think we've missed something."

My love for Rayelle keeps me going. Some coffee would help. I pray my body doesn't give out on me. Marge and Ken are probably twenty years older than me. I hope they can stay awake, but Marge reminds me that they both get up much later in the day than I do. It hasn't been as long for them. Still, they must be tired.

We're on Amsterdam Avenue, and I'm fading. My eyes flutter, trying to close. The buildings are starting to blend into one murky metropolitan mess. I'm an idiot for believing I'd find them here, and while Marge and Ken are trying to help, they're only enabling my madness. But there's nowhere else to look, and I can't give up. I'd never forgive myself for not exhausting every single clue, for abandoning Rayelle when she needs me the most, for never being able to see her grow up, and for depriving us both of all we mean to one another.

Three minutes later, to my great surprise, a store sign, right underneath the scaffolding, pulls me out of my stupor. I gasp at what the rising sun reveals, my heartbeat quickening.

"That's it!" I scream. "That's where they are if they're anywhere!"

"Where?" Marge looks around frantically.

"That antique store. Vintage Postcards." I bounce in my seat like an excited child.

"Are you sure, Liam? How do you know?"

"I don't think I told you that I was in the Times Square souvenir store Royce Senior owns. Sherita told me about it. I found him behind a counter toward the back. He was on the phone, and I pretended to be looking at art while I listened to him. I thought he was talking about actual postcards he had in *that* store. Valuable ones.

Now that I run the tape in my brain back, it all makes sense. He said nobody has asked about vintage postcards and the antique market isn't exactly booming. I just wish I put that together earlier."

"You couldn't have known," Marge says with kindness. "No way. Remember, Liam. Things happen as they do for a reason."

"I hope so." My heart is racing. "I can't believe my eyes. I wonder if they're there. Please, let them still be there." I can't help it. I pop my seat belt and grab the door handle.

Ken stops the car. "I gotta find a place to park. You two get out. Hurry! I'll meet you there."

As Marge and I get out, she takes my hand. "We're gonna find them, Liam. This is the break you've been waiting for."

CHAPTER SIXTEEN

Saturday, 5:30 a.m.

Marge and I stand in front of the store.

"I hope Ken can pick this lock without anyone noticing," she says.

I try the handle. "He won't have to. It's open."

"Really?" Marge tries the handle herself. "Great."

"Not if they left in a hurry and forgot. Besides, the door to the apartment might be locked."

"We'll find out." Marge speaks quietly as she looks down the street and motions to Ken who's hurrying toward us. "Just wait a few seconds."

"This is odd." Ken catches up to us and eyes the open door. "Did you find it like this?"

"It was closed," I explain. "But not locked."

"You want me to go in first?" he asks.

"No, I need to do it," I say emphatically. "Just close it behind you so we don't attract unwanted attention."

"Of course." Ken follows and shuts the door.

We look around the antique store, crowded with treasures. At one end, there's a brick wall. It's cleverly made, along with graffiti, to look like an alley. An old Radio Flyer red wagon sits there, next to a vintage Schwinn bike, a football, an old baseball and bat. I don't know why, but the scene mesmerizes me until my eyes land on the antique mahogany door behind the counter. "Over there. That door. Behind the glass display case. That has to be it."

The three of us walk stealthily to the end of the counter, then around it to access the door. I feel like I'm in a movie, and some knife-wielding lunatic is going to jump out at us. As we reach the door, I turn the knob. Just like with the front door, it's closed but unlocked. I nod toward the top of the stairs to show Marge and Ken that the door to the apartment is open.

A thought slices through me. What if I find their dead bodies? Maybe Ray and Carly got into a fight and he killed her, along with Rayelle, so no one would know where he's going. I can't believe I never even considered that. *Stop catastrophizing, Liam. Things are bad enough as they are.*

Something is really off. As we quietly climb the stairs, I can see a red-and-blue Persian rug and an antique mahogany buffet against the left wall. I turn to Marge before I go any farther. I'm emboldened by the you-can-do-it-Liam look she gives me. I take a deep breath and walk into the room. My jaw drops.

Right in front of me, sitting toward the left of a long, sapphire-blue couch, his face buried in the palms of his hands, is Chaz.

Hearing us, he looks up. If I didn't know better, I'd swear he'd been crying. "Holy fuck, Tallamore. You escaped again." His eyes appear to bug out as he sees Marge. The two of them stare at each other for a moment before Chaz turns back to me. "I see you had a rescue team. Well, I'm glad you're out of that fucking basement. I didn't want to put you there. I don't know how the hell you found this place, Houdini, or maybe I should say Sherlock, but you're too late. They're gone."

"Where are they?" I'm poised to reverse course and run down

the stairs.

"Chill. They've been gone for at least an hour. No clue where they went. I'm not in the loop anymore. We've both been fucked over." He nods toward the empty seats. "You might as well all sit. I'll tell you what I know."

I take a seat on the couch while Marge and Ken quickly settle into two chairs at a right angle.

Chaz is digging his nails into the palms of his hands. "So, first, about Mack. He's worked for my old man for years, but we barely exchanged two words with one another. I'd say hello, and he'd grunt at me. Charming shit like that. When Mack showed up at Baradino's, suddenly speaking in semi-whole sentences, that's the first time we ever had anything resembling a conversation. Said he was there to play pool. Idiot me; I bought it. Turns out the old man had sent him to cozy up to me. Know why? Didn't trust me." He bites his lip so hard, I'm afraid it will bleed. "I don't have the moral compass my felon sibling does, so I needed watching. Rich, huh?" He reddens. "I'm the one who's been loyal to our father my entire life. I'm the one who didn't go to prison. I'm the one who helped build the family business, but still, he blames me for my brother's fucked-up lot in life. Then, recently, he decided to sic his lunatic wise guy on me to further protect the prodigal jailbird."

Marge looks oddly nervous. "Why does he blame *you*?"

Chaz is chewing his lip. He exhales. "See, when Ray robbed the grocer, I was only sixteen. I heard him tell his friend, Dean Cox, that he was going to rob the store, down to the exact time he was going to do it. So I went there. I don't know what the hell I thought I'd accomplish, but I needed to see for myself. I snuck in through the alley. The owner had left the back door partially open because he'd just gotten a delivery and was making trips to the dumpster." He looks at me. "Sorry to reference—"

"Just go on, Chaz."

"He'd just unboxed a shipment of paper towels when the bell over the front door sounded, and he went up front. Left me the perfect hiding place." He pauses. "About ten minutes later, sure enough, what Ray said would happen did happen. Only much worse. The poor guy was killed. It was devastating. Probably the worst day of my life. I felt guilty that I hadn't said something when I'd overheard the plans, but Ray would have called me a liar, and the old man would have *never* believed me." He pauses to get his bearings. "It never occurred to me anyone would die. Not ever. My brother's a whole lot of things, but not a cold-blooded killer."

"Things go awry in the blink of an eye," Ken says. "Been a witness to it myself. Not easy to see that kind of thing happen before your eyes, especially to watch the life snuffed out of a good man."

Chaz nods. "Yeah, the grocer was a stellar human being. Unlike my brother and father." He inhales a calming breath. "A part of me wanted Ray to go to prison or to at least to incur our father's wrath. I thought maybe I'd finally have the old man's love and respect. Once Ray was arrested, Cox, who wasn't any kind of angel himself, flipped on my brother to say it was pre-meditated, and that Ray had been bragging about his plans. You know, he flipped to squirm out of his own shit. Ray was already fucked, but Cox's testimony only made everything worse, and got Ray more time. But I won't get into everything that went down."

"No," Marge says. It's almost like she's sending him a secret message with her eyes, but I'm sure that's my wild imagination going at it again. "Not the time for all of that."

I'm oddly thrown off balance by his story and want him to get back to what's most important. "I'm confused. What about Carly and my daughter? How does Mack play into all of this? I've got to find them, Chaz. I can't give up."

"I'll be quick about it, but I'm giving you this brief history because you need to understand where things stand and why. About five years after my brother was incarcerated, I was a stupid ass and confided in a so-called friend, Freddie, that I'd seen the whole thing go down and still felt guilt over not stopping it. I hadn't told any of my friends a thing, and I was bursting for a confidant. It was a lot to hold inside. I needed someone to tell me it wasn't my fault, you know?" Chaz grabs a jade dodo bird from the coffee table, fiddles with it, then puts it back. "Freddie didn't waste any time going to my father. Told him I'd confessed to a whole lot and that for a hefty chunk of change, he'd tell all. Of course, my father jumped on the opportunity and paid Freddie what he'd asked for. That's when he learned I'd been in that back room during the robbery. He was furious that I didn't protect Ray by saying whatever needed to be said to keep his ass out of prison." He seethes. "Only I *wanted* his ass in prison after what went down, and I wasn't going to lie and get thrown in there my damn self."

"I'm very certain you made the right decision for all concerned." She fixes her gaze on him. "Very certain."

They exchange weird looks again, and this time I'm not imagining it.

Chaz punches a fist into the palm of his right hand. "You know, with Cox flipping on Ray, Freddie selling our friendship for money, I should have learned not to have confidence in anyone. But life goes on, you know, and I do have a few people I *can* trust. Like my buddy Rick who works at Baradino's."

"I remember him," I say. "He seems like a good guy."

"He is. Unlike Mack who only fits the *wise*-guy profile. I shouldn't have let him buddy up to me. But since we found ourselves in the same place, he was always there to help me out. Like one night, I got mugged on the street, and Mack supposedly 'beat the crap out of the guy,' and I got my money back. Now I know that was a fucking setup. Damn, I'm an idiot. Anyway, when you showed up, Tallamore, I needed help keeping you away so you wouldn't ruin everything I've worked for—and Mack was the perfect temporary ally, or so I thought." He looks disgusted with himself. "Like I told you, find them on your own, but you involve me, I'm done. Only I didn't know I was *already* done for. Mack told the old man I was soft on you, despite locking you in a trash dumpster and later in a cold basement. When my father took in Mack's assessment of me, he said that buying you food was all the proof he needed that I was a traitor and a fucking weakling. Not sure why you needed to go hungry on top of being stuck in a basement prison. But Mack's a sadistic SOB, and I guess my father is too."

I'm seeing an entirely new side of Chaz, though I'm not all that surprised. "I'm so sorry that happened. I ate the sandwich, and I appreciated it. Being locked up—not so much. But I was starving. It helped a lot. I still have the chips. I have a question, if it's not too intrusive."

"Shoot." Chaz puts both palms up. "Metaphorically speaking, of course."

Ken cracks a smile.

"I'm just wondering why a goon like Mack would work for a Times Square souvenir shop and antique store owner. Doesn't seem like a likely combination."

Chaz looks uncomfortable, and I'm about to retract my question when he responds. "I'll tell you what I know, and believe it or not, it's not much. First, my father had a rough childhood that he *never* talks about, so there's that, meaning I don't know who the hell he knows. Second, when he was looking for someone to work in the Times Square store to scare away the shoplifters and other unwanted guests, Mack just showed up. Never did know if the old man put out a call for someone or what. In no time at all, Mack became his right-hand man. Yeah, no doubt the guy has other 'associations' besides my father, but that's about all I know and want to know."

"Thanks for answering. Maybe it doesn't matter, but I was curious." I turn to Ken. "Would it be terrible of me to ask you to pick up some coffee across the street?"

Ken stands. "You read my mind. Was just gonna ask. I know Margie and I could use a cup. Think we all can."

"Thanks. I can't sleep until I find my daughter." I notice he calls her Margie again and called her 'babe' earlier. They're more than good friends. Not that it matters worth a damn now, not to mention their relationship being none of my business.

"There's cream and sugar here," Chaz says, "so you can just get black for everyone, if that's easier."

"I'll get something to eat as well." Ken watches Chaz reach into his pocket. "No need. This is on me. I'm Ken, by the way."

"Chaz."

As Ken hurries down the stairs, Marge introduces herself too. Only I get the feeling they already know one another.

I've never been more impatient in my life. I look at Chaz. "So why are you sitting here all by yourself? I get why your head is fucked up, but what am I missing?"

"Well, you were with me when I went to see that guy in the basement apartment to pick up a package."

"Fake passports and whatever." I stare at him to gauge his reaction.

"Oh." His mouth opens in surprise. "You figured that out."

"Yeah."

"So, a while later, after Mack and I hid you in the basement of that brownstone under renovation, we split up. He said he was heading home. I went to the Souvenir Tiger where I was instructed to bring the documents. Of course, the store was closed, but I called and the old man let me in. He sleeps there sometimes. Having me come to the store was a fucking setup, though. He took the package, then told me to come here, to his secret apartment, say good-bye to my brother, spend a little time with him, and then take the three of them to JFK in the early afternoon. But when I got here, they were gone."

Chaz's revelation gives me hope. My shoulders relax as I exhale in relief, knowing they're not out of the country yet, but then I wonder if that was a lie.

"Did you see the fake names on the passports?" I ask.

"Yeah." Marge lurches in his direction. "Did you?"

"Nope. They were wrapped up, sealed, tied tightly with string, then wrapped up some more. There's no way even someone like Houdini here"—he looks at me—"could have opened that mess and put it back together. Sorry, man. They had me jumping through all kinds of hoops to cover their tracks. Like sending me to that guy to borrow money." He thinks. "Holy shit!" He slaps his forehead. "Mack knew you were with me! I don't think that guy in the hoodie was trying to rob us. My father, with Mack's help, faked the loan, then hired some punk to shoot at us. I don't know if he just wanted to kill us or keep us out of the way. Or maybe my father just wanted to keep me away, and Mack arranged the shooting on his own without my father's knowledge. Sounds more like it, knowing Mack. No clue what the plan was, but I'm sure the package I got was filled with blank paper. The passport guy didn't even look inside because he'd already been paid. He knew there was nothing in there, and that I was a fucking patsy. I should have known. Damn! Sons of bitches! You saved us both, Houdini." He looks guilty. "Sorry I had to treat you the way I did. I've been a real dick to you."

"I'm still thinking about the guy who shot at us. It would've been a real bonus for Carly to have me dead or out of the way too."

"Well, we're both alive. None of that shit matters now."

"Only my daughter matters."

"She does."

We all look up as Ken returns with two bags, one with coffee, the other with food. His hair is wet, and water drips from his face. Ken puts everything on the coffee table, a bunch of tiny creamer cups and sugar packets falling out. "I thought this would make things easier," he tells Chaz. "Oh, and in case you all haven't noticed, it's raining again." He looks out the window. "Guess you didn't need me to tell you that."

"Thanks, man." Chaz takes a cup of coffee and a bagel. "I was just telling Marge and Liam that my old man— or Mack—or both— set me up. Just figured it out while you were getting us a caffeine fix. He tried to have Liam and me killed or injured. No time to repeat it. Marge can tell you."

"Holy shit." Ken shares a look with Marge. He whispers something to her.

I pour some cream into a cup and take several sips before turning to Chaz. "So, rewind to when you got here. Did you figure out that you were betrayed because everyone was gone? Did your father call you?"

Chaz reaches between two couch cushions and pulls out a crumpled-up piece of yellow, lined paper from a legal pad. "Nah. I had this 'Dear Chaz, Fuck You' letter waiting for me."

Marge tears a packet of sugar and pours it into her coffee. "I won't ask to read that. You want to paraphrase?"

Chaz stuffs the letter back between the cushions. "Yeah. Get this. Seems the old man is leaving for wherever with them and is planning to sell his share of these businesses back to his brother and nephew. Says he's been deprived of his son long enough." He scarfs down a quarter of his bagel as if he's ravenous. "My parents have been separated forever. Nobody even told me when their divorce came through years ago. Guess it wasn't exactly news, only a legal formality. Before I can tell him to get back on the topic, he shakes off his wandering thoughts, something I'm all too familiar with, and keeps talking. "Anyway, the old man said he knows I faked love and loyalty for money." Chaz looks at me. "I know you're thinking he's right, Houdini, but for most of these years, I really did want him to love me the way he does his felon offspring. When Ray came out of prison and

I saw how things were, it was like, 'Well, Chaz, you might as well stay in the game to secure your kids' future.'" He looks sadly at me. "They live with their mom, but I see them all the time. They're my world, like Rayelle is yours."

I have a thought. "Wait. When your father said he was leaving with Carly and Ray, did he happen to say where they were going? That would help narrow things down."

"Had the balls to tell me 'somewhere in the world.' Nice, huh?"

I feel sorry for the guy, but I've got to find Rayelle. "Do you think they're all together now?"

"Not necessarily. In fact, probably not. He had a whole pile of crap on his desk at the souvenir store. But he's too wily to hang around for very long. Might go to another location before he joins the felon."

I stand. "I need to hit the head."

"Through the kitchen," Chaz says. "On your left."

That coffee went through me. I take care of business and hurry back. "So he'll probably be long gone when the store opens, but isn't there a chance he might still be there now?"

"Yeah. But Mack could be with him. And seeing how they probably had that punk shoot at us, there's nothing to stop them from trying again. And I'm sure Mack's a lot more experienced than the hoodie punk was."

I pause. "Wait. Mack thinks I'm still in the basement, right?"

"*I* thought you were still there, so yeah. I guess he does."

"I've got to figure this out." I'm too nervous to sit, and I start pacing the room. "Oh my God," I scream.

"What?" Marge says as Chaz and Ken sing the chorus.

I look behind the end table, and pull out the little red boots with Rayelle's Paddington Bear attached to them. I hug it as if it were her. Tears well in my eyes and threaten to do way more, but I force them away. "I wonder why they made her leave that here."

"Easier to spot a kid with a Paddington Bear at JFK if she's holding him, you know? They're pretty distinctive. And probably no room left in her luggage. Especially when you're leaving for good."

"And because I bought this for her, and it's her favorite toy." I look at Paddington's face. "We'll find her, buddy." I pick up my backpack. First, I pull the two small bags of potato chips out. I mean to throw them on the couch, but they land on the floor. I zip the bear inside. There's just enough room for him and nothing else. I can't let him get ruined in the rain.

Marge excuses herself and hurries to use the facilities while I try to figure out a plan. I wait until she comes back to speak aloud. I don't want her to miss anything.

I'm hyperventilating, so I sit back on the couch. "Rayelle always says she she's too old to carry a toy, but whenever she gets upset, which is often, the bear's her greatest support, and she doesn't care who sees her with it. She loves Paddington, like I just said, because I gave him to her, and she knows how deeply I love her."

"You just said Rayelle gets upset often. Why?" Marge's brow creases in concern.

"Because she doesn't think her mother loves her the way she loves Oliver, who I now know is Ray's biological child. Rayelle was right all along. Such an intuitive kid. I kept telling myself that a mother's relationship with her son is different from one with her daughter. Self-delusion, I guess."

"Don't be too hard on yourself," Marge says. "We've got to

figure out our next move."

"Sure do." Ken runs a hand through his thick salt-and-pepper hair. "Sounds like we examine the options—quick like too."

I turn to Chaz. "If your parents are divorced, is it possible Ray would go say good-bye to your mother, especially if he's planning to bolt forever?"

"Yeah. He would." He shoots a glance at the two small snack bags on the floor. "He's a master at shit when the chips are down."

I want to laugh, but I can't. I offer half a smile and pick up the chips. "Something I don't get, Chaz. If the guy's on parole, why not wait it out and leave legally?"

Chaz shakes his head in disgust. "He doesn't confide jack shit to me. But he has his reasons. No time to get into them and can't say I know all of them either. We're not exactly close."

"We need to split up," Ken says. "Maybe I should go with Liam to Times Square, just in case Mack's there with Senior. Marge, you should go to Chaz's mother's place."

"No!" Chaz says forcefully. "Marge should stay here with me. I might be able to come up with another plan of action, then we'll go together."

Marge is oddly compliant when I expected her to say no. I'm not going to ask. Everything is getting muddled in my brain again. "Okay, then, I'll go to Times Square, and Ken can go check out Chaz's mother's house."

"That's better," Marge says.

Chaz stands, walks over to a drawer, and pulls out my cell. "Guess you'll need this."

I take the phone. "Thanks, but I have a burner. Got a pen and paper? I'll write down the number for everyone." I jot down the burner number quickly. "I don't want to turn on my regular phone, even for a second. Now, more than ever, after hearing everything you told me, I don't need Mack, your father, or anyone else tracking my location." I look at Marge and Ken. "But I'm forever grateful that the two of you did."

"Good thinking." Chaz nods. "And you sure looked destroyed when I took it away from you."

"Couldn't let you know that what matters most to me about the phone are all of the photos of my daughter. Using it now—not so much. You might have figured out I had another phone. Not that I could get any signal down in that dungeon anyway."

"Look, Liam." Ken reaches around to his back. "After hearing that you two were shot at, I'm even more worried for your safety. If you're going to Times Square, you need to protect yourself." He reaches behind his back. "You need to take this. Don't worry; I'm carrying two tonight."

What's going on? "No!" The big man pulls out a gun and extends his arm to hand it to me. I wave my hands in front of me. "I don't want it!" The sight of the cold metal gun terrifies me, and my blood runs cold. I don't even know how to use one. I don't want anyone to die. Everything blurs, and it's like I'm blacking out with my eyes still open. How is that even possible?

I don't know who I am or why I'm freaking out. Why does this man want to give me a gun? I can't see him, but I know another man is chasing me. Why? What did I do? Am I in trouble? Are they going to kill me? Why would this man want to give me a gun if he wanted me dead? I don't understand. But I know the man I can't see is going to hurt me. I'm sure of it. He's calling for me to stop like I did something wrong.

Who am I? I drop this big backpack I'm holding. They must be after me thinking I stole it. Only I didn't! I swear! Whose is it? Why are these people looking at me like I'm crazy? Am I? Who are they?

I've got to get away from them! There's a flight of steps. That's my way out! "Leave me alone!" I scream as I take two steps at a time. "Leave me alone!"

"Let me go after him," the red-headed lady says. She means business too. "You two stay here!"

I don't know why she's chasing me. Maybe it was her backpack. I just need to hide.

CHAPTER SEVENTEEN

I might know where I am now. I see the brick wall. I recognize the red wagon. It belongs to that kid with all the freckles who always wears clothes that are too big for him. He told me he never gets anything new. Only hand-me-downs from his older brother. I don't have an older brother, but I doubt I get much that's new. Do I even have parents? Maybe I'm old enough to buy my own clothes. I feel like I'm bigger than I used to be. I don't know. I can't even remember my name. I'm just scared to death.

I know who put that graffiti on the wall. The guys who bully me spray-paint that stuff everywhere. One is tall with long, greasy hair, and the short-haired one wears tanks in the summer to show off his muscles. And when it gets colder, he wears shirts that are a size too small. Just so he can show off his six-pack. He tells me I'll never have one being a fucking wimp. They both call me "pussy wussy" and "chicken shit loser." Names like that. Those are the only two I can think of because they say them the most. They've thrown me against the wall, pushed me to the ground, and kicked me more times than I want to count. Other kids who see it won't help because they don't want to get kicked too. I hate bullies. I want to punch them, only I know they'd kill me. But I'll show them some day! I swear I will. I worry they're going to jump out of wherever they're hiding and beat me up. I don't have the strength to take on two guys, but one-on-one, well, I'll give it everything I've got.

That's not my bike against the wall. But the kid who owns it better come get it before someone steals it. The guys who bully me call it a "sissy ride." I'm not the only one they bully, but it doesn't make me feel any better. I know that people who don't like themselves are usually the meanest. Only that doesn't make me feel better either. I just know a smart person told me that.

My heart is beating so fast. I wipe my sweaty hands on my pants. Something is very wrong. I feel like I'm in another person's body. Maybe I'll just sit up against that wall. It's the only thing that looks familiar. I wonder if people who lose their minds ever find them.

The red-headed lady is walking toward me. Very slowly. Is she afraid I'll hurt her? She looks more like she's afraid of scaring *me*. Oh, no. She's sitting down next to me like it's something we do every day.

I'm lost for words, so I sit and tremble. Maybe I am a pussy wussy. I hate that name. And I'm not one. But I'm scared. I don't want that man to give me his gun.

"Liam." She leans toward me, but stops short of touching my hand. "It's okay. You're okay. It's Marge. Remember me? I know it feels like we've known each other forever, but we only met last night when you came into my restaurant: Marge's Place. Take a deep breath. Think. I'm sure it'll come to you."

I can only stare at her. She must be telling the truth because she looks familiar. But wait. That's no guarantee. Lots of people I've seen before lie.

"You told me you were searching for your daughter. I sent you to my friend Sherita. Remember?"

I have a daughter? How can that be possible? I'm too young. I don't even have a sister. Maybe she's mistaking me for someone else.

She still wants to touch my hand, but she's afraid she'll scare me. I know that. She's very gentle as she speaks. "My friend Ken and I rescued you from a basement, and then we ended up here."

I have a vague picture in my head. "You're the lady who always rescues me from the basement. Aren't you?"

Now she touches my hand. "I rescued you tonight. With my friend."

I'm still confused. She's very nice, but now she's getting agitated and trying to hide it.

"Liam. Look at me. You're Liam Tallamore from Trenton, New Jersey, and I'm your new friend, Marge O'Toole. We're in New York City on Amsterdam Avenue. Your wife, Carly, has taken your daughter, Rayelle, and they plan to leave the country with Ray Royce Junior. We have to find them before they go. We don't have any time to waste. Please, Liam. Tell me I'm getting through to you. We have to find your little girl! *Nothing* is more important right now."

"Oh!" I've somehow been zapped back into reality. "Marge. Yes, Carly took Rayelle, and I have to find them." I look around the antique store and realize who I am and where I am. "Why the hell are we sitting down here? What just happened?"

She's distracted by something as she looks out the storefront window. Before she can answer my question, she pulls me up, pushes me to the right, and puts a finger to her mouth. We sit behind a large mahogany wardrobe. What's going on?

Her finger touches her lips again to remind me to stay silent.

Oh, shit! Mack is here. I see him. He just came through the front door, and he's carrying some old leather-and-canvas tool bag. Looks like it's filled with stuff. He's pissed that he's all wet, wildly shaking the water off as he mumbles a few expletives. This guy would threaten rain if he could. He'd take a gun and shoot it.

"Yo, Chazzie!" he yells as he heads toward the upstairs door. "You'd better still be here! I'm coming for you." He stomps loudly up the stairs.

Marge waits until we hear him reach the top. She grabs my hand and we quietly get as close to the door as we can and kneel behind an antique dressing table with a built-in mirror on top.

Luckily, we can hear everything as both doors are open, and Mack has a very loud voice. "I just went to check on our friend in da basement. Da lock bar was broken, and da mothafucka was gone. Dem t'ings don't break demselves."

There's a pause. I wish I could see what's going on.

"I have dis here bag for a reason. Was gonna tie him up and gag him case he tried any monkey business. Only his ass wasn't there. You broke him out, didn't ya, Chazzie?"

"No, I didn't! I swear on my kids!"

"Youse a lyin' bastard. Well, lookee what we've got here. It's da mothafucka's little-boy backpack. You not only let him out, you brought him here, dint cha?"

"No," Chaz says loudly, which I realize is for our benefit. "Actually, I went to check on him because I had the same worry you did. Yeah, someone had obviously broken him out, and he clearly didn't have time to take his backpack. So I brought it here. End of story."

"Where's Ken?" I whisper to Marge.

"I'm sure he hid when he heard Mack coming up the stairs." She pauses. "And not because he's a coward. Trust him, Liam."

"Oh, really," Mack shouts. "So dat's your story, Chazzie?" He snorts loudly. "I'm gonna open dis little bitch's bag and see what's inside."

I start to hyperventilate as Marge puts a calming hand on my shoulder. "Try to breathe normally, Liam. Please."

"Well, look who's a mothafuckin' liar. Dis stupid bear in da red hat and blue jacket was left here in dis damn apartment. So no way it could have been in his bag in da basement. I remember dis dumb bear real well. After I brought dem back from saying good-bye to your motha, Carly told her little girl ain't no way she was bringin' it wid dem, but she had da rest of the day to play wid it until dey left. When I came back to take dem where dey are now, the girl was still cryin' about da stupid bear. Carly told da brat like ten times before we left to shut up and stop askin'.

"Da girl went into a corner all sulky and crybaby like and den started drawing a picture of da bear like for a freakin' souvenir. Had da stupid t'ing standin' up, posin' for her. Carly t'ought she was making a good-bye picture. But den, when we was leaving, da kid was still clutching da damn t'ing. Carly got real mad and t'ru it over dere. I was surprised when da brat didn't even cry. Guess she knew she'd get smacked. Like yesterday, she was a real pain when she went to see your motha. Kept huggin' her and tryin' to whisper shit to her. Carly was spittin' mad and pulled her away. And den we left. Kid was a damn bigger pain today. I got no damn time for brats. Just like me, Carly ain't got time for dat crybaby nonsense. Told da kid to zip her yapper."

I ball my hands into fists as I imagine punching Mack's face, then try to push away the words I have for Carly. Too much to deal with now. But my blood is boiling. How could she treat Rayelle this way? I don't understand why she didn't just leave her with me and go off with her lover. She knows how much we love each other. Or was that the point? To inflict as much pain on us both as possible. Still, why bring Ray-Ray along feeling the way she does? Why would she want our daughter to be with her and her lover? To abuse her? I unfurl my fists and wipe more sweat on my pants. Why didn't I see all of this sooner? Probably because she was never this cruel. I'm shaking with rage as Marge puts an arm around me, her eyes pleading with me to stay put—and silent.

"Where did you take them?" Chaz asks. "Tell me!"

Mack bursts out laughing. "Yeah, like I'm gonna tell you, squishy soft dough boy. You is just like Raymond said you was." The silence that stretches out makes me nervous. I release a breath when he speaks again. "While we's talkin' about da man, he wrote a message for you. Ain't gonna give it to you, but I'll show it to you."

"You've got a message from my father stuffed in your pocket?" I know Chaz is phrasing the question that way so we know what's going on.

"Yeah. Here, I'll hold it up. Hope you know how to read—"

"I know *you* are not making fun of *my* English abilities."

"Oh, you understand me, Chazzy. I know how to communicate. I ain't no orwriter and don't need to be."

"Orator?"

"Shut da hell up! Here's what your daddy wrote."

"So you're not going to read it to me?"

"Read it for yourself before I whack you for bein' a smart ass."

Chaz reads aloud. "Charles, you have proven yourself disloyal to our family. You stay far away and let us do what we need to do.

Don't even think about double-crossing me or your brother. Even though I'm leaving, I have eyes everywhere."

"Dat's real sweet. Two of dem eyes is mine, just sos you know."

"Just be quiet, will you?"

"I ain't gonna shut up. And I want you to give me back dat letter from poppa Royce dat I left here for you."

"I burnt it," Chaz says.

"Youse a lyin' little bastard. Gimme da letter, or I'll go pay a visit to your kiddies. And I ain't playin,' marshmallow boy."

"Here, you son of a bitch."

"Awww, Chazzie got his feewings all hurt and crumpled Daddy's letter up in a ball. Stuffed it between da sofa cushions."

"What else do you want from me? Just get out of here!"

Mack breaks out into sick laughter. "I call da shots here. And now I'm gonna tell you what happens next. I'm gonna tie your ass up and take dis backpack and bear wid me. If I had time, I'd drown it in da Central Park Lake. Or maybe I'll just wait for a sunny day and behead da damn thing, den t'ro it on a playground so I can watch da kiddies cry. Boo hoo!" He laughs again.

Sick, sadistic, one-dimensional sonofabitch. I've never met anyone with so little substance or empathy. I'll bet a 3D printer could spit out something or someone more human. I know he's bigger than me, but listening to him fills me with rage, enough to at least make me feel like I could take him. I've been trying to breathe right, but hearing this just does me in. I want to go up there and have it out with him, but Marge grips my shoulders tightly.

"Stay put, Liam," she whispers. "If you make yourself a human target for that man, he'll kill you without blinking, and you and

Rayelle will *never* see each other again. I can't be any clearer. Hear me?"

I nod. She's right. But it's really hard to stay put.

"Damn, Mack, give me a break," Chaz shouts. "You don't need to fucking tie me up!"

"Oh yeah I do. Can't trust you. You lied to me."

"I didn't! I found the pack in the basement, like I said, and brought it here. Then, later, when I saw the bear behind the end table, I thought I'd put it in there for Tallamore to have after they'd left the country. Since he'll never see his daughter again, I thought at least he could have her bear. That's the truth."

"Awwwww. Ain't dat sweet? Only a pussy man t'inks of somethin' like dat. You proved my damn point. Dat's why I'm tyin' your ass up!"

"No you're not! There's no reason to. I don't know where anyone is. Not Tallamore, not my brother and Carly—not even the old man. I only know where you are because your ugly-ass face is threatening me."

"Don't you be calling me ugly! You got a choice, Chazzy. I brought all dis equipment t'inking I'd be tyin' Tallamore up again. Was gonna muzzle him and cover his eyes with a black scarf too. Don't know where he is, but now I got all dis for you. Funny how t'ings work out."

"No, you don't need to do this!"

"What will it be, Chazzy? Does your ass get tied up or shot?" The sound of a loud slap makes me jump. I'm more certain than ever that Mack had that guy in a hoodie shoot at us. It doesn't matter now, except it punctuates the fact that this guy doesn't play.

"Fuck, Mack. Put the gun away, will you? And you don't need to hit me again."

"Dat smacker was for you to hurry up and make a damn choice. You don't make one, I'll just shoot youse right in your babymaker."

"Okay," Chaz says, "Tie me up."

Marge turns to me. "He's doing the right thing. He knows Ken is there."

"Wait," Chaz says. "Once you do all this shit to me, then what?"

"Den I'm gonna go help my boss and his family get outta da country."

My breathing is out of control again. Fighting the fear that threatens to cripple me, I tremble, looking desperately at Marge for permission to act.

She remains calm and steady. "No, Liam. We do nothing. Hear me."

Mack has obviously chosen to gag Chaz first. I can only hear him grunting while his smothered voice begs for mercy. I hear a thud and some rattling. Mack must be going through his tool bag for rope, tape, and whatever else he needs.

It doesn't take more than five minutes before Mack speaks again. "Dere we go. You look so perty 'n all. Just gotta do your legs and ankles, and I'll be on my way."

"Put your hands up, you son of a bitch! I'm no softie, and I'll kill you soon as look at your mug!"

Oh, thank God. Ken to the rescue. I was hoping this is what would happen, but I wasn't sure.

Marge whispers to me. "He had to wait until Mack dropped the gun and was distracted. My man is no dummy."

"Who da damn hell are you?" Mack says. "Where'd you materialize from?"

I'm surprised Mack knows the word "materialize."

"Hands up or I'll kill your ass!" Ken shouts. "And while we're at it, why don't you tell me where Carly, Ray, and the child are."

"Man, I don't know. Raymond don't be givin' me all da information at once – just for situations like dis. I do one job, den I get what I need to know for da next."

"Then how about you call him, say you took care of business, then get the address. He won't have to know you betrayed him. We'll follow you."

"Mack ain't no damn pussy rat and never will be. You might as well shoot me, mothafucka, I ain't doin' shit like that. Ain't in my blood. Never will be. Ain't no rat. And if I die, least I won't be remembered as one. No type-R blood in t'ese veins. No pussy blood either. Ain't gonna snitch. And Raymond's phone ain't turned on now neither."

There's suddenly silence. I slump in defeat. I thought Ken was going to get it out of him. But guys like Mack don't spill shit. Even I know that.

"Okay, Liam," Marge says. "Hear me. You stay hidden. Ken and Chaz need my help, and Mack can't know you were *ever* here. Trust me; we've got this. Not our first rodeo."

I press my lips together and look down.

"Tell me you'll stay here, Liam." She raises my chin and gives me a hard stare. "Liam? I need to know you'll trust us—and stay put."

I exhale. I know she's right, but doing so goes against my every instinct. "I will. Promise."

Marge looks into my eyes, then races up the stairs.

"Who da hell is dis red bitch?"

"None of your damn business!" Ken says. "You don't want to talk, so get in the fucking chair!"

In what feels like an eternal wait, but is probably only five or six minutes, I listen to the rumbling upstairs and now I hear Chaz's voice along with Marge and Ken's. The grumbling and muffled threats are now Mack's, and I know he's being tied up. Another minute passes, and I hear the upstairs door shut.

Marge and Ken come running down the stairs, then Chaz about five seconds behind them. Marge has my backpack. It's partially open, and I see Paddington is still inside. Chaz pulls a key out of his pocket and locks the downstairs door.

He opens a closet and grabs two black umbrellas, handing one to Marge and the other to me. "I've got the key to the shop. Locking that too. C'mon, people, let's get the hell out of here."

CHAPTER EIGHTEEN

Saturday, 6:53 a.m.

We follow Ken uptown on Amsterdam and around the corner to where his Escape is parked. The rain is absolutely brutal again. I tell Marge to sit up front with Ken as Chaz and I jump in the back.

I turn to him. "I can't assume anything when my little girl's life is on the line. Am I being a fucking idiot thinking I can trust you?"

Chaz looks down as if guilt is sweeping through him. "Despite my acting like a mini-Mack when our paths crossed all those times, though maybe one with better English, I was always with you." He puts a palm up. "Yeah, I know. I had one hell of a way of showing you, but think about it. I didn't lie to you. Listen, man, everything I was doing was for my kids—and yeah, for me too. It wasn't that I didn't feel your pain, but I was selfishly putting money for my kids' future before your daughter's welfare. That sucks, but that's where my head was at. I was clutching at my perceived consolation prize for all the years of wasted loyalty to the old man. I forgot that I can provide for my kids without the bastard."

"I've no doubt you can," Marge says.

"Being honest about it, my old man wouldn't have helped me put them through college or done anything else. My kids have never been of interest to him. If they'd belonged to the felon, well, that would have been different."

"That's pretty clear," I tell him. Out of nowhere, I remember what Chaz said at Baradino's about how he's always been my best friend, but now isn't the time to ask him to elaborate. But it was one hell of a weird thing to say considering we only met yesterday. "I appreciate the explanation."

"Good. So know I'm with you, man. Now we need to put our heads together and figure out a next move."

"What do you have for us?" Marge asks. "Did that eloquent thug drop any clues, or is that just my wishful thinking?"

"That was my question too," I say.

"Two things," Chaz says. "They clearly said good-bye to my mother yesterday, so they're not there now. I want to call her and see if she can tell us anything. She and my father barely speak, but unlike him, she loves me. We're quite close."

"Good to hear." Marge smiles. "You don't deserve the ugliness from your father. But we all go through life carrying burdens we don't deserve."

"Ain't that the truth, Margie." Ken cracks the windows a bit and turns on the air to keep the windows from getting foggier. "Sorry, folks. Gotta do this."

"A few drops of rain is the least of our worries." Marge smiles lovingly at him.

"What's the second thing, Chaz?" My right leg shakes uncontrollably.

"So, I'm guessing everyone heard me reading that love note from my father that Mack held up for me." Disgust shows on his face. "He doesn't want me to have a shred of physical evidence of anything, even if it's as worthless as that piece of paper. You probably heard Mack ask for my father's letter back."

"Yeah, we did. I figured that was the reason." I look at him.

"And?"

"Well, I don't need to have that second note in my possession to have gotten a clue from it. He's not at the Souvenir Tiger anymore. He was at his girlfriend Gloria's place when he wrote that and probably still is."

"You could tell that how?" Marge asks.

"It was written in purple ink," Chaz explains. "All of her pens are in some shade of purple or turquoise. The old man brags about her collection, and is always looking for new pens to give to her. Then he forgets we know about it. We catch him in all kinds of lies just by the color ink he's used on take-home paperwork. Nobody gives a damn where he spends his nights, but he likes to give his staff the impression that he never leaves the store. Like that's some incentive for them to work harder to impress him."

"Does he use her pens at work?" I ask.

"No way. They're expensive fountain pens with special cartridges. She never lets anyone take them, for one, because the replacement cartridges are often hard to find. And they're not cheap. The pens are like children to her. When she comes into the store to help him with paperwork, she won't even bring one with her. Really, I'm sure he is or was at her place."

"Make sense," I mutter. The clock is running down on the time left to find Rayelle, and I can't believe we're sitting in a stationary car talking ink color and fancy pens. But why should this moment be any less bizarre than the ones before it?

"So, what should I do?" Ken turns his head to speak to Chaz. "You planning to go to Gloria's place and confront him, or are you thinking of waiting outside and following? I mean, if he's no longer there, that's time lost. Just saying. Also, where does she live?"

A crack of thunder explodes in the sky, and I jump.

"This madness will end, Liam," Marge says. "And the sun will shine again too." She looks at Chaz. "What Ken just said. What's your take?"

"She lives off 42nd Street. Near Ninth or Tenth. Don't know the address, but I'll know the building if I see it. I was there once years ago. He laughs. "Sorry, this isn't funny, but I think it was to bring him a freakin' pen he'd taken home by mistake. Didn't wanna get caught." He pauses to think. "As for your other question, there's no way in hell I'll go up there. Senior hasn't heard from Mack, so if I show up, that'll clue him in that I might have had something to do with it. Plus, I don't know that he does have another hooligan lurking nearby who wouldn't pull a gun on me, then tie me up in a storage closet or basement. Or worse. I'm thinking this: It's a high-rise apartment building, and there's a doorman. I don't think the guy would turn down a Benjamin or two to say whether he's left or not."

"Great, I've got plenty of them," I offer, happy that my cash stash is going to be more helpful than my upper lip stache was. "I'll pull out five hundred. Who's going to bribe him?"

"I will," Ken says.

I look at Chaz. "And if your father's there," I say, "where do we wait so we can follow him? It's not like you can park in front of the entrance, and waiting around casually in the rain isn't much of an option."

Ken starts the car and we're finally on our way. "We'll head over there now. Listen, Liam. One step at a time. Each outcome determines our next move. Too hard to plan in advance based on what we don't know." He turns his head to speak to Chaz. "You said 42nd Street near Ninth or Tenth, right?"

"I did."

"While he's driving," Marge tells Chaz, "call your mother. See what happened yesterday when they visited her. Maybe they left a clue behind."

Saturday, 6:59 a.m.

We're going south on Columbus. The car is barely moving while the rain lashes down, but at least the windows are closed again. Even with the windshield wipers on high, Ken is struggling to see the cars and trucks in front of him. There is unending road construction. Traffic sucks on a good day, and there's some kind of accident or stopped car ahead. I can't tell. I only know this is brutal. We're not even at 70th Street yet, and while the near crawl is sending my anxiety through the roof, listening to Chaz on the phone with his mother as he explains our situation, then questions her, is really doing me in. Now he's listening as she speaks, and he's gone quiet. What is she saying? More silence. His face tells me it's nothing good. I can tell he's hanging on her every word. Now he's asking her some quick questions, but not the kind I can glean information from. At last! He's winding up the call.

"I love you too, Mom. And I'll let you know. Thanks for trusting me with all of this. Soon as I can, I'll come by to visit. Yeah, of course. I'll bring the kids. Bye." He ends the call, turns off his phone, and looks at me.

"What, Chaz? What did she say?"

Marge turns around, but doesn't say anything.

Chaz shakes his head in disgust. "What didn't she say? I'll start with Ray and Carly. Just like Mack said, they were there yesterday. Earlier in the day. Ray told her they were leaving the country, and he didn't think he'd ever see her again. My mom said he didn't seem too choked up about it, like he was telling her he was going on a vacation. That was a gut punch for her, but at the same time not too much of a surprise. She was kind of expecting it actually. But I'll get to that." He chews his lip like he did back at the apartment. "Before I go on, I need to tell you this part. When they went to leave, Rayelle ran over to my mother, gave her a big hug, and whispered in her ear, 'tell Daddy help me!'"

My throat narrows, but I get the words out. "What your mother said confirms my worst fears. My girl is really scared. And I'm fucking petrified. We have to find her!" I look out the window. We've only gone one block. In the distance, a police siren gets louder. Marge's face twists in pain.

"When Carly saw her whispering, she yanked Rayelle away, asking her what the fuck she said. And yeah, that's exactly how she phrased it."

"Damn her. How did Rayelle respond?"

"Said she was telling my mother what a pretty lady she was. When Carly screamed, 'Bullshit! Stop lying,' my mother cut her off and said, 'That's exactly what the child told me. Word for word! She's telling you the absolute truth.'"

"Did Carly buy it?"

"My mother feels sure of it. And for the record, Rayelle *did* say that, right before she asked for help. Carly then let go of Rayelle's arm, looked somewhat embarrassed, then changed the subject." Chaz pauses.

Lines form on his face. Shit. What else is coming?

"Oh, my mother said Rayelle was clutching Paddington the entire time."

I can't put my rage on display, so I ask Ken a useless question. "We can't move any faster, can we?"

"Sorry, Liam. It's New York. I don't know what to say. I wish this car could sprout wings and fly over this mess. I'd do anything to get you there more quickly."

"He would," Marge agrees.

"I don't know what I'd been doing now without the two of you. I think the universe sent you to me, and I have to believe it's for a reason."

"It is." Marge turns to me with hopeful eyes. "There's no doubt. And we'll find your daughter."

"Thanks." I focus on Chaz who isn't done telling me everything. I can see he's eager to continue. "Go on, finish what you were saying."

"So listen, man, my mother said that she tried to honor Rayelle's request to contact you, but nobody answered your home phone. Plus, she figured you were out looking for them anyway. You had to be."

Marge looks stunned, but leaves the talking to me.

"Wait! There's a big chunk of something missing. I can't believe that Carly or Ray would have given your mom her last name. So how would she have had any notion who I was?"

"You're not gonna like this."

"I don't like anything that's happened since yesterday after lunch, so that hardly matters now." The police sirens unnerve me as they draw closer. They stop down the street, and thankfully, the sirens have stopped too. The rain is still coming down with a fury.

Chaz continues. "First, I didn't know any of this until right now. Truth."

"I believe you. Just tell me whatever it is."

"Well, obviously Carly kept this from you, but when Oliver was eighteen, he expressed his curiosity about a biological father or any known paternal grandparents. He never believed he was the product of rape, and that's when Carly told him the truth. That his biological father was her first love, and that no, she wasn't raped, but that by law, it would have been considered statutory rape. But how it was never that to her. Then she begged him not to say anything. And Oliver obliged because he didn't want to hurt you. He was pretty sure his mother was still hung up on the guy or that she thought she was."

My heart sinks, but I don't want anyone to notice. "Makes sense. So, wait, your parents must know Oliver then."

"Yeah. I'm shocked as hell actually. Didn't have a clue. My mother just explained that Carly started writing to Ray in prison, over two years ago, when Oliver turned eighteen. She was secretly thrilled that he was curious about his biological father and his family. It gave her an excuse to be in touch with Ray again."

Got your blinders off now, Liam? Damn, love really did make you blind. "Looking back, it was all there. I should have seen it. Go on, Chaz."

"First, Carly wrote to Ray to tell him that he had a son and let that sink in. He was happy, but damn, he was mega pissed that he'd been deprived of knowing him all these years. After he calmed down a bit, a month or so later, Carly told him their son wanted to meet his grandparents and for them to be aware he existed. She didn't dare tell Ray that Oliver had no interest in knowing *him,* and that his curiosity only went as far as learning his roots slash identity."

A wave of relief crashes over me, knowing that Oliver didn't want to replace me with Ray. "How the hell did Carly keep such a secret? What if I'd gotten the mail before her and saw his letter from prison?"

"Wouldn't have happened. Apparently she opened a P.O. box to write to him. And if they ever talked, I'm sure the calls didn't go to any phone you knew about."

"No." All concern for my son comes flooding back. "Oliver's a great kid. I haven't been able to reach him for almost two months. I thought he'd shut me out of his life. I legally adopted him, but I've always worried he'd prefer his biological father." I hate displaying my insecurities like this, but I feel compelled to be honest.

"No. Just the opposite. He went into hiding of some sort when Felonious Hunk came out of prison. He knew for sure his mother was not only having an affair, but was completely obsessed with him too. My mom said Oliver lost a whole lot of respect for her. Also, after meeting my father about two years ago, he'd taken an instant dislike to him when the old man immediately tried to mold him into some version of himself and Ray. Not to mention that my father was insistent from jump that Oliver change his last name from Tallamore to Royce."

I drop my face into the palm of my hands, then lift my head, hoping my rage is no longer visible. Only it is.

"Yeah, I feel your pain, Houdini. But Oliver didn't want anything to do with that, and my father's aggressive demands quickly turned him off. But he adored his grandmother, and they've secretly stayed in touch. My mom has him on her phone as Dr. Sumore. You know, for Oliver Twist. 'Please, sir. I want some more.'"

I offer a quick smile. I'm heartened to hear this but confused. "How come your mom never told you any of this before?" I ask. "I mean, you're his uncle. Didn't Oliver want to know you?"

"He wasn't presented with that option." Chaz shakes his head. "My father and brother didn't want you, me, or anyone else to know introductions had been made. Too afraid that if we did, we'd brainwash Oliver into thinking his father was really a criminal." His lips twist in disgust. "Yeah, like we're the ones who wanted to control him. Not. He thought staying silent was the simplest way to keep things under control. And as he didn't know *me*, that part was easy for the time being."

I'm stunned. And I'm realizing that my son is a grown man now. I'm so proud of him. After taking a moment to let Chaz's words sink in, I digress and talk to Ken. "You doing okay with the driving?"

"Best as I can. This traffic's a bitch. And these idiots honking as if any of us have the power to go faster. Sheesh. People piss me off, and this rain doesn't wanna stop. Even my windshield wipers are like, 'Please, dude, can we take a coffee break?'" He sighs. "I just want to get you where you need to be."

"Ken's a champion," Marge says with a grin I haven't seen before. "Now don't change the subject again, and let Chaz continue."

She's right. I just needed my brain to take a breather.

Chaz wipes his brow with the back of his hand. "Aside from

telling Liam what he has a right to know, I gotta add that Oliver called my mom last night. Said he couldn't stop worrying about his baby sister. Had a friend ring the house several times to see who answered and got freaked when nobody did from Friday afternoon until now. The reason Oliver said he's hiding away isn't just because he doesn't like his father or grandfather. It's because they've both told him, in separate conversations, that leaving the country to start a brand-new life would be wonderful. Oliver didn't like the sound of that and was afraid they'd kidnap him. He knew Ray wanted his son, and he was convinced his mother would leave Rayelle with you. He's freaking out about being wrong. Feels guilty as fuck. My mom knew nothing about this until last night." Chaz exhales in frustration. "I know this doesn't help us find them, but this getaway was obviously planned for months."

Self-loathing punches me in the gut. "Which makes me a bigger idiot for not seeing all of the signs. And I don't even have words for how much I hate that Oliver's put any of this on himself."

"Don't beat yourself up, Liam. There are enough other people in the world to do it for you," Marge says.

Her words hit me hard. After having that breakdown a while ago, I know now that I was bullied and made to feel like shit. Is that why I can't remember my earlier childhood? It wasn't a sports accident. Why did my parents lie to me? It's no wonder I've felt so much rage all my life, never knowing where to direct it. But I know now, and I've got to use it to my advantage. "You're right," I tell her.

Chaz clears his throat. "So let me wrap up what my mother said, before I forget."

"Please do."

"Your son said he misses you and his sister something fierce. My mom would have passed on the message, but of course, she had no clue that you and I were in touch. Anyway, now that she does, she said we should fill her in on any progress we make. She wants to call Oliver and let him know that you and I are looking for her together, if that's okay with you. She said she won't do anything until I text her that it's okay."

"Yeah, that's good. Maybe I should give her my burner number or get his. Wouldn't that work?"

"Not yet. Let my mom handle this for now. I'm just saying, considering I was the one to take your phone from you once, if for any reason that would happen again, meaning someone else would get it, you don't want any trace of Oliver to be found, right? The guy is really afraid of his felonious sperm donor kidnapping him or getting someone to do it for him."

"I didn't even think of that. Okay, so you take the phone then."

Chaz shakes his head. "Better idea. We need a line of communication with my mother, whose name is Allegra by the way, in case she hears anything from Oliver or anyone else. And of course, to call her if we have information to share. I don't know if the old man still thinks I'm tied up in the Amsterdam Avenue apartment, but the more time that elapses without hearing from Mack, well, trust me, he'll send someone there for a status check. And no way do we want him tracking us down."

"Definitely not," Marge says.

Chaz nods. "So, I'll text my mom, tell her to fill Oliver in, and make sure she only uses this number."

"Go for it. And please, thank her for me, and ask her to tell

Oliver I love him very much and am going to find his sister."

"Traffic's moving a bit faster," Ken says. "Not *fast*, but we're making progress. Hang in there, Liam."

CHAPTER NINETEEN
Saturday, 7:29 a.m.

"That building! Right there." Chaz points to a red-brick, high-rise building. "Her name is Gloria Menhardt. She lives on the tenth floor. I don't remember the apartment number. Just in case you cross paths, you should know she's about five six, early fifties, and has long, dark wavy hair mixed with some silver. Hippie vibe. Pretty lady."

"Gotcha." Ken squints, peering out of the windshield. "I've got to pull over and let someone else drive. Don't see anywhere I can park this baby, especially not in this rain."

"I'll take over," Chaz says. "Get behind that stopped truck. You jump out, and I'll keep driving until you text Marge and tell us where to pick you up."

I reach into my backpack and pull out five one-hundred-dollar bills. "Here. Use as much as you need to."

Ken puts his right hand over his shoulder and takes the money, looking at it briefly. "Doubt I'll need this much, but better to have too much than not enough."

Before I can blink, Chaz is driving, and Ken's on the street, black umbrella up, rushing toward the building. We wait about a minute for the truck to move; then Chaz begins driving around the block.

"I want to be positive," I say, "and it sure as hell isn't about the money, but I don't know what this is going to get us. I mean, if the guy *has* left the building, it's not like he's going to leave his itinerary with the doorman."

Marge turns around. "Honey, listen to me. If you've learned anything in the past day and night, it's that any clue, no matter how small, can matter. Hell, if you've watched police dramas, you know that much."

"I do, only those shows have a formula, and they've only got so many minutes to track down the bad guys and solve the crime. My life right now is like a longer show of undetermined minutes, with no formula and no guarantee. I'm really terrified. I know we've made progress, but are we really any closer to finding them?"

"Liam, your breath is breaking again. Please. Slow down. And yes, we're going to find them."

For a moment, I'm in another place again, and I've heard that before. I'm scared, but I have to stay in the present. My little girl's life depends on it.

Marge is craning her neck to keep an eye on me. I don't know what she thinks can happen to me in the back seat of Ken's Ford Escape. I just know if I start breathing regularly, she'll stop furrowing her brow like that. Not to mention looking so sad. It's unsettling and messing with my head.

Ten minutes, which feel more like sixty, pass. Marge gets a text from Ken, and we drive to where he's waiting on Ninth Avenue.

Just like before, Ken and Chaz reassign their butts with speed. Guess you learn to move fast when you live in New York. Ken's driving again, and Chaz is in the back seat next to me. We pass a sign for the Lincoln Tunnel, and we keep driving until Ken can find a temporary place to pull over. Luckily, the rain is a soft drizzle again.

"Just give me a minute." Ken focuses on the road. "I'll tell you what I learned as soon as we can stop."

A cab that has just let a passenger out, goes on its way, and Ken quickly takes the space and stops. We're on a side street now, but I don't know where. Only that we're south of the Tunnel entrance.

Ken turns around and hands my money back. "Okay, so as it turns out, I didn't need this. Soon as I walked into the building, I saw a woman fitting Gloria's description to a T. She says to the doorman, 'Guess you saw the bastard leave,' and he tells her yeah, that Raymond ran out of the building, picked up the three suitcases he'd paid him to watch, but didn't catch a car in front of the door like he usually does."

"Didn't want anyone to track him," Chaz says. "I know how that goes."

"What else?" I ask.

"Sorry, Liam. We just missed him by ten minutes. I stood there as long as I could, pretending to make a phone call. All I heard was her telling the doorman that Raymond's planning to leave the country forever, but if he changes his mind and comes back, to never let him in again. Said that he told her he was going to stay with her forever, just to get one last romp in the hay, then spilled the truth before he left for good. She's livid. Went on about how she wasted eight years of her life on the guy. I wanted to listen longer, but the doorman started to get suspicious of me, so I pretended I had an emergency and was canceling my visit to the phantom resident I was supposedly on my way to visit."

Disappointment punches me in the gut. "I can't believe we just missed him. This is the worst news."

"Not necessarily. Because I overheard them, we know it's the truth. I didn't want to say this before, but we couldn't have been positive that he wouldn't give us some phony story just to get the money. You never really know where someone's loyalties might lie, Liam. It's not always where you think they do."

Chaz must see the concern on my face. "I hear what you're thinking, Houdini, but you need to believe that everyone in this car is with you. I know, says the guy who locked you up twice and threatened your ass, but you're good. You really are."

I believe him. Oddly, I don't doubt myself for having faith in him.

"Okay, so we know for sure Raymond really left," Marge says. "Where do we go from here?"

The burner phone rings.

"Maybe my mother's thought of something." Chaz answers the call. "Hi, Mom. Yeah. Didn't think it was too wise to use my own phone anymore. What?" His face distorts in pain. "Oh, geez, Rayelle doesn't have Paddington anymore. We heard through Dad's hired thug, Mack, that Carly yanked him right out of her arms and threw him against the wall before they left. The bear's actually in the car with us." He listens for another moment. "I know. Cruel and then some. Just tell Oliver, and please assure him that the moment we have any information, we'll let you know so you can pass it on. That's a promise. Love you, too, Mom. And we'll find her."

I don't know what Oliver said to his grandmother, but my heart is breaking as I wait for Chaz to tell me.

Chaz releases a weary breath. "Seems that Oliver is becoming more distraught over his sister, and his guilt is increasing exponentially by the minute. He said that the one small thing that comforted him was knowing Rayelle had the bear. She'd told her brother that Paddington hears all of her secrets, and he hoped having him would keep her calm, not to mention make her easier to spot in a crowd. Mom's not looking forward to telling Oliver that Rayelle doesn't have him anymore, but she'll do it. She promised the truth. All of it."

I pound my fist into the palm of my hand as I watch the misty rain on the windshield. "I hate that Oliver is blaming himself. If anyone should have stopped this, it was me. But no, I've been wearing blinders—"

Marge turns around to give me some serious shade. "What did I tell you before about beating yourself up? Now, you want to do something for Rayelle? Take the bear out of the knapsack and hug him for her."

"Go ahead, man," Chaz says. "C'mon. I'm not going to razz you for that. And Mack isn't here, so you're good."

I zip open the knapsack, and Paddington almost pops out as if self-ejecting.

"After you hug him, let him sit next to you," Marge says.

I hold Paddington and look him in the eyes. "This is for Rayelle, fella." I clutch the bear to my chest and can't seem to let go."

It's tough not to notice the way Chaz is looking at me. Staring is more like it. Maybe I was an idiot for believing he's on my side.

"Houdini, there's a little white triangle sticking out of the bear's hood. Check it out."

I turn the bear around and look into the plaid-lined hood of his red jacket. My heart is beating faster. There's a piece of paper, and it's been folded many times. Only the very corner is showing. I'm grateful for Chaz's eagle eyes.

"Please let this be something." Marge turns to watch.

"Glad I'm not driving." Ken turns around as well.

I quickly unfold the paper. It's Rayelle's drawing of Paddington. "This must be the picture Mack was talking so rudely about—the one my girl was drawing before they left. This is weird though."

"What?" Marge asks.

"Just that Rayelle made the outer jacket plaid and scribbly. That's nothing she would ever do unless… Holy shit!"

"Tell us!" Chaz says.

"Look! She scribbled a crazy design in Paddington's coat in hopes that Carly wouldn't see that she's hidden some text in here. It says, 'shertin or big apple royel then it lee. Help me daddy!!!' Oh, my poor girl!" I pause a second to play back that goon's taunting words. "Mack was surprised Rayelle wasn't as upset as he expected when her mother threw the bear. Now I know why!"

Marge stretches her arm out. "Liam, please. May I see that?"

I hand the paper to Marge who can't read it fast enough. "Sheraton or Big Apple Royale Hotel. Then—"

"Italy," Chaz finishes for her. "Yup. The old man has friends in Palermo and Calabria. And God only knows where else. Likely planning to tuck themselves away where no one would think to look."

"What do we do now?" I ask, trying not to hyperventilate.

Marge hands the paper back to me. "Sherita told me to call her any time at all if there was even the remotest possibility she could help. As the lady has friends all over the New York hospitality industry, especially in the vicinity of Times Square, there's no better person to come to our rescue.

"She's probably just gone to sleep after working the night shift," I say. "But yeah, we have to call her."

"Sleep is the last thing any of us care about right now, Liam. Besides, if it makes you feel any better, Sherita is off on Saturday nights."

"Listen up, people." Ken eases the car into the street. "Just saw someone pull out of a legal space, and I'm grabbing it. There's only mist falling now, and I know a place not too far—just around the corner on Eighth. We can have breakfast. I don't think any of us will say no to a second cup of coffee and something to eat while Sherita does some digging."

That sounds good to me, but I'm racked with concern we're wasting time.

Marge reads me so well. "Liam, Ken is right. I think we have time to eat and strategize. We all need fuel. And if we get any kind of alert on their exact whereabouts, we'll leave."

"Yeah," I say, relieved Ken's pulled into the legal parking space. "Of course we will. I'll pay the check quickly."

We get out of the car. Ken locks it. Chaz is on the phone updating his mother, and Marge's face is lined with worry. My God, what if Sherita doesn't answer?

Saturday, 8:11 a.m.

We enter the small diner-like restaurant and the server, a kind woman with Jasmine on her name tag, leads us to a booth and asks me if I want the window seat. I nod as Chaz and I trade barely perceptible smirks. It would be humorous if the situation weren't so dire. But still,

I'm happy to have my "winder seat." I slide across the booth and look out at the rain. Chaz sits next to me as Marge and Ken occupy the other side.

I'm thinking of 'Captain Bob' who I met less than twenty-four hours ago in real time—eons ago in crisis time. I contemplate calling him if the need arises and put my hand in my pants pocket. His card is still there—Robert F. Dansworth, Attorney at Law. Burning the name into my brain, in case I lose the card, I carefully slide it back inside. I get lost in thought for a second as I count the ways he's already helped me. Then I notice the panic on Marge's face. "You can't reach Sherita?"

"I've called three times. It just goes to voicemail. Something's wrong. She told me she'd leave the phone on and turn the volume up. Maybe I should go to her place."

"Call again, honey." Ken puts a comforting hand on hers.

She presses Sherita's name and just looks at him despairingly when it goes to voicemail again.

"Wait a few minutes, Margie. I know that sounds like an eternity at the moment, but keep the faith. She'll answer."

Marge is really trying to hold it together for me, but I see she's about to break. She waits all of two minutes and calls for the fifth time. "Sher? My God! I was in an absolute panic when you didn't pick up!"

To my great relief, and everyone else's, Sherita's distinctive chatter is heard.

Marge looks at us. "Her dog fell asleep on the phone, and his butt muffled the sound."

"Thank goodness." Ken offers a lopsided grin. "That everything is okay, not about the dog's butt smothering the ring."

Marge smiles lovingly at him, then returns to her call. "I'll tell you what we found out, Sher. If anyone can help us, it's you."

The three of us sit in silence while Marge explains Rayelle's hidden message as quickly and as precisely as she can. When she finishes, she listens intensely as Sherita responds.

"Okay, Sher. Thank you so much. We're at a restaurant on Eighth Avenue. Gonna refuel and caffeinate ourselves to kingdom come. Ken will text you his number as a backup. Let us know as soon as you have anything at all. And thanks, my friend. I owe you—again." Marge hangs up and slides her phone sideways to Ken so he can see Sherita's number and text her.

"What is she going to do?" I ask.

After Ken returns her phone, Marge leaves it on the table. We quickly give our orders to Jasmine as she pours our coffee. None of us cares what we eat, so we all order one of the two breakfast specials advertised on the flyer that's clipped onto the front of the menu. I can't help but notice that Jasmine looks as tired as we do.

Marge pours a small amount of sugar into her coffee, a larger amount of milk, then takes a sip. "First, Sher is going to call one of her friends at the Sheraton while her husband calls the Big Apple Royale. We'll know shortly whether they've registered under their real names, though I think it's safe to say they haven't."

"I could've made that call," I say, feeling stupid I didn't.

"No, Liam. You couldn't have, and it's a very good thing you didn't. First, hotels won't confirm whether someone is staying there or not. If you have the guest's name, they'll transfer your call to the room, but you still wouldn't know which room that is. So, you'd actually be helping Carly and Ray by alerting them with a ringing house phone. That's not something we want to do. They could flee long before you'd ever find them."

I sigh. "Of course. Where's my brain?" I caution myself to think things over before I react impulsively—something I've had trouble with my entire life. If there were ever a time to get myself in check, it would be now. "I hear you. What else did Sher say?"

"That it's hotel policy for guests to have identification that matches the name they register with. So, Ray and Carly couldn't have come up with a last-minute alias."

"Damn," Chaz says. "Wish like hell I could press Rewind and go back to when those forged documents were in my hand. True, they were tightly wrapped and sealed, but I could have found someone capable of undoing and redoing the package without anyone being the wiser—if I hadn't been in full-dick mode."

Now *I'm* the voice of reason. "No, you couldn't have. Don't forget. Mack was right by your side, not to mention your father was waiting for you to deliver the package. That would have been impossible."

"Right. It would have. More than I even knew then. Way more."

"We're going forward." Marge sips her coffee. "We can't rewrite the past or dwell on it. But this is what's going to happen. First, Sher and her husband will confirm that Ray and Carly aren't in either place under their real names, which we're almost sure is the case. As she's got contacts at both hotels, they'll filter down the possibilities. You know, see who paid in cash, which rooms have a child, etcetera. Sher says it's likely Raymond took an adjoining room. It's the most plausible scenario but not necessarily the correct one. They're going to check for two adults and a child with an adjoining single and every combination possible. Who knows, maybe someone she can trust remembers checking them in."

I'm hopeful, but still nervous. "Is Sherita sure someone will help her?"

"She is. Help goes both ways, Liam. Sher's done her share of favors. Hear me?"

A young man places our food on the table as Jasmine stands behind him with a coffee pot.

"Thank you." Marge slides her coffee cup over. "How did you know?"

"I see a bunch of tired people at this hour. Lots come in after working night shifts or doing whatever else they do. Today, I'm a bit weary myself. Had two cups." She smiles. "Anything else I can get you folks?"

"I'll take the check," I tell her. "We may have to leave in a hurry."

"I get that. Give me a quick second or two." She walks the coffee pot over to the counter, places it down, then, pulling a pad out of her pocket, tears off a page, comes back to our table, and hands it to me.

Marge takes in a mouthful of eggs. "Just like my aunt Tonya used to make." After another bite, she looks at me. "You know, Liam, I have no idea what Rayelle looks like. Got a photo?"

"I've got hundreds on my phone but can't turn that on." I reach into my pocket for my wallet. "But there's a favorite one of the two of us at Mill Hill Park. It was taken a month ago on her last birthday."

I hand it to Marge, and she and Ken admire it. I'm not prepared to see Marge react so sentimentally to a child she never knew existed until last night. She almost looks teary-eyed, but, no doubt, jumping into a stranger's life to help save his daughter can do that to a person.

"What a gorgeous little girl who loves her daddy." Marge puts her hand over her heart. "I can see she has a beautiful soul. It radiates. And I can't imagine any photo expressing a father's love for his daughter more than this one does."

"Yeah," I say, trying not to choke up. "That was a special day. We went to the park together. Carly didn't want to come—now I know why. I was pissed, but later glad she didn't. Right after I took that selfie, Rayelle asked me if we could write a secret song together. One to remember the day. She's an amazing child—human being. We sing the song together when I kiss her goodnight." I choke back more emotion. "Anyway, that photo, that day, is special to us both. That's why I carry it. Ray-Ray had a framed copy of it in her room, but Carly made her leave it behind in Trenton."

"I'm so sorry." Marge attempts a smile. "Is this the only photo you have?"

"Only one I have in my wallet. I've never been in a position where I couldn't turn my phone on before." I pull another photo out. "This is me at my fourth birthday party. These are my parents. Think I was cute?"

Marge's eyes glisten with tears as she sniffs. "You were. I can see your parents are good people. They clearly have lots of love for you, just like you have for Rayelle. No doubt their love has helped you to become such an amazing dad." She holds both photos and looks back and forth at them. "These are treasures."

"May I see?" Ken asks.

Marge, almost as if she were reluctant to let go, hands them to him.

"Aw, look at your daughter. What a beauty. Reminds me of my baby sister." He smiles. "She's forty-seven now, but she'll always be Little Baby Dara to me."

"Chaz." Marge looks at him. "How about your children?"

"Benjamin and Kismet: twelve and nine. The loves of my life." He looks sad. "Unlike Houdini here, my photos are only on my phone." He shakes off the emotion. "Hope I'll be able to show you later, after we rescue Rayelle. By the way, I need to update my mother. I'll send her a text from the burner for now."

As Chaz texts his mother, Marge hands me back the photos, and I look lovingly at both, before sliding them into my wallet.

We eat our food in silence until three minutes later, when Marge gets a text from Sherita.

CHAPTER TWENTY

Marge picks up her phone, reads the text, then puts it down. "It'll come as no surprise to anyone that Ray and Carly didn't register under their real names. Sher has spoken with friends at both hotels. They're going to look at everyone who checked in, how they paid, how many were registered, and anything else that might help to identify them. We have time to finish our breakfasts, have as much coffee as we need, and take care of business. I'm guessing it won't take them too long to narrow this down." She opens a packet of strawberry jam and spreads it onto a piece of toast.

"Just praying they didn't decide on a different hotel." I finish the last of my orange juice.

"Let's not go down any roads we don't need to at the moment." Marge bites into the bread. "We need to finish our meals and be ready to go."

I fish some money out of my pocket and leave a large tip for Jasmine. I can't help but notice that Ken is craning is neck to look at someone working the grill through the open kitchen window. Everything makes me panic, and this is no exception. "Is something wrong?"

"Quite the contrary. I think one of the cooks is an old friend of mine, Darren. Ironically, his last name is Cook. He used to manage the kitchen at a club where I worked. Took ill with something serious, left the job, and we lost touch. I never knew if he survived and feared the worst. Pretty certain that's him. Sure hope I'm right, but it's been a while. Look, I'm just going to hit the men's room and see if I can say a quick hello if it's not his doppelganger. He's busy, and I am too. But I'd like to at least reconnect. Had a real strong bond with the man."

"I hope it's him, honey. You've mentioned Darren so many times." Marge gets up to let him out of the booth, and I see a good-looking fifty-something Black man in the kitchen grin widely as he notices Ken standing there. Ken smiles back. It *is* his friend. I feel happy for the two of them. How nice reunions are. Ken hurries toward the kitchen, and I can hear their animated voices as Darren disappears from view for a few moments. They're incredibly happy to see one another. Darren is back on the grill again, still smiling, and Ken is in the men's room.

To my left, Jasmine is behind the counter wiping it down after a customer has just left. Her eyes open wide, and she gasps. Looking straight ahead, I see a bedraggled and soaking wet man in his forties, his hair tousled and his eyes glazed over. He's come through the front door and is staggering toward her. He's drunk as fuck. Oh, no. He's holding a gun behind his back. He stops at the counter, right in front of her. My palms are sweaty again. I'm trembling. I can't look away. I can't go away. I can't watch another nice person die. Wait, who did I watch die? Why is my brain saying things I don't understand? I'm never around guns. I hate them. I don't even like seeing them in a cop's holster. They scare me. Oh, please, I can't let anyone see me lose control again. The gun is in his left hand, against his thigh. Jasmine hasn't seen it yet.

"Jesus, Marty! What are you doing here? You look like a wet rag that needs to be wrung out. And what part of 'we're over' didn't you get last night? Not to mention 'don't even think about coming to my job?' Please, I'm working!"

He stands back a couple of feet so she can see the gun at his side.

"What the hell? My God, where did you get that, and why did you bring it here?" Jasmine's hand goes to her throat. "Get *it* and yourself out of here!"

"Seriously, Jazzers? You think you can end our relationship like you did last night, after three and a half years, and I'm shh-posed to be fucking okaaay about it? I've given you everything under the shh-un, and now I'm not even worth talking to? Whaaat the fuck?"

"Marty! Put. The. Gun. Away. Now!"

"Thash not what I call talking." He sways to one side.

She tries to calm herself. Her breathing is erratic. Of course she's petrified. So am I. So is everyone else—we're all staring at the unfolding drama. She obviously doesn't want things to escalate. Her tone softens. "I've 'talked about it' with you a million times. You know how I feel. I can't tolerate excess drinking and the rotten behavior that goes along with it. Your drinking has gotten way worse, and every time you have more than two drinks, you become very mean, negating all of the good things we've shared." She lets her face fall in disgust. "This shining moment in time being a stellar example."

"Bullshit! I'm n-not drunk. Jush been up all night!"

I hear her mutter "drinking" to herself.

"What did you jush shhay?"

Now she's pleading with him. "How many more slurred words and angry rages was I supposed to take, Marty? What in the world was left to talk about? Sometimes the bad just outweighs the good to such a degree that there are no longer pros and cons to be weighed. Like right now. You're fucking drunk!"

He quickly turns the corner, yanks her arm, and pulls her out from behind the counter. His right arm is around her neck, and his left hand is pointing the gun at her head. "Brazen bisssh!" His face reddens with rage. He wobbles but stays steady enough to hold her hostage.

"Stop!" She blanches. "Okay, I'm sorry I said that. I didn't mean it. Listen, we'll go somewhere and talk. I promise. Just put the gun away! In case you're not aware of it, you're committing a crime."

"Too late to de-crime-a-late myself now, isn't it?" Marty's eyes scan the restaurant. "Any of you people try to leave or call the poleesh, I won't hesitate to kill her. Don't tesssst me. It'll save me from having to sheee her with another man."

An older couple rushes out the door from the other side of the diner, and a mother and her child cower under a table. I'm sure someone has managed to call, but there's a hush among the customers until a man in a back booth calls out to him. "Put the gun down, and let the lady go!"

As Marty turns to his right to respond to the man, a text dings on Marge's phone. Sherita must have some information. There's no time to waste, but if this menacing creep sees Marge touch her phone, he'll think she's calling the police and kill Jasmine and God only knows who else. No way we can let that happen.

Another minute goes by. Marty's gun is still jammed to the side of her head while my burner phone, that Chaz is using, sounds as well. It has to be his mother. It's got to be something important, but we can't risk anyone's life and touch the phones. My breath is breaking again, looking at Jasmine's terrified face and thinking about Rayelle, wondering what *her* face looks like. The longer we wait, the greater the risk that I'll never see my little girl again. But this lovely woman's life is in jeopardy. I can't ignore that. What's in the texts from Chaz's mom and Sherita? Every single second is precious. I can't believe this is happening. Like I haven't been through enough?

Marge's worried eyes are telling me to calm down. This woman doesn't play. She has the most expressive eyes of anyone I've ever met. Suddenly, it all makes sense.

I see Ken and Darren in the hallway behind the counter that goes left to the kitchen and back to the restrooms. They're waiting for the perfect moment for Marty to face forward. Jasmine's back is still pressed to his chest, the crook of his arm under her neck, nearly choking her.

Before I can even process what I think the men are going to do, Ken makes a quick and fluid grab for the gun while Darren kicks Marty's knees from behind.

I hold my breath.

Marty's leg's buckle. He screams, and the cringing sound of cracking bone fills the restaurant as Marty falls face down onto the hard floor. Jasmine, who reacts quickly, runs into the arms of a co-worker. She comforts her as the tears roll.

Ken says something to Darren, who stands with his foot on Marty's back, and signals to all of us to leave immediately. Nobody has to tell me twice. I grab my backpack and slide out of the booth. We're gone.

Saturday, 8:49 a.m.

We pass two NYPD officers hurrying into the restaurant as we rush out into the teaming rain. Our umbrellas quickly go up as we head for Ken's car.

A minute later, fueled by caffeine and adrenaline, we hop inside and close the doors.

"You, mister," Marge says to Ken as she pulls her phone out of her jacket pocket, "need to lay off the liquids."

"Why's that?"

"So you don't need to use the men's room anymore." She chuckles. "Damn, honey, the last two times you've come out of one, you've had to stop a crime in progress."

"I was thinking the same thing." He snaps his seatbelt into place. "Crazy. But I found my friend again."

"That you did." She smiles.

Marge and Chaz are now both checking their phones to read the texts that came in when we were briefly being held hostage.

"Holy shit," they both say only seconds apart.

"You first," Chaz says to Marge.

"Well, it's good news. Carly, Ray, Rayelle, and Raymond are at the Big Apple Royale on the Eighth floor—under aliases. Sher says she's leaving her apartment now to meet us in the lobby at the Curtain Call Hotel where she works. Says she'll give us all the information and help us formulate a plan. She's withholding the room numbers for now. Doesn't want any of us to go there half-cocked and blow this whole thing up."

I know that was meant for me. Once again, I chastise myself. Sherita is right. We need a plan. If I had the exact room numbers, I'd be on my way to the hotel, prepared to beat down the door. How stupid that would have been. Again, I remind myself how very dangerous my impulsiveness can be.

"What does *your* text say?" Marge asks Chaz.

"Not good. Mom said that a guy from the Souvenir Tiger called her to say that my dad's girlfriend, Gloria, was shot and rushed to the hospital. She's in surgery right now. It's serious. An attempted murder." Chaz has a faraway look in his eyes for a moment. "This is horrific. Please, everyone, say some kind of prayer that she'll be okay. Who would do this? Let me call my mom. We just need to know what's going on and also to figure out if any of this is tangled up with our stuff."

"Wow!" Ken shakes his head in shock. "What a gut punch. I just saw the lady and she was fine. Raymond had left a while ago. Can't imagine he'd come back to try and kill her. That would certainly complicate his departure. But I don't know these people, so who am I to speculate. I know nothing about her, much less who would want her dead. Yeah, Chaz. Call your mom before we head to the Curtain Call."

I'm a wreck. I feel sick to know this lady was shot. And I feel guilty for even thinking it, but now there's another delay in getting to Rayelle. It's a brief one but could matter. I slow my breathing. We're all silent as Chaz talks to his mother.

"No way! Are you fucking kidding me? Thanks for telling me, Mom. Listen. Just know this much. The person the cops are looking for is *not* the man who shot her. I know nothing else, but I know *that* for a fact. Can't explain now. You just stay safe, and don't open the door for anyone you don't know. And tell Oliver we found out that

Carly and Ray are staying at the Big Apple Royale under their phony names. Right now, we're headed to the Curtain Call Hotel on Eighth to meet Marge's friend Sherita who works there. She's off work today, but she's meeting us in the lobby to give us all the details and help figure out how to proceed. I'll let you know the plan as soon as we have one." He looks at the despair on my face. "Oh, yeah. And tell Oliver his dad Liam loves him. Catch you later, Mom. I love you too."

"Thanks for that," I tell him.

"I still can't believe someone shot that lovely woman," Ken says. "What kind of monster would do that?"

Chaz goes pale. "That's the thing, Ken. Right now, you're the main person of interest. They have you on security video leaving the lobby."

For a moment, we all sit in stunned silence.

"What the actual bloody fuck?" he screams. "Yeah, I'd imagine they would, but they don't have me on security video killing anyone, do they? Why would I *want* to kill her? I don't even know her! Not to mention the minor fact I don't kill *anyone.* They call me 'Karma Ken' for giving bad guys what they deserve, mostly delivering them to law enforcement. I'm not a damn murderer. Never have been. Do they know my name? Are you sure they think it's me? What the hell did I do to become suspect numero uno besides stand in the lobby? Did the doorman mention anyone else? This is some kind of major fuckery."

"Outrageous." Marge puts a comforting hand on his arm. "But you're only a person of interest, not a main suspect, sweetheart, and this can be easily cleared up. Let Chaz tell you what he knows. And if you don't think you're calm enough to drive, let Chaz take the wheel."

Ken undoes his seatbelt and swivels around to face Chaz

sitting behind him. "Can you tell me exactly what your mother said?"

"I will, but first, let me just preface it with what you already know. You went into Gloria's building to question the doorman, but you didn't end up questioning him because she was there talking to him."

"Right." Ken's face is red with anger. "That's exactly what happened. Nothing more."

"And you said that you left because you thought the doorman appeared suspicious of you."

Ken slaps his forehead. "Bloody fucking hell! The doorman being suspicious and me being on camera does not a guilty man make!"

"Apparently, they asked him if he saw anyone who didn't belong there, and tag, you were it. Told them you were standing nearby for several minutes while he and Gloria spoke. The guy thinks you probably left to wait outside for her."

"Well, that's fucking great." He smacks the steering wheel. "I go from breaking up one crime, to being a 'person of interest' for attempted murder, to stopping another crime."

"Please don't worry too much," Marge says. "I have a feeling they'll catch the culprit before they ever find you. And nobody's going to bring in the sketch artist, on well, such sketchy details. It'll be okay. I know it."

"They have me on camera, making a fake phone call." A vein bulges on the side of his neck. "No need for a sketch artist."

"How did your mother come to know all of this," Ken asks.

"One of my father's employees, Mike, who works a few nights a week, is also NYPD. After Gloria was shot, knowing she was Mike's boss's girlfriend, a cop friend called Mike to let him know what happened. For one, he was afraid the shooter might be after my mom as well. Mike's sent a friend to watch out for her. Of course, nobody could reach my father. I think we've all turned off our phones for the same reason."

Ken wipes the sweat off his forehead with his sleeve. "My God. I hope your mother isn't in this criminal's line of sight."

"I don't think she is, but we can't be too careful," Chaz says. "I know you're worried about them looking for you, but it'll be okay."

"This shit is unreal, and if they do catch up with me, like Margie said, I can prove I had nothing to do with it." He exhales and says nothing for several seconds, then puts his seatbelt back on. "I'm okay to drive. We've got to rescue Liam's daughter. Nothing's more important than that. And the rain has slowed a bit. We're good to go." He starts the car and carefully pulls out of the space as a few expletives spill from his lips and dissolve into the tense air that surrounds us.

CHAPTER TWENTY-ONE

Miraculously, we drive the ten-something blocks uptown in the light rain without anything unexpected or disastrous happening. Being able to park at the hotel saves us from having to worry about finding a space on the street.

We're sitting in a corner of the Curtain Call lobby with Sherita. Marge has just filled her in on Gloria being shot and Ken being a person of interest.

"Curses on that cockwomble doorman for saying it could be you," Sherita says to Ken.

"Can't blame the guy." Ken twists his lips. "I'm sure I'd have mentioned me too in his position."

"Well, they'll find out who shot the poor woman. We've got to pray she wakes up after surgery, and then hopefully she can identify the trigger-happy piece of diseased camel saliva who tried to snuff her out. Okay, so I've been thinking nonstop about the best way to rescue Liam's daughter."

That was a hell of a segue. "You're not the only one. I can't thank you enough for all you're doing to help me find my little girl. I know you've barely had any sleep."

"I'd get up at the ass crack of dawn any day of the week for my friend Marge and anyone who's important to her. Especially to save a child."

"Thank you seems inadequate. Have you come up with

anything yet?"

Sherita looks around. "I have several thoughts, but considering that Ken's an innocent person of interest, and we don't know who could be looking for you or Chaz, I think we should stay out of sight. There's a small conference room down the hall that's not being used. We can go in there. I've got the key. We need to take every possible precaution."

"You're always on the ball," Marge says as she and Ken get up. "Yes, sounds good."

I grab my backpack and stand, taking only one step forward, when someone calls out. "Dad! Wait up! Dad!"

My eyes widen. A tear rolls down my face—the first one I've allowed to fall since this ordeal began. Oliver, three inches taller than I am, his dark hair flopping in front of his eyes, rushes toward me. He looks a bit disheveled in his torn jeans, sweatshirt, and navy-blue rain jacket, but he's never looked more wonderful to me in all of these years.

We embrace one another and have a mutual, but quick, manly welling of tears. It's not enough for me. I give him one more squeeze before letting go. I swallow the lump in my throat as he squeezes me back.

"I'm so glad I found you, Dad. Looks like I would have missed you if I was like ten seconds later. I was at the Marriott when Grandma Allegra called to tell me Mom and Ray-Ray are at the Big Apple Royale under fake names, but that you were all meeting here to make a plan. Looks like you're leaving already."

I shake my head. "I'll be forever grateful that you didn't miss us. Best timing ever, and I couldn't be happier to see you." I gesture toward the hall. "No, we're not leaving. Just relocating to a conference room. I'll explain later. Ol, these are my friends Marge, Ken, Sherita, and Chaz. I don't know where I'd be without them." I look at the four smiling faces. "And this is my son, Oliver."

"Hey, kid." Chaz's eyes fill with unshed tears as he soaks in Oliver's appearance. "Guess you probably know I'm your uncle."

Oliver stops to take a good look at his face. "Yeah. Grandma Allegra told me all about you. Your dad and brother didn't want me to know you, so I knew it had to be because you're a good guy." Oliver surprises me by throwing his arms around Chaz. I'm blown away by how warmly Chaz reciprocates, but I understand how special the moment is for both of them.

"Come on." Chaz drapes an arm around Oliver's shoulder, giving him a squeeze. "Let's follow Sherita and get out of sight."

We walk across the lobby and down the hall. I keep turning to look at my son, making sure that I didn't have another crazy delusion and imagine him. Sherita unlocks the door to the Limelight Room, and we follow her into a modest-sized room with Broadway show posters on the walls. "I need the most macho men here to take one of those round tables up against the wall and open it. Someone else can de-stack six of those black chairs, and we're good to go."

Before Sherita is finished speaking, Ken has already grabbed the large table without waiting for help and opens it on the red-and-gold star-patterned carpet.

"You so did that on purpose," Marge whispers to Sherita. "You knew he'd bite with that 'most macho' bullshit. You're still a piece of work after all of these years, and I couldn't love you more."

"You too, Margie." Sherita winks.

Oliver sits between me and Chaz. "I'm really sorry I stayed away, Dad. I was afraid they'd kidnap me, and thought I could hide until they left. Sperm donor and his dad kept trying to entice me to leave the country with them. I said no every time, but then they said some things that gave me the effin' chills, you know, and I got to thinking I might not have a choice. I'm sure my gut was right. I just never thought they'd take my baby sister because she's your biological child. No surprise that Mom would sacrifice my life for her lover, just to keep him in her …." His face turns scarlet. "Um, never mind that last part. You know."

"None of this is remotely your fault." I squeeze his hand. "Remember that. Where have you been hiding out?"

"In Astoria. At my friend Jack's place on Ditmars Blvd. You know, in Queens. When Grandma Allegra said you were in the city looking for Ray-Ray, I got on the train and came here. Then, I went from one hotel to another, looking at every face I could. Like I said before, I was checking out the Marriott when she called and said you were here. We gotta find her, Dad."

"We will, kid," Marge says before I can. "No wusses at this table. We'll figure something out."

"What Marge said," I add. "We will. Failure's not in our playbook."

"Okay, people," Sherita says. "Here's what I've got. They're on the eighth floor of the Big Apple Royale in adjoining rooms. I'm sure Carly, Ray, and Rayelle are in 827 because that easily stows two adults and a kid. The smaller room is next door: 829. Probably where Chaz's *padre* is holed up. Now, we could knock on the doors, but I don't think any excuse in the world will get them to open up. Unless they order room service, we've got no shot. And any pretense of being maintenance, they'd see through and vamoose. Or be on the defense and be dangerous. Can't chance it."

"No," I say. "Definitely not. So what do we do?"

Sherita holds up her index finger. "I'm thinking we need to create some activity in the hallway to bring them out. Something to make Rayelle too excited to stay in the room."

"Okay, that makes sense," Chaz says. "*But* ... let's say you get them to open the door. The minute Ray sees any of us, well, I don't even want to think about what he might do. My felonious sibling is known for reacting before thinking. Get my drift?"

"I hear you," Sherita says. "So I came up with what I think is a brilliant plan, only I don't know if you'll all want to go for it."

"Anything that will put that little girl into her father's and her brother's arms is something I'll sign up for. Stating that right up front," Marge says emphatically.

"Ditto." Ken nods.

Sherita turns to me. "Liam. When you came to me last night, I'm sure you remember when Sir Clank-a-lot came over and asked me if I had a room for the knight."

"First time ever seeing a so-called man of armor. How could I forget?"

"Didn't think you would. So, after his royal appearance, I mentioned how we've got all kinds of fun-loving convention-going dressers-uppers who come to New York to do their thing, right?" She doesn't wait for me to answer. "I know I told you about the Furries—the grown-ass people who clomp around dressed up in animal costumes."

"Not easier to forget that either."

Chaz smirks. "They probably have better disguises than you did."

I turn around. "Payback is coming. No time for it now, smart ass."

Sherita continues. "You should also remember me telling you that when the Furries convention was held here, on the last night, several of them de-furred and left their lifeless furry animal 'outards' behind while their blood-and-guts innards hurried to catch their respective planes. And they never called us after they got home. Don't ask me why I didn't confiscate those lovable costumes after the requisite 45-day waiting period, but something in me decided to lock them away for a rainy day." She half-laughs. "No joke intended. Anyway, I'm thinking today is that day. It's time to unleash the beasts."

I see where she's going, and it sounds insane and brilliant at the same time.

"Keep talking." Marge gives her a loving smile. "Not that you need any prompting. Never did."

"There's a reason no one's ever called me 'Silent Sher.'" She chuckles. "I sure met my match when I met you, girlfriend. Okay, so listen up, people. My friend Lorenzo at the Apple Royale has a room for us to hide out in at the end of the hall on the eighth floor. He also said that the hotel was busy when Carly and Ray checked in, so chances are they had to see there are Furries in the house." She smirks. "Heck, one day I'll learn to say that with a straight face. "Anyway, having seen them already should make them less suspicious that they're the intended audience for the show I've got in mind. I figure if we all make some happy ruckus in the hallway, either the kid is gonna want to come out and join in the fun, or Carly and Ray might open the door and tell us to shut up. Either way would probably work, but it would be far better if the little girl runs out to join in the fun, or uses it to make her escape. Of course, there are other guests on the eighth floor, but we can't worry about them. I'm sure they'll understand and maybe even enjoy themselves. I just wish there was some secret signal we could send to let Rayelle know that her dad was part of the ruckus." She turns to me. "You got anything, Liam? Anything at all?"

Ten hopeful eyes meet my two.

"Yes." I jump halfway out of my seat. "I know exactly what to do. Rayelle will immediately know I'm out there, and no one else will have a clue! In fact, I just mentioned it at breakfast."

Everyone looks expectantly at me as I prepare to explain.

"Wait!" Marge blurts out. "The secret song you two wrote on her eighth birthday, last month, at the park in Trenton. Is that it?"

"Sure is."

"You sure Carly never got wind of it?" Ken asks.

"No, she was usually downstairs on her iPad or doing something else when I would put Ray-Ray to bed. All she'd ever do is blow her a kiss, often without even looking up from what she was doing."

"That's cold," Sherita says.

"Like an arctic chill," Marge adds.

"Yeah." I have a flashback of Carly saying goodnight via hand gesture, and it sickens me. "It was important to both me and Ray-Ray that our song *be* secret, so when we sang it every night, we did so very softly. Carly would have needed super-bionic ears to have heard anything at all."

"No time like the present to teach it to us. Melody and all." She curls her fingers toward her. "Bring it on."

My instinct is to look at Chaz. "My daughter wrote ninety percent of this. Don't even think about laughing."

"C'mon, Houdini. I'm past that." He smirks. "For the moment, anyway. I'm just thinking of my own kids, and nothing would be funny about a song that would save them. So go for it."

I inhale. This is weird, but I've got to do it.

"It's special when we're together

In any kind of weather,

But we love it most in the sun,

Cause that means the fun has begun.

But even in the rain,

We never have to explain

 Cause being together is the best it can be

When I'm with you and you're with me."

Nobody says a word, so I keep talking. "After we'd sing it, we'd say goodnight. She'd say, 'I love you, Daddy,' and I'd say, 'I love you more, pumpkin.' And that's been our routine. Every night since her birthday." I pause to fume. "Except last night. Of course, I've always been there to tuck her in or read her stories. Long before the song was written."

"What a beautiful relationship you two have." Sherita wipes away a tear.

I know Marge wants to say something, but she's too emotional.

"That sounds just like something Rayelle would write," Oliver says. "On my twentieth birthday, she wrote me a poem about how I wasn't a teenager anymore. It was really cute. Just like she is."

"That's our girl," I say.

"Okay." Sherita shakes off her nerves. "I'll grab some paper and a pen out of the supply cabinet, and Liam can write down the lyrics. I'll photocopy them for everybody. Then, I'll have someone drive all of you to the Big Apple Royale where you'll take the service elevator to your eighth-floor headquarters. Before I go any further, I need to ask Chaz a question."

"Shoot."

Sherita rolls her eyes. "There's irony for you. Chaz, I just wanted to know if your father or brother could be carrying."

Chaz sighs. "I strongly doubt it. First, the old man has never been one to pack heat, in spite of his rough childhood. I've watched him. He's uneasy around a piece. That's why he hires people like Mack. As for Ray, not worth the risk. If he carries a gun and is stopped for any reason and found to be on parole, he's royally screwed. And third, as they're all planning to leave the country, there's no way they'd carry or leave anything in a suitcase. Can't be one-hundred percent sure of anything, but I really don't think so. That said, it's not like my family and I are close. So everyone should still proceed as if they do have a weapon or two."

Ken nods. "Always better to err on the side of caution, but I'm happy the odds are against it."

Sherita blows out a big puff of air. "I was hoping Chaz would say something like that, but Ken is right." She straightens in her chair. "Back to my plan. I'll be at the storage locker here, grabbing the merchandise, as gross as it might be. There are nine costumes. I know there's a bear, a fox, and a wolf. That's all my brain has allowed me to keep in the ol' memory bank. Oh, and I've got some toy musical instruments stashed, so I'm gonna include those. I'll sanitize them first. Everything will go into some trunks, and a driver buddy of mine will deliver them to you at the Royale. I'll be with him. So, memorize that song, practice the heck out of it, and after I arrive with the costumes, we'll get the show on the road. Operation Save Rayelle. And no one's gonna stop us."

Saturday, 10:16 a.m.

We're in a spacious corner room at the Big Apple Royale with two queen-size beds. Marge and Ken are sitting against the headboard on one, and I've got the other one to myself. Oliver insisted. He and Chaz are sitting on either side of a small desk. It does feel good to stretch my legs out, especially considering the less-than-cozy circumstances I've been in throughout the night, but we're only here a short time, and resting is the last thing on my mind. I turn my gaze to the window. I still can't believe the intensity of the rain. It started when I got on the train at Trenton and hasn't really stopped since.

Sherita's driver brought the five of us here. We were escorted in through a side entrance and taken by freight elevator to the eighth floor. The driver checked the hallway to make sure no one was there. After getting us safely installed in this room, he headed back to the Curtain Call to retrieve the costumes Sherita is packing in trunks. And Sherita herself.

I can't believe my little girl is right down the hall, and I'm sitting here on the bed while everyone is looking at photocopies of our song lyrics. Rayelle is so close, and all I want to do is run down the hall, pound on the door, and tell them to release my little girl. Ordinary people would have called the authorities. I'm not ordinary, and now, more than ever, I'm convinced that I was right to take this job on myself, especially as I'm this close. Besides, if any authorities broke down the door, God only knows what might happen to Rayelle. I'm not as optimistic as Chaz that nobody has a gun. For all I know, Ray or his dad might shoot her. Or maybe even Carly. Who knows? That means I can't think of trying to break down the door either. I won't let impulsiveness drag me down the hall and introduce me to rampant stupidity. Rayelle has already been traumatized. I know that. Her rescue is going to be as loving and easy as possible. What happens after that may be frightening, but Oliver is here to shield her from that while I take care of business.

Meanwhile, Sherita has someone monitoring the hallway cameras just in case they decide to bolt.

Ten minutes pass, and everyone is reading the lyrics, over and over again. Marge is closing her eyes and whispering them to herself.

Oliver looks up from the paper. "Okay, Dad, I've got the words down pat."

"You've got the youngest brain here." Marge clicks her tongue. "Easiest for you."

Not quite used to Marge, Oliver isn't sure how to respond.

"I've almost got them," Marge tells him. "See, the longer you're alive, the more there is to clutter your noggin." Seeing his blank face, she elaborates. "Your head. Brain. Storage capacity. File cabinets. Gray matter."

"Oh." He tries to work up a smile. "Yeah, I got it. But I've sure had a lot of stuff in my brain these last two years. Especially these past two months."

"I'll bet you have," Marge says sympathetically. "How could you not?"

"I think it's time for you to start singing." Chaz looks at me with a deadpan face, but I know that once Rayelle is safe, he's going to razz me. This is no time to be shy. I get off the bed and sit on the bottom end of it. "Okay, I'll sing it twice; then everyone can join me."

I'm pleased that they're all committed to getting this right. The first rehearsal goes great. We're just about to try again when there's a knock on the door.

"It's Sherita," Ken says. "I'll get it."

I know Ken isn't one-hundred percent certain or he wouldn't have volunteered to let her in. But after poor Gloria being shot, we're even less sure of everything than we were before, especially knowing there's a would-be murderer on the loose. As expected, it's Sherita, followed by her driver who drags in two trunks and a large garment bag. One of the trunks is covered in stickers from every city in the world that ever existed. I feel like I've been through as much in one night as that trunk has in years. But I can handle it. What has my little girl been through? She's so close, but she might as well be a million miles away until she's in my arms.

"Thanks, Lucas! I owe you one," Sherita calls after her driver. "You delivered for me again—literally. And send my love to Lizz."

Having the two trunks and bag in front of me, I know I'm that much closer to getting my Ray-Ray back and freeing her from the grips of her mother. I slow my breathing. I know how easily it can escalate.

"Okay, people, here are the costumes." Sherita opens her arms as if she's presenting an act. "Don't fight over them. What did I miss?"

"You just need to memorize the lyrics," Oliver says.

"Already did that back at the Curtain Call and on the way over. Bonita Sherita Mamacita doesn't let any grass grow under her feet. Every moment is valuable. Come on, people, we gotta get the garb on, and then Liam can teach me the melody. We'll be good to go." Sherita wastes no time flipping the latches on the trunks open. "Dig in. Choose your friendly beast."

"You mentioned back at your hotel there was a bear?" I say. "That's the first animal Rayelle will be attracted to."

"Sure is." Sherita yanks a bear head out of the trunk and tosses it to me. "I'm sure the rest of him is in here." Within seconds, she's dug out the bear body and flings it onto the bed. "As you can see, these costumes go beyond what you might wear on Halloween with your kids. These babies are made to satisfy bigger urges, like actually *becoming* the animal, but we don't need to go there now. Or ever."

While everyone else is looking through the trunks, I slip into the bear costume, but leave the head off until it's time to go.

"You should take this one." Ken lifts something orange and furry out of the second trunk and holds it up in front of Marge. "The sexy fox with the long eyelashes could be your spirit animal. I'll be the wolf only because this costume looks big enough for me to stuff myself into."

"Good call, honey."

"I'll be the tiger." Oliver unzips the garment bag.

"And I'll take the March Hare." Chaz looks sad. "My kids loved him when I used to read *Alice in Wonderland* to them."

Sherita looks around. "Glad to see everyone moving so fast. And I'll be Nuts the squirrel. Smallest costume here. People near and dear would say the name fits. And if anyone says so who's not in my love circle, well, that leaves me with some serious ass to kick."

Marge shakes her head with a smile.

I look at Sherita. "I can't thank you enough."

"Don't thank me for anything until we rescue your daughter. And even then, not necessary. Seeing the two of you together will be all the thanks I could ever want. Now, everyone grab an instrument out of the travel-stickered trunk. Before we practice the song, I have one very important instruction. The devil is in the detail, so I've had this whole thing choreographed by a friend who works here. We can't afford to mess up. When we leave the room, everyone needs to start singing 'Row, Row, Row Your Boat.' By the time that's over, we should just be approaching Room 821. That's when you need to start singing Rayelle's song. Not before. Everyone got that?"

We all agree.

"I've had a card key made for each one of us. Liam, you already have yours. Everyone else, come take one. We can't know who will need to get in the room when, so everyone needs access. Just be careful who sees you. Also, before we go, I have some escape routes in place. My friends and I have left no stone unturned. I'll get to that in a moment. But before I forget, be sure to stow your valuables into the closet safe if you haven't already, speak up if you have burning-ass questions, say a prayer or two if you're so inclined, and after I go over things, we'll get this show on the road."

The six of us leave the room, immersed in an alternate reality as our bizarre rescue parade begins. I lead the way, singing the nursery rhyme. In no time at all, doors on the floor are opening. Two children stand in the first doorway, their father behind them, gleeful delight on all three faces. That's a very good sign. A few solitary adults open their doors as well. It's nearly 11:00 a.m., and while most guests have vacated, the few that remain look as if they partied hard the night before and aren't sure if what they're seeing isn't a by-product of something they may have ingested. At least that's my twisted take. One guy, in boxers and a T-shirt, his eyes glazed over, will probably think this was a dream when he exits from his self-induced stupor. Another woman stands with her dropped jaw, looking as if she's never seen a musical animal parade in a hotel hallway before. Meanwhile, we're almost finished rowing the boat gently down the stream. Two housekeepers stand by their carts with smiles. Nobody told them what's going down, but having seen a lot in their profession, neither looks surprised.

Just as we're ready to begin Rayelle's song and the few still-occupied rooms have likely opened their doors, I see someone who clearly doesn't belong. He's a large man wearing a sopping-wet, oversized gray raincoat, a fishing hat with neck flaps, and a face mask. Because who doesn't dress for a day at the lake in a Manhattan hotel? Something is very wrong. I can tell by his movements that he's antsy and angered by the unexpected crowd. He stands awkwardly and tries to blend in. God only knows who or what is under that coat. Wait, maybe it's Raymond, taking pains not to be recognized en route to his last stop before JFK. Oh no! What if he's the one who tried to kill Gloria? I feel terrible, but I can't do anything about that now.

Proceeding as planned, right outside of Room 827, I lead the group in song. "It's special when we're together, in any kind of weather …."

"I told you he'd come to get me! Told you!"

"Don't you even think about leaving this room!"

Even through a door, wearing a bear's head on top of my own, I have no trouble recognizing Carly's and Rayelle's voices.

"But we love it most in the sun, cause that means the fun has begun …."

"Daddy's here!" Rayelle screams joyfully.

"I warned you! Don't you dare open—"

It's too late for Carly to stop her. The door flies open, and Rayelle comes racing through. Thank you, God! Thank you!

My precious girl, her long brown hair back in a ponytail, wearing embroidered jeans and a Big Apple T-shirt, looks with amazement as she steps out into the hallway a split second before Carly attempts to yank her back in the room. "Let me go, Mommy! I want to be with Daddy! I know he's here!"

"No he's not! He told me to take you away! Why would he come get you?" Carly shouts. "Get back in here!"

How dare she!

Rayelle looks around. Her gaze stops as she sees me, or, rather the bear. I drop the plastic horn, squat down, and put my arms out for her embrace. With no hesitation, she runs to me. "Daddy!"

I take her into my arms and stand. "Yes! It's me, baby girl. It's Daddy! I came with my friends to save you. I got the message you left in Paddington's hood. You were so clever to make that picture and leave it with him. You're so brave and so smart."

"Take the bear head off." Tears are running down her face. "I want to see you, Daddy."

I undo all but one fastener and reveal my own face. "See? It's me, pumpkin. I've missed you more than anyone in my life." I kiss her more times than I can count.

Rayelle buries her face in my bear chest. "Mommy said I would never see you again!"

I shoot an angry glance at Carly. I'm fuming, rage welling up inside me, but this joyful moment belongs to me and Rayelle. I'll deal with Carly shortly. I give Rayelle my full attention. "I'm sure she did say that, honey, and it was very wrong of her. You're not going anywhere with Mommy. But see this tiger standing next to me?"

"Hey, baby sister," Oliver says.

"Oliver!" she cries, clinging to me with her left hand and touching his striped fur with her right as if it's the most natural thing in the world. "I missed you so much! Mommy said you would be coming with us, only not on the same airplane."

Oliver was right. They *were* planning to kidnap him or force his hand somehow.

"I would have only come to find you." Oliver lovingly strokes the underside of her chin. "And when I found you, I would've brought you home." I hear the anger in his voice, but he's tamping it down for his sister.

"Don't ever let me go, Daddy." She grabs a fistful of my bear fur. "You either, Oliver."

"Honey, that will never happen. And we'll have lots of time to be together soon, but Daddy has to take care of things and make sure that you always stay with me and Oliver. I don't ever want to lose you. Not ever. I have to make sure that Mommy and her friend never try to take you away again."

"Her stupid *boy*friend," Rayelle says through her tears. "They do kissy naked things in the bathroom and think I don't know. He's so mean to me. So is Mommy."

Rage surges through my veins, but I know my priorities. I have to control my impulses. "Pumpkin, you go with your brother, okay? Daddy will join you both when he finishes what he has to do." I inhale a quick but calming breath, then glare at Carly to let her know I mean business.

Her eyes transmit fury. "Oh hell no, Liam! You stay here with me, Rayelle! And that's an order."

Rayelle, still in my arms, turns to face Carly. "No, Mommy! You can't make me!"

Carly's face inflates with rage. "Just watch me, little girl!"

Taking big, angry strides toward us, Carly reaches out to grab Rayelle from me as Ken, Marge, Chaz, and Sherita make an animal wall in front of us, obstructing Carly's mobility and her view.

"Let me take my daughter back, you Bronx Zoo rejects!" I know Carly, and her body language tells me she wants to physically fight everyone but knows a losing battle when she sees one. Instead, she flares her nostrils, gives us the finger, then mumbles the crudest expletives she can muster.

In that brief window of opportunity, I hand Rayelle to Oliver, and he disappears with her through the stairwell door behind us—one of the escape routes Sherita had told us about. Oliver will come back to our room when it's safe, and he's been briefed on where to go in the meantime.

Everyone keeps singing, even louder, only they've moved on to "Ring Around the Rosy." We'd decided on this in advance too—silence not being the best bet at the precise moment everything has hit the fan. The animal wall blocks Carly for another minute, giving Oliver the time to disappear.

"Where's my son taking my daughter?" Carly screams at me. She turns to a fox, wolf, March Hare, and squirrel she can't identify. "Stop singing, and go fuck yourselves. Or each other for all I care." Being in her sight again, her eyes narrow as she stares at me. "What are you doing, you fucking lunatic? How did you find us?"

A man, who must be Ray comes out of the room behind her. He's tall, just like Chaz and his father. He's run off with *my* wife and child, yet he stares at me with the contempt I should have for *him*. Meanwhile, the man in the raincoat, who I perceive to be Raymond, goes into the room. Ray is still staring at me … sneering. I get the feeling he wants to lurch forward and grab me, but he's tightly controlling his impulses. If anyone knows how that works, I do. But damn, there's something about this guy that's sickeningly familiar to me, only I can't place him. My heart rate is escalating as his hateful scrutiny confirms that I'm right. Fear still courses through me. My palms are sweating, but I don't want him to see how nervous he's making me. I let fear play all the games it needs to play. I only know I can't allow another cerebral power outage.

"Who else is hiding behind these bullshit costumes?" Ray screams, looking away from me for the first time.

Something about him gives me the chills. Oh, no! Raymond is in their room. He had to have come through the room next door. Damn. I've jumped to conclusions about the mystery man's identity. Shit! My stomach is flipping. I'm lightheaded. Disoriented. *You can't lose it now, Liam. Stay strong. Everything you care about is on the line!*

The mystery man in the raincoat wastes no time approaching Raymond. Something ugly is going down. I can't hear what the men are saying to one another, but Raymond screams for Ray and Carly to hurry back inside. Panic radiates from his eyes.

Expressions of joy on the hotel guests' faces have morphed into stunned, frightened, and fearful expressions. One door after another quickly closes. A child cries. I shudder as the mood darkens.

I'm going into that room. The Royces and the mystery man be damned. I'm having it out with Carly to end this nightmare.

Squirrely Sherita heads down the hallway. I know she's on her way to make sure my kids are okay. Ken, Marge, and Chaz, still wearing their animal heads, follow me into the room, closing the door, but not firmly shutting it behind us.

"You want to talk to me?" Carly rages, her long dark hair unkempt with strands hanging in front of her face. "You lose the Sherwood Forest brigade. Oh, silly me. F.A.O. Schwartz!"

I say nothing. I've always wanted to take Rayelle to that toy store, but never got the chance. I'll have it soon.

Suddenly, the man in a raincoat rips his hat and mask off. "Dey wanna stay, den good. It's huntin' season here in dis room, and I got me a gun and all kinds of ammo. Well, lookee here, if it ain't Tallamore and his baby toys all come to life."

Shit! I should've known! I knew he'd only be tied up so long before someone came looking for him. But I've got nothing to say to Mack, and while I know Chaz does, he's not revealing himself, and neither are Marge and Ken. Of course, Mack could easily guess who they are, but his mind is elsewhere as he fixates on Raymond who's shaking with rage.

"Do something about these furry losers," Raymond says to Mack. "Don't stand there hurling insults at them. That won't get us anywhere. What the hell are you waiting for? This shit is second nature to you."

Mack bursts out in raucous laughter. "Oh, dis is funny, you piece o' garbage. You still be t'inking I work for you. Da whole job's been a ruse, but youse all been too stupid."

"What are you talking about, Mack?" Raymond stares at him defiantly. "Don't you even think of calling me stupid again, you babbling bully. Of course you work for me, and I've paid your thug-ass well."

Mack's face almost looks like a puffer fish as he reddens and bloats his cheeks. "T'ug ass?! Babblin' bully? You shut da damn hell up, and don't be callin' me dem names. You is a bad man. You was quite da criminal when youse was young, just like Junior here fresh outta da slammer."

At the mention of prison, Ray glares at me. His stare is lethal. I think he's trying to get some kind of reaction, but I still won't play.

"You don't know anything about my childhood," Raymond barks at Mack. "Save that tough-guy crap for other people. You don't intimidate me. And since when are you the law-abiding voice of morality?"

"Since I say so, dat's when. I follow Mack's laws. Dat's right. My own, mothafucka. I don't care 'bout anyone else's. But your big mouth got my older brutha killed, and for a whole lot of years, I didn't know da name of da filt'y rat who opened his yapper. My brutha was da only good person in my life. I ain't never stopped missin' him."

Thankfully, Ray turns his focus to his father. "What the hell is he talking about?"

Raymond frowns. "I wasn't a good kid, son. I got into trouble every which way I went. That's why I've been so protective of you— obsessively so. I never wanted you to go down the same path I did and blamed myself when it happened. But I have no clue what kind of decomposing garbage Mack is spewing at the moment. None. And that's the truth."

Mack pulls out a gun and points it at Ray, Carly, and Raymond. "Youse t'ree go sit on da edge of da bed while I tells you a story." He snarls. "And hurry da hell up!"

Raymond's entire countenance changes before my eyes. He's cowering as it suddenly dawns on him Mack isn't joking. "C'mon, man… I didn't mean—"

"Sit on da edge of da bed!" Mack takes a step closer.

Raymond sits, nodding for Ray and Carly to do the same. The three remain silent as they try to process the threat. I know Carly. She's petrified and looking at Ray to save her. His face is pinched in anger, but Raymond, slumping, looks terror-stricken, the shock of Mack's one-eighty showing on his face as his jaw drops and freezes in place.

I'm surprised Mack seems so unfazed by me and my three

animal friends behind him, but he's intent on having this out with Raymond, and it's clear he's been anticipating the confrontation for years—with a vehemence stronger than any retribution he might wish for the people who tied him up.

Raymond closes his mouth and sits up straighter. He's going to say something; I know it. Bet he thinks he can talk Mack down. "Mack, my friend and associate. Can we please talk without the piece? I'm happy to compensate you for anything I may have done to upset you. This is unnecessary."

"I ain't your damn friend, and you ain't never been mine. And compensate me?" Mack has the reddest, angriest face I've ever seen. "You t'ink dere is anyt'ing you could give me or say to me? Ain't nothin'. Now you shut da hell up unless I ask you to speak. Ain't afraid to pull no trigger, mothafucka!"

Raymond shrinks in abject fear again, putting the palms of both hands up, silently begging Mack not to shoot. Now he's trembling, his momentary courage dissolved into nothingness.

Ray squeezes Carly's hand. I know he can't be as calm as he seems, but after twenty years in prison, I'm sure he's learned to play it cool. I don't know if he took her hand to calm her, or to stop her from making any impetuous moves. She can be worse than me when she's scared.

Mack glowers at Raymond. "You remember coming to steal from your church when you was t'irteen? On a Monday afternoon after a whole lotta cash was collected on dat Sunday before?"

Raymond turns scarlet and looks down at his lap. Oh, yeah. He sure does. His body language is screaming in guilt.

"Well, someone got dere before you. Dunk. You remember

Dunk?"

The name Dunk means nothing to me, but the name Hunk comes to mind as I look more closely at Ray. I have to put that at the back of my mind for now.

"Uh … yeah. Dunk the punk, they called him. We used to hang at times. But he was several years older than me and had his own crowd. I'm sorry, Mack. With all due respect, so what?"

"So what?!" Mack screams so loud that Ray drops Carly's hand to keep his father upright on the bed.

Raymond can only swallow the lump in his throat as Mack's rage escalates into unrestrained fury.

"Did you say 'So what?' You say 'so what' again and I'll put one between Junior's eyes. Dat was my brutha! Dunk was my brutha! We didn't have no money for food, and da landlord was gonna t'row us out. Dunk did what he hadda do for his family. You knew we was dirt poor and our fatha in prison. Our motha only knew one way to make money, but da men beat her half da time or didn't pay her. Dunk's friends knew dat. You hadda know dat. But didn't nuthin' stop you from tellin' da damn cop you seen Dunk punch out da priest when he wouldn't give up da church's money!"

"Hey, man, I'm really sorry. I won't lie to you. Guess I did. Trust me. Didn't want to say shit, but I was left with no choice. I was already on paper-thin ice when the cop nabbed me. I was just a stupid kid!" He stares at the gun. I can tell he wants to say something but stops himself.

Ray stares at his father, his eyes wide and mouth open. I can only imagine what Chaz's face looks like under the March Hare head.

"Youse a stupid man if you t'ink I care why you did dat. You ratted out my brutha to save yourself. He went to prison, and he got killed dere 'cause some of them boys don't like no one messing with da man of God. One of dem was da priest's damn nephew! Oh man, you killed your friend who was my brutha."

"I didn't kill him, Mack!"

"You got him killed. Same as if you done it wid your own two hands! Den we was t'rown on da streets. My mutha disappeared one day, and dat was it. I was on my damn own, livin' with my mean drunk uncle 'cause he wanted the foster money. Put on dis whole act to get himself certified with da state. I got raised on da street. I's been fighting da world for years. All because of you. I didn't never forget who to blame. You don't like Mack? You made Mack!"

Raymond waves his hands as if doing so will quiet Mack or pre-empt anything else he has to say. "No, I don't take responsibility for who you are! Sorry, that's not on me. But I will be forever sorry I ratted out Dunk."

Mack doesn't acknowledge a word. "Wasn't till da cop retired and got old dat I finally found him. Paid him a real special visit. He said he didn't remember who ratted out Dunk, but den I said a few words, real nice like, showed him what I'd be packin', and his memory come back like magic. Real amazin' like. After dat, he didn't have no trouble rememberin' nothin'. I got him to say real clear who ratted out my brutha." Mack pauses. He's choked up. Quite the quandary for a one-dimensional piece of cardboard, though he makes slightly more sense to me now. "He was da only person who was good to me, my brutha Duncan. And you got him whacked! When I found out it was you, I came to find you so dat I could turn on you one day like you turned on him. And yeah, I made some good cash in da meantime."

"Give me a break!" Senior says. "We were kids, Mack. I never imagined Dunk would get killed. The cop was going to beat the shit out of me, and I feared for my life. If the law didn't kill me, my old man would've. I had enough crap with my own home life. I didn't think much about anyone else's. Yeah, I guess I knew your father was in prison, but I didn't know you mother was a—"

"Youse better stop right dere! What she hadda do ain't who she was! And I still don't be knowin' if she's dead or alive. So shut da damn hell up!"

"Sorry. Didn't mean anything by it. I was just trying to explain that—"

"Shut up! I's doin' da talkin."

"Man, please! I was just a scared kid trying to save myself. How was I supposed to know what would happen?"

"You knew damn well what would happen, you lyin' sack o' shit. Hell's Kitchen didn't raise dumbasses. Ev'ry damn one of us went to da school of hard knocks. You knew, and you didn't care. And now it's payback time. I did a real good job of bein' your friend, just like you did wid Dunk, until you sold him out to cover your ass. I waited years so I could kill da people you love just like you did to me! My motha might as well be dead cause I ain't never seen her again. T'anks to you. I already whacked your girlfriend. Dat Gloria chick be dead on the street! Too bad 'cause she was real pretty."

Mack must have fled the scene quickly to believe that he killed her instantly. I say a quick prayer and hope she's made it through surgery.

"What?! You killed my beautiful Gloria!" Raymond's hands fly to his head and squeeze it. "She's the love of my life!"

Right. That's why you left her.

Raymond stands, trying to block Ray and Carly from Mack's gun. "I can't believe you killed her! She never did anything to you! Such a good woman! I can't even imagine the world without her. I'll fucking kill you, Mack!" He shifts his stance, exposing Ray and Carly again. "I'll tear you limb by limb. I'll decapitate you so quickly that your mouth will still be screaming when your head falls from your neck onto the floor. Then I'll kick it out the window and come back for the rest of you!"

That's about as likely to happen as a cockroach threatening to dismantle the refrigerator that sits on top of it. Mack is a damn fridge. And Raymond is out of his mind with rage and grief.

"Oh, shit," Ray says as he and Carly exchange worried looks.

Mack walks up to Raymond and puts the gun to his forehead. "Sit down, mothafucka. And don't make me be tellin' youse again!" With his hand pressed to Raymond's chest, Mack pushes him back onto the bed with such force that Ray has to help his father to sit again.

"Youse got quite da imagination dere. Don't t'ink youse gonna do nuttin to me. I got da damn gun on all youse, and I's much stronger den you. I woulda whacked Gloria in front of your damn face, but it was too much trouble to get her here. She died hatin' your guts t'ough. When she saw me, she t'ought you'd sent me to bring her to you. Oh man, she sure called you some whoppers. Den, when she saw da gun, she was crying and beggin' for me to let her live. She said, 'Why'd Raymond send you to kill me?' and I told her, 'Because he didn't want nobody hangin' around to talk shit about him. Youse be knowing too much.' And she believed me. Den bang! And now I's gonna kill Junior here, 'cause you love him more den anyone."

"No!" Carly screams. "I've waited for over twenty years to be with him again. Don't you dare! Ray is my whole heart and soul."

I'm surprised her words sting, knowing what I do, but I'm able to brush them off for now.

"Do you t'ink I care, little missy, dat you waited twenty years for some more damn Royce dick while he was shovin' it into da female prison guards … or maybe just waited til his buddies dropped dere soap in da shower. You t'ink about dat? Hope you enjoyed what youse gotten so far, 'cause I like shootin' da babymakers off mothafuckas before the final whack. T'ough it might be better to let dem live like dat."

"No!" Carly screams.

They're all arguing back and forth so vociferously that it's a loud chaotic jumble to me. I'm lost in the threats, bad English, accusations, pleas, excuses, name-calling, and screaming. I'm surprised that Ray and his father are both so vocal with a gun pointed at them. I see the wolf and the March Hare move closer to one another, and I know they're planning something. There's movement on the side of Ken's costume, and I know he's hard at work. In no time at all, having slipped his arm out of the wolf costume, he's taken a knife from his pocket, cut a hole on the side, then handed Chaz the knife.

I'm shocked that Mack is so undeterred by who might be behind him, but it's clear that he's living his wet dream, and his street smarts have taken a back seat to his pent-up rage.

Carly is in tears over the threat to her lover's life. She's consumed with her fear of losing him. Rayelle is already in her rear-view mirror; that's obvious.

Ken and Chaz now drop the bodysuits to the waist to free their hands, and as Ken, in a move similar to the one in the diner, grabs the gun from Mack. But this time, Chaz slashes the knife across the back of Mack's legs, enough to rip his pants, draw blood, and cripple him in one fell swoop. Mack howls in pain as he goes down, his leg twisting as it hits the floor and he collapses on his back. Unlike the inebriated Marty in the diner, Mack has a lot more determination to get up, despite his agony.

Chaz puts a foot on Mack's big stomach while Ken holds him at gunpoint. "Don't even think about trying to get up!"

"You broke my knee and cut my legs, you mothafucka!"

Ken and Chaz rip off their animal heads, while Ray and his father are so riled up they're nearly unintelligible as they scream over one another.

Mack stays focused. "I knew it was Batman and Chazzy behind me. Who's under dat damn fox? I'll bet dat's da red bitch. Oh, youse all came to get the kid." He stares at Chaz, his face tight with pain. "I would have killed you, mothafucka, but dat mighta made your old man happy, and Mack ain't about making dreams come true. But now, after you cut me like dis, I wish I'd killed youse anyway."

Talking about things that cut deeply, I can see Mack's words are painful to Chaz, and I know he's waiting for his father to counter—to tell Mack that he's wrong. But Raymond says nothing. And here I'm thinking Chaz must've been feeling good that he saved his family, just like I felt when I saved Chaz from the hooded guy who shot at us. Only he's hurting.

"You're a traitor," Raymond screams at Chaz as Ray glares at me again. "I asked you to keep Tallamore away from us, and what do you do? Install yourself as president of his fucking fan club. You're a pathetic disgrace. Look at you, dressed up like some fucking ninja rabbit coming here to destroy your brother's future after he's suffered for twenty years."

"How about the man he killed? How about that man's family? They didn't suffer? I don't care what either one of you do or where you go," Chaz shouts. "But I'm here because taking someone's child is a deal breaker."

"Too bad nobody ever took you!"

Chaz gulps.

"My Gloria is dead! That's all that matters to me." Tears roll freely down his face.

"Dat's your fault." Mack's squirming under Chaz's foot, almost oblivious to Ken, who is still pointing a gun at him.

Ray shoots daggers at his brother, then back at me. I swallow the lump in my throat. Why is he so intimidating to me? He looks at Chaz again, then nods in my direction. "This loser BFF of yours still doesn't know shit, does he? He wallows in more ignorance than bullshit." He looks as if he wants to spit.

What the hell are they talking about? What could Ray possibly know about me, other than whatever garbage Carly might have told him? How can he show no shame for taking another man's wife?

"Let me da fuck up!" Mack bellows, still struggling to get free as his bloodied legs stain the hotel carpet. "I ain't messin' widchu people!"

Before Mack can spew more threats, two uniformed cops announce themselves, tell everyone to drop their guns, then rush in to find the object of their search on the floor. Ken puts his gun down, and he and Chaz move to the side. The larger cop speaks to Mack while they both pull him up. "Robin Francis MacElroy, you're under arrest for the attempted murder of Gloria Menhardt. You have the right to remain silent ...."

I tune out as Mack is given his Miranda rights, and more cops come in. I want to get back to Rayelle and Oliver, but I know that once Mack is taken away and we've given statements to the other cops, I have to take care of business with Carly or nothing will matter.

"Robin Francis?!" Chaz says incredulously. "Seriously? Robin? Francis? That's your name?"

"Shut da damn hell up, Chazzie!"

"Take care, little birdie. Enjoy the cage."

"Mothafucka," Mack mumbles, moaning in pain and limping badly as the first two cops take him away.

Carly is holding onto Ray, profusely sobbing. Raymond is asking a remaining officer to confirm that "attempted murder" means that Gloria is still alive. Hearing that she's in surgery, he collapses onto a bed in relief and prays for her life and for God to forgive him.

Ken puts his arm around Marge, who has taken the fox head off, and Chaz looks at his brother and father as if they're complete strangers to him—because they are. As his family indulges in their own pain, they're oblivious to his presence. I feel for him. He just came to their rescue, and they haven't offered thanks in any way. They only blame him. He's an outlier, but then I remember his mother, Allegra. She's wonderful, and she adores him and Oliver both. But still, the look on his face devastates me. Marge has noticed and puts her arm around him as she whispers something in his ear. She's the sweetest tough woman I've ever known.

I know we're going to have to talk to the cops and give

statements before any of us can leave. That will be tricky. I doubt that I'll tell them that I knew Ray and Carly were taking my daughter to Italy. I don't want him thrown back in prison for planning to violate parole, because that would leave Carly in our lives. They can live a long, happy life wherever—as long as I'm granted custody of Rayelle. Maybe I'll tell them that she took my daughter to New York City without asking my permission, and I was angry that she left me for another man. It's not exactly a lie, and they don't need to know everything. I'll play it by ear. I doubt Ray, Carly, or Raymond want to say any more.

Ken looks at a text on his phone and gives me a thumbs up. I exhale and feel weak in the knees. My kids are safe with Sherita and whoever else she has guarding them.

Never in my life have I felt the relief I do now. I've saved my daughter and reconnected with my son. So why, when I look at Ray, who stares back with such contempt, do I feel as if my entire world and everything I've known is about to blow up before my eyes?

CHAPTER TWENTY-THREE

The police have left, and everyone is drained. As statements were being taken, the police received a call that Gloria has awakened from surgery and was able to confirm the witness's report that Mack is the man who shot her. Her prognosis is good. Hearing that, Raymond lets the tears flow again, so immersed in his grief and relief that he barely remembers his plans to leave her forever.

Carly made sure the police heard her story first, and I was good with that. I let her say everything she wanted. She knows what I want, and I know what she wants.

True to form, she told the cops that I went to extremes to find my daughter because I'm too neurotic and out of control to have waited until they came home on Sunday night. Then, the character assassination really began. She went on and on about how I have a horrible habit of blowing everything out of proportion and that tracking her down in this hotel is a perfect example. I'm pitiful because I won't accept that the marriage was over, even after more than two years of no sex. She left out the part about never telling me we were over. I felt only numbness as she continued to stumble over her excessive and unsolicited explanation. Few insults went unspoken. Being the impulsive and overdramatic man that I am, I organized this "New York animal Mardi Gras" to stage a fake rescue so Rayelle would think of me as some superhero from the books I read to her. And sadly, our daughter's personality is much more like mine, and she's likely eaten up her emancipation with a big spoon. There was way more to Carly's fusillade of accusatory rhetoric than shaming me. That was actually the least important part of it. She was telling me what story we were going with while simultaneously warning me not to implicate her lover in anything. I know that. She's just lucky the cops were so focused on Mack. She's lucky I want her gone and didn't show her letter to the cops—which would have negated everything she said about just taking a weekend getaway.

The officer who read Mack his Miranda rights finally shut her down. They hadn't burst in to find out why we were dressed like animals or who Carly was having an affair with. They came to arrest Mack after a witness identified him as Gloria's shooter. They wanted to know about Mack and Raymond's relationship and to make sure Mack wasn't acting on his former boss's orders. For a moment, I thought Chaz might interject that his father possibly hired someone to shoot at us, but with no proof, it would have just complicated things. And it probably was Mack. That makes more sense. But who knows?

They were all instructed not to go anywhere. As clearly as Ray and Carly intend to ignore the warning, I'm sure Raymond is grateful for the out. It's pretty obvious he's staying in New York in hopes of reconciling with Gloria. Though I don't think Ray's figured that out yet.

I've already forgotten so much of what was said by the Royces because it didn't concern me, and I can't stop thinking about my children. I just hate that I experience a jolt to my system every time Ray speaks or sends death stares my way. It's horrible to endure things that you can't slap a name on or recognize, which until this day, has been my life story.

Normally, I'd feel so alone, but Marge and Chaz were keenly aware of my facial expressions and body language which no doubt clued them into the turmoil churning inside me. There were times when I almost thought Marge was going to ask for a break, but she didn't. She just watched me like a hawk, and Chaz wasn't far behind her. Ken paid the most attention to what was happening, probably because the rest of us were so distracted, and one of us needed to "take minutes."

The cops discovered that Ray is on parole, but as he wasn't breaking any laws, they warned him not to start now. Yeah, right.

Now it's the seven of us. The officers have left. Raymond is sitting on one of the beds, his head down, his feet on the floor, lost in his own world. Marge and Ken sit by the desk, and Chaz stands by my side.

Carly snarls at me. "Tell the animal brigade to take a hike."

"Are your lover and his father gonna go hiking as well?"

Ray looks like he wants to lurch at me again, but he stays still.

"No! Of course not," she says, flinging her hair behind her shoulders. "I want them to hear this conversation for themselves."

I stare at her, trying to keep my anger in check. "So, you want *your* witnesses, but mine should leave?"

Carly shoots a look at Marge and Ken. "As long as they stay quiet."

"They're not here to talk. Can we sit down?"

Ray gestures for Carly to sit next to Raymond on the edge of the bed. As he sits on the other side of her, I sit on the opposite bed. We're face-to-face. It's unnerving. I wait for Carly to start the real conversation. I can't help but notice her eye makeup is smudged. Not that it matters, but it occurs to me that she's been wearing more of it these past two years than ever. How stupid I was not to pick up on that. Not to mention the new clothes she was buying.

"Not that you can't figure this out for yourself, Liam." She's spitting her words. "But I want a divorce."

"So do I."

"Good." She lets out a sigh of relief. "Glad we're in agreement." She releases the scowl on her face from captivity. "As a matter of fact, I've had divorce papers drawn up. I was going to have them sent to you, but since you're here, you can sign them now." She makes a move to get up.

"Whoa! Hold on. I'm not signing anything until I get sole custody of Rayelle. And I want half of the cash back that you took from our joint accounts and the safe."

Carly's body jerks as if she's just been tased. "But we need that to live on!" The scowl returns before it can get too far away.

"So your husband-to-be needs *my* money to support you? Really? And you don't think your daughter needs money?"

Ray sneers and nods in my direction. "Give him his fucking money, Carly. We don't need shit from him except his signature and his silence. We still have your half, and I have my own money. Not to mention, I'll make a lot more."

Defeated, she mumbles her acquiescence.

I straighten my posture. I'm proud of myself. I knew phrasing my opposition that way would get under Ray's skin. "Okay, I'll call my lawyer and have him draw up custody papers—"

"Oh my God, Liam!" Carly laughs. "You're such a pathetic liar.

You don't have an attorney. You went all half-cocked and came here looking for me. I don't even think you know any attorneys, much less have one to call. You just don't want to admit you were hoping I'd come back to you." She looks at Ray. "He totally was!"

"No, Carly, I wasn't." I reach into my pocket and pull out Bob's card. "Robert Fitzgerald Dansworth," I say, holding up the card but making sure she doesn't take it. "He's a powerful New York attorney. Not only is he representing me, but we rode from Trenton to Penn Station together on the train."

"Bullshit!"

"I did. I swear on the life of Rayelle and Oliver. And really, Carly, does it matter? I have an attorney."

"Whatever." She stops to release some of the steam building up in her kettle-like head. "Do you think I don't love my daughter? Because I do!"

"In your own twisted way, yeah, probably. But Rayelle is low on your priority list. You took her from the only home she's ever known, and you traumatized her. And I don't think you purposely wanted to hurt her, but you wanted to hurt me and didn't care what happened to her in the process. That's the problem."

"Rayelle's always liked you better," Carly snaps. "I hate that! I only wanted her to forget you and learn to love me more."

"By kidnapping her and telling her that her adoring father never wants to see her again? Are you delusional? Do you not think that's about as selfish a motive as there is? She's a human being with feelings. Not a carnival prize. And if you think she prefers me, maybe it's because she's always known you prefer Oliver. Because he's Ray's biological son. A day doesn't go by when you haven't ignored her in one way or another."

"Oh, really. Give me an example!"

"For one, you're never interested in putting her to bed. You'd rather snuggle with your iPad. For me, that's the best part of every day: spending quality time with my little girl before she nods off."

Carly shoots me a dirty look. "You've brainwashed her, so why should I even try to put her to bed and be shot down?"

"Seriously. That's the best you can do? I wouldn't think of brainwashing my children. This is on you, Carly. Even though nobody understood what was behind your actions, it's clear now that Oliver has always been a walking, breathing souvenir from your teenage days with Ray. It all makes sense, and even without a label, that obsessive love has been on display for years. Your feelings have not only made Rayelle uncomfortable, but Oliver's never felt loved for being his own person, even before he was able to grasp why. So there's that. The kid went into hiding because he didn't want to go anywhere with either one of you or his newly minted grandfather. He didn't want to change his last name. He just never expected you'd take his sister."

"Aren't you the all-knowing oracle—of bullshit!"

I'm trying not to make eye contact with Ray, even as I speak his name. Every time our eyes meet, I shrink inside myself and want to run. It's a horrible feeling. I can't let him rattle me. I know Chaz understands why I'm feeling this way, but I hardly have time to pull him aside now for an explanation. I don't know why I keep thinking of the name Hunk. Then I remember how twice Chaz called his brother Felonious Hunk, a play on the jazz pianist Thelonious Monk's name. I thought it was just wordplay, but maybe Ray was called Hunk back in the day. I remember Sherita telling me he got Carly pregnant at fifteen, but that he regularly had sex with a bunch of girls who were legal. Yeah, Hunk was probably an appropriate name.

Wait! What the hell is wrong with me! I'm *not* remembering Hunk from long ago, I'm just remembering the name from Friday night, and my convoluted brain is trying to make it into something else. I need to stop doing things like this. But wait; if I'm only remembering a nickname from a recent conversation, why is Ray so eerily familiar? He definitely knows me and not because I'm married to his girlfriend. I feel dazed and defeated, but I return to the conversation. "Carly, everyone in this room is *really* tired. Why don't we just come to an agreement and skip the part where we hurl insults at one another? Can we do that?"

"I'm not signing anything that says I can't ever see my daughter again!"

I remind myself to stay calm. I look at Carly, and while she's still exotic and beautiful, my attraction to her has disappeared into thin air. "I'm not asking you to. When you get wherever you're going, if you're in a calm, kind, and rational state of mind, you can video chat with her. You can visit with her if you come back to this country—if she wants to see you. I love our little girl, Carly, and I have her best interests at heart. And having her mother in her life, in whatever way that fits, is part of that. It doesn't have to be in any traditional sense. I think it remains to be seen what will work out."

She can only bring herself to give me another dirty look, but I know that's because she doesn't have an appropriate answer or retort.

"Look, Carly, give me an address where I can reach you. And your attorney, too, when you get one. Our attorneys can work together to make sure we both get what we want."

"Do you really think I trust you not to fuck me over and send the law after Ray?"

"You probably don't trust me with anything. But know this: I want the two of you to be happy. I don't want my daughter's life to be disrupted again. Why would I want Ray back in prison and you miserable and vengeful? Think about that, Carly. How would that benefit me? I'll tell you: it wouldn't."

A few moments pass before she responds. "Okay, but I'm still not giving you our new address."

"Fine. But make sure you do give me all of Rayelle's belongings before I leave."

She snickers at me in contempt.

Raymond, who's returned to the realm of awareness, speaks up. "I can serve as the conduit, liaison, or whatever is necessary. I'm not going anywhere. I was wrong to want to be a part of my son's new life. And I was very wrong to leave the woman who has loved me for so many years. I'm praying that she recovers and that she'll give me a chance to make it up to her."

I was wondering when he'd fess up.

"I get it, but wow, really? You're not coming, Dad?" Ray's disappointment is obvious. "I was looking forward to having that time with you."

Carly suppresses a smile. It's not surprising she's happy about this change in plans.

"Believe me, I was looking forward to it as well, son, but my life is in New York. I'll always be here for you. In any and every way you need me to be."

Chaz shakes off a chill. His father won't even acknowledge

him. I'm lucky to have such loving parents. I can't imagine his devastation.

"So, listen." Carly shifts her hips and puts her hand on the left one. "Just to be clear." She pauses to snicker. "I'll leave the divorce papers with Ray's dad, and he'll find us an attorney. That's what we're agreeing to, right?"

"That's it."

"Okay, well, then I need to say good-bye to my daughter. And let Ray and I talk to our son."

What a nasty gut punch. "He's *our* son, Carly. A grown man who can make up his own mind." I take a breath. "And I think he already has."

Ray is squeezing his fists together. He looks angry enough to implode, but he's biting his tongue.

"Then let me see my daughter. You can at least do that. No excuses."

"I'm not going to make excuses, Carly. Just listen to me." I stiffen as I prepare to tell her something she probably doesn't want to hear. "We're leaving this hotel shortly. I'm happy for you to say good-bye to Rayelle if that's what she wants. I'm going to ask her, and hear me when I tell you, I have no intention of swaying her either way. Our sweet girl has been through so much, and I'm not forcing her to do one more thing that might traumatize her."

"Saying good-bye to her mother isn't traumatic!" Carly growls.

"It could be. If that mother is one and the same who took her away from everything that matters to her and told lies about her father. Yeah, it could be."

I look at Marge, who smiles sympathetically and nods. She and

Ken haven't said a word, and rightly so, but I've felt their support so strongly.

I stand to go as Ray gets up as well. Carly remains seated and stares at me while Ray walks to the closet, opens the safe, and counts out a lot of money. He walks to me. The anger in his eyes unnerves me even more. "Here's fifty grand. Hold on."

Without thinking, I turn and hand the money to Ken.

Ray goes back to the closet, pulls out Rayelle's luggage, then drops it in front of me, giving me a you-bastard-take-your-crap-and-go look.

I nod and turn to Carly. "I *will* ask Rayelle if she wants to say good-bye. *And* Oliver. If you think I won't do it, understand that I would never want my children to resent me for not giving them the choice. If I'm not back in ten minutes, well, you know."

Carly, slumping where she sits, says nothing as Ray sits and puts his arm around her.

Immediately, Ken takes the luggage from me and heads to the door.

Marge offers me a comforting arm as we follow. Staying behind, for only a moment, is Chaz. Even though I'm heading out the door and unable to see him or anyone else, I know he's taking last looks at his family. Sadly, I'm quite sure they're not looking at him. I don't understand their cruelty. There has to be more to this story, rational or not. That's just the way life ... and families ... seem to be sometimes.

Saturday, 12:46 p.m.

Twenty-four hours ago, I was having an Italian hoagie and Dr. Pepper with a work buddy before going to the bank to cash my paycheck. It's beyond phantasmagorical what's happened since.

I hurry down the hall with Marge, Ken, and Chaz. I can't get to my kids fast enough. My fist taps out my no-longer-secret knock with Rayelle, and she calls out for someone to let me in, which Oliver does.

My little girl flies into my arms as everyone takes the first seat they can. Sherita, with a huge grin, watches as we reunite for the second time. She's had extra chairs brought in, and a guard I've not seen before sits quietly in the room.

Rayelle pulls me over to the bed where Paddington is lying, and we sit. I know he was happy to see her again.

"It felt like forever for you to come back, Daddy. I was afraid they'd try to take you away too."

How adorable. She's just so precious. "No, honey, believe me, I'm the last person they want with them."

"I thought like maybe they'd take you so we couldn't be together."

"Not a chance, baby."

"But isn't that why they took me?"

I feel a thud in my gut. What a perceptive child. "I don't know for sure. But I do know that we're together again. And we're going to stay together. That's a promise."

Rayelle hugs me.

"I hate to interrupt," Sherita says, "but it's probably best that the three of you head back to my hotel and not spend any more time here. That's why I don't have any food waiting. If you're hungry, my kitchen staff at the Curtain Call is ready to rock 'n' roll."

"That's so thoughtful," I say as I ponder how underwhelming the word is to describe my appreciation and gratitude to everyone in the room. "And leaving here is exactly what I'd planned to do. I just have to ask Rayelle and Oliver something before we go anywhere." I swallow the lump in my throat. "I have to ask you both if you want to say—"

"No way," Oliver says.

Rayelle looks confused. "What, Daddy?"

I summon my courage. The question isn't as easy as I thought it would be. "We're leaving here to go to another hotel. Mommy is still down the hall in her room, and she's still going away with her *friend*. She really wants to say good-bye. I told her that wasn't my decision to make and that I would ask the two of you. That's what I'm doing."

"No! I don't want to see her. Please, don't make me, Daddy!"

Oliver exhales. "Nobody will make you do anything you don't want, Ray-Ray. Didn't I tell you that?"

I look at both of them. "I know your mom has hurt you, but I need to be really sure you don't want to take advantage of this opportunity. She's still your mom. I don't want you to regret anything later. I can't say when you'll get another chance."

"I'm super-duper sure." Rayelle squeezes Paddington in a tight hug. "Double triple and that other word."

"Quadruple," I say.

"Yeah, that one!"

Oliver says nothing, but his darkened eyes say everything.

"Okay, then. That's fine." I stroke Rayelle's hair and look into her beautiful brown eyes. "If you're both sure it's what you want."

"One-hundred," Oliver mumbles.

Rayelle appears to have forgotten what we were talking about. "Guess what, Daddy?"

"What, honey?"

"As soon as Oliver got me away from Mommy and her stupid boyfriend, guess what happened?"

"Tell me!"

"Look!" She points to the window. "The sun came out!"

I glance outside and smile. Indeed, the rain's gone, and the sun's shining brightly. My mother taught me that there are no coincidences, and if there was ever a moment to believe that, it is right now.

Oliver, who's hyperaware that I'm fading fast, takes Rayelle and introduces her to Marge, Ken, and Chaz. They welcome her like the family they've become to me.

Ken spends only a moment with Rayelle, then turns to look in my direction. Patting his chest, he reminds me that he has my money tucked away and gestures toward the safe in the closet. I nod, agreeing that he should put my money in the backpack once he opens it. He does exactly that, then hands it to me.

"I can't thank you enough, Ken. I don't want to think about how things would have turned out without you."

"Then don't. It's all good." He smiles, then returns to Marge, who's still chatting with Rayelle.

I pull out my cell phone and turn it on. A lot of missed calls from my parents. There's a text from my boss telling me I'm fired for never coming back to work, never calling again, and refusing to explain why I couldn't. I let him know I had a crisis. That's enough.

It's still none of his business, and I won't miss the job. I turn the phone off again. Not taking any chances right now.

All I want is to spend time with my children, but I have to face the inevitable; I'm ready to crash—and hard. Everything that matters is in this room with me, and I wish I could just let the rest vanish into thin air.

But something is gnawing at me. Ray. Hunk. Whatever name he goes by. It was no coincidence that I had such a visceral reaction to him. And it wasn't because Carly and he are together. It has nothing to do with her. He clearly hates me with every fiber of his being. The more I think about it, the more fear squeezes me. It's getting tighter and tighter, and it won't let go. Please, God, not now. I just got my children back. Let me be sane and happy, please.

Marge sees my pained face and comes over to me, leaving Ken and Chaz to occupy Rayelle, as they happily do.

She sits in the spot Rayelle vacated. "Honey, listen to me. We're all wrecked, but I don't think any of us have ever been so tired for such a glorious reason. Ken, Chaz, and I are going to leave. Sherita's going to have you driven back to her hotel. She's got a couple men here who are going to tail Carly and Ray to make sure they take off for Italy. Meanwhile, just to be safe, someone will be guarding your room at the Curtain Call. This is only a precaution—I don't think there's anything to worry about. And I've got a nose for trouble; trust me."

I look at her face and see a whole lot more than fatigue. I know she has a nose for trouble, and that's why I'm so concerned. There's something she is reluctant to tell me. But she needs to. "What else is there, Marge? Please."

She puts her right hand on my shoulder, and her eyes shower me with love. "We all need to sleep. For a long time. Tomorrow is Sunday. I live in the brownstone with the green door that's to the right of my restaurant. Why don't you come by? Say twelve thirty? Sherita's offered to come by your room at the Curtain Call around noon or before to take your kids out for the afternoon. She'll bring them back to my place after I let her know all's well.

After all is well? What in the world is she talking about? This has to be connected to my intense reaction to Ray and vice versa—as well as everything else that is a mystery in my life. But how would Marge know any of this? Then I remember: after she rescued me from that basement, I asked her point blank if there had been previous times. She never said no. She only said that it wasn't the time to talk about it. I'm guessing tomorrow is the time. My anxiety should be through the roof now, but it's as tired as I am. I feel my eyelids closing. "This is huge, isn't it?"

She just smiles. "Tomorrow around twelve-thirty."

"I am seriously crashing. I don't know how to thank any of you," I say.

Marge's tired eyes look lovingly at me. "We've already been thanked. The moment Oliver called out to you in the lobby and Rayelle ran to you in the hallway, we felt it."

My shoulders droop as my fatigue climbs another rung or two toward the top of the tired ladder. "I'm going to eat a quick bite and go to sleep. I feel so guilty when I want to be with the kids."

"They're reuniting with one another as well. Your amazing son will take great care of your beautiful daughter while you have a long, deep sleep. You'll have plenty of time to be together. There's nothing else you need to do right now."

I remember the missed calls from my mother when I finally turned on my phone. "Well, there's my mom. She must be so worried. I spoke to her briefly last night, but that feels like another lifetime. I had seven missed calls from her just now. I'd call her, but she'll have way too many questions, and I'm way too tired. So tired."

"I know, honey."

Marge stands to address everyone in the room. "Time for us all to get going. Grab whatever you brought with you and the cash from any pockets you picked." She laughs. "Kidding! Just making sure you're all still awake. Check that the safe is empty and nothing is left around. Nothing personal in the trash baskets either."

As everyone stands, Marge turns to me. "I'll call your mom for you. Don't worry."

Chaz, Ken, and Marge give me huge hugs and leave. Sherita will be driving back to the hotel with us. While Rayelle uses the bathroom, the driver takes her luggage out of the room which now looks as empty as it did when we arrived.

Five minutes later, after having made sure we're not being watched, we're in the freight elevator going down. Because I don't have enough going on in my head, I allow a strange thought to enter without knocking. Marge said she'd call my mom. She never even asked for her number. She doesn't know her first name, yet she sounded like it was the most natural thing in the world.

CHAPTER TWENTY-FOUR

When we got to our adjoining rooms at the Curtain Call yesterday, I couldn't help but note that it had been twenty-four hours since my world fell apart and was put back together again.

We ordered some food, and I talked as much as I could until my kids ordered *me* to sleep. I think I closed my eyes around 2:00 p.m. and I didn't open them again until 8:00 a.m. this morning. I don't ever remember having slept eighteen hours before, but then again, I don't remember the first fourteen years of my life. So there's that. I'm awake and happy, but a strong feeling of trepidation sits in the pit of my stomach.

Sherita came by around 10:30 a.m. I gave Oliver a wad of cash and told him to make sure that his sister and this lovely woman have an incredible afternoon. They've booked tickets for the 1:30 p.m. Circle Line Tour, the same one in the brochure that Sherita gave me Friday night. They're going to have lunch in the café on the boat. Oh, and I was assured that Carly and Ray left on a flight the night before, just shy of midnight, to Naples, Italy. And Raymond was seen entering the hospital where Gloria was admitted and hasn't left yet. Word is that she's going to make it. I hope so.

After Sherita left with my kids, I ran down to the haberdashery off the lobby that Sherita recommended. I bought two new outfits, then came back to the room and took the longest shower I'd ever had … followed by a shave. Putting on new clothes felt wonderful. The sun is shining, and my world is good again. I just know that something is about to drastically change. But no matter what I'm about to learn, nothing could be worse than what I've been through. That much I know.

Sunday, 12:35 p.m.

I'm standing outside Marge's green front door with the prettiest, most colorful bouquet of flowers I could find. I know Ken and Chaz are inside with her. I've bonded with these people in a way few people ever do, yet I'm terrified to go in and see them anew. It's almost like meeting them all over again, and I've always had a problem with new people.

Just as I'm about to ring the bell, Marge opens the door. "Well aren't you a sight for sore eyes. Come in, Liam. I was going to wait it out and see how long it took for you to let us know you were here, but I decided to put you out of your misery. You look as bright-eyed and bushy-tailed as the rest of us." She eyes the bouquet. "Are those beauties for me?"

"They are." I hand them to her. Despite her warm welcome, I'm still standing outside. Marge laughs, takes me by the arm, and pulls me in. Ken is sitting on the couch, and Chaz, who no longer looks like the scruffy guy I first saw, is settled comfortably in one of two matching armchairs.

"I'm going to put these in a vase with some water." Marge hurries to the kitchen.

The room is warm and loving. There's a huge brown, green, and orange-red area rug over the hardwood floors. Three walls are painted sage, the fourth one bare brick with a fireplace. Plants hang in the bay windows, and there are photos and art everywhere. I'm far from being a decorator, but I've always thought that a person's home says a lot about them. The warmth of being surrounded by earthy colors assuages some of my fears.

"Well, you clean up good," Chaz says. "Who knew a shower and a shave would be the best disguise of all. I barely recognize you, man."

"And you barely resemble the big scruff of a guy I first saw in Sweep's. In fact, I thought of you as Scruff until I learned your name."

"You could have called me a lot worse," Chaz says.

"Who says I didn't?" I grin.

"Touché."

"Hey, Liam, good to see you." Ken stands, walks over, and gives me a strong hug. "Have a seat. No matter how much sleep you got, I know you don't want to stand."

I sit in a comfortable chair that matches the one Chaz is in.

For me, there's an unsettling awkwardness between me and the people who I speed-bonded with during the most emergent and frightening time of my remembered life. I still feel the intense connection, but it's in a light-of-day reality. I have to get to know them all over again. Maybe it's what waking up after a one-night stand is like, only I've never done one of those. I was always shy, on the traditional side.

The doorbell rings. I snap back into panic mode, my heart racing, but it turns out to be a friend of Marge's who she calls "Sammio," the manager of an Italian restaurant who brings over a charcuterie board that she'd specifically ordered for lunch. He apologizes for running late. Together, they clear off the coffee table and set everything up in no time, including a small tray with drinks and trays for eating. Sammio quickly leaves as Marge's profuse thanks follow him to the front door.

I never even knew the word "charcuterie" before, but seeing the spread of cheeses, salami, cold cuts, grapes, pickles, crackers, bread, dips, and so much more tells me that I've indeed known charcuterie boards before; we've just never been formally introduced. Why am I having this inane conversation with myself? Because I'm scared. I know that.

"Everyone, help yourselves." Marge takes a small plate and leads the way.

I'm still glancing around. As I see the art, I can't help but remember my middle-of-the-night adventures in the two apartments I visited with Chaz. But Marge's home is warm and inviting, and I tell her that.

"This house is finally a home again," she says. "Ever since I threw that beer-guzzling, tail-chasing nightmare out of here. Our marriage has been long over, but the bastard wouldn't leave. Finally, I got his ass out of here, but that doesn't stop him from doing the wobbly dance into my restaurant every week and begging for me to take him back. Came in last night. Just after you left."

"Oh. Aren't you getting divorced soon? Has he stopped fooling around?" I ask, knowing my question is an awkward time filler and that she and Ken are clearly together.

"Yes we are, and hell no, he hasn't. Just wants to live in this beautiful house again, and that ain't gonna happen. I got over that man a very long time ago. That's why I put that tracker in a couple of his jackets when I did. Needed proof for the divorce I'll be getting soon."

I shove some salami and cheese into my mouth while I can still eat and wash it down with some of the Italian lemonade. I have a feeling that whatever is coming will render me unable to put food in my stomach for a while. I take a piece of bread and smear it with some garlic herb spread. Delicious. It takes my mind off my current situation for all of two seconds.

Everyone else looks nervous too, but mostly Marge and Chaz.

"Okay," Marge says, inhaling then exhaling what seems like all the breath in her body. "There are a million places to begin; I just don't know which one of them to choose."

Chaz looks at her with concern. "There's no easy way to do this. You've just got to rip the Band-Aid off."

Whatever Chaz is talking about, I know one thing: the Band-Aid is mine.

CHAPTER TWENTY-FIVE

"You're right, Chaz," Marge says softly. "I think I can do this."

"You can, honey." Ken speaks softly as they make eye contact. "Go at your own pace."

She glances at him before giving me her full attention. "Liam, it's time for me to tell you a little bit about my life." She takes a few sips of coffee. "Can't pretend I'm too tired to speak. This java is powerful stuff, and I've had way more than forty winks. Never been so damn wide awake actually." She exhales. "Okay, no more diverting course. I'll start with my high school days in Manhattan." She offers a self-conscious smile that's incongruous with her big personality. "That's where I met the love of my life, Ken Julson. I knew he was my forever guy right from the get-go." She looks at him ever so briefly. "But when we graduated, his father moved the family to Vegas." Frowning, Marge turns to him again, this time with pleading eyes.

Ken smiles. "Let me take over here, honey." He stops to finish a piece of melon he was eating. "See, my dad had a lifelong dream of owning a nightclub on the Strip. He'd been looking into all kinds of opportunities for years. Every one of them would fall through, so I never told Margie because I didn't think it would ever be a reality. Neither did my mother, brother, or sister. We thought we were just humoring him as he chased a dream. But then, the stars aligned, and my dad found exactly what he was looking for. Honestly, I was in a state of shock, but I hid that from him. He was up there on cloud nine;

I couldn't destroy his euphoria." He lets out a painful sigh. "Let me tell you, with every cell of my being, I hated leaving my girl, but I'd made a promise to my dad to be by his side if he got a club. I figured I'd just help him get things rolling, then get rolling myself—back to New York. Only *things* took an unexpected nosedive for a while after he got shot outside one of the casinos. An unfortunate situation of just being in the wrong place at the wrong time. Nothing to do with him personally, but he took the bullet. I couldn't go anywhere. Had to work even harder at the club and for longer hours. My family needed me, and it was a pretty intense recovery. So, my brother, sister, and I stayed on." A wicked smile appears on his lips. "And yeah, that's when I started carrying and becoming the beefy, take-no-prisoners but adorable Karma Ken you see before you."

Marge laughs, and her eyes fill with love.

Ken reaches over to the board and casually spreads some cheese on a cracker. "Eventually, I had a talk with my brother, Al, and he told me I'd sacrificed enough. Said he and my dad were good on their own if I needed to go. So, finally feeling I could leave free of guilt, I came back to New York for a visit. When I learned Margie was married, I was devastated but not surprised. Never so much as let her know I was in the city. Just made a U-turn back to the desert after catching up with some friends here. And I resumed my job at the club."

This isn't what I expected to hear, and I'm not sure how it concerns me, but I know more will be revealed if I don't pass out from anticipation and nerves first.

"I've got it from here." Marge smiles at Ken. "Thanks, honey." She puts a hand on her forehead and gazes down. "I was an idiot." She looks up at me. "No, that's too kind a word for the foolish, brash, headstrong Margaret Maeve O'Toole. Sure, I grew up knowing more about life than most kids my age ever will, but I was so devastated about Ken leaving that I didn't stop to reassess my options. I didn't consider going with him because I knew we'd have zero time together with his brutal work schedule. And yeah, I love New York. As I tried to make sense out of everything, I decided only fools and suckers waited, and I didn't believe Ken would ever come back. With all of those women in Vegas, I'd be an idiot to think he wouldn't meet someone. How could he not? Why wait like a fool and throw away my young life? 'I'll show him,' I told myself." She stops and takes a few sips of coffee. "So what did I do? I threw away my young life. Didn't waste any time doing so. Got myself involved with some loser-boozer guy: Harry tail-chasing, money-washing, human-beer receptacle Salinksy—and all of the havoc he wreaked."

Nausea swirls in my stomach. I don't know why, but the name knocks on the door of my brain demanding attention. I'm jittery and anxious, so I reach for a few green grapes to at least occupy my hands.

"Harry was a looker back then, and he had big bucks to spend. I told myself Ken would be sorry he left me, but I didn't realize I'd be a lot sorrier for taking up with the likes of Harry." She sighs. "Ken and I had made a clean break. I insisted on it. But there were many times when I considered calling him in hopes of reuniting, then flying to Vegas and having Elvis marry us in some fantasy chapel. But I stopped those thoughts after a while. I knew I had to put him out of my mind to survive. And then I married Harry, had a child, and began life with a criming maniac. I'd made my choice and stepped up to embrace the life I'd chosen."

I glance at Chaz, and he's not making eye contact with me. He's just nibbling at the food on his plate, waiting for Marge to tell more of her story.

"Would I be wrong in guessing that being married to Harry was how you ended up doing time?" I ask.

"Bingo! Sure was. I went along with all kinds of nutso garbage despite being angry at him a good deal of the time. Harry and his cohorts ruffled every red feather I had. Young Margie bird wasn't as savvy as she thought. Chirping nonstop about something you don't want to do doesn't matter in the eyes of the law if you go ahead and do it. You know? I was idiotic to believe my spoken protests would somehow absolve me of my guilt if the law caught up to me. Nobody cared that I was somewhat coerced. I did the crimes, so I did the time. And that's all you need to know, except that I was dumb enough to be suckered back into the same habits after my first release. Didn't do much to lower the prison's recidivism rates." She pushes the coffee cup away. "Enough caffeine." She pours herself a small glass of lemonade. "By the way, I went by Margie when I was first incarcerated, but that name was too sweet for prison life, so I became Marge. Has more of a tough ring to it."

"Still Margie to me." Ken sends her a loving look that reveals his shared pain.

"What happened to your child when you went to prison," I ask, feeling like a heavyweight boxing match is going on in my stomach.

Marge smiles uneasily. "The first time, my mother and grandmother stepped in and took over. Harry was sentenced at the same time, but even if he hadn't been, I'd never have left a child in his care. That aside, it about killed me not to see my kid." She cuts a small slice of brie. "It's times like this when I'm glad I quit smoking all those years ago. I'd have gone through two packs by now." She pops the cheese in her mouth.

"Tell me about it," Chaz says. "I quit twelve years ago, then broke down and had half a pack Friday night dealing with all of my family's shit. Then I realized I wasn't going to let them mess me up any more than they had. So I quit. On the same day I started again." He makes a face. "Sorry, Marge. Go back to what you were saying."

Marge politely finishes chewing. "I loved my son with every breath of my body. I still do."

I don't know why I was sure she had a boy, but this is the first mention of her child's gender. The bell rings, and Round Two begins in my stomach.

"My circumstances didn't allow me to be the mother he deserved. I was so busy with my husband and his associates that I was oblivious to the troubles my boy had at school and in the neighborhood."

"He was bullied," I say matter-of-factly, as if I was there to witness it. "The kids were really mean to him."

"They were, Liam. And when he was fourteen, this older guy, who knew the hell my kid was going through, befriended him for no other reason than to take advantage. He knew my son spent a lot of time in the presence of criminals. Told him that he'd be forever grateful to whatever 'cool kid' out there could get him a gun for protection. He knew my child was bullied and coveted the 'cool' label more than anything. This guy said that if my son helped him, he'd make sure nobody ever fucked with Eddie Salinksy again."

There's a powerful jolt to my system. The boxers are still throwing punches. I stop to breathe. I remember the woman in the pink bathrobe from Friday night when I was on my way to Baradino's. She was screaming the name Eddie, and I got lost in some kind of momentary fog. Some man walking by with his wife wanted to call and get me help. They thought I was crazy. *This* is crazy. There can't be any connection. Eddie is such a common name. But I know more about him than I should. I know kids used to beat the crap out of him.

Marge has stopped talking, and I'm sure it's because she can see my face distorting as my brain fights to understand.

"You okay, Liam?" Ken asks. "Because Margie can wait for a better time if that's what you'd like."

There is no better time. Postponing the inevitable, whatever that may be, is the dead last thing I need. I can't see my kids again with my thoughts sizzling like stir-fry vegetables in a wok. "Please, tell me whatever I need to know."

"I think I should take over now," Chaz says.

Wait, what? How can Chaz take over Marge's story? How does that compute?

"I'd appreciate it." Putting a hand to her neck, she exhales, then slumps. She looks as overwhelmed as I feel.

Chaz is nervous. He reminds me of myself. "Well, Houdini, to say you've met my older brother is an understatement. For the record, he's four years older than you and two years older than me."

I'm wondering why Chaz is so precise about age, but I expect I'll find out. Shortly.

"Back when he was around, everyone in the neighborhood called him Hunk."

I'm feeling sicker by the moment. Like both boxers just punched me instead of each other.

"Carly was his number one. He met her uptown at this private school where he worked part-time doing maintenance. She recognized him from a job he once did in her apartment building a few years earlier. They started talking, and yeah, before long, they started doing a whole lot more than that, but not in their own hood where anyone would know them. Not to mention, most of their time was spent indoors." Chaz clears his throat. "Sorry, Liam." I give him my best no-problem look, and he resumes talking. "Back in the hood, Ray also had a small harem of girls he could be openly seen with ... girls that allowed him to get some, uh, you know, whenever he wanted it. That Sandy chick you saw at Baradino's was one of them. She was madly in love with him, but her anatomy was the only thing he cared about. As Marge just told you, the company you keep can really fuck up your life."

"Sure as hell can," she says. "Excuse my big mouth. The floor is yours."

Chaz lightly waves his hands in a don't-worry gesture. "Well, aside from the legit maintenance jobs he got and the supposed right path he was on, Ray started hanging with the wrong kind of friends when he was about thirteen or so. I never understood why my father seemed to love him more for it, but he did. From what the old man spilled yesterday, he didn't want Ray to break bad the way he apparently did at that age." His face reddens. "I'm not sure how treating your younger son like dirt helps to that end, but that's the road my father walked. I'm guessing it's because his own father was on the abusive side, so he decided that coddling Ray no matter what would bring different results. You know, like he was afraid Ray would rebel if he dissed his trouble-making friends, so he just heaped the love on him instead. Thought being some kind of steady fatherly presence in Ray's life would keep him on the straight and narrow. But fuck any fatherly presence he might show with his younger son. Yeah, fuck *him!*" Chaz tries to shrug off his anger. "Sorry. Anyway, my father had to work, and despite being the great dad to Ray he thought he was, he had no clue how bad his oldest son's friends really were. These guys Ray hung with quickly went from shoplifting to robbing businesses at gunpoint. Nice, huh?"

I shiver. I can't let my emotions show on my face or be revealed with any erratic body movements. I try to remain impassive, then wish myself luck with that one as I grab a wedge of cheddar to deter me from exposing my fear.

"You're doing great, Chaz. You okay to keep going?" Marge asks.

"Gotta do this. Not just for Houdini, but for all of us." He spreads his fingers apart and stretches them, as if he's warming up to play the piano or something. "I was obsessed with having my father's love. I hated that my brother routinely fucked up and that my father would respond by paying even more attention to him. Anyway, one day, when Ray was eighteen, and I think I told you some of this next part on Friday night, I overheard Ray telling a friend he didn't want to be sucked into the family business and needed a chunk of cash to do his own thing. So he was going to rob this grocer. Ray said he told this naïve kid with criminal parents that if he got him a gun for protection, he'd stop all the bullies from bothering him again—*and* be his friend. I remember Ray kind of snickering, saying that kids of criminals usually have better bullshit detectors, but this one was different. Kind of a sad loner."

I suppress a vocal response, but just barely.

Marge buries her head in her hands for moment, then looks at Chaz. "Please, don't stop now."

His fingers now interlocked, Chaz stretches his arms, then stops. He draws a breath. "This shit is harder than I thought, and I didn't think it would be easy."

"You're doing great," Ken assures him.

I want to say something, but keeping sane is the best I can do. The break between boxing rounds has begun. I'm a bit calmer.

"So, when I heard this robbery was going down, I needed to see it for myself. I wasn't sure if Ray was just laying it on thick to impress his friend, or if he was really going through with it. Two days later, a half hour before the time he'd told his friend what would happen, I watched Ray like a hawk, then followed at a distance. I put on old clothes he wouldn't recognize and wore a Yankee cap since I'm a diehard Mets fan. The streets were crowded, and it was easy to follow him and not be noticed. Then, when I saw him go down this alley, I hid behind this, uh, dumpster...."

"You have a long history with them," I say to Chaz, unsure if I'm trying to be funny or not.

"Uh, yeah." Chaz doesn't acknowledge the humor, but I know he got it. He's just as messed up as I am right now.

He starts to reach for something off the charcuterie board, then thinks twice about it. "Even before I hid, while I was still a good distance behind, I could see Eddie nervously looking around as he watched Ray approaching." Chaz appears to shiver in revulsion as his mind plays back the scene. "Once I'm behind the dumpster, close enough to hear, my brother wastes no time with small talk, not even a fucking hello, and tells the kid to show him the goods. Eddie pulls the gun out from underneath his jacket. It was wrapped in a white T-shirt. The kid's a wreck and a half. Hates guns. Tells Ray that he needs to promise he'll take the bullets out if there are any. Not knowing anything about guns, Eddie didn't know how to check and was petrified of doing the wrong thing. Ray tells him to stay put, then walks several yards away and pretends to be removing bullets. He was even laughing at how naïve Eddie was. Not that I was a mind reader, but I knew my brother." Chaz's eyes close, and a pained look comes over him. "Next thing I know, Ray is telling Eddie they're going inside to talk to the owner. At that moment, the kid understands what's going down, finds his anger, and says a loud and firm, 'No way!' Ray's stunned to learn Eddie has a voice, but by that time, he doesn't give a flying fuck. He points the gun at him and tells him they're going in through the back door, through the storage room, into the store." Chaz sighs and looks away from all of us. "The only reason the back door was open is because the owner, Jack Keneally, had been unloading deliveries and putting boxes in the dumpster after flattening them." Chaz looks sick to his stomach. "Ray had been watching him for a while, so he knew what day he got deliveries." He sighs in disgust. "I ran into the room and hid in an empty paper towel carton that Keneally had just unpacked."

For a moment, I have an out-of-body experience, and I'm inside the grocery store. Mr. Keneally's pallid, stunned face is in front of me as the tears threaten to roll. I take a deep breath and return to Marge's living room.

"Within seconds, Ray and Eddie are inside, and I hear the kid begging Ray to leave. He's scared out of his fucking mind as he realizes that Hunk lied to him, and he's an unwitting accomplice in a robbery. That's when I learned that the kid lived behind the store, and Mr. Keneally knew him well. Man, Eddie was distraught that his friend would think he would ever rob him, and he's begging Ray to put the gun down, crying his eyes out as Ray calls him a fucking crybaby pussy. Keneally, trying desperately to stop the robbery, tells Eddie he thought they were friends and says his address aloud, you know, to remind Eddie he knows exactly where to find him or to send the police. I'm shocked he lives so close. In tears, Eddie asks Ray if he really took the bullets out and gets fucking laughed at in the most demoralizing way before Ray calls him a pussy again."

"Nooooo!" I shout.

Everyone looks at me.

"You want me to stop?" Chaz says. "I will. I know this is really tough."

"Yes, but no," I say, my breath hitching. "Keep talking." My head feels like it's about to explode. Forget the boxing match in my stomach. I think the ref killed both fighters. Why do I have to analogize everything? Why can't I just deal with reality? I think about Rayelle and Oliver and hope they're having a good time on the boat with Sherita. I think about my parents. I think about everything good in my life and pray it will stop the oncoming freight train. There I go again. I'm so confused. I look at Chaz who's waiting for permission to continue. He didn't believe I meant it the first time. "Seriously, go on."

Chaz gulps. "I get it. This is a whole fucking lot to process."

"Go on," I repeat.

"Okay, so I make this hole in the fold of the carton, and I see there's a customer in the store. Nobody I've ever seen before. A forty-something-year-old Black dude, nicely dressed. He's hiding in the canned vegetables and meats aisle. Scared out of his mind. And I know my brother thinks the store is empty save for him and Eddie."

"Dear God," Marge cries softly.

"Anyway, I can't remember every word. I'd be lying if I said I did. But next thing I know, Ray is telling the grocer he won't think twice about killing him if he doesn't hand over the contents of the register. And that's when the kid, freaks out, screams 'No,' and tries to grab the gun from Ray. Not expecting him to have this kind of fight, Ray panics and shoots Keneally, who instantly collapses to the floor. One bullet hit the poor guy smack in his heart. My fucking brother runs to the register to make a grab for the money. He doesn't even look to see if the man is alive. Eddie runs out the way he came in, through the back room and into the alley. The customer in hiding chases him outside, calling after him that it wasn't his fault. When the guy tries to collar Eddie, just to talk to him, the kid is so wired and out of control that he falls against the concrete wall. Hits his head hard. The guy isn't sure if Eddie's alive, and I'm not either, but I know he could be. Dude says something to Eddie about how he's sorry, he'll call an ambulance for him and Keneally, but he can't stay because nobody will ever believe he was just trying to help. He takes off."

"I didn't know all of this," Marge says. "All of these years, and I didn't know these details. There was no time."

The room is spinning, and I feel as if I'm going to pass out … worse … disassociate. But I know I can't do that. Not again. I flash back to the day before when Ray came out of the hotel room, sneering at me as if he hoped looks could kill. I'm surprised I didn't twig when I saw him then, but yeah, denial is a powerful thing. I need to let my mind go blank for a moment. I do. I take a few breaths, then nod to let Chaz know it's okay to go on.

He continues. "I didn't wait to see what my fucked-up brother would do. And I couldn't wait to see if the guy would call an ambulance or when. So I hurried into the alley to pick up the kid. I performed CPR on him, and he quickly started breathing but looked completely out of it. I picked him up and ran with him to the address I'd heard Keneally mention. Luckily, I got away unseen. If he hadn't started breathing when he did, everything would've been different. *Everything.* Anyway, moving on with the story, just as I got to the Salinksy house, I saw three men leaving. I waited long enough for them to jump into a black Cadillac Escalade and take off; then I ran to the front door."

"And I opened it," Marge said. "And I saw my son and nearly lost my breath and my own life. Eddie opened his eyes and looked at me blankly. It was like he couldn't see me. I called 911. The EMTs came right away. Within minutes, Eddie was taken to the hospital. I was so eager to follow that I had little time to get the full story from Chaz, but I have been forever grateful to him for saving my son's life. We never saw one another again until Friday night."

I focus on Chaz, but he won't make eye contact with me. I can do the math, but I don't want to. How much further can this story go?

Marge is speaking again. "I'm not going to lay out all of the details here. In fact, I'm going to be as brief as I can because this isn't, as they say, the time or the place. I will say that Eddie was given every test for head trauma, and I was told he was physically fine. But then they told me he couldn't remember who he was. Said he was in a dissociative fugue, something that was almost always temporary, but in rare cases of psychological trauma, could be permanent." She looks at me. "Do you want me to tell you the rest?

I nod and try to pretend there's not a tornado going on in my head and that I'm not seeing pieces of my younger life being whipped around like flying debris. I've got to stop these annoying analogies. I have enough junk in my head. I know the term dissociative fugue. I use it. The first time I heard it, it felt like something I should remember. I related to it instantly, but I didn't know why. Maybe because I've had a whole bunch of mini fugues inside a big one. After Rayelle was taken, I'd chalked up my crazy thoughts and departures from reality to stress-induced hallucinations. Being in New York under extreme duress triggered the past to come out of hiding. Only I wasn't ready to handle it. I'd let each memory take a peek at my current life, but I'd force it away because I had to focus on getting my child back. I have to stay calm or Marge will stop talking. I need to know more. I nod for her to continue. Words don't come.

"After leaving the hospital, I didn't want to take Eddie home. Even imagining how Harry might act, scared me to no end. And when the doctors told me the most important thing was to create a safe environment for my son, well, there was no choice."

"Were you afraid your husband would put Eddie in the basement?" I surprise myself by asking this question. I can't bring myself to refer to Eddie in anything but the third person. At least for now.

Tears roll down Marge's cheeks. "Yes, sweetheart. He did that often when his thug-sociates came for a visit. The basement had a lock on the door; Eddie's room didn't. He wanted a guarantee that nobody would be a witness to what was said. Locking up his son was no solution. It was cruel and horrible, but I couldn't stop him. All I could do was scream at him to let Eddie out when the coast was clear. You were right when you asked about previous rescues. There were many. And then, after Eddie lost his memory, I thought it best for him never to see Harry again."

Marge is still referring to Eddie in the third person too. And I understand why. In so many ways, Eddie was an entirely different human being. Also, I suspect she's afraid I'll lose it if she changes tenses. I have the same fear, but I know it won't happen. Memories are flashing before me. The bullying, the name calling, the horrible people in my home, being locked in the basement, being shy and sensitive, stealing the gun, Ray lying to me, trying to stop the robbery ... then nothing. Absolutely nothing. I look at Chaz. "So what happened with Ray back in the store?"

He guzzles half of his drink. "Well, I didn't see any of the aftermath. I was long gone. But from all later witness accounts, as soon as the gunshot went off, people on the streets panicked. Nobody looked in the window for a bit because they were afraid of being shot, not knowing what had just happened. The cops got there pretty damn quick, though. They caught Ray with the gun and the money, standing over the poor grocer's dead body, cursing. He was arrested on the spot, and, of course, had GSR on his hands—you know, residue—so he couldn't lie about having shot the grocer. The gun was never traced back to the Salinsky's because the serial number had been filed off. Oh, and the ambulance the customer had called got there right before the cops did. I'd taken Eddie away, and Mr. Keneally was dead. I heard that most of the people there were crying when they saw him leave in a body bag. He was well loved. A fixture in the neighborhood."

I look down at the floor as I remember what a wonderful man Jack Keneally was.

Chaz stops to wipe his forehead with the back of his hand. "It was horrific. Every moment of it. Afterward, I was so sure my father would finally see Ray for who he was and start loving me. But that never happened. He loved Ray even more. I was *persona non grata*, or maybe I should just say *son non grata.*"

I'm terrified to ask the next question, but I get it out. "And your brother. Did he try to implicate … *Eddie* … in the robbery?"

"I'll answer that," Marge says. "Harry had an associate visit Ray in jail right after his arrest. He told him if there was any mention of *any* Salinsky, Ray could expect his time behind bars to be a hell unlike anything he'd ever known. Mind you, this was for Harry's benefit, not Eddie's."

"So he never said a word," Chaz says, "but even if Harry Salinsky's associates didn't get to him from jump, I doubt Ray would have said anything. He knew they were a notoriously tough group." He stops to wash down the words he's just spoken. "But to this day, my brother thinks he could have just robbed the guy without killing him had, uh, Eddie not freaked out or tried to stop him. He's got a grudge that he's carried for over twenty years. That's the reason he was happy for Carly to take Rayelle. Payback. Oh, and if you're wondering what Ray's told Carly, my bet is absolutely nothing. Yeah, he made some crack in the hotel room about you still being ignorant, but if she picked up on that and asks him, he'll BS his way out of it. Or maybe he already did. I know that much. The last thing he wants to do is rock his own boat or give Carly what he perceives as any reason to feel empathy for you. I'll just leave that there for now."

"One more thing." I swallow my fear. "When did you all know that Liam Tallamore and Eddie Salinsky were one and the same?"

Chaz fills his glass with more lemonade. I know it's just to buy time. "Yeah that." He takes a few sips, then puts the glass down. "So, when Carly contacted Ray in prison after all of the lost years, the first thing she told him was that they had a son. After the shock settled in, my brother wanted to know who she'd married and who was raising his boy. Carly told him your name, and he wasted no time having the old man check you out. Just so you know, he never told her he was doing that nor what he subsequently learned." Chaz slowly shakes his head. "As you can imagine, Ray became unhinged to the moon and back when he found out Carly was married to Eddie … um … you. He not only blamed you for his crime, but now you'd married the love of his life. You: the dumb punk kid he thought to be way inferior to himself. And he was sure your parents changed your name solely to keep you from being named as an accomplice."

Marge's face tightens. "Bullshit."

My head is spinning. "I can only imagine how pissed he was. I guess this is a minor issue, but I hate that all of you knew who I was before I did."

"Yeah, it's fucked, Houdini. But listen. Things work out like they do for a reason. Remember I told you, back at the apartment, how five years later, my so-called friend, Freddie, sold me out to my father when I confided in him? As soon as the old man discovered that I'd been at the grocery store and had seen everything go down, and that 'some kid' had been there too, he demanded to know who you were—

right after he cursed me out for lying to him for five years. He asked
Ray who you were, but he said you were just some punk he'd met on
the street that day who tagged along. Trust me, Ray was still scared
shitless of Harry Salinksy and his gang. Meanwhile, my father,
clueless, was just desperate to blame someone else in hopes of getting
Ray out of prison. He was relentless. Told him again that I never got a
look at the kid's face. Luckily, I'd never told Freddie who you were or
what happened afterward. I'll always be grateful for that. The old man
kept hounding me. Ad nauseum, I repeated that the kid was an
unwilling accomplice and that Ray forced him to be there—with a gun
at his back. He sure didn't like that and accused me of still lying. He
wanted to beat the shit outta me. He didn't, though, because he knew
I was stronger than he was and that I wouldn't have hesitated to fight
back. Truth be damned. It had no home with my father if it went
against my brother's word."

"And that's another reason he treats you so bad, isn't it?" I ask.
"Because he thinks you could have saved Ray."

"Yeah, something like that. But hear me, Houdini, it was all
Ray's fault. He deserved every minute of his sentence. Luckily for you,
after all of those years, after my father ran the check on you, and Ray
finally spilled the whole story after his early release, my father wanted
a new life with his son way more than he wanted to take misplaced
revenge on an innocent fourteen-year-old kid. So that shit fell by the
wayside. He just wanted you out of the way so they could leave the
country." He sighs. "So like I just said; don't worry about who knew
what when. Things could have gone a whole different way. Scary
different. Just saying. And really sorry you had to see your friend get
murdered. And it's a damn shame that you ever got mixed up with the

likes of my brother all of those years ago."

Unsteadiness overwhelms me as I hear Chaz's words and see Jack Kenneally's frightened face in my mind's eye. But I refuse to lose consciousness. My twenty-one-year break from reality has gone on long enough. "I didn't know!" I shout, jumping to my feet. "I was so fucking stupid. Battered and bruised emotionally from almost every direction. I really thought having Hunk on my side would change everything. Mr. Keneally was my friend. Every time I went into the store, he'd give me something and tell me crazy stories about his childhood. He was a really funny guy. I never knew robbing him was what Ray had in mind. Never! It seemed like only seconds after I gave him the gun for 'protection,' he was pointing it at my back, pushing me into the store. I was such a lame kid. Stupid. Ignorant. Idiotic. Unworthy of life. Fucked up beyond fucked up! Desperate to be accepted. My friend is dead because I was so stupid!" I stop.

An aura of light forms in front of me. Mr. Keneally stands in it, smiling, his gentle eyes so loving. He's gone again. Lightheaded, but amazed, I fall back into my seat.

Chaz vehemently shakes his head. "No, this is on Ray. Trust me, everything would have gone down without you. And who knows, maybe more people would have been killed had Ray brought one of his friends along instead of you."

I hear Chaz's words, but I ignore their veracity. "I'm no better than Harry."

"No! You're a million times better! Don't ever say that again!" Marge gets up from the couch and runs over to me. I stand as she hugs me and begs me to stop the self-deprecating. I put my arms around her and sob.

"Sweetheart." She leads me to the couch where she's sitting with Ken. "Have a seat, please."

I sit on her right as Ken stays seated to her left.

Marge is fighting back tears. "I am thankful every day that you didn't pick up that man's horrible ways. So grateful. I didn't know you were being bullied; I only knew you were nothing like Harry and his friends. Or me, sadly, for that matter. I'm not so innocent."

"I'm surprised I didn't turn out like him. After all, I have his genes."

Marge pales, slowly shakes her head, then lets her face drop. She turns to Ken whose mouth falls open in shock. Oh. My. God.

"You don't have Harry Salinsky's genes," she says softly. "A much better man gave you life." Swallowing, she looks at Ken again.

His eyes widen, and he can only look back at her. After several long moments, he speaks. "Oh, sweetheart, you should have told me." He's choked up something major. "You really should have."

Marge stammers, unable to voice an immediate response as she gets up, and sits on the opposite side of me so Ken can slide over. He does so, hugging me as tightly as he can, tears welling in his eyes.

As our embrace ends, I get up to let Ken sit next to Marge again, now taking an empty space on the other side of her.

Ken waits for her to find her voice again.

"I didn't know until you were gone. If you'd still been in New York, I would've. I know that much. But I thought it was way too late for so many reasons. Sorry, my love. Don't have much more than that. Not at this moment anyway. Don't think it hasn't haunted me."

Ken lowers his eyes, agony etched on his face. "Now I understand why Rayelle looks like my sister Dara did as a child. And you take after my mother's side of the family. They weren't big hulking guys like I am." He offers a shy smile, then pauses to recover. "I'm sorry, this isn't the most important thing right now. Margie, you need to continue. Liam, I can't say I'm not overjoyed, and yes, stunned, to learn this, but I do mourn the lost years. And I know Margie didn't want me to mourn, hence she didn't tell me. If I understand anything, it's that. Not gonna lie. It hurts like hell, but it doesn't change my love for this extraordinary woman."

"How do you know me so well and forgive me so easily?" She runs a hand tenderly down the side of his face. "I don't deserve your love and kindness."

Ken is still choked up, but the words come. "Of course you do. And yes, we have a lot to talk about, and we will, but I know your heart, Margie." He squeezes her hand. "Right now, I'm sure Liam has many more questions. Pressing ones. Liam, you stay here by Margie. I'll take your chair and make some more room on the couch. Not that I haven't enjoyed our game of musical chairs." He smiles through the awkwardness.

I feel as if I'm floating. After a moment, I manage a few words as I look at the woman next to me. "How did I become—?"

Marge nods, then turns to face me. "My best friend in school was Amanda Stanley. As you know, Liam, Amanda is very different from me, but opposites attract. She grounded me—in a good way— and I offered her a taste of the crazy fun she'd never have dared to enjoy on her own. There was a lot of trust between us. Still is. After high school, Amanda met and married Bryce Tallamore, then moved to the Trenton area with him. He had a job offer there, and she decided to study art."

I'm mesmerized and astounded.

"Amanda was originally your godmother when you were born. But because I never wanted her near Harry and his associates, all your birthday parties were held at her house. We'd visit often, and you had more friends in her Jersey neighborhood than your own in New York. That's why there are so many photos of you with your parents as a young kid."

I feel lighter than I ever can remember being. "I always wondered why my birthday parties were by far and away the bits of my childhood I could vaguely recall. Maybe it's because of the photos I had. But even those memories faded, but I pretended they hadn't." I look at Marge. "Tell me the rest."

"Well, by the time you were five, Amanda had earned her master's in art and decided it was time to start their family. She tried for years, sadly losing the two babies she was able to conceive. It crushed her into little pieces."

I remember something. "A couple of times I asked her if she had an easy pregnancy, and she always looked uncomfortable. She'd say pregnancy isn't for everyone or something nonspecific like that. I just figured that carrying me made her sick, and she didn't want to hurt my feelings."

"No, sweetheart. And let me just add that carrying you was joyful." Marge's bright smile fills me with happiness. "Still want me to keep yakking?"

"Definitely."

"Well, when you came out of the hospital not knowing who you were, I decided to take you to Amanda and Bryce's because I sure wasn't taking you home. Plus, I needed time to think, especially as my second trial was scheduled for the following week, and I knew I was going back to prison. Like I said, I was a reluctant accomplice the second time around, not to mention an idiot for letting myself fall back into Harry's world."

"Did he care that you were taking me away?"

"In a word: no." She looks at me as if she can hear my silent question. "Yes, he's always believed you're his biological son." She winces. "Anyway, I told him what the doctors had said about creating a safe environment for you, and he was all too happy to go along with that."

A chill races up my spine. "Kept him from having to lock me up too."

She sighs and nods, but I can see it hurts her to do so.

"Anyway, I packed up some of your things, rented a car, and we headed to Amanda and Bryce's. I needed a safe place to think and to decide what was best for you while I gave my encore performance in the hoosegow. The Tallamore's or my mother's house? I wasn't sure. The closer we got to Trenton, the more confused I became. I pulled off the highway and drove to a park. Having a peaceful environment to talk, to think, was important to me." She looks at me as if to see if I have anything to say, but I don't. Not yet.

Marge exhales, making an effort to stay calm. "We sat in the car; I asked if you remembered what had happened. Still having no conception of who you were, you got anxious very quickly, started to hyperventilate, and couldn't catch your breath. That was something that always scared me silly. My grandmother, who lost my grandfather tragically when a panic attack turned into a fatal heart attack, had always reminded me that people die if they can't breathe. It may sound obvious, but it isn't always. When I would become too excited or upset about something, she would always say something like, 'Once a broken breath, you might barely survive. But broken again, you may not be alive.' If my breathing got really bad, she'd say it a different way, 'Twice a broken breath, portends a certain death. Always take time to breathe, Margaret. Always breathe.' And that scared the hell out of me. Still does."

"Oh my God." Another piece of the puzzle lands in front of me. "Yes, I remember you telling me that all the time. I've even remembered the saying, only not where it came from."

Marge takes my hands in hers. "It was at that moment that I knew my late grandmother's words could save my son's life. There was no way I could allow you to live with my mother as Eddie Salinsky. You, losing your breath like that, made it all clear. The universe was talking to me. I looked into your lost eyes and told myself I was saying good-bye to protect and save you. I explained the whole thing, hoping that somewhere inside your traumatized mind, you'd understand or remember at a future time. At that moment, though filled with soul-crushing angst and the worst pain of my life, I decided to take you to live with Amanda and Bryce. And, I knew that if you failed to get your memory back, then you would become Liam Bryce Tallamore. That's what Amanda always wanted to name a son. Harry was happy to sign away his custodial rights, and I signed away mine to give you, Amanda, and Bryce the family you all needed and deserved. You already loved one another. And yes, it shattered my heart, and my mother's, but I never regretted doing it. It killed me not to see you when I came out of prison, but I'd promised those close to me that I would never interfere with your upbringing. You've turned into a wonderful and loving man, something that may never have happened if Harry Salinsky had found his way back into your life, or if you stayed in a neighborhood anywhere near, well, certain people. This may sound crazy, but I'm glad I went back to prison, Liam. Your life was so much better because I did."

Her words hit me hard. I want to tell her she's wrong, but I know she isn't. I have no appropriate response, so I look at Chaz. "You always knew who I was. And you never told anyone you saw me at the grocery store. You took me out of the alley. I guess you *have* been my best friend all these years. You put your lips on mine to save me."

For the first time, Chaz looks embarrassed. "Let's leave that out of the narrative, shall we?" He smirks. "You can thank my ninth-grade health teacher for making us learn CPR."

"Was I your Sleeping Beauty?" I say, trying to find some levity.

"Taking a raincheck on payback for that one," Chaz says. "You just wait."

"Seriously, Chaz, everything you told me about being my best friend. I've never had a better one."

Chaz is now scarlet red. "That was hyperbole for the most part, but yeah, I always thought you needed protecting, even though years passed before I found out what had become of you. You'd had enough hell. I know. I still deal with the trauma of seeing Mr. Kenneally being shot too. Not an easy vision. In many ways, I feel responsible for not speaking up before it happened, but after being idiot enough to confide in Freddie, this is the first time in over fifteen years I'm mentioning it."

Marge gasps. "How selfish of me not to think about all you've been through … what you still go through. But your brother killed that lovely man. Not you."

Chaz puts the palms of his hands up. "Don't worry. Please, let's not talk about my situation now."

His kind words warm my heart, but I won't embarrass him by getting emotional. Another thought comes to me. "Seems like Houdini's first great escape was facilitated by you."

"Touché again." Chaz wears the hint of a smile. "Never quite thought of it that way before. It's been over two decades and all. I'll accept that if you leave the Sleeping Beauty shit in the dust and promise never to prick your finger again."

Chaz knows his fairytales. That happens when you have kids. My mind is racing with questions, emotional responses, and things I can't even identify. I turn back to Marge. "Yesterday afternoon, you said you would call my mother to let her know I was okay. It wasn't until I got on the elevator to leave that I wondered why you never asked for her number." Panic stirs in my gut. "So, does she know what happened? Does she know what you were going to tell me today? Are they upset? Are they okay?"

"They're just fine. And I can't say I wasn't overjoyed to hear her voice again. Believe it or not, Liam, aside from being relieved Rayelle and Oliver are okay, your parents want you to be whole again and to reclaim your lost years, even if they weren't happy ones. They hated telling you that sports-injury story, but they had no choice."

"Good. I'll call them later. But I have so many questions. Like Friday night, when I came into your restaurant, did you recognize me?"

"I was about ninety percent sure. Then I began to doubt myself, thinking that maybe I was seeing who I wanted to see, the person who I never stopped looking for as I passed strangers on the street and greeted my customers. It wouldn't have been the first time the universe played dirty tricks on me. But when you told me your last name, well, that removed all doubt. The last photo I'd seen of you was your high school graduation photo." She smiles. "Someone may have slipped and sent it to me. But even without that, yes, I do believe I would've known you."

"I thought you were looking at me strangely. Come to think of it, so was Sherita. I remember feeling like I was a museum relic or something. She knew, too, right?"

"Yes. When I called her, I told her, but until Friday night, she never knew your new name. I've been very careful to protect your privacy all these years. But I had good reason to tell her. I hope you're okay with that."

"Of course. I don't know if I'd have found Rayelle without her help." I tremble as I imagine a different outcome, then stop myself. "Sherita's such an incredible person, and I'll always be grateful to her." I have a thought. "I keep thinking about how time is Irish once an hour, because it's O'clock. Does that mean something?"

"Your grandmother, my mother, beat that one to death, but I'd heard it said so many times that I couldn't help reviving it whenever I saw the big hand on the twelve." She smiles. "You remember that, obviously."

"Not until I heard you say it Friday night." I fidget with my fingers, realizing I've never taken off my wedding ring. I do so and shove it into my pocket as if it's loose change.

Chaz gives me a subtle thumbs up.

I smile, then look at Marge again. "I'm not a heavy drinker, but it's been a heavy day so far. Got some Johnny Walker or Dewars I might nurse? Restore my brain cells."

"Booze does just the opposite. You know that, right?" Chaz laughs.

"Yeah, I do. But today, understanding the circumstances, I think it'll work with me."

"I think you're right, Houdini. The booze will cut us all a break. We can toast to its magical powers."

"A short drink, everyone," Marge reminds us. "No more."

"I'm good with that. Just something for intermission." I pause. "Is there a second act?"

Marge looks wistfully at me. "There is, Liam. It's called the rest of your life."

CHAPTER TWENTY-SIX

Sunday, 2:15 p.m.

After we pour our drinks, the room becomes silent. Answers beg more questions, but I remind myself that there's time. There's just so much that the brain can take in. I remember from science class that there's a saturation point when a substance can't receive any more of another. Something like that.

I care deeply for everyone in this room now, and I know I'm not the only one who's had their life turned upside down. I'm trying to process that I've now got two sets of wonderful parents when many people don't even get one. Memories are coming back quickly. I'm trying to push them aside, hoping for a trickle, not a flood.

Chaz has helped me so much, and yet, he remains tortured by his father's disdain for him and his own guilt over what his brother did. I have an inkling he may also feel responsible for what happened to me, though he hasn't said it aloud. We'll get to those topics eventually. I'll be there for him. We'll spar with smiles until we're old men. I want everyone here to be a constant in my life; I know that much. I hope they feel the same. I think they do.

I'm shocked by how easily Ken seems to adjust to the news that he has a son. I imagine that with time, if not in the very immediate future, he'll have more questions. He said he would. But for now, he knows Marge kept his fatherhood a secret out of love for him … and for me.

Meanwhile, she's kept her pain tucked inside for years. I

wonder, after I disappeared, what did she tell all the people who knew she had a son? Knowing Marge, she probably told them to mind their own business. I'm curious, but it's hardly a priority at this moment. Just as she tried hard not to let every nuance of my past rain down on me at once, I have to be gentle with her too. This isn't all about me, no matter how I spin it.

Despite the memories returning, I feel calmer than I ever have, but I'm not naïve. I know there's a long road to healing and that I should get some help. Maybe we all should. But at the moment, my immediate future is staring me in the face, asking me what I'm going to do with it. I don't know. Just as I'm about to think about it some more, Marge jumps in as if she were reading my mind.

"I can see the question marks circling your head." She smiles. "You're thinking about what comes next, yes?"

I smile at her. "Well, if there was ever a time to make a change, now would be it. Not only in light of everything that happened, but this is summer, and I wouldn't have to pull Rayelle out of school mid-year if we relocate. Not to mention that I lost my job for not coming back to work Friday."

"Really?" Chaz sips his drink. "Did you let them know you had a problem?"

"Oh, yeah. But my boss wanted to know my reason so he could decide if I had grounds. Nosy SOB. Always has been. The entire staff of the auto parts store would have known my business within five minutes. Not to mention the customers and *their* families."

Chaz helps himself to a few pieces of salami. "Yeah. I'd hate that shit. Did you like the job?"

"Not especially. It was just that: a job. Not a career path. Just a paycheck. I didn't know who I was, so I guess I didn't know where I was going or where I wanted to go. Some days I felt like I was waiting at a railroad station for a ghost train. I knew it, but I waited anyway."

"I hear ya. Well, I wouldn't mind having you around." Chaz looks at the ground, as if he's embarrassed.

"Really? You wouldn't, huh?"

Chaz's reddened cheeks return to normal. "Yeah. I mean, there are thousands of dumpsters I haven't locked you in yet. What fun could I have if you stay in Trenton?"

"You've got a point, Scruff." I offer half a smile knowing there's plenty of time for him to earn a whole one.

He's still abashed by the show of affection, but enjoying our repartee. I think we'd both love to have a brother and best friend in one another.

Marge and Ken are holding hands. It makes me happy to see how deeply they love one another. Maybe someday, I'll find someone to love me that way and vice versa. That would be nice, but I'm not ready for that any time soon.

"So," Marge says, "I'll ask my question more specifically since Chaz just mentioned it, and I did hear you say the word 'relocate' a minute or so ago. I know you're going back to Trenton, but permanently?"

I shrug. "Can't say the thought excites me very much. In fact, it rather makes me sick. I also don't want to live in the home I shared with Carly. I don't think that would be healthy for Rayelle, either."

"Would I be out of line to say I hope you'd consider coming back home, now that you know where home is? To have you here in New York would mean the world to us. I know the city is very different from the suburbs." She frowns. "I suppose it would be a huge adjustment for everyone though."

"I don't see how it could be a bigger adjustment than coming to terms with everything I've just learned or have been through these past few days. I don't feel uncomfortable here anymore, despite all of it. Carrying the unknown with me for twenty-one years is what made life so difficult."

"But you carried on," Ken says. "One need only look at your children to see how much they love you."

"Thanks for that. Oliver is off on his own now, but wherever we live, I always want him to have a place to call home. I can't imagine living anywhere but New York now. I never thought I'd feel this way, but it's true. Rayelle's got a say in all of this, of course. I want to give her time to make sure she'd be okay with it. For one thing, she's always wanted a dog, but Carly had no interest in helping her take care of one. If she's still interested, which I'm sure is the case, after we get resettled and things feel right, a trip to the pound may be in our future." I smile, imagining how happy this will make Rayelle. "Tonight, I think we'll just chill and hang out. I have two important calls to make as well. There's a whole lot to get in order. I'll probably go back to Jersey on Tuesday or Wednesday and see my parents." I turn to Marge. "My mom has always wanted to live in North Jersey, to be more proximate to the city, especially the art galleries and theaters. They never did it because they wanted to stay close to us. This could work out for everyone."

Marge wipes a tear from her eye. "I would love to have Amanda in my life again, but only if it wouldn't be awkward for you. She said pretty much the same thing when we spoke yesterday. As I told you, Liam, when I took you to her all those years ago, I had to let our friendship go. Not in my heart, but it wouldn't have been good then for any of us if we'd stayed in touch. The only time I heard from her was when I got your graduation photo. There was a note attached saying, 'He's a wonderful young man.' She put two xx's after that, and we didn't communicate again until last night."

"Wow. I didn't think of this before, but Mom used to talk about a best friend she'd lost contact with. Every time, I would offer to help her find the friend on the Internet. And she'd always make some excuse not to have me do it. But I knew she missed her friend, and it made me sad. I could see the pain in her eyes."

Marge starts to respond, but puts a hand up to dismiss the words that won't come. I get it. She's too emotional to talk. I'm so happy to know she's missed my mother just as much as my mom's missed her. I'm overwhelmed thinking about how the worst thing in my life, having my girl taken, my son in hiding, and my wife leaving me, has likely ended up in what I believe will be a better life than any of us could ever have imagined.

Ken looks at his phone. "Sherita just texted. Wants to know if it's okay to bring the kids by when the boat trip is over." He smiles. "Oh, and they're having a great time."

"Absolutely," I tell him. "Can't wait to see them."

Marge looks a bit anxious. "Liam, I was wondering if you and the kids would come by for dinner tomorrow night. Before you head back." She looks at Chaz. "You too, of course. And if you want to bring Kismet and Benjamin, that would be terrific."

"I'll talk to their mother," he says. "I think she'll be down with that."

"Sounds like a plan," I say. "I may have something very important to do in the early afternoon, but dinner should work just fine." Marge, Ken, and Chaz are staring at me. They want to know what's going on. I can't jinx anything by talking about it.

There are some things that cannot be left undone.

CHAPTER TWENTY-SEVEN

Last night was the best of my life. Being with Rayelle and Oliver brought more joy than I've ever known. We were going to have dinner at an Italian restaurant, but the kids opted for room service so that we didn't have to share one another with anyone. Sherita had the kitchen prepare a feast, and she wouldn't let me pay for anything. The kids already love her, and I have no doubt she'll always be in our lives.

My children and I had no pre-planned agenda. We laughed, we got silly, and we cried thinking about how dangerously close we came to losing one another. Again, I let Rayelle and Oliver know that I hope that their mother will find her way to have a positive and steady role in their lives again. No doubt, Carly probably thinks I'm gloating as I plot against her, but she'd be very wrong. When you love your kids, you do what's best for them, not for yourself. I realize that's exactly what Marge did for me. Her second stint in prison was only fifteen months, but she let me go forever because she loved me that much. I wonder if I would do the same, and I have to admit I can't quite answer that question.

Oliver told Rayelle that there's no limit to how many people the heart can hold. What a proud moment. He loves having so many grandparents now. I told him that if he ever wants to connect with Raymond, he's free to do so. He wasn't too keen about it, but I told him to leave the door open. The kids were both a bit nervous about Carly's parents, who live in Hawaii, not knowing where they stand with the whole situation, or if they even know. Oliver doesn't think Carly's told them yet, saying that his mother wouldn't want to hear their objections or get into an argument over it. He thinks she's way more likely to spill when everything is a "done deal." I think he's right. I told the kids that if they want to speak to their grandparents any time soon, I'd be happy to call first and find out where things stand. I get why they'd be afraid to wade in awkward waters with the Kawais. I'll do everything I can for them to the best of my ability. I'll never be perfect, but I'll never stop trying to be the best father I can.

The three of us had a video chat with my parents. Even my dad was weepy hearing all that happened. My mother is the one who usually cries buckets, but he shed his fair share of tears. After the kids went into the other room, I told my parents what I foresee for the future. They love the idea of us moving to New York or North Jersey, and my father is calling his realtor soon so they can do the same. My mother's countenance looked so much lighter. I never realized that she was holding so many secrets inside and that doing so had taken such a toll, just as it has on Marge. She's thrilled at the prospect of being closer to New York, to be able to have her best friend back—with everything out in the open.

The kids and I were together all night long. I only stepped away for twenty minutes to make another important call. It went better than expected. Now, it's Monday afternoon, and I'm walking with my kids on the West Side. We're heading toward Baradino's. I have a very good feeling.

He sees me coming before I see him. "Liam!" he cries. "You found your daughter!" Isaiah, who had been sitting on his wooden box, jumps up and runs toward us, throwing his arms around me. "My friend, I prayed for you something fierce these past days. Looks like God heard me." He looks upward. "Thank you!" He smiles at Rayelle and Oliver. "Miracles never cease to happen if you believe they can."

I'm not crying, but I might as well be. "Kids, I want you to meet Isaiah Calbert Jones. We met on Friday night and became instant friends. If it wasn't for him, I'm not sure we'd be together now. He's a very good person." I look at the man with glistening eyes. "Isaiah, this is my daughter, Rayelle, and my son, Oliver."

The three of them make a big deal over one another, and I step aside to send a very important text. I glance at my children and take a moment to soak in the joy that radiates from the three of them. I've never been more fulfilled.

Monday, 12.59 p.m.

The kids are hitting it off with Isaiah like he's their long-lost and beloved uncle. I told Isaiah I'd tell him the entire story about Rayelle's rescue later. He was good with that. He's happy the sun's shining and said we should rejoice in it.

As the three of them laugh, I'm nervous as I see the approaching cab slow down and stop.

The passenger jumps out and hugs me, just the way Isaiah did, only with the addition of a big slap on the back. "Liam, my weary traveling friend. You look like a much happier man than the one I said good-bye to on the train. As I told you last night on the phone, I know you never planned to see me again, but when I got off at Penn Station and left you my card, I had a sneaky kind of suspicion you'd be calling."

"Who had the sneaky suspicion?" I ask with a smile, "You or Captain Bob?"

Bob pats me on the back again. "I reckon I'm not as different from that crazy captain as I thought."

I introduce everyone, and I'm amazed at how well my kids are interacting with him as well. It's not surprising. Both men have gregarious, warm, and giving personalities. Isaiah and Bob are really hitting it off, and I'm overjoyed. After several minutes of conversation, Bob asks us all to head down the street to the diner to have a bite of lunch with him.

Isaiah hesitates. "Well, I don't know. Some of these establishments don't take well to homeless men coming in."

Bob puts his arms around Isaiah. "I don't know who you're talking about. Come on, friend, I have something very important to talk to you about."

As we head toward a booth, I ask Bob if he wants his "winder seat."

He chuckles. "Nope, don't need it now, Liam. That was only for the times when I felt so lonely that I needed to look out the window at the scenery so nobody noticed my sadness. I think life is changing for all of us."

We order lunch and the conversation flows beautifully throughout. The kids think Bob is really funny, and I see a light in Isaiah's eyes that I imagine hasn't been there for a long time. I know it's about to get even brighter.

"Isaiah," Bob says, once the server has taken our plates away. "I met our friend Liam here on Friday. We rode on the train together from Trenton to Penn Station. Liam wasn't particularly happy to have a seat mate, much less one as silly as I was being that day. He was going through a trauma I'd never have imagined, and there I was, trying desperately to have a conversation. I was so focused on my own pain that I neglected to think that the stranger beside me might have some of his own. I'll try to never let that happen again. Oliver, Rayelle, I'll tell you this: be kind to everyone; you never know what someone might be going through. It's not an original piece of advice, but it's one that will always be important to remember."

Isaiah is mesmerized by his words. So are the kids.

"Liam wasn't interested in anything about me, but still, I gave him the brief story of my life, explaining how I'd devised a silly second personality named Captain Bob to get through my pain. I explained that after the death of my wife, Janine, and the shame that my son and nephew brought to us, all I wanted in life was some companionship. It's been pretty lonely for me. Said a friend or two and a roommate would be nice."

I watch as Isaiah is beginning to understand why I've introduced the two men.

"Liam called me last night. After he told me about the legal matters he needs help with, he told me he'd met a fine man named Isaiah Calbert Jones. He explained that Isaiah had lost everything when his wife took sick, yet remained a grateful man, even having to sleep in a wooden shed in an alley. He asked me if I might know of a job for Isaiah so he could get off the streets. The moment I heard this, my brain started going full speed, like it did when I was a young lawyer." He picks up a napkin and wipes away a tear that hasn't fallen. "Honestly, I was quite sure Liam and I had met for a reason. A very good one. Because he didn't indulge my silly conversational whims, I made an on-the-spot decision to retire my alter ego, Captain Bob. But after we parted ways, I felt ashamed. This stranger, wrapped in worry and pain, had been the catalyst to help me, but I'd done nothing for him except leave a business card and a red umbrella." He looks a bit embarrassed. "I didn't feel like it was a very fair trade. And really, who would trust an attorney who acted as bonkers as I did?" He makes a face.

I look at my kids, then at Isaiah. "But as I told Bob on the phone last night, our serendipitous"— I see Rayelle's puzzled face— "lucky meeting, set everything in motion for me to find you and Oliver again."

Isaiah looks upward and smiles. "He sure does work in mysterious ways."

"Daddy is very mysterious," Rayelle says, and we all laugh. I make a mental note to explain things to her later.

As everyone soaks in the moment, I realize that I've also shed an alter ego, that of a confused man who kept trying to figure out who he was. And while I understand more than I ever have, I still have a long way to go. I think Bob, Isaiah, and I will all be on a similar, but different journey. Bob's looking at me. He's waiting for an okay to keep talking. I give him the nod.

The former sea captain breaks out in a big smile. "Now, getting back to our phone conversation last night. When Liam told me a good man named Isaiah Calbert Jones needed a job, being a lawyer, I went online this morning and did a check on the name. Standard procedure and all that." He winks. "Not surprising at all, everything was exactly as I was told it was." He smiles. "Isaiah, you managed a community center for over twenty-five years. Inspired children and adults alike.

Won several awards for your service too."

Isaiah looks embarrassed. "I just did my best; that's all."

Bob isn't finished. "And you have a business degree from Hunter, not to mention many continuing education classes you've taken over the years. Were you hoping to get a master's degree?"

"It was something I considered. But when my Nellie took sick, our entire world changed. Eventually, I couldn't even keep the job I loved so much. Those people were my second family. It was a dark day when I left the Center, but an even darker day when the love of my life died. I really thought she'd be okay, and I could go back to work." He looks down. "It didn't work out that way at all, as you can see. I hid away; I didn't want anyone to know how monumentally I'd failed."

Bob smiles sympathetically. "It's not your failure when life's pressures and demands far exceed your assets. And it is certainly not your fault that your beloved wife died."

"Still miss her like crazy. Every day. Always will. But I'm a lucky man to have had her."

Bob looks directly at Isaiah. "You're also a very good man, Isaiah Calbert Jones. Your battles have been greater than mine, yet you've endured in ways I honestly don't know I could have. In fact, I'll be even more honest. I'm quite sure I couldn't have. Infinite respect, my new friend."

Isaiah's eyes are watering, but he says nothing. Rayelle and Oliver hang onto Bob's every word. I'm remembering when Oliver still lived at home and he and Ray-Ray watched TV together, intoxicated by some of the shows they'd watch as they waited to see if the bad guys would get caught, the good ones rewarded.

"I've been fortunate, Isaiah, and I've also been very sad. Here's the thing. I have a beautiful three-bedroom apartment on the sixteenth floor of a doorman building here on the Upper West Side. Used to work in a law firm, but now that I'm semi-retired, I work part-time out of my home. Sure would like a friend to move in with me. A good man, someone I can relate to." He looks down. "We've both lost our wives. We need to rebuild. We have that in common and much more."

Isaiah nods.

"Do you have any children?" Bob asks.

"I have a daughter who lives in London. Serena Jones-Faulkner. Married an Englishman. She handles Human Resources for a large architectural firm. I just learned she's pregnant with their first child. Such a blessing. I've told her I have a modest place in this neighborhood, that I have a roof over my head. That's the God's honest truth; I do. Just don't think she'd do well hearing it's a wooden shed." He looks sad for a brief moment, then revives his smile. "Haven't ever given her an address. Only a post office box. I think she suspects my situation isn't as it should be, but I don't want her worrying about me. Especially being so far away and with a baby coming soon. Gotta say, it pains me not to be completely honest with her, but I just do the best I can with what the good Lord gives me."

"Exactly how I feel. Please hear me, Isaiah. I'd sure like a roommate and a friend. You'd have your own room and bathroom, not to mention a glorious view of the Manhattan skyline. How does that sound?"

Isaiah momentarily looks as if all of the breath in his body has been taken away. I silently tell him to breathe. Good news should never bring forth a broken breath. And definitely not two.

"It sounds like paradise, Bob." Isaiah hangs his head. "But I have no means to pay my way. And that's always been very important to me, even as I am now."

"You do, and you will," Bob says. "Just told you I work out of home. I could really use an assistant, both professionally and personally. Don't worry; I wouldn't ask too much from you. But you'd be helping me out in every way. I'll give you a place to stay and a modest weekly salary. It would be your home to come and go from any time. How about it, Isaiah?" He pauses as if to feel the weight of his words. "I think we both met Liam for a reason, don't you?" He's a bit overcome as he searches Isaiah's eyes. "I could really use a friend. Might you as well?"

Saying nothing, Isaiah looks upward, then smiles at Bob. "This is more than I ever prayed for. I only asked for the life I was meant to have, and for all whom I care for to be blessed."

Bob wipes away a tear that *has* fallen. "I want to believe this is the life you're meant to have now." He offers a crooked smile. "You're welcome to vet me online as I did you. Matter of fact, I'll give you a laptop to do the deed on and then to have as your own. This is a two-way street."

Isaiah smiles. "You've been vetted, my friend. I've been told what no computer check could reveal. Thank you. It's with great humility and thanks that I accept this blessing. I think we'll be very good friends indeed."

Monday, 2:15 p.m.

Rayelle and Oliver walk with Bob, who regales them with tales of

Captain Bob's adventures as he tries to squeeze some life lessons into his stories. I walk behind with Isaiah, who wears a brilliant smile.

He touches my arm, and we stop for a moment. "Like I told you, Liam. I'm a lucky man." His eyes sparkle as he looks at me for confirmation.

My heart is full. "Me too, Isaiah. Me too."

THE END

Illustration by Shykia Bell

Dear, Reader:

If you enjoyed this book, I would be deeply grateful for a short review on Amazon.com. It *really* helps. Thank you!

ABOUT THE AUTHOR

LISETTE BRODEY was born and raised in the Philadelphia area. She lived in New York City for ten years and now resides in Los Angeles. She is the multi-genre author of thirteen books. Her titles include: *Crooked Moon; Squalor, New Mexico; Molly Hacker Is Too Picky!;* The Desert Series (*Mystical High, Desert Star, Drawn Apart*); *Hotel Obscure: A Collection of Short Stories; Love, Look Away; The Sum of our Sorrows; The Waiting House: A Novel in Stories; All That Was Taken; and Twice a Broken Breath.*

She has also published two short stories in an anthology called *Triptych's (Mind's Eye Series, Book 3*).

All of her books are available in both Kindle and paperback.

Website & contact: lisettebrodey.com
Twitter / X: twitter.com/lisettebrodey
Facebook: facebook.com/BrodeyAuthor
Instagram: @ca_lisette
Pinterest: pinterest.com/lisetteca/

www.ingramcontent.com/pod-product-compliance
Lightning Source LLC
Chambersburg PA
CBHW070915260626
47162CB00007B/2674